Praise for *New York Times* bestselling author Diana Palmer

"Palmer proves that love and passion can be found even in the most dangerous situations."
—*Publishers Weekly* on *Untamed*

"You just can't do better than a Diana Palmer story to make your heart lighter and smile brighter."
—*Fresh Fiction* on *Wyoming Rugged*

"Diana Palmer is a mesmerizing storyteller who captures the essence of what a romance should be."
—*Affaire de Coeur*

"The popular Palmer has penned another winning novel, a perfect blend of romance and suspense."
—*Booklist* on *Lawman*

"Diana Palmer's characters leap off the page. She captures their emotions and scars beautifully and makes them come alive for readers."
—*RT Book Reviews* on *Lawless*

Dear Reader,

I can't believe that it has been thirty years since my first Long, Tall Texan book, *Calhoun*, debuted! The series was suggested by my former editor, Tara Gavin, who asked if I might like to set stories in a fictional town of my own design. Would I! And the rest is history.

As the years went by, I found more and more sexy ranchers and cowboys to add to the collection. My readers (especially Amy!) found time to gift me with a notebook listing every single one of them, wives and kids and connections to other families in my own Texas town of Jacobsville. Eventually the town got a little too big for me, so I added another smaller town called Comanche Wells and began to fill it up, too.

You can't imagine how much pleasure this series has given me. I continue to add to the population of Jacobs County, Texas, and I have no plans to stop. Ever.

I hope all of you enjoy reading the Long, Tall Texans as much as I enjoy writing them. Thank you all for your kindness and loyalty and friendship. I am your biggest fan!

Love,

Diana Palmer

NEW YORK TIMES BESTSELLING AUTHOR

DIANA PALMER

LONG, TALL TEXANS:

Leo

Jordan

HARLEQUIN® SPECIAL RELEASE

ISBN-13: 978-1-335-62185-6

Long, Tall Texans: Leo/Jordan

Copyright © 2019 by Harlequin Books S.A.

First published as Lionhearted
by Harlequin Books in 2002
and Cattleman's Pride by Harlequin Books in 2004.

The publisher acknowledges the copyright holder
of the individual works as follows:

Lionhearted
Copyright © 2002 by Diana Palmer

Cattleman's Pride
Copyright © 2004 by Diana Palmer

Recycling programs
for this product may
not exist in your area.

Printed in U.S.A.

www.Harlequin.com

CONTENTS

A prolific author of more than one hundred books, **Diana Palmer** got her start as a newspaper reporter. A *New York Times* bestselling author and voted one of the top ten romance writers in America, she has a gift for telling the most sensual tales with charm and humor. Diana lives with her family in Cornelia, Georgia. Visit her website at www.dianapalmer.com.

Visit the Author Profile page at Harlequin.com for more titles.

LEO

PROLOGUE

LEO HART FELT alone in the world. The last of his bachelor brothers, Rey, had gotten married and moved out of the house almost a year ago. That left Leo, alone, with an arthritic housekeeper who came in two days a week and threatened to retire every day. If she did, Leo would be left without a biscuit to his name, or even a hope of getting another one unless he went to a restaurant every morning for breakfast. Considering his work schedule, that was impractical.

He leaned back in the swivel chair at his desk in the office he now shared with no one. He was happy for his brothers. Most of them had families now, except newly married Rey. Simon and Tira had two little boys. Cag and Tess had a boy. Corrigan and Dorie had a boy and a baby girl. When he looked back, Leo realized that women had been a missing commodity in his life of late. It was late September. Roundup was just over, and there had been so much going on at the ranch, with business, that he'd hardly had time for a night out. He was feeling it.

Even as he considered his loneliness, the phone rang.

"Why don't you come over for supper?" Rey asked when he picked up the receiver.

"Listen," Leo drawled, grinning, "you don't invite your brother over to dinner on your honeymoon."

"We got married after Christmas last year," Rey pointed out.

"Like I said, you're still on your honeymoon," came the amused reply. "Thanks. But I've got too much to do."

"Work doesn't make up for a love life."

"You'd know," Leo chuckled.

"Okay. But the invitation's open, whenever you want to accept it."

"Thanks. I mean it."

"Sure."

The line went dead. Leo put the receiver down and stretched hugely, bunching the hard muscles in his upper arms. He was the boss as much as his brothers on their five ranch properties, but he did a lot of the daily physical labor that went with cattle raising, and his tall, powerful body was evidence of it. He wondered sometimes if he didn't work that hard to keep deep-buried needs at bay. In his younger days, women had flocked around him, and he hadn't been slow to accept sensual invitations. But he was in his thirties now, and casual interludes were no longer satisfying.

He'd planned to have a quiet weekend at home, but Marilee Morgan, a close friend of Janie Brewster's, had cajoled him into taking her up to Houston for dinner and to see a ballet she had tickets for. He was partial to ballet, and Marilee explained that she couldn't drive herself because her car was in the shop. She was easy on the eyes, and she was sophisticated. Not that Leo was tempted to let himself be finagled into any sort of intimacy with her. He didn't want her carrying tales of his private life to Janie, who had an obvious and uncomfortable crush on him.

He knew that Marilee would never have asked him to take her any place in Jacobsville, Texas, because it was a small town and news of the date would inevitably get back to Janie. It might help show the girl that Leo was a free agent, but it wouldn't help his friendship with Fred Brewster to know that Leo was playing fast and loose with Janie's best friend. Some best friend, he thought privately.

But taking Marilee out would have one really good consequence—it would get him out of a dinner date at the Brewsters' house. He and Fred Brewster were friends and business associates, and he enjoyed the time he spent with the older man. Well, except for two members of his family, he amended darkly. He didn't like Fred's sister, Lydia. She was a busybody who had highfalutin ideas. Fortunately, she was hardly ever around and she didn't live with Fred. He had mixed feelings about Fred's daughter Janie, who was twenty-one and bristling with psychology advice after her graduation from a junior college in that subject. She'd made Cag furious with her analyses of his food preferences, and Leo was becoming adept at avoiding invitations that would put him in her line of fire.

Not that she was bad looking. She had long, thick light brown hair and a neat little figure. But she also had a crush on Leo, which was very visible. He considered her totally unacceptable as a playmate for a man his age, and he knocked back her attempts at flirting with lazy skill. He'd known her since she was ten and wearing braces on her teeth. It was hard to get that image out of his mind.

Besides, she couldn't cook. Her rubber chicken dinners were infamous locally, and her biscuits could be classified as lethal weapons.

Thinking about those biscuits made him pick up the phone and dial Marilee.

She was curt when she picked up the phone, but the minute he spoke, her voice softened.

"Well, hello, Leo," she said huskily.

"What time do you want me to pick you up Saturday night?"

There was a faint hesitation. "You won't, uh, mention this to Janie?"

"I have as little contact with Janie as I can. You know that," he said impatiently.

"Just checking," she teased, but she sounded worried. "I'll be ready to leave about six."

"Suppose I pick you up at five and we'll have supper in Houston before the ballet?"

"Wonderful! I'll look forward to it. See you then."

"See you."

He hung up, but picked up the receiver again and dialed the Brewsters' number.

As luck would have it, Janie answered.

"Hi, Janie," he said pleasantly.

"Hi, Leo," she replied breathlessly. "Want to talk to Dad?"

"You'll do," he replied. "I have to cancel for dinner Saturday. I've got a date."

There was the faintest pause. It was almost imperceptible. "I see."

"Sorry, but it's a long-standing one," he lied. "I can't get out of it. I forgot when I accepted your dad's invitation. Can you give him my apologies?"

"Of course," she told him. "Have a good time."

She sounded strange. He hesitated. "Something wrong?" he asked.

"Nothing at all! Nice talking to you, Leo. Bye."

Janie Brewster hung up and closed her eyes, sick with disappointment. She'd planned a perfect menu. She'd practiced all week on a special chicken dish that was tender and succulent. She'd practiced an exquisite crème brûlée as well, which was Leo's favorite dessert. She could even use the little tool to caramelize the sugar topping, which had taken a while to perfect. All that work, and for nothing. She'd have been willing to bet that Leo hadn't had a date for that night already. He'd made one deliberately, to get out of the engagement.

She sat down beside the hall table, her apron almost stiff with flour, her face white with dustings of it, her hair disheveled. She was anything but the picture of a perfect date. And wasn't it just her luck? For the past year, she'd mounted a real campaign to get Leo to notice her. She'd flirted with him shamelessly at Micah Steele's wedding to Callie Kirby, until a stabbing scowl had turned her shy. It had angered him that she'd caught the bouquet Callie had thrown. It had embarrassed her that he glared so angrily at her. Months later, she'd tried, shyly, every wile she had on him, with no success. She couldn't cook and she was not much more than a fashion plate, according to her best friend, Marilee, who was trying to help her catch Leo. Marilee had plenty of advice, things Leo had mentioned that he didn't like about Janie, and Janie was trying her best to improve in the areas he'd mentioned. She was even out on the ranch for the first time in her life, trying to get used to horses and cattle and dust and dirt. But if she couldn't get Leo to the house to show him her new skills, she didn't have a lot of hope.

"Who was that on the phone?" Hettie, their house-keeper, called from the staircase. "Was it Mr. Fred?"

"No. It was Leo. He can't come Saturday night. He's got a date."

"Oh." Hettie smiled sympathetically. "There will be other dinners, darlin'."

"Of course there will," Janie said and smiled back. She got out of the chair. "Well, I'll just make it for you and me and Dad," she said, with disappointment plain in her voice.

"It isn't as if Leo has any obligation to spend his weekends with us, just because he does a lot of business with Mr. Fred," Hettie reminded her gently. "He's a good man. A little old for you, though," she added hesitantly.

Janie didn't answer her. She just smiled and walked back into the kitchen.

LEO SHOWERED, SHAVED, dressed to the hilt and got into the new black Lincoln sports car he'd just bought. Next year's model, and fast as lightning. He was due for a night on the town. And missing Janie's famous rubber chicken wasn't going to disappoint him one bit.

His conscience did nag him, though, oddly. Maybe it was just hearing Janie's friend, Marilee, harp on the girl all the time. In the past week, she'd started telling him some disturbing things that Janie had said about him. He was going to have to be more careful around Janie. He didn't want her to get the wrong idea. He had no interest in her at all. She was just a kid.

He glanced in the lighted mirror over the steering

wheel before he left the sprawling Hart Ranch. He had thick blond-streaked brown hair, a broad forehead, a slightly crooked nose and high cheekbones. But his teeth were good and strong, and he had a square jaw and a nice wide mouth. He wasn't all that handsome, but compared to most of his brothers, he was a hunk. He chuckled at that rare conceit and closed the mirror. He was rich enough that his looks didn't matter.

He didn't fool himself that Marilee would have found him all that attractive without his bankroll. But she was pretty and he didn't mind taking her to Houston and showing her off, like the fishing trophies he displayed on the walls of his study. A man had to have his little vanities, he told himself. But he thought about Janie's disappointment when he didn't show up for supper, her pain if she ever found out her best friend was stabbing her in the back, and he hated the guilt he felt.

He put on his seat belt, put the car in gear, and took off down the long driveway. He didn't have any reason to feel guilty, he told himself firmly. He was a bachelor, and he'd never done one single thing to give Janie Brewster the impression that he wanted to be the man in her life. Besides, he'd been on his own too long. A cultural evening in Houston was just the thing to cure the blues.

CHAPTER ONE

LEO HART WAS half out of humor. It had been a long week as it was, and now he was faced with trying to comfort his neighbor, Fred Brewster, who'd just lost the prize young Salers bull that Leo had wanted to buy. The bull was the offspring of a grand champion whose purchase had figured largely in Leo's improved cross-breeding program. He felt as sad as Fred seemed to.

"He was fine yesterday," Fred said heavily, wiping sweat off his narrow brow as the two men surveyed the bull in the pasture. The huge creature was lying dead on its side, not a mark on it. "I'm not the only rancher who's ever lost a prize bull, but these are damned suspicious circumstances."

"They are," Leo agreed grimly, his dark eyes surveying the bull. "It's just a thought, but you haven't had a problem with an employee, have you? Christabel Gaines said they just had a bull die of unknown causes. This happened after they fired a man named Jack Clark a couple of weeks ago. He's working for Duke Wright now, driving a cattle truck."

"Judd Dunn said it wasn't unknown causes that killed the bull, it was bloat. Judd's a Texas Ranger," Fred reminded him. "If there was sabotage on the ranch he co-owns with Christabel, I think he'd know it. No, Christabel had that young bull in a pasture with a lot of clover and she hadn't primed him on hay or tannin-containing forage beforehand. She won't use antibiotics, either, which would have helped prevent trouble. Even so, you can treat bloat if you catch it in time. It was bad luck that they didn't check that pasture, but Christabel's shorthanded and she's back at the vocational school full-time, too. Not much time to check on livestock."

"They had four other bulls that were still alive," Leo pointed out, scowling.

Fred shrugged. "Maybe they didn't like clover, or weren't in the same pasture." He shook his head. "I'm fairly sure their bull died of bloat. That's what Judd thinks, anyway. He says Christabel's unsettled by having those movie people coming next month to work out a shooting schedule on the ranch and she's the only one who thinks there was foul play." Fred rubbed a hand through his silver hair. "But to answer your question—yes, I did wonder about a disgruntled ex-employee, but I haven't fired anybody in over two years. So you can count out vengeance. And it wasn't bloat. My stock gets antibiotics."

"Don't say that out loud," Leo chuckled. "If the Tremaynes hear you, there'll be a fight."

"It's my ranch. I run it my way." Fred looked sadly toward the bull again. He was having financial woes the likes of which he'd never faced. He was too proud to tell Leo the extent of it. "This bull is a hell of a loss right now, too, with my breeding program under way. He wasn't insured, so I can't afford to replace him. Well, not just yet," he amended, because he didn't want Leo to think he was nearly broke.

"That's one problem we can solve," Leo replied. "I've got that beautiful Salers bull I bought two years ago, but it's time I replaced him. I'd have loved to have had yours, but while I'm looking for a replacement, you can borrow mine for your breeding season."

"Leo, I can't let you do that," Fred began, overwhelmed by the offer. He knew very well what that bull's services cost.

Leo held up a big hand and grinned. "Sure you can. I've got an angle. I get first pick of your young bulls next spring."

"You devil, you," Fred said, chuckling. "All right, all right. On that condition, I'll take him and be much obliged. But I'd feel better if there was a man sitting up with him at night to guard him."

Leo stretched sore muscles, pushing his Stetson back over his blond-streaked brown hair. It was late September, but still very hot in Jacobsville, which was in southeastern Texas. He'd been helping move bulls all morning, and he was tired. "We can take care of security for him," Leo said easily. "I've got two cowboys banged up in accidents who can't work cattle. They're still on my payroll, so they can sit over here and guard my bull while they recuperate."

"And we'll feed them," Fred said.

Leo chuckled. "Now that's what I call a real nice solution. One of them," he confided, "eats for three men."

"I won't mind." His eyes went back to the still bull one more time. "He was the best bull, Leo. I had so many hopes for him."

"I know. But there are other champion-sired Salers bulls," Leo said.

"Sure. But not one like that one." He gestured toward the animal. "He had such beautiful conformation—" He broke off as a movement to one side caught his attention. He turned, leaned forward and then gaped at his approaching daughter. "Janie?" he asked, as if he wasn't sure of her identity.

Janie Brewster had light brown hair and green eyes. She'd tried going blond once, but these days her hair was its natural color. Straight, thick and sleek, it hung to her waist. She had a nice figure, a little on the slender side, and pretty little pert breasts. She even had nice legs. But anyone looking at her right now could be forgiven for mistaking her for a young bull rider.

She was covered with mud from head to toe. Even her hair was caked with it. She had a saddle over one thin shoulder, leaning forward to take its weight. The separation between her boots and jeans was impercepti-ble. Her blouse and arms were likewise. Only her eyes were visible, her eyebrows streaked where the mud had been haphazardly wiped away.

"Hi, Daddy," she muttered as she walked past them with a forced smile. "Hi, Leo. Nice day."

Leo's dark eyes were wide-open, like Fred's. He couldn't even manage words. He nodded, and kept gap-ing at the mud doll walking past.

"What have you been doing?" Fred shouted after his only child.

"Just riding around," she said gaily.

"Riding around," Fred murmured to himself as she trailed mud onto the porch and stopped there, calling for their housekeeper. "I can't remember the last time I saw her on a horse," he added.

"Neither can I," Leo was forced to admit.

Fred shook his head. "She has these spells lately," he said absently. "First it was baling hay. She went out with four of the hands and came home covered in dust and thorns. Then she took up dipping cattle." He cleared his throat. "Better to forget that altogether. Now it's riding. I don't know what the hell's got into her. She was all geared up to transfer to a four-year college and get on with her psychology degree. Then all of a sudden, she announces that she's going to learn ranching." He threw up his hands. "I'll never understand children. Will you?" he asked Leo.

Leo chuckled. "Don't ask me. Fatherhood is one role in life I have no desire to play. Listen, about my bull," he continued. "I'll have him trucked right over, and the men will come with him. If you have any more problems, you just let me know."

Fred was relieved. The Harts owned five ranches. Nobody had more clout than they did, politically and financially. The loan of that bull would help him recoup his losses and get back on his feet. Leo was a gentleman. "I'm damned grateful, Leo. We've been having hard times lately."

Leo only smiled. He knew that the Brewsters were having a bad time financially. He and Fred had swapped and traded bulls for years—although less expensive ones than Fred's dead Salers bull—and they frequently did business together. He was glad he could help.

He did wonder about Janie's odd behavior. She'd spent weeks trying to vamp him with low-cut blouses and dresses. She was always around when he came to see Fred on business, waiting in the living room in a seductive pose. Not that Janie even knew how to be seductive, he told himself amusedly. She was twenty-one, but hardly in the class with her friend Marilee Morgan, who was only four years older than Janie but could give Mata Hari lessons in seduction.

He wondered if Marilee had been coaching her in tomboyish antics. That would be amusing, because lately Marilee had been using Janie's tactics on him. The former tomboy-turned-debutante had even finagled him into taking her out to eat in Houston. He wondered if Janie knew. Sometimes friends could become your worst enemy, he thought. Luckily Janie only had a crush on him, which would wear itself out all the faster once she knew he had gone out with her best friend. Janie was far too young for him, and not only in age. The sooner she realized it, the better. Besides, he didn't like her new competitive spirit. Why was she trying to compete with her father in ranch management all of a sudden? Was it a liberation thing? She'd never shown any such inclination before, and her new appearance was appalling. The one thing Leo had admired about her was the elegance and sophistication with which she dressed. Janie in muddy jeans was a complete turnoff.

He left Fred at the pasture and drove back to the ranch, his mind already on ways and means to find out what had caused that healthy bull's sudden demise.

JANIE WAS LISTENING to their housekeeper's tirade through the bathroom door.

"I'll clean it all up, Hettie," she promised. "It's just dirt. It will come out."

"It's red mud! It will never come out!" Hettie was grumbling. "You'll be red from head to toe forever! People will mistake you for that nineteenth-century Kiowa, Satanta, who painted everything he owned red, even his horse!"

Janie laughed as she stripped off the rest of her clothes and stepped into the shower. Besides being a

keen student of Western history, Hettie was all fire and
wind, and she'd blow out soon. She was such a sweetheart. Janie's mother had died years ago, leaving behind Janie and her father and Hettie—and Aunt Lydia
who lived in Jacobsville. Fortunately, Aunt Lydia only
visited infrequently. She was so very house-proud,
so clothes-conscious, so debutante! She was just like
Janie's late mother, in fact, who had raised Janie to be a
little flower blossom in a world of independent, strong
women. She spared a thought for her mother's horror
if she could have lived long enough to see what her
daughter had worn at college. There, where she could
be herself, Janie didn't wear designer dresses and hang
out with the right social group. Janie studied anthropol-
ogy, as well as the psychology her aunt Lydia had insisted on—and felt free to insist, since she helped pay
Janie's tuition. But Janie spent most of her weekends
and afternoons buried in mud, learning how to dig out
fragile pieces of ancient pottery and projectile points.

But she'd gone on with the pretense when she was
home—when Aunt Lydia was visiting, of course—proving her worth at psychology. Sadly, it had gone awry
when she psychoanalyzed Leo's brother Callaghan last
year over the asparagus. She'd gone to her room howling
with laughter after Aunt Lydia had hung on every word
approvingly. She was sorry she'd embarrassed Cag, but
the impulse had been irresistible. Her aunt was *so* gullible. She'd felt guilty afterward, though, for not telling
Aunt Lydia her true interests.

She finished her shower, dried off, and changed into
new clothes so that she could start cleaning up the floors
where she'd tracked mud. Despite her complaints, Hettie
would help. She didn't really mind housework. Neither

did Janie, although her late mother would be horrified if she could see her only child on the floor with a scrub brush alongside Hettie's ample figure.

Janie helped with everything, except cooking. Her expertise in the kitchen was, to put it mildly, nonexistent. But, she thought, brightening, that was the next thing on her list of projects. She was undergoing a major self-improvement. First she was going to learn ranching—even if it killed her—and then she was going to learn to cook.

She wished this transformation had been her idea, but actually, it had been Marilee's. The other girl had told her, in confidence, that she'd been talking to Leo and Leo had told her flatly that the reason he didn't notice Janie was that she didn't know anything about ranching. She was too well-dressed, too chic, too sophisticated. And the worst thing was that she didn't know anything about cooking, either, Marilee claimed. So if Janie wanted to land that big, hunky fish, she was going to have to make some major changes.

It sounded like a good plan, and Marilee had been her friend since grammar school, when the Morgan family had moved next door. So Janie accepted Marilee's advice with great pleasure, knowing that her best friend would never steer her wrong. She was going to stay home—not go back to college—and she was going to show Leo Hart that she could be the sort of woman who appealed to him. She'd work so hard at it, she'd have to succeed!

Not that her attempts at riding a horse were anything to write home about, she had to admit as she mopped her way down the long wooden floor of the hall. But she was a rancher's daughter. She'd get better with practice.

SHE DID KEEP TRYING. A week later, she was making biscuits in the kitchen—or trying to learn how—when she dropped the paper flour bag hard on the counter and was dusted from head to toe with the white substance.

It would have to be just that minute that her father came in the back door with Leo in tow.

"Janie?" her father exclaimed, wide-eyed.

"Hi, Dad!" she said with a big grin. "Hi, Leo."

"What in blazes are you doing?" her father demanded.

"Putting the flour in a canister," she lied, still smiling.

"Where's Hettie?" he asked.

Their housekeeper was hiding in the bedroom, supposedly making beds, and trying not to howl at Janie's pitiful efforts. "Cleaning, I believe," she said.

"Aunt Lydia not around?"

"Playing bridge with the Harrisons," she said.

"Bridge!" her father scoffed. "If it isn't bridge, it's golf. If it isn't golf, it's tennis… Is she coming over today to go over those stocks with me or not?" he persisted, because they jointly owned some of his late wife's shares and couldn't sell them without Lydia's permission. If he could ever find the blasted woman!

"She said she wasn't coming over until Saturday, Dad," Janie reminded him.

He let out an angry sigh. "Well, come on, Leo, I'll show you the ones I want to sell and let you advise me. They're in my desk…damn bridge! I can't do a thing until Lydia makes up her mind."

Leo gave Janie a curious glance but he kept walking and didn't say another word to her. Minutes later, he left—out the front door, not the back.

JANIE'S SELF-IMPROVEMENT CAMPAIGN continued into the following week with calf roping, which old John was teaching her out in the corral. Since she could now loop the rope around a practice wooden cow with horns, she was progressing to livestock.

She followed John's careful instruction and tossed her loop over the head of the calf, but she'd forgotten to dig her heels in. The calf hadn't. He jerked her off her feet and proceeded to run around the ring like a wild thing, trying to get away from the human slithering after him at a breakneck pace.

Of course, Leo would drive up next to the corral in time to see John catch and throw the calf, leaving Janie covered in mud. She looked like a road disaster.

This time Leo didn't speak. He was too busy laughing. Janie couldn't speak, either, her mouth was full of mud. She gave both men a glare and stomped off toward the back door of the house, trailing mud and unspeakable stuff, fuming the whole while.

A bath and change of clothes improved her looks and her smell. She was resigned to finding Leo gone when she got out, so she didn't bother to dress up or put on makeup. She wandered out to the kitchen in jeans and a loose long-sleeved denim shirt, with her hair in a lopsided ponytail and her feet bare.

"You'll step on something sharp and cripple yourself," Hettie warned, turning from the counter where she was making rolls, her ample arms up to the elbows in flour.

"I have tough feet," Janie protested with a warm smile. She went up and hugged Hettie hard from behind, loving the familiar smells of freshly washed cotton and flour that seemed to cling to her. Hettie had been around since Janie was six. She couldn't imagine life without the gray-haired, blue-eyed treasure with her constantly disheveled hair and worried expression. "Oh, Hettie, what would we do without you?" she asked on a sigh, and closed her eyes.

"Get away, you pest," Hettie muttered, "I know what you're up to... Janie Brewster, I'll whack you!"

But Janie was already out of reach, dangling Hettie's apron from one hand, her green eyes dancing with mischief.

"You put that back on me or you'll get no rolls tonight!" Hettie raged at her.

"All right, all right, I was only kidding," Janie chuckled. She replaced the apron around Hettie's girth and was fastening it when she heard the door open behind her.

"You stop teaching her these tricks!" Hettie growled at the newcomer.

"Who, me?" Leo exclaimed with total innocence.

Janie's hands fumbled with the apron. Her heart ran wild. He hadn't left. She'd thought he was gone, and she hadn't bothered with her appearance. He was still here, and she looked like last year's roast!

"You'll drop that apron, Janie," Leo scolded playfully.

Janie glanced at him as she retied the apron. "You can talk," she chided. "I hear your housekeepers keep quitting because you untie aprons constantly! One kept a broom handle!"

"She broke it on my hard head," he said smugly. "What are you making, Hettie?"

"Rolls," she said. She glanced warily at Leo. "I can't make biscuits. Sorry."

He gave her a hard glare. "Just because I did something a little offbeat…"

"Carried that little chef right out of his restaurant, with him kicking and screaming all the way, I heard," Hettie mused, eyes twinkling.

"He said he could bake biscuits. I was only taking him home with me to let him prove it," Leo said belligerently.

"That's not what he thought," Hettie chuckled. "I hear he dropped the charges…?"

"Nervous little guy," Leo said, shaking his head. "He'd never have worked out, anyway." He gave her a long look. "You sure you can't bake a biscuit? Have you ever tried?"

"No, and I won't. I like working here," she said firmly.

He sighed. "Just checking." He peered over her shoulder fondly. "Rolls, huh? I can't remember when I've had a homemade roll."

"Tell Fred to invite you to supper," Hettie suggested.

He glanced at Janie. "Why can't she do it?"

Janie was tongue-tied. She couldn't think at all.

The lack of response from her dumbfounded Leo. To have Janie hesitate about inviting him for a meal was shocking. Leo scowled and just stared at her openly, which only made her more nervous and uncertain. She knew she looked terrible. Leo wanted a woman who could do ranch work and cook, but surely he wanted one who looked pretty, too. Right now, Janie could have qualified for the Frump of the Year award.

She bit her lower lip, hard, and looked as if she were about to cry.

"Hey," he said softly, in a tone he'd never used with her before, "what's wrong?"

"Have to let this rise," Hettie was murmuring after she'd covered the dough and washed her hands, oblivious to what was happening behind her. "Meanwhile I'm going to put another load of clothes in the washer, darlin'," she called to Janie over her shoulder.

The door into the dining room closed, but they didn't notice.

Leo moved closer to Janie, and suddenly his big, lean hands were on her thin shoulders, resting heavily over the soft denim. They were warm and very strong.

Her breath caught in the back of her throat while she looked up into black eyes that weren't teasing or playful. They were intent, narrow, faintly glittering. There was no expression on his handsome face at all. He looked into her eyes as if he'd never seen them, or her, before—and she looked terrible!

"Come on," he coaxed. "Tell me what's wrong. If it's something I can fix, I will."

Her lips trembled. Surely, she could make up something, quick, before he moved away!

"I got hurt," she whispered in a shameful lie. "When the calf dragged me around the corral."

"Did you?" He was only half listening. His eyes were on her mouth. It was the prettiest little mouth, like a pink bow, full and soft, just barely parted over perfect, white teeth. He wondered if she'd been kissed, and how often. She never seemed to date, or at least, he didn't know about her boyfriends. He shouldn't be curious, either, but Marilee had hinted that Janie had more boyfriends than other local girls, that she was a real rounder.

Janie was melting. Her knees were weak. Any minute, she was going to be a little puddle of love looking up at his knees.

He felt her quiver under his hands, and his scowl grew darker. If she was as sophisticated as Marilee said she was, why was she trembling now? An experienced woman would be winding her arms around his neck already, offering her mouth, curving her body into his...

His fingers tightened involuntarily on her soft arms. "Come here," he said huskily, and tugged her right up against his tall, muscular body. Of all the Harts, he was the tallest, and the most powerfully built. Janie's breasts pressed into his diaphragm. She felt him tauten at the contact, felt his curiosity as he looked down into her wide, soft, dazed eyes. Her hands lightly touched his shirtfront, but hesitantly, as if it embarrassed her to touch him at all.

He let out a soft breath. His head was spinning with forbidden longings. Janie was barely twenty-one. She was the daughter of a man he did business with. She was off-limits. So why was he looking at her mouth and feeling his body swell sensuously at just the brush of her small breasts against him?

"Don't pick at my shirt," he said quietly. His voice was unusually deep and soft, its tone unfamiliar. "Flatten your hands on my chest."

She did that, slowly, as if she were just learning how to walk. Her hands were cold and nervous, but they warmed on his body. She stood very still, hoping against hope that he wasn't going to regain the senses she was certain he'd momentarily lost. She didn't even want to breathe, to do anything that would distract him. He seemed to be in a trance, and she was feeling dreams come true in the most unexpected and delightful way.

He smiled quizzically. "Don't you know how?"

Her lips were dry. She moistened them with just the tip of her tongue. He seemed to find that little movement fascinating. He watched her mouth almost hungrily. "How…to…do what?" she choked.

His hand went to her cheek and his thumb suddenly ran roughly over her lips, parting them in a whip of urgent, shocking emotion. "How to do this," he murmured as his head bent.

She saw the faint smile on his hard mouth as his lips parted. They brushed against hers in tiny little whispers of contact that weren't nearly enough to feed the hunger he was coaxing out of her.

Her nails curled into his shirt and he tensed. She felt thick hair over the warm, hard muscles of his chest. Closer, she felt the hard, heavy thunder of his pulse there, under her searching hands.

"Nice," he whispered. His voice was taut now, like his body against her.

She felt his big hands slide down her waist to her hips while he was playing with her mouth in the most arousing way. She couldn't breathe. Did he know? Could he tell that she was shaking with desire?

Her lips parted more with every sensuous brush of his mouth against them. At the same time, his hands moved to her narrow hips and teased against her lower spine. She'd never felt such strange sensations. She felt her body swell, as if it had been stung all over by bees, but the sensation produced pleasure instead of pain.

He nibbled at her upper lip, feeling it quiver tentatively as his tongue slid under it and began to explore.

One lean hand slid around to the base of her hips and slowly gathered them into his, in a lazy movement that made her suddenly aware of the changing contours of his body.

She gasped and pulled against his hand.

He lifted his head and searched her wide, shocked green eyes. "Plenty of boyfriends, hmm?" he murmured sarcastically, almost to himself.

"Boy…friends?" Her voice sounded as if she were being strangled.

His hand moved back to her waist, the other one moved to her round chin and his thumb tugged gently at her lower lip. "Leave it like this," he whispered. His mouth hovered over hers just as it parted, and she found herself going on tiptoe, leaning toward him, almost begging for his mouth to come down and cover hers.

But he was still nibbling at her upper lip, gently toying with it, until he tilted her chin and his teeth tugged softly at the lower lip. His mouth brushed roughly over hers, teaching it to follow, to plead, then to demand something more urgent, more thorough than this slow torment.

Her nails bit into his chest and she moaned.

As if he'd been waiting patiently for that tiny little sound, his arms swallowed her up whole and his eyes, when they met hers, glittered like candlelight from deep in a cave.

His hand was in her ponytail, ripping away the rubber band so that he could catch strands of it in his strong fingers and angle her face just where he wanted it.

"Maybe you are old enough…" he breathed just before his mouth plunged deeply into hers.

She tautened all over with heated pleasure. Her body

arched against him, no longer protesting the sudden
hardness of him against her. She reached up to hold
him, to keep that tormenting, hungry mouth against her
lips. It was every dream she'd ever dreamed, coming
true. She could hardly believe it was happening here, in
broad daylight, in the kitchen where she'd been trying
so hard to learn to make things that would please him.
But he seemed to be pleased, just the same. He groaned
against her lips, and his arms were bruising now, as if
he wasn't quite in control. That was exciting. She threw
caution to the winds and opened her mouth deliberately
under the crush of his, inviting him in.

She felt his tongue go deep into the soft darkness,
and she shivered as his mouth devoured hers.

Only the sound of a door slamming penetrated the
thick sensual fog that held them both in thrall.

Leo lifted his head, slowly, and looked down into a
face he didn't recognize. Janie's green eyes were like
wet emeralds in her flushed face. Her lips were swollen, soft, sensual. Her body was clinging to his. He had
her off the floor in his hungry embrace, and his body
was throbbing with desire.

He knew that she could feel him, that she knew he
was aroused. It was a secret thing, that only the two
of them knew. It had to stay that way. He had to stop.
This was wrong…!

He let go of her slowly, easing her back, while he
sucked in a long, hard breath and shivered with a hunger he couldn't satisfy. He became aware of the rough
grip he had on her upper arms and he relaxed it at once.
He'd never meant to hurt her.

He fought for control, reciting multiplication tables

silently in his mind until he felt his body unclench and relax.

It troubled him that he'd lost control so abruptly, and with a woman he should never have touched. He hadn't meant to touch her in the first place. He couldn't understand why he'd gone headfirst at her like that. He was usually cool with women, especially with Janie.

The way she was looking at him was disturbing. He was going to have a lot of explaining to do, and he didn't know how to begin. Janie was years too young for him, only his body didn't think so. Now he had to make his mind get himself out of this predicament.

"That shouldn't have happened," he said through his teeth.

She was hanging on every word, deaf to meanings, deaf to denials. Her body throbbed. "It's like the flu," she said, dazed, staring up at him. "It makes you... ache."

He shook her gently. "You're too young to have aches," he said flatly. "And I'm old enough to know better than to do something this stupid. Are you listening to me? This shouldn't have happened. I'm sorry."

Belatedly, she realized that he was backtracking. Of course he hadn't meant to kiss her. He'd made his opinion of her clear for years, and even if he liked kissing her, it didn't mean that he was ready to rush out and buy a ring. Quite the opposite.

She stepped away from him, her face still flushed, her eyes full of dreams she had to hide from him.

"I... I'm sorry, too," she stammered.

"Hell," he growled, ramming his hands into his pockets. "It was my fault. I started it."

She moved one shoulder. "No harm done." She

cleared her throat and fought for inspiration. It came unexpectedly. Her eyes began to twinkle wickedly. "I have to take lessons when they're offered."

His eyebrows shot up. Had he heard her say that, or was he delusional?

"I'm not the prom queen," she pointed out. "Men aren't thick on the ground around here, except old bachelors who chew tobacco and don't bathe."

"I call that prejudice," he said, relaxing into humor.

"I'll bet you don't hang out with women who smell like dirty horses," she said.

He pursed his lips. Like hers, they were faintly swollen. "I don't know about that. The last time I saw you, I recall, you were neck-deep in mud and sh—"

"You can stop right there!" she interrupted, flushing.

His dark eyes studied her long hair, liking its thick waves and its light brown color. "Pity your name isn't Jeanie," he murmured. "Stephen Foster wrote a song about her hair."

She smiled. He liked her hair, at least. Maybe he liked her a little, too.

She was pretty when she smiled like that, he thought, observing her. "Do I get invited to supper?" he drawled, lost in that soft, hungry look she was giving him. "If you say yes, I might consider giving you a few more lessons. Beginner class only, of course," he added with a grin.

CHAPTER TWO

JANIE WAS SURE she hadn't heard him say that, but he was still smiling. She smiled back. She felt pretty. No makeup, no shoes, disheveled—and Leo had kissed her anyway. She beamed. At least, she beamed until she remembered the Hart bread mania. Any of them would do anything for a biscuit. Did that extend to home-made rolls?

"You're looking suspicious," he pointed out.

"A man who would kidnap a poor little pastry chef might do anything for a homemade roll," she reminded him.

He sighed. "Hettie makes wonderful rolls," he had to admit.

"Oh, you!" She hit him gently and then laughed. He was impossible. "Okay, you can come to supper."

He beamed. "You're a nice girl."

Nice. Well, at least he liked her. It was a start. It didn't occur to her, then, that a man who was seriously interested in her wouldn't think of her as just "nice."

Hettie came back into the room, still oblivious to the undercurrents, and got out a plastic bowl. She filled it with English peas from the crisper. "All right, my girl, sit down here and shell these. You staying?" she asked Leo.

"She said I could," he told Hettie.

"Then you can go away while we get it cooked."

"I'll visit my bull. Fred's got him in the pasture."

Leo didn't say another word. But the look he gave Janie before he left the kitchen was positively wicked.

But if she thought the little interlude had made any permanent difference in her relationship with Leo, Janie was doomed to disappointment. He came to supper, but he spent the whole time talking genetic breeding with Fred, and although he was polite to Janie, she might as well have been on the moon.

He didn't stay long after supper, either, making his excuses and praising Hettie for her wonderful cooking. He smiled at Janie, but not the way he had when they were alone in the kitchen. It was as if he'd put the kisses out of his mind forever, and expected her to act as if he'd never touched her. It was disheartening. It was heartbreaking. It was just like old times, except that now Leo had kissed her and she wanted him to do it again. Judging by his attitude over supper, she had a better chance of landing a movie role.

SHE SPENT THE next few weeks remembering Leo's hungry kisses and aching for more of them. When she wasn't daydreaming, she was practicing biscuit-making. Hettie muttered about the amount of flour she was going through.

"Janie, you're going to bankrupt us in the kitchen!" the older woman moaned when Janie's fifth batch of biscuits came out looking like skeet pigeons. "That's your second bag of flour today!"

Janie was glowering at her latest effort on the baking sheet. "Something's wrong, and I can't decide what.

I mean, I put in salt and baking powder, just like the recipe said…"

Hettie picked up the empty flour bag and read the label. Her eyes twinkled. "Janie, darlin', you bought self-rising flour."

"Yes. So?" she asked obliviously.

"If it's self-rising, it already has the salt and baking powder in it, doesn't it?"

Janie burst out laughing. "So that's what I'm doing wrong! Hand me another bag of flour, could you?"

"This is the last one," Hettie said mournfully.

"No problem. I'll just drive to the store and get some more. Need anything?"

"Milk and eggs," Hettie said at once.

"We've got four chickens," Janie exclaimed, turning, "and you have to buy eggs?"

"The chickens are molting."

Janie smiled. "And when they molt, they don't lay. Sorry. I forgot. I'll be back in a jiffy," she added, peeling off her apron.

She paused just long enough to brush her hair out, leaving it long, and put on a little makeup. She thrust her arms into her nice fringed leather jacket, because it was seasonally cool outside as well as raining, and popped into her red sports car. You never could tell when you might run into Leo, because he frequently dashed into the supermarket for frozen biscuits and butter when he was between cooks.

SURE ENOUGH, AS SHE started for the checkout counter with her milk, eggs and flour, she spotted Leo, head and shoulders above most of the men present. He was wearing that long brown Australian drover's coat he favored in wet weather, and he was smiling in a funny sort of way.

That was when Janie noticed his companion. He was bending down toward a pretty little brunette who was chattering away at his side. Janie frowned, because that dark wavy hair was familiar. And then she realized who it was. Leo was talking to Marilee Morgan!

She relaxed. Marilee was her friend. Surely, she was talking her up to Leo. She almost rushed forward to say hello, but what if she interrupted at a crucial moment? There was, after all, the annual Jacobsville Cattleman's Ball in two weeks, the Saturday before Thanksgiving. It was very likely that Marilee was dropping hints right and left that Janie would love Leo to escort her.

She chuckled to herself. She was lucky to have a friend like Marilee.

If JANIE HAD known what Marilee was actually saying to Leo, she might have changed her mind about the other woman's friendship and a lot of other things.

"It was so nice of you to drive me to the store, Leo," Marilee was cooing at Leo as they walked out. "My wrist is really sore from that fall I took."

"No problem," he murmured with a smile.

"The Cattleman's Ball is week after next," Marilee added coyly. "I would really love to go, but nobody's asked me. I won't be able to drive by then, either, I'm sure. It was a bad sprain. They take almost as long as a broken bone to heal." She glanced up at him, weighing her chances. "Of course, Janie's told everybody that you're taking her. She said you're over there all the time now, that it's just a matter of time before you buy her a ring. Everybody knows."

He scowled fiercely. He'd only kissed Janie, he hadn't proposed marriage, for God's sake! Surely the girl wasn't going to get possessive because of a kiss? He hated gossip, especially about himself. Well, Janie could forget any invitations of that sort. He didn't like aggressive women who told lies around town. Not one bit!

"You can go with me," he told Marilee nonchalantly. "Despite what Janie told you, I am no woman's property, and I'm damned sure not booked for the dance!"

Marilee beamed. "Thanks, Leo!"

He shrugged. She was pretty and he liked her company. She wasn't one of those women who felt the need to constantly compete with men. He'd made his opinion about that pretty clear to Marilee in recent weeks. It occurred to him that Janie was suddenly trying to do just that, what with calf roping and ranch work and hard riding. Odd, when she'd never shown any such inclination before. But her self-assured talk about being his date for the ball set him off and stopped his mind from further reasoning about her sudden change of attitude.

He smiled down at Marilee. "Thanks for telling me about the gossip," he added. "Best way to curb it is to disprove it publicly."

"Of course it is. You mustn't blame Janie too much," she added with just the right amount of affection. "She's very young. Compared to me, I mean. If we hadn't been neighbors, we probably wouldn't be friends at all. She seems so…well, so juvenile at times, doesn't she?"

Leo frowned. He'd forgotten that Marilee was older than Janie. He thought back to those hard, hungry kisses he'd shared with Janie and could have cursed himself for his weakness. She was immature. She was building a whole affair on a kiss or two. Then he remembered something unexpectedly.

He glanced down at Marilee. "You said she had more boyfriends than anybody else in town."

Marilee cleared her throat. "Well, yes, *boy*friends. Not men friends, though," she added, covering her bases. It was hard to make Janie look juvenile if she was also a heartbreaking rounder.

Leo felt placated, God knew why. "There's a difference."

Marilee agreed. A tiny voice in her mind chided her for being so mean to her best friend, but Leo was a real hunk, and she was as infatuated with him as Janie was. All was fair in love and war, didn't they say? Besides, it was highly unlikely that Leo would ever ask Janie out—but, just in case, Marilee had planted a nice little suspicion in his mind to prevent that. She smiled as she walked beside him to his truck, dreaming of the first of many dances and being in Leo's arms. One day, she thought ecstatically, he might even want to marry her!

JANIE WENT THROUGH two more bags of flour with attempts at biscuits that became better with each failed try. Finally, after several days' work, she had produced an edible batch that impressed even Hettie.

In between cooking, she was getting much better on horseback. Now, mounted on her black-and-white quarter horse, Blackie, she could cut out a calf and drive it into the makeshift corral used for doctoring sick animals. She could throw a calf, too, with something like professionalism, despite sore muscles and frequent bruises. She could rope, after a fashion, and she was riding better all the time. At least the chafing of her thighs against the saddle had stopped, and the muscles had acclimatized to the new stress being placed on them.

Saturday night loomed. It was only four days until the Cattleman's Ball, and she had a beautiful spaghetti-strapped lacy oyster-white dress to wear. It came to her ankles and was low-cut in front, leaving the creamy skin of her shoulders bare. There was a side-slit that went up her thigh, exposing her beautiful long legs. She paired the dress with white spiked high heels sporting ankle straps which she thought were extremely sexy, and she had a black velvet coat with a white silk lining to defend against the cold evening air. Now all she lacked was a date.

She'd expected Leo to ask her to the ball after those hungry kisses, despite his coolness later that day. But he hadn't been near the ranch since he'd had supper with her and her father. What made it even more peculiar was that he'd talked with her father out on the ranch several times. He just didn't come to the house. Janie assumed that he was regretting those hard kisses, and was afraid that she was taking him too seriously. He was avoiding her. He couldn't have made it plainer.

That made it a pretty good bet that he wasn't planning to take her to any Cattleman's Ball. She phoned Marilee in desperation.

The other woman sounded uneasy when she heard Janie's voice, and she was quick to ask why Janie had phoned.

"I saw you with Leo in the grocery store week before last," Janie began, "and I didn't interfere, because I was sure you were trying to talk him into taking me to the ball. But he didn't want to, did he?" she added sadly.

There was a sound like someone swallowing, on the other end of the phone. "Well, actually, no. I'm sorry." Marilee sounded as if she were strangling on the words.

"Don't feel bad," Janie said gently. "It's not your fault. You're my best friend in the whole world. I know you tried."

"Janie…"

"I had this beautiful white dress that I bought specially," Janie added on a sigh. "Well, that's that. Are you going?"

There was a tense pause. "Yes."

"Good! Anybody I know?"

"N…no," Marilee stammered.

"You have fun," Janie said.

"You…uh…aren't going, are you?" Marilee added.

Her friend certainly was acting funny, Janie thought. "No, I don't have a date," Janie chuckled. "There'll be other dances, I guess. Maybe Leo will ask me another time." After he's got over being afraid of me, she added silently. "If you see him," she said quickly, "you might mention that I can now cut out cattle and throw a calf. And I can make a biscuit that doesn't go through the floor when dropped!"

She was laughing, but Marilee didn't.

"I have to get to the hairdresser, Janie," Marilee said. "I'm really sorry…about the ball."

"Not your fault," Janie repeated. "Just have enough fun for both of us, okay?"

"Okay. See you."

The line went dead and Janie frowned. Something must be very wrong with Marilee. She wished she'd been more persistent and asked what was the matter. Well, she'd go over to Marilee's house after the dance to pump her for all the latest gossip, and then she could find out what was troubling her friend.

She put the ball to the back of her mind, despite the disappointment, and went out to greet her father as he rode in from the pasture with two of his men.

He swung out of the saddle at the barn and grinned at her. "Just the girl I wanted to see," he said at once. He pulled out his wallet. "I've got to have some more work gloves, just tore the last pair I had apart on barbed wire. How about going by the hardware store and get me another pair of those suede-palmed ones, extra large?"

"My pleasure," Janie said at once. Leo often went to the hardware store, and she might accidentally run into him there. "Be back in a jiffy!"

"Don't speed!" her father called to her.

She only chuckled, diving into her sports car. She remembered belatedly that she didn't have either purse or car keys, or her face fixed, and jumped right back out again to rectify those omissions.

Ten minutes later, she was parking her car in front of the Jacobsville Hardware Store. With a wildly beating heart, she noticed one of the black double-cabbed Hart Ranch trucks parked nearby. Leo! She was certain it was Leo!

With her heart pounding, she checked her makeup in the rearview mirror and tugged her hair gently away from her cheeks. She'd left it down today deliberately, remembering that Leo had something of a weakness for long hair. It was thick and clean, shining like a soft brown curtain. She was wearing a long beige skirt with riding boots, and a gold satin blouse. She looked pretty good, even if she did say so herself! Now if Leo would just notice her…

She walked into the hardware store with her breath catching in her throat as she anticipated Leo's big smile at her approach. He was the handsomest of the Hart brothers, and really, the most personable. He was kindness itself. She remembered his soft voice in her kitchen, asking what was wrong. Oh, to have that soft voice in her ear forever!

There was nobody at the counter. That wasn't unusual, the clerks were probably waiting on customers. She walked back to where the gloves were kept and suddenly heard Leo's deep voice on the other side of the high aisle, unseen.

"Don't forget to add that roll of hog wire to the order," he was telling one of the clerks.

"I won't forget," Joe Howland's pleasant voice replied. "Are you going to the Cattleman's Ball?" Joe added just as Janie was about to raise her voice and call to Leo over the aisle.

"I guess I am," Leo replied. "I didn't plan to, but a pretty friend needed a ride and I'm obliging."

Janie's heart skipped and fell flat. Leo already had a date? Who? She moved around the aisle and in sight of Leo and Joe. Leo had his back to her, but Joe noticed her and smiled.

"That friend wouldn't be Janie Brewster, by any chance?" Joe teased loudly.

The question made Leo unreasonably angry. "Listen, just because she caught the bouquet at Micah Steele's wedding is no reason to start linking her with me," he said shortly. "She may have a good family background, she may be easy on the eyes, she may even learn to cook someday—miracles still happen. But no matter what she does, or how well, she is never going to appeal to me as a woman!" he added. "Having her spreading ludicrous gossip about our relationship all over town isn't making her any more attractive to me, either. It's a dead turnoff!"

Janie felt a shock like an electric jolt go through her. She couldn't even move for the pain.

Joe, horrified, opened his mouth to speak.

Leo made a rough gesture with one lean hand, burning with pent-up anger. "She looks like the rough side of a corncob lately, anyway," Leo continued, warming to his subject. "The only thing she ever had going for her were her looks, and she's spent the last few weeks covered in mud or dust or bread flour. She's out all hours proving she can compete with any man on the place and she can't stop bragging about what a great catch she's made with me. She's already told half the town that I'm a kiss short of buying her an engagement ring. That is, when she isn't putting it around that I'm taking her to the Cattleman's Ball, when I haven't even damned well asked her! Well, she's got her eye on the wrong man. I don't want some half-baked kid with a figure like a boy and an ego the size of my boots! I wouldn't have Janie Brewster for a wife if she came complete with a stable of purebred Salers bulls, and that's saying something. She makes me sick to my stomach!"

Joe had gone pale and he was grimacing. Curious, Leo turned...and there was Janie Brewster, staring at him down the aisle with a face as tragic as if he'd just taken a whittling knife to her heart.

"Janie," he said slowly.

She took a deep, steadying breath and managed to drag her eyes away from his face. "Hi, Joe," she said with a wan little smile. Her voice sounded choked. She

couldn't possibly look for gloves, she had to get away!
"Just wanted to check and see if you'd gotten in that
tack Dad ordered last week," she improvised.

"Not just yet, Janie," Joe told her in a gentle tone.
"I'm real sorry."

"No problem. No problem at all. Thanks, Joe. Hello,
Mr. Hart," she said, without really meeting Leo's eyes,
and she even managed a smile through her tattered dignity. "Nice day out, isn't it? Looks like we might even
get that rain we need so badly. See you."

She went out the door with her head high, as proudly
as a conquering army, leaving Leo sick to his stomach
for real.

"Why the hell didn't you say something?" Leo asked
Joe furiously.

"Didn't know how," Joe replied miserably.

"How long had she been standing there?" Leo persisted.

"The whole time, Leo," came the dreaded reply. "She
heard every word."

As if to punctuate the statement, from outside came
the sudden raucous squeal of tires on pavement as Janie
took off toward the highway in a burst of speed. She was
driving her little sports car, and Leo's heart stopped as
he realized how upset she was.

He jerked his cell phone out of his pocket and dialed
the police department. "Is that Grier?" he said at once
when the call was answered, recognizing Jacobsville's
new assistant police chief's deep voice. "Listen, Janie
Brewster just lit out of town like a scalded cat in her
sports car. She's upset and it's my fault, but she could
kill herself. Have you got somebody out on the Victoria

road who could pull her over and give her a warning? Yeah. Thanks, Grier. I owe you one."

He hung up, cursing harshly under his breath. "She'll be spitting fire if anybody tells her I sent the police after her, but I can't let her get hurt."

"Thought she looked just a mite too calm when she walked out the door," Joe admitted. He glanced at Leo and grimaced. "No secret around town that she's been sweet on you for the past year or so."

"If she was, I've just cured her," Leo said, and felt his heart sink. "Call me when that order comes in, will you?"

"Sure thing."

Leo climbed into his truck and just sat there for a minute, getting his bearings. He could only imagine how Janie felt right now. What he'd said was cruel. He'd let his other irritations burst out as if Janie were to blame for them all. What Marilee had been telling him about Janie had finally bubbled over, that was all. She'd never done anything to hurt him before. Her only crime, if there was one, was thinking the moon rose and set on Leo Hart and taking too much for granted on the basis of one long kiss.

He laughed hollowly. Chances were good that she wouldn't be thinking it after this. Part of him couldn't help blaming her, because she'd gone around bragging about how he was going to marry her, and how lucky he was to have a girl like her in his life. Not to mention telling everybody he was taking her to the Cattleman's Ball.

But Janie had never been one to brag about her accomplishments, or chase men. The only time she'd tried to vamp Leo, in fact, had been in her own home, when her father was present. She'd never come on to him when they were alone, or away from her home. She'd been old-fashioned in her attitudes, probably due to the strict way she'd been raised. So why should she suddenly depart from a lifetime's habits and start spreading gossip about Leo all over Jacobsville? He remembered at least once when she'd stopped another woman from talking about a girl in trouble, adding that she hated gossip because it was like spreading poison.

He wiped his sweaty brow with the sleeve of his shirt and put his hat on the seat beside him. He hated what he'd said. Maybe he didn't want Janie to get any ideas about him in a serious way, but there would have been kinder methods of accomplishing it. He didn't think he was ever going to forget the look on her face when she heard what he was saying to Joe. It would haunt him forever.

MEANWHILE, JANIE WAS setting new speed records out on the Victoria road. She'd already missed the turnoff that led back toward Jacobsville and her father's ranch. She was seething, hurting, miserable and confused. How could Leo think such things about her? She'd never told anybody how she felt about him, except Marilee, and she hadn't been spreading gossip. She hated gossip. Why did he know so little about her, when they'd known each other for years? What hurt the most was that he obviously believed those lies about her.

She wondered who could have told him such a thing. Her thoughts went at once to Marilee, but she chided herself for thinking ill of her only friend, her best friend. Certainly it had to be an enemy who'd been filling Leo's head full of lies. But…she didn't have any enemies that she knew of.

Tears were blurring her eyes. She knew she was going too fast. She should slow down before she wrecked the car or ran it into a fence. She was just thinking about that when she heard sirens and saw blue lights in her rearview mirror.

Great, she thought. Just what I need. I'm going to be arrested and I'll spend the night in the local jail.…

She stopped and rolled down her window, trying unobtrusively to wipe away the tears while waiting for the uniformed officer to bend down and speak to her.

He came as a surprise. It wasn't a patrolman she knew, and she knew most of them by sight at least. This one had black eyes and thick black hair, which he wore in a ponytail. He had a no-nonsense look about him, and he was wearing a badge that denoted him as the assistant chief.

"Miss Brewster?" he asked quietly.

"Y…yes."

"I'm Cash Grier," he introduced himself. "I'm the new assistant police chief here."

"Nice to meet you," she said with a watery smile. "Sorry it has to be under these circumstances." She held out both wrists with a sigh. "Want to handcuff me?"

He pursed his lips and his black eyes twinkled unexpectedly. He didn't look like a man who knew what humor was. "Isn't that a little kinky for a conversation? What sort of men *are* you used to?"

She hesitated for just a second before she burst out laughing. He wasn't at all the man he appeared to be. She put her hands down.

"I was speeding," she reminded him.

"Yes, you were. But since you don't have a rap sheet, you can have a warning, just this once," he added firmly. "The speed limit is posted. It's fifty on all county roads."

She peered up at him. "This is a *county* road?" she emphasized, which meant that he was out of his enforcement area.

Nodding, he grinned. "And you're right, I don't have any jurisdiction out here, so that's why you're getting a warning and a smile." The smile faded. "In town, you'll get a ticket and a heavy scowl. Remember that."

"I will. Honest." She wiped at her eyes again. "I got a little upset, but I shouldn't have taken it out on the road. I'm sorry. I won't do it again."

"See that you don't." His dark eyes narrowed as if in memory. "Accidents are messy. Very messy."

"Thanks for being so nice."

He shrugged. "Everybody slips once in a while."

"That's exactly what I did..."

"I didn't mean you," he interrupted. His lean face took on a faintly dangerous cast. "I'm not nice. Not ever."

She was intimidated by that expression. "Oh."

He wagged a finger at her nose. "Don't speed."

She put a hand over her heart. "Never again. I promise."

He nodded, walked elegantly to his squad car and drove toward town. Janie sat quietly for a minute, getting herself back together. Then she started the car and went home, making up an apology for her father about his gloves without telling him the real reason she'd come home without them. He said he'd get a new pair the next day himself, no problem.

Janie cried herself to sleep in a miserable cocoon of shattered dreams.

As LUCK WOULD have it, Harley Fowler, Cy Parks's fore-man, came by in one of the ranch pickup trucks the very next morning and pulled up to the back door when he saw Janie walk out dressed for riding and wearing a broad-brimmed hat. Harley's boss Cy did business with Fred Brewster, and Harley was a frequent visitor to the ranch. He and Janie were friendly. They teased and played like two kids when they were together.

"I've been looking for you," Harley said with a grin as he paused just in front of her. "The Cattleman's Ball is Saturday night and I want to go, but I don't have a date. I know it's late to be asking, but how about going with me? Unless you've got a date or you're going with your dad...?" he added.

She grinned back. "I haven't got a date, and Dad's away on business and has to miss the ball this year. But I do have a pretty new dress that I'm dying to wear! I'd love to go with you, Harley!"

"Really?" His lean face lit up. He knew Janie was sweet on Leo Hart, but it was rumored that he was avoiding her like measles these days. Harley wasn't in love with Janie, but he genuinely liked her.

"Really," Janie replied. "What time will you pick me up?"

"About six-thirty," he said. "It doesn't start until seven, but I like to be on time."

"That makes two of us. I'll be ready. Thanks, Harley!"

"Thank you!" he said. "See you Saturday."

He was off in a cloud of dust, waving his hand out the window as he pulled out of the yard. Janie sighed with relief. She wanted nothing more in the world than to go to that dance and show Leo Hart how wrong he was about her chasing him. Harley was young and nice looking. She liked him. She would go and have a good time. Leo would be able to see for himself that he was off the endangered list, and he could make a safe bet that Janie would never go near him again without a weapon! As she considered it, she smiled coldly. Revenge was petty, but after the hurt she'd endured at Leo's hands, she felt entitled to a little of it. He was never going to forget this party. Never, as long as he lived.

CHAPTER THREE

THE ANNUAL JACOBSVILLE Cattleman's Ball was one of the newer social events of the year. It took place the Saturday before Thanksgiving like clockwork. Every cattleman for miles around made it a point to attend, even if he avoided all other social events for the year. The Ballenger brothers, Calhoun and Justin, had just added another facility to their growing feedlot enterprise, and they looked prosperous with their wives in gala attire beside them. The Tremayne brothers, Connal, Evan, Harden, and Donald, and their wives were also in attendance, as were the Hart boys; well, Corrigan, Callaghan, Rey and Leo at least, and their wives. Simon and Tira didn't attend many local events except the brothers' annual Christmas party on the ranch.

Also at the ball were Micah Steele, Eb Scott, J. D. Langley, Emmett Deverell, Luke Craig, Guy Fenton, Ted Regan, Jobe Dodd, Tom Walker and their wives. The guest list read like a who's who of Jacobsville, and there were so many people that the organizers had rented the community center for it. There was a live country-western band, a buffet table that could have fed a platoon of starving men, and enough liquor to drown a herd of horses.

Leo had a highball. Since he hadn't done much drinking in recent years, his four brothers were giving him strange looks. He didn't notice. He was feeling so miserable that even a hangover would have been an improvement.

Beside him, Marilee was staring around the room with wide, wary eyes.

"Looking for somebody?" Leo asked absently.

"Yes," she replied. "Janie said she wasn't coming, but that isn't what your sister-in-law Tess just told me."

"What did she say?"

Marilee looked worried. "Harley Fowler told her he was bringing Janie."

"Harley?" Leo scowled. Harley Fowler was a courageous young man who'd actually backed up the town's infamous mercenaries—Eb Scott, Cy Parks and Micah Steele—when they helped law enforcement face down a gang of drug dealers the year before. Harley's name hadn't been coupled with any of the local belles, and he was only a working-class cowboy. Janie's father might be financially pressed at the moment, but his was a founding family of Jacobsville, and the family had plenty of prestige. Fred and his sister-in-law Lydia would be picky about who Janie married. Not, he thought firmly, that Janie was going to be marrying Harley....

"Harley's nice," Marilee murmured. "He's Cy Parks's head foreman now, and everybody says he's got what it takes to run a business of his own." What Marilee didn't add was that Harley had asked her out several times before his raid on the drug lord with the local mercenaries, and she'd turned him down flat. She'd thought he bragged and strutted a little too much, that he was too immature for her. She'd even told him so. It had made her a bitter enemy of his.

Now she was rather sorry that she hadn't given him a chance. He really was different these days, much more mature and very attractive. Not that Leo wasn't a dish. But she felt so guilty about Janie that she couldn't even enjoy his company, much less the party. If Janie showed up and saw her with Leo, she was going to know everything. It wasn't conducive to a happy evening at all.

"What's wrong?" Leo asked when he saw her expression.

"Janie's never going to get over it if she shows up and sees me with you," she replied honestly. "I didn't think how it would look…"

"I don't belong to anybody," Leo said angrily. "It's just as well to let Janie know that. So what if she does show up? Who cares?"

"I do," Marilee sighed.

Just as she spoke, Janie came in the door with a tall, good-looking, dark-haired man in a dark suit with a ruffled white shirt and black bow tie. Janie had just taken off her black velvet coat and hung it on the rack near the door. Under it, she was wearing a sexy white silk gown that fell softly down her slender figure to her shapely ankles. The spaghetti straps left her soft shoulders almost completely bare, and dipped low enough to draw any man's eyes. She was wearing her thick, light brown hair down. It reached almost to her waist in back in a beautiful, glossy display. She wore just enough makeup to enhance her face, and she was clinging to Harley's arm with obvious pleasure as they greeted the Ballengers and their wives.

Leo had forgotten how pretty Janie could look when she worked at it. Lately, he'd only seen her covered in mud and flour. Tonight, her figure drew eyes in that dress. He remembered the feel of her in his arms, the eager innocence of her mouth under his, and he suddenly felt uneasy at the way she was clinging to Harley's arm.

If he was uncomfortable, Marilee was even more so. She stood beside Leo and looked as if she hated herself. He took another long sip of his drink before he guided her toward Harley and Janie.

"No sense hiding, is there?" he asked belligerently.

Marilee sighed miserably. "No sense at all, I guess."

They moved forward together. Janie noticed them and her eyes widened and darkened with pain for an instant. Leo's harsh monologue at the hardware store had been enough to wound her, but now she was seeing that she'd been shafted by her best friend, as well. Marilee said Janie didn't know her date, but all along, apparently, she'd planned to come with Leo. No wonder she'd been so curious about whether or not Janie was going to show up.

Everything suddenly made perfect sense. Marilee had filled Leo up with lies about Janie gossiping about him, so that she could get him herself. Janie felt like an utter fool. Her chin lifted, but she didn't smile. Her green eyes were like emerald shards as they met Marilee's.

"H-hi, Janie," Marilee stammered, forcing a smile. "You said you weren't coming tonight."

"I wasn't," Janie replied curtly. "But Harley was at a loose end and didn't have a date, so he asked me." She looked up at the tall, lean man beside her, who was some years younger than Leo, and she smiled at him with genuine affection even through her misery. "I haven't danced in years."

"You'll dance tonight, darlin'," Harley drawled, smiling warmly as he gripped her long fingers in his. He looked elegant in his dinner jacket, and there was a faint arrogance in his manner now that hadn't been apparent before. He glanced at Marilee and there was barely veiled contempt in the look.

Marilee swallowed hard and avoided his piercing gaze.

"I didn't know you could dance, Harley," Marilee murmured, embarrassed.

He actually ignored her, his narrow gaze going to Leo. "Nice turnout, isn't it?" he asked the older man.

"Nice," Leo said, but he didn't smile. "I haven't seen your boss tonight."

"The baby had a cold," Harley said. "He and Lisa don't leave him when he's sick." He looked down at Janie deliberately. "Considering how happy the two of them are, I guess marriage isn't such a bad vocation after all," he mused.

"For some, maybe," Leo said coldly. He was openly glaring at Harley.

"Let's get on the dance floor," Harley told Janie with a grin. "I'm anxious to try out that waltz pattern I've been learning."

"You'll excuse us, I'm sure," Janie told the woman who was supposed to be her best friend. Her eyes were icy as she realized how she'd been betrayed by Marilee's supposed "help" with Leo.

Marilee grimaced. "Oh, Janie," she groaned. "Let me explain...."

But Janie wasn't staying to listen to any halfhearted explanations. "Nice to see you, Marilee. You, too, Mr. Hart," she added with coldly formal emphasis, not quite meeting Leo's eyes. But she noted the quick firming of his chiseled lips with some satisfaction at the way she'd addressed him.

"Why do you call him Mr. Hart?" Harley asked as they moved away.

"He's much older than we are, Harley," she replied, just loudly enough for Leo to hear her and stiffen with irritation. "Almost another generation."

"I guess he is."

Leo took a big swallow of his drink and glared after them.

"She'll never speak to me again," Marilee said in a subdued tone.

He glared at her. "I'm not her personal property," he said flatly. "I never was. It isn't your fault that she's been gossiping and spreading lies all over town."

Marilee winced.

He turned his attention back to Janie, who was headed onto the dance floor with damned Harley. "I don't want her. What the hell do I care if she likes Harley?"

The music changed to a quick, throbbing Latin beat. Matt Caldwell and his wife, Leslie, were out on the dance floor already, making everybody else look like rank beginners. Everybody clapped to the rhythm until the very end, when the couple left the dance floor. Leo thought nobody could top that display until Harley walked to the bandleader, and the band suddenly broke into a Strauss waltz. That was when Harley and Janie took the floor. Then, even Matt and Leslie stood watching with admiration.

Leo stared at the couple as if he didn't recognize them. Involuntarily, he moved closer to the dance floor to watch. He'd never seen two people move like that to music besides Matt and Leslie.

The rhythm was sweet, and the music had a sweeping beauty that Janie mirrored with such grace that it was like watching ballet. Harley turned and Janie followed every nuance of movement, her steps matching his exactly. Her eyes were laughing, like her pretty mouth, as they whirled around the dance floor in perfect unison.

Harley was laughing, too, enjoying her skill as much as she enjoyed his. They looked breathless, happy—young.

Leo finished his drink, wishing he'd added more whiskey and less soda. His dark eyes narrowed as they followed the couple around the dance floor as they kept time to the music.

"Aren't they wonderful?" Marilee asked wistfully. "I don't guess you dance?"

He did. But he wasn't getting on that floor and making a fool of himself with Marilee, who had two left feet and the sense of rhythm of a possum.

"I don't dance much," Leo replied tersely.

She sighed. "It's just as well, I suppose. That would be a hard act to follow."

"Yes."

The music wound to a peak and suddenly ended, with Janie draped down Harley's side like a bolt of satin. His mouth was almost touching hers, and Leo had to fight not to go onto the floor and throw a punch at the younger man.

He blinked, surprised by his unexpected reaction. Janie was nothing to him. Why should he care what she did? Hadn't she bragged to everyone that he was taking

her to this very dance? Hadn't she made it sound as if
they were involved?

Janie and Harley left the dance floor to furious,
genuine applause. Even Matt Caldwell and Leslie congratulated them on the exquisite piece of dancing. Apparently, Harley had been taking lessons, but Janie
seemed to be a natural.

But the evening was still young, as the Latin music
started up again and another unexpected couple took
the floor. It was Cash Grier, the new assistant police
chief, with young Christabel Gaines in his arms. Only
a few people knew that Christabel had been married
to Texas Ranger Judd Dunn since she was sixteen—
a marriage on paper, only, to keep herself and her invalid mother from losing their family ranch. But she
was twenty-one now, and the marriage must have been
annulled, because there she was with Cash Grier, like
a blond flame in his arms as he spun her around to the
throbbing rhythm and she matched her steps to his expert ones.

Unexpectedly, as the crowd clapped and kept time for
them, handsome dark-eyed Judd Dunn himself turned
up in evening dress with a spectacular redhead on his
arm. Men's heads turned. The woman was a supermodel, internationally famous, who was involved in a
film shoot out at Judd and Christabel's ranch. Gossip
flew. Judd watched Christabel with Grier and glowered.
The redhead said something to him, but he didn't ap-
pear to be listening. He watched the two dancers with
a rigid posture and an expression more appropriate for
a duel than a dance. Christabel ignored him.

"Who is that man with Christabel Gaines?" Marilee
asked Leo.

"Cash Grier. He used to be a Texas Ranger some years ago. They say he was in government service as well."

Leo recalled that Grier had been working in San Antonio with the district attorney's office before he took the position of assistant police chief in Jacobsville. There was a lot of talk about Grier's mysterious past. The man was an enigma, and people walked wide around him in Jacobsville.

"He's dishy, isn't he? He dances a *paso doble* even better than Matt, imagine that!" Marilee said aloud. "Of course, Harley does a magnificent waltz. Who would ever have thought he'd turn out to be such a sexy, mature man…"

Leo turned on his heel and left Marilee standing by herself, stunned. He walked back to the drinks table with eyes that didn't really see. The dance floor had filled up again, this time with a slow dance. Harley was holding Janie far too close, and she was letting him. Leo remembered what he'd said about her in the hardware store, and her wounded expression, and he filled another glass with whiskey. This time he didn't add soda. He shouldn't have felt bad, of course. Janie shouldn't have been so possessive. She shouldn't have gossiped about him…

"Hi, Leo," his sister-in-law Tess said with a smile as she joined him, reaching for a clear soft drink.

"No booze, huh?" he asked with a grin, noting her choice.

"I don't want to set a bad example for my son," she teased, because she and Cag had a little boy now. "Actually, I can't hold liquor. But don't tell anybody," she added. "I'm the wife of a tough ex-Special Forces guy. I'm supposed to be a real hell-raiser."

He smiled genuinely. "You are," he teased. "A lesser woman could never have managed my big brother and an albino python all at once."

"Herman the python's living with his own mate these days," she reminded him with a grin, "and just between us, I don't really miss him!" She glanced toward her husband and sighed. "I'm one lucky woman."

"He's one lucky man." He took a sip of his drink and she frowned.

"Didn't you bring Marilee?" she asked.

He nodded. "Her wrist was still bothering her too much to drive, so I let her come with me. I've been chauffeuring her around ever since she sprained it."

Boy, men were dense, Tess was thinking. As if a woman couldn't drive with only one hand. She glanced past him at Marilee, who was standing by herself watching as a new rhythm began and Janie moved onto the floor with Harley Fowler. "I thought she was Janie's best friend," she mentioned absently. "You can never tell about people."

"What do you mean?"

She shrugged. "I overheard her telling someone that Janie had been spreading gossip about you and her all over town." She shook her head. "That's not true. Janie's so shy, it's hard for her to even talk to most men. I've never heard her gossip about anyone, even people she dislikes. I can't imagine why Marilee would tell lies about her."

"Janie told everybody I was bringing her to the ball," he insisted with a scowl.

"Marilee told people that Janie said that," Tess corrected. "You really don't know, do you? Marilee's crazy about you. She had to cut Janie out of the picture before she could get close to you. I guess she found the perfect way to do it."

Leo started to speak, but he hesitated. That couldn't be true.

Tess read his disbelief and just smiled. "You don't believe me, do you? It doesn't matter. You'll find out the truth sooner or later, whether you want to or not. I've got to find Cag. See you later!"

Leo watched her walk away with conflicting emotions. He didn't want to believe—he *wouldn't* believe—that he'd been played for a sucker. He'd seen Janie trying to become a cattleman with his own eyes, trying to compete with him. He knew that she wanted him because she'd tried continually to tempt him when he went to visit her father. She flirted shamelessly with him. She'd melted in his arms, melted under the heat of his kisses. She hadn't made a single protest at the intimate way he'd held her. She felt possessive of him, and he couldn't really blame her, because it was his own lapse of self-control that had given her the idea that he wanted her. Maybe he did, physically, but Janie was a novice and he didn't seduce innocents. Her father was a business associate. It certainly wouldn't be good business to cut his own throat with Fred by making a casual lover of Janie.

He finished the whiskey and put the glass down. He felt light-headed. That was what came of drinking when he hadn't done it in a long time. This was stupid. He had to stop behaving like an idiot just because Fred Brewster's little girl had cut him dead in the receiving line and treated him like an old man. He forced himself to walk normally, but he almost tripped over Cag on the way.

His brother caught him by the shoulders. "Whoa, there," he said with a grin. "You're wobbling."

Leo pulled himself up. "That whiskey must be 200 proof," he said defensively.

"No. You're just not used to it. Leave your car here when it's time to go," he added firmly. "Tess and I will drop Marilee off and take you home. You're in no fit state to drive."

Leo sighed heavily. "I guess not. Stupid thing to do."

"What, drinking or helping Marilee stab Janie in the back?"

Leo's eyes narrowed on his older brother's lean, hard face. "Does Tess tell you everything?"

He shrugged. "We're married."

"If I ever get married," Leo told him, "my wife isn't going to tell anybody anything. She's going to keep her mouth shut."

"Not much danger of your getting married, with that attitude," Cag mused.

Leo squared his shoulders. "Marilee looks really great tonight," he pointed out.

"She looks pretty sick to me," Cag countered, eyeing the object of their conversation, who was standing alone against the opposite wall, trying to look invisible. "She should, too, after spreading that gossip around town about Janie chasing you."

"Janie did that, not Marilee," Leo said belligerently. "She didn't have any reason to make it sound like we were engaged, just because I kissed her."

Cag's eyebrows lifted. "You kissed her?"

"It wasn't much of a kiss," Leo muttered gruffly. "She's so green, it's pathetic!"

"She won't stay that way long around Harley," Cag

chuckled. "He's no playboy, but women love him since he helped our local mercs take on that drug lord Manuel Lopez and won. I imagine he'll educate Janie."

Leo's dark eyes narrowed angrily. He hated the thought of Harley kissing her. He really should do something about that. He blinked, trying to focus his mind on the problem.

"Don't trip over the punch bowl," Cag cautioned dryly. "And for God's sake, don't try to dance. The gossips would have a field day for sure!"

"I could dance if I wanted to," Leo informed him.

Cag leaned down close to his brother's ear. "Don't 'want to.' Trust me." He turned and went back to Tess, smiling as he led her onto the dance floor.

Leo joined Marilee against the wall.

She glanced at him and grimaced. "I've just become the Bubonic Plague," she said with a miserable sigh. "Joe Howland from the hardware store is here with his wife," she added uncomfortably. "He's telling people what you said to Janie and that I was responsible for her getting the rough side of your tongue."

He glanced down at her. "How is it your fault?"

She looked at her shoes instead of at him. She felt guilty and hurt and ashamed. "I sort of told Janie that you said you'd like her better if she could ride and rope and make biscuits, and stop dressing up all the time."

He stiffened. He felt the jolt all the way to his toes. "You told her that?"

"I did." She folded her arms over her breasts and stared toward Janie, who was dancing with Harley and apparently having a great time. "There's more," she added, steeling herself to admit it. "It wasn't exactly true that she was telling people you were taking her to this dance."

"Marilee, for God's sake! Why did you lie?" he demanded.

"She's just a kid, Leo," she murmured uneasily. "She doesn't know beans about men or real life, she's been protected and pampered, she's got money, she's pretty...." She moved restlessly. "I like you a lot. I'm older, more mature. I thought, if she was just out of the picture for a little bit, you...you might start to like me."

Now he understood the look on Janie's face when he'd made those accusations. Tess was right. Marilee had lied. She'd stabbed her best friend in the back, and he'd helped her do it. He felt terrible.

"You don't have to tell me what a rat I am," she continued, without looking up at him. "I must have been crazy to think Janie wouldn't eventually find out that I was lying about her." She managed to meet his angry eyes. "She never gossiped about you, Leo. She wanted you to take her to this party so much that it was all she talked about for weeks. But she never told anybody you were going to. She thought I was helping her by hinting that she'd like you to ask her." She laughed coldly. "She was the best friend I ever had, and I've stabbed her in the back. She'll never speak to me again after tonight, and I deserve whatever I get. For what it's worth, I'm really sorry."

Leo was still trying to adjust to the truth. He could talk himself blue in the face, but Janie would never listen to him now. He was going to be about as welcome as a fly at her house from now on, especially if Fred found out what Leo had said to and about her. It would damage their friendship. It had already killed whatever feeling

Janie had for him. He knew that without the wounded, angry glances she sent his way from time to time.

"You said you didn't want her chasing you," Marilee reminded him weakly, trying to find one good thing to say.

"No danger of that from now on, is there?" he agreed, biting off the words.

"None at all. So a little good came out of it."

He looked down at her with barely contained anger. "How could you do that to her?"

"I don't even know." She sighed raggedly. "I must have been temporarily out of my mind." She moved away from the wall. "I wonder if you'd mind driving me home? I... I really don't want to stay any longer."

"I can't drive. Cag's taking us home."

"You can't drive? Why?" she exclaimed.

"I think the polite way of saying it is that I'm stinking drunk," he said with glittery eyes blazing down at her.

She grimaced. No need to ask why he'd gotten that way. "Sorry," she said inadequately.

"You're sorry. I'm sorry. It doesn't change anything." He looked toward Janie, conscious of new and painful regrets. It all made sense now, her self-improvement campaign. She'd been dragged through mud, thrown from horses, bruised and battered in a valiant effort to become what she thought Leo wanted her to be.

He winced. "She could have killed herself," he said huskily. "She hadn't been on a horse in ages or worked around cattle." He looked down at Marilee with a black scowl. "Didn't you realize that?"

"I wasn't thinking at the time," Marilee replied. "I've always worked around the ranch, because I had to. I never thought of Janie being in any danger. But I guess she was, at that. At least she didn't get hurt."

"That's what you think," Leo muttered, remembering how she'd looked at the hardware store.

Marilee shrugged and suddenly burst into tears. She dashed toward the ladies' room to hide them.

At the same time, Harley left Janie at the buffet table and went toward the rest rooms himself.

Leo didn't even think. He walked straight up to Janie and caught her by the hand, pulling her along with him.

"What do you think you're doing?" she raged. "Let go of me!"

He ignored her. He led her right out the side door and onto the stone patio surrounded by towering plants that, in spring, were glorious in blossom. He pulled the glass door closed behind him and moved Janie off behind one of the plants.

"I want to talk to you," he began, trying to get his muddled mind to work.

She pulled against his hands. "I don't want to talk to you!" she snapped. "You go right back in there to your date, Leo Hart! You brought Marilee, not me!"

"I want to tell you…" he tried again.

She aimed a kick at his shin that almost connected.

He sidestepped, overbalancing her so that she fell heavily against him. She felt good in his arms, warm, delicate and sweetly scented. His breath caught at the feel of her soft skin under his hands where the dress was low-cut in back.

"Harley will…be missing me!" she choked.

"Damn Harley," he murmured huskily and the words went into her mouth as he bent and took it hungrily.

His arms swallowed her, warm under the dark evening suit, where her hands rested just at his rib cage. His mouth was ardent, insistent, on her parted lips.

He forced them apart, nipping the upper one with his teeth while his hands explored the softness of her skin. He was getting drunk on her perfume. He felt himself going taut as he registered the hunger he was feeling to get her even closer. It wasn't enough....

His hands went to her hips and jerked them hard into the thrust of his big body, so that she could feel how aroused he was.

She stiffened and then tried to twist away, frantic at the weakness he was making her feel. He couldn't do this. She couldn't let him do it. He was only making a point, showing her that she couldn't resist him. He didn't even like her anymore. He'd brought her best friend to the most talked-about event in town!

"You...let me go!" she sobbed, tearing her mouth from his. "I hate you, Leo Hart!"

He was barely able to breathe, much less think, but he wasn't letting go. His eyes glittered down at her. "You don't hate me," he denied. "You want me. You tremble every time I get within a foot of you. It's so noticeable a blind man couldn't mistake it." He pulled her close, watching her face as her thighs touched his. "A woman's passion arouses a man's," he whispered roughly. "You made me want you."

"You said I made you sick," she replied, her voice choking on the word.

"You do." His lips touched her ear. "When a man is this aroused, and can't satisfy the hunger, it makes him sick," he said huskily, with faint insolence. He dragged her hips against his roughly. "Feel that? You've got me so hot I can't even think…!" Leo broke off abruptly as Janie stomped on his foot.

"Does that help?" she asked while he was hobbling on the foot her spiked heel hadn't gone into.

She moved back from him, shaking with desire and anger, while he cursed roundly and without inhibition.

"That's what you get for making nasty remarks to women!" she said furiously. "You don't want me! You said so! You want Marilee. That's why you're taking her around with you. Remember me? I'm that gossiping pest who runs after you everywhere. Except that I'll never do it again, you can bet your life on that! I wouldn't have you on ice cream!"

He stood uneasily on both feet, glaring at her. "Sure you would," he said with a venomous smile. His eyes glittered like a diamondback uncoiling. "Just now, I could have had you in the rosebushes. You'd have done anything I wanted."

He was right. That was what hurt the most. She pushed back her disheveled hair with a trembling hand. "Not anymore," she said, feeling sick. "Not when I know what you really think of me."

"Harley brought you," he said coldly. "He's a boy playing at being a man."

"He's closer to my age than you are, Mr. Hart!" she shot back.

His face hardened and he took a quick step toward her.

"That's what you've said from the start," she reminded him, near tears. "I'm just a kid, you said. I'm just a kid with a crush, just your business associate's pesky daughter."

He'd said that. He must have been out of his mind.

Looking at her now, with that painful maturity in her face, he couldn't believe he'd said any such thing. She was all woman. And she was with Harley. Damn Harley!

"Don't worry, I won't tell Dad that you tried to seduce me on the patio with your new girlfriend standing right inside the room," she assured him. "But if you ever touch me again, I'll cripple you, so help me God!"

She whirled and jerked open the patio door, slamming it behind her as she moved through the crowd toward the buffet table.

Leo stood alone in the cold darkness with a sore foot, wondering why he hadn't kept his mouth shut. If a bad situation could get worse, it just had.

CHAPTER FOUR

JANIE AND HARLEY were back on the dance floor by the time Leo made his way inside, favoring his sore foot.

Marilee was standing at the buffet table, looking as miserable as he felt.

"Harley just gave me hell," she murmured tightly as he joined her. "He said I was lower than a snake's belly, and it would serve me right if Janie never spoke to me again." She looked up at him with red-rimmed eyes. "Do you think your brother would mind dropping us off now? He could come right back…"

"I'll ask him," Leo said, sounding absolutely fed up.

He found Cag talking to Corrigan and Rey at the buffet table. Their wives were in another circle, talking to each other.

"Could you run Marilee home now and drop me off on the way back?" he asked Cag in a subdued tone.

Corrigan gaped at him. "You've never left a dance until the band packed up."

Leo sighed. "There's a first time for everything."

The women joined them. Cag tugged Tess close. "I have to run Leo and Marilee home."

Tess's eyebrows went up. "Now? Why so early?"

Leo glared. His brothers cleared their throats.

"Never mind," Cag said quickly. "I won't be a minute…"

"Rey and I would be glad to do it…" Meredith volunteered, with a nod from her husband.

"No need," Dorie said with a smile, cuddling close to her husband. "Corrigan can run Leo and Marilee home and come right back. Can't you, sweetheart?" she added.

"Sure I can," he agreed, lost in her pretty eyes.

"But you two don't usually leave until the band does, either," Leo pointed out. "You'll miss most of the rest of the dance if you drive us."

Corrigan pursed his lips. "Oh, we've done our dancing for the night. Haven't we, sweetheart?" he prompted.

Dorie's eyes twinkled. She nodded. "Indeed we have! I'll just catch up on talk until he comes back. We can have the last dance together. Don't give it a thought, Leo."

Leo was feeling the liquor more with every passing minute, but he was feeling all sorts of undercurrents. The women looked positively gleeful. His brothers were exchanging strange looks.

Corrigan looked past Leo to Cag and Rey. "You can all come by our house after the dance," he promised.

"What for?" Leo wanted to know, frowning suspiciously.

Corrigan hesitated and Cag scowled.

Rey cleared his throat. "Bull problems," he said finally, with a straight face. "Corrigan's advising me."

"He's advising me, too," Cag said with a grin. "He's advising both of us."

All three of them looked guilty as hell. "I know more about bulls than Corrigan does," Leo pointed out. "Why don't you ask me?"

"Because you're in a hurry to go home," Corrigan improvised. "Let's go."

Leo went to get Marilee. She said a subdued, hurried goodbye to Cag and Rey and then their wives. Leo waited patiently, vaguely aware that Cag and Rey were standing apart, talking in hushed whispers. They were both staring at Leo.

As Marilee joined him, Leo began to get the idea. Corrigan had sacrificed dancing so that he could pump Leo for gossip and report back to the others. They knew he was drinking, which he never did, and they'd probably seen him hobble back into the room. Then he'd wanted to leave early. It didn't take a mind reader to put all that together. Something had happened, and his brothers—not to mention their wives—couldn't wait to find out what. He glared at Corrigan, but his brother only grinned.

"Let's go, Marilee," Leo said, catching her by the arm.

She gave one last, hopeful glance at Janie, but was pointedly ignored. She followed along with Leo until the music muted to a whisper behind them.

WHEN MARILEE HAD been dropped off, and they were alone in the car, Corrigan glanced toward his brother with mischievous silvery eyes and pursed his lips.

"You're limping."

Leo huffed. "You try walking normally when some crazy woman's tried to put her heel through your damned boot!"

"Marilee stepped on you?" Corrigan said much too carelessly.

"Janie stepped on me, on purpose!"

"What were you doing to her at the time?"

Leo actually flushed. It was visible in the streetlight they stopped under waiting for a red light to change on the highway.

"Well!" Corrigan exclaimed with a knowing expression.

"She started it," he defended himself angrily. "All these months, she's been dressing to the hilt and waylaying me every time I went to see her father. She damned near seduced me on the cooking table in her kitchen last month, and then she goes and gets on her high horse because I said a few little things I shouldn't have when she was eavesdropping!"

"You said a lot of little things," his brother corrected. "And from what I hear, she left town in a dangerous rush and had to be slowed down by our new assistant chief. In fact, you called and asked him to do it. Good thinking."

"Who told you that?" Leo demanded.

Corrigan grinned. "Our new assistant chief."

"Grier can keep his nose out of my business or I'll punch it for him!"

"He's got problems of his own, or didn't you notice him step outside with Judd Dunn just before we left?" Corrigan whistled softly. "Christabel may think she's her own woman, but Judd doesn't act like any disinterested husband I ever saw."

"He's got a world famous model on his arm," Leo pointed out.

"It didn't make a speck of difference once he saw Christabel on that dance floor with Grier. He was ready to make a scene right there." He glanced at Leo. "And *he* wasn't drinking," he emphasized.

"I am not jealous of Janie Brewster," Leo told him firmly.

"Tell that to Harley. He had to be persuaded not to go after you when Janie came back inside in tears," Corrigan added, letting slip what he'd overheard.

That made it worse. "Harley can mind his own damned business, too!"

"He is. He likes Janie."

"Janie's not going to fall for some wet-behind-the-ears would-be world-saver," Leo raged.

"He's kind to her. He teases her and picks at her. He treats her like a princess." He gave his brother a wry glance. "I'll bet he wouldn't try to seduce her in the rosebushes."

"I didn't! Anyway, there weren't any damned rosebushes out there."

"How do you know that?"

Leo sighed heavily. "Because if there had been, I'd be wearing them."

Corrigan chuckled. Having had his own problems with the course of true love, he could sympathize with his brother. Sadly, Leo had never been in love. He'd had crushes, he'd had brief liaisons, but there had never been a woman who could stand him on his ear. Corrigan was as fascinated as their brothers with the sudden turn of events. Leo had tolerated Janie Brewster, been amused by her, but he'd never been involved enough to start a fight with her, much less sink two large whiskeys when he hardly even touched beer.

"She's got a temper, fancy that?" Corrigan drawled.

Leo sighed. "Marilee was telling lies," he murmured. "She said Janie had started all sorts of gossip about us. I'd kissed her, and liked it, and I was feeling trapped.

I thought the kiss gave her ideas. And all the time...
Damn!" he ground out. "Tess knew. She told me that
Marilee had made up the stories, and I wouldn't listen."

"Tess is sharp as a tack," his older brother remarked.

"I'm as dull as a used nail," Leo replied. "I don't even
know when a woman is chasing me. I thought Janie
was. And all the time, it was her best friend Marilee."
He shook his head. "Janie said I was the most conceited man she ever met. Maybe I am." He glanced out
the window at the silhouettes of buildings they passed
in the dark. "She likes Harley. That would have been
funny a few months ago, but he keeps impressive company these days."

"Harley's matured. Janie has, too. I thought she handled herself with dignity tonight, when she saw you
with Marilee." He chuckled. "Tira would have emptied
the punch bowl over her head," he mused, remembering his redheaded sister-in-law's temper.

"Simon would have been outraged," he added. "He
hates scenes. You're a lot like him," he said unexpectedly, glancing at the younger man. "You can cut up, but
you're as somber as a judge when you're not around us.
Especially since we've all married."

"I'm lonely," Leo said simply. "I've had the house
to myself since Rey married Meredith and moved out,
almost a year ago. Mrs. Lewis retired. I've got no biscuits, no company..."

"You've got Marilee," he was reminded.

"Marilee sprained her wrist. She's needed me to
drive her places," Leo said drowsily.

"Marilee could drive with one hand. I drove with a
broken arm once."

Leo didn't respond. They were driving up to the main

ranch house, into the driveway that made a semicircle around the front steps. The security lights were on, so was the porch light. But even with lights on in the front rooms of the sprawling brick house, it looked empty.

"You could come and stay with any of us, whenever you wanted to," Corrigan reminded him. "We only live a few miles apart."

"You've all got families. Children. Well, except Meredith and Rey."

"They're not in a hurry. Rey's the youngest. The rest of us are feeling our ages a bit more."

"Hell," Leo growled, "you're only two years older than me."

"You're thirty-five," he was reminded. "I'll be thirty-eight in a couple of months."

"You don't look it."

"Dorie and the babies keep me young," Corrigan admitted with a warm smile. "Marriage isn't as bad as you think it is. You have someone to cook for you, a companion to share your sorrows when the world hits you in the head, and your triumphs when you punch back. Not to mention having a warm bed at night."

Leo opened the door but hesitated. "I don't want to get married."

Corrigan's pale eyes narrowed. "Dorie was just a little younger than Janie when I said the same thing to her. I mistook her for an experienced woman, made a very heavy pass, and then said some insulting things to her when she pulled back at the last minute. I sent her running for the nearest bus, and my pride stopped me from carrying her right back off it again. She went away. It was eight long years before she came home, before I was able to start over with her." His face hardened. "You know what those years were like for me."

Leo did. It was painful even to recall them. "You never told me why she left."

Corrigan rested his arm over the steering wheel. "She left because I behaved like an idiot." He glanced at his brother. "I don't give a damn what Marilee's told you about Janie, she isn't any more experienced than Dorie was. Don't follow in my footsteps."

Leo wouldn't meet the older man's eyes. "Janie's a kid."

"She'll grow up. She's making a nice start, already."

Leo brushed back his thick, unruly hair. "I was way out of line with her tonight. She said she never wanted to see me again."

"Give her time."

"I don't care if she doesn't want to see me," Leo said belligerently. "What the hell do I want with a mud-covered little tomboy, anyway? She can't even cook!"

"Neither can Tira," Corrigan pointed out. "But she's a knockout in an evening gown. So is our Janie, even if she isn't as pretty as Marilee."

Leo shrugged. "Marilee's lost a good friend."

"She has. Janie won't ever trust her again, even if she can forgive her someday."

Leo glanced back at his older brother. "Isn't it amazing how easy it is to screw up your whole life in a few unguarded minutes?"

"That's life, *compadre*. I've got to go. You going to be okay?"

Leo nodded. "Thanks for the ride." He glowered at Corrigan. "I guess you're in a hurry to get back, right?"

Corrigan's eyes twinkled. "I don't want to miss the last dance!"

Or the chance to tell his brothers everything that had happened. But, what the hell, they were family.

"Drive safely," Leo told Corrigan as he closed the car door.

"I always do." Corrigan threw up his hand and drove away.

Leo disarmed the alarm system and unlocked the front door, pausing to relock it and rearm the system. He'd been the victim of a mugging last October in Houston, and it had been Rey's new wife, Meredith, who had saved him from no worse than a concussion. But now he knew what it was to be a victim of violent crime, and he was much more cautious than he'd ever been before.

He tossed his keys on his chest of drawers and took off his jacket and shoes. Before he could manage the rest, he passed out on his own bed.

JANIE BREWSTER WAS very quiet on the way home. Harley understood why. He and Janie weren't an item, but he hated seeing a woman cry. He'd wanted, very badly, to punch Leo Hart for that.

"You should have let me hit him, Janie," he remarked thoughtfully.

She gave him a sad little smile. "There's been enough gossip already, although I appreciate the thought."

"He was drinking pretty heavily," Harley added. "I noticed that one of his brothers took him and Marilee home early. Nice of him to find a designated driver, in that condition. He looked as if he was barely able to walk without staggering."

Janie had seen them leave, with mixed emotions. She

turned her small evening bag in her lap. "I didn't know he drank hard liquor at all."

"He doesn't," Harley replied. "Eb Scott said that he'd never known Leo to take anything harder than a beer in company." He glanced at her. "That must have been some mixer you had with him."

"He'd been drinking before we argued," she replied. She looked out the darkened window. "Odd that Marilee left with him."

"You didn't see the women snub her, I guess," he murmured. "Served her right, I thought." His eyes narrowed angrily as he made the turn that led to her father's ranch. "It's low to stab a friend in the back like that. Whatever her feelings for Hart, she should have put your feelings first."

"I thought you liked her, Harley."

He stiffened. "I asked her out once, and she laughed."

"What?"

He stared straight ahead at the road, the center of which was lit by the powerful headlights of the truck he was driving. "She thought it was hilarious that I had the nerve to ask her to go on a date. She said I was too immature."

Ouch, she thought. A man like Harley would have too much pride to ever go near a woman who'd dented his ego that badly.

He let out a breath. "The hell of it is, she was right," he conceded with a wry smile. "I had my head in the clouds, bragging about my mercenary training. Then I went up against Lopez with Eb and Cy and Micah." He grimaced. "I didn't have a clue."

"We heard that it was a firefight."

He nodded. His eyes were haunted. "My only experience of combat was movies and television." His lean hands gripped the wheel hard. "The real thing is less… comfortable. And that's all I'll say."

"Thank you for taking me to the ball," she said, changing the subject because he'd looked so tormented.

His face relaxing, he glanced at her. "It was my pleasure. I'm not ready to settle down, but I like you. Anytime you're at a loose end, we can see a movie or get a burger."

She chuckled. "I feel the same way. Thanks."

He pursed his lips and gave her a teasing glance. "We could even go dancing."

"I liked waltzing."

"I want to learn those Latin dances, like Caldwell and Grier." He whistled. "Imagine Grier doing Latin dances! Even Caldwell stood back and stared."

"Mr. Grier is a conundrum," she murmured. "Not the man he seems, on the surface."

"How would you know?" he asked.

She cleared her throat. "He stopped me for speeding out on the Victoria road."

"Good for him. You drive too fast."

"Don't you start!"

He frowned. "What was he doing out there? He doesn't have jurisdiction outside Jacobsville."

"I don't know. But he's very pleasant."

He hesitated. "There's some, shall we say, unsavory gossip about him around town," he told her.

"Unsavory, how?" she asked, curious.

"It's probably just talk."

"Harley!"

He slowed for a turn. "They say he was a government assassin at one point in his life."

She whistled softly. "You're kidding!"

He glanced at her. "When I was in the Rangers, I flew overseas with a guy who was dressed all in black, armed to the teeth. He didn't say a word to the rest of us. I learned later that he was brought over for a very select assignment with the British commandos."

"What has that got to do with Grier?"

"That's just the thing. I think it *was* Grier."

She felt cold chills running up her arms.

"It was several years ago," he reiterated, "and I didn't get a close look, but sometimes you can tell a man just by the way he walks, the way he carries himself."

"You shouldn't tell anybody," she murmured, uneasy, because she liked Grier.

"I never would," Harley assured her. "I told my boss, but nobody else. Grier isn't the sort of man you'd ever gossip about, even if half the things they tell are true."

"There's more?" she exclaimed.

He chuckled. "He was in the Middle East helping pinpoint the laser-guided bombs, he broke up a spy ring in Manhattan as a company agent, he fought with the freedom fighters in Afghanistan, he foiled an assassination attempt against one of our own leaders under the nose of the agency assigned to protect them…you name it, he's done it. Including a stint with the Texas Rangers and a long career in law enforcement between overseas work."

"A very interesting man," she mused.

"And intimidating to our local law enforcement guys. Interesting that Judd Dunn isn't afraid of him."

"He's protective of Christabel," Janie told him. "She's sweet. She was in my high school graduating class."

"Judd's too old for her," Harley drawled. "He's about

Leo Hart's age, isn't he, and she's just a few months older than you."

He was insinuating that Leo was too old for her. He was probably right, but it hurt to hear someone say it. Nor was she going to admit something else she knew about Christabel, that Judd had married the girl when she was just sixteen so that she wouldn't lose her home. Christabel was twenty-one and Judd had become her worst enemy.

"Sorry," Harley said when he noticed her brooding expression.

"About what?" she asked, diverted.

"I guess you think I meant Leo Hart's too old for you."

"He is," she said flatly.

He looked as if he meant to say more, but the sad expression on her face stopped him. He pulled into her driveway and didn't say another word until he stopped the truck at her front door.

"I know how you feel about the guy, Janie," he said then. "But you can want something too much. Hart isn't a marrying man, even if his brothers were. He's a bad risk."

She turned to face him, her eyes wide and eloquent. "I've told myself that a hundred times. Maybe it will sink in."

He grimaced. He traced a pattern on her cheek with a lean forefinger. "For what it's worth, I'm no stranger to unreturned feelings." He grimaced. "Maybe some of us just don't have the knack for romance."

"Speak for yourself," she said haughtily. "I have the makings of a Don Juanette, as Leo Hart is about to discover!"

He tapped her cheek gently. "Stop that. Running wild won't change anything, except to make you more miserable than you are."

She drew in a long breath. "You're right, of course. Oh, Harley, why can't we make people love us back?"

"Wish I knew," he said. He leaned forward and kissed her lightly on the lips. "I had fun. I'm sorry you didn't."

She smiled. "I did have fun. At least I didn't end up at the ball by myself, or with Dad, to face Leo and Marilee."

He nodded, understanding. "Where is your dad?"

"Denver," she replied on a sigh. "He's trying to interest a combine in investing in the ranch, but you can't tell anybody."

He scowled. "I didn't realize things were that bad."

She nodded. "They're pretty bad. Losing his prize bull was a huge financial blow. If Leo hadn't loaned him that breeding bull, I don't know what we'd have done. At least he likes Dad," she added softly.

It was Harley's opinion that he liked Fred Brewster's daughter, too, or he wouldn't have been putting away whiskey like that tonight. But he didn't say it.

"Can I help?" he asked instead.

She smiled at him. "You're so sweet, Harley. Thanks. But there's not much we can do without a huge grub-stake. So," she added heavily, "I'm going to give up school and get a job."

"Janie!"

"College is expensive," she said simply. "Dad can't really afford it right now, and I'm not going to ask him to try. There's a job going at Shea's…"

"You can't work at Shea's!" Harley exclaimed. "Janie,

it's a roadhouse! They serve liquor, and most nights there's a fight."

"They serve pizza and sandwiches, as well, and that's what the job entails," she replied. "I can handle it."

It disturbed Harley to think of an innocent, sweet girl like Janie in that environment. "There are openings at fast-food joints in town," he said.

"You don't get good tips at fast-food joints. Stop while you're ahead, Harley, you won't change my mind," she said gently.

"If you take the job, I'll stop in and check on you from time to time," he promised.

"You're a sweetheart, Harley," she said, and meant it. She kissed him on the cheek, smiled, and got out of the cab. "Thanks for taking me to the ball!"

"No sweat, Cinderella," he said with a grin. "I enjoyed it, too. Good night!"

"Good night," she called back.

She went inside slowly, locking the door behind her. Her steps dragging, she felt ten years older. It had been a real bust of an evening all around. She thought about Leo Hart and she hoped he had the king of hangovers the next morning!

THE NEXT DAY, Janie approached the manager of Shea's, a nice, personable man named Jed Duncan, about the job.

He read over her résumé while she sat in a leather chair across from his desk and bit her fingernails.

"Two years of college," he mused. "Impressive." His dark eyes met hers over the pages. "And you want to work in a bar?"

"Let me level with you," she said earnestly. "We're in financial trouble. My father can't afford to send me back to school, and I won't stand by and let him sink without trying to help. This job doesn't pay much, but the tips are great, from what Debbie Connor told me."

Debbie was her predecessor, and had told her about the job in the first place. Be honest with Jed, she'd advised, and lay it on the line about money. So Janie did.

He nodded slowly, studying her. "The tips are great," he agreed. "But the customers can get rowdy. Forgive me for being blunt, Miss Brewster, but you've had a sheltered upbringing. I have to keep a bouncer here now, ever since Calhoun Ballenger had it out with a customer over his ward—now his wife—and busted up the place. Not that Calhoun wasn't in the right," he added quickly. "But it became obvious that hot tempers and liquor don't mix, and you can't run a roadhouse on good intentions."

She swallowed. "I can get used to anything, Mr. Duncan. I would really like this job."

"Can you cook?"

She grinned. "Two months ago, I couldn't. But I can now. I can even make biscuits!"

He chuckled. "Okay, then, you should be able to make a pizza. We'll agree that you can work for two weeks and we'll see how it goes. You'll waitress and do some cooking. If you can cope, I'll let you stay. If not, or if you don't like the work, we'll call it quits. That suit you?"

She nodded. "It suits me very well. Thank you!"

"Does your father know about this?" he added.

She flushed. "He will, when he gets home from Denver. I don't hide things from him."

"It's not likely that you'll be able to hide this job from him," he mused with a chuckle. "A lot of our patrons

do business with him. I wouldn't like to make more enemies than I already have."

"He won't mind," she assured him with a smile. She
crossed her fingers silently.

"Then come along and I'll acquaint you with the job,"
Jed said, moving around the desk. "Welcome aboard,
Miss Brewster."

She smiled. "Thanks!"

CHAPTER FIVE

FRED BREWSTER CAME home from Denver discouraged. "I couldn't get anybody interested," he told Janie as he flopped down in his favorite easy chair in the living room. "Everybody's got money problems, and the market is down. It's a bad time to fish for partners."

Janie sat down on the sofa across from him. "I got a job."

He just stared at her for a minute, as if he didn't hear her. "You what?"

"I got a job," she said, and smiled at him. "I'll make good money in tips. I start tonight."

"Where?" he asked.

"A restaurant," she lied. "You can even come and eat there, and I'll serve you. You won't have to tip me, either!"

"Janie," he groaned. "I wanted you to go back and finish your degree."

She leaned forward. "Dad, let's be honest. You can't afford college right now, and if I went, it would have to be on work-study. Let me do this," she implored. "I'm young and strong and I don't mind working. You'll pull out of this, Dad, I know you will!" she added gently. "Everybody has bad times. This is ours."

He scowled. "It hurts my pride..."

She knelt at his feet and leaned her arms over his

thin, bony knees. "You're my dad," she said. "I love
you. Your problems are my problems. You'll come up
with an angle that will get us out of this. I don't have
a single doubt."

Those beautiful eyes that were so like his late wife's
weakened his resolve. He smiled and touched her hair
gently. "You're like your mother."

"Thanks!"

He chuckled. "Okay. Do your waitress bit for a few
weeks and I'll double my efforts on getting us out of
hock. But no late hours," he emphasized. "I want you
home by midnight, period."

That might be a problem. But why bother him with
complications right now?

"We'll see how it goes," she said easily, getting to
her feet. She planted a kiss on his forehead. "I'd better
get you some lunch!"

She dashed into the kitchen before he could ask any
more questions about her new employment.

But she wasn't so lucky with Hettie. "I don't like
the idea of you working in a bar," she told Janie firmly.

"Shhhh!" Janie cautioned, glancing toward the open
kitchen door. "Don't let Dad hear you!"

Hettie grimaced. "Child, you'll end up in a brawl,
sure as God made little green apples!"

"I will not. I'm going to waitress and make pizzas
and sandwiches, not get in fights."

Hettie wasn't convinced. "Put men and liquor together, and you get a fight every time."

"Mr. Duncan has a bouncer," she confided. "I'll be
fine."

"Mr. Hart won't like it," she replied.

"Nothing I do is any of Leo Hart's business anymore," Janie said with a glare. "After the things he's said about me, his opinion wouldn't get him a cup of coffee around here!"

"What sort of things?" Hettie wanted to know.

She rubbed her hands over the sudden chill of her arms. "That I'm a lying, gossiping, man-chaser who can't leave him alone," she said miserably. "He was talking about me to Joe Howland in the hardware store last week. I heard every horrible word."

Hettie winced. She knew how Janie felt about the last of the unmarried Hart brothers. "Oh, baby. I'm so sorry!"

"Marilee lied," she added sadly. "My best friend! She was telling me what to do to make Leo notice me, and all the time she was finding ways to cut me out of his life. She was actually at the ball with Leo. He took her…" She swallowed hard and turned to the task at hand. Brooding was not going to help her situation. "Want a sandwich, Hettie?"

"No, darlin', I'm fine," the older woman told her. She hugged Janie warmly. "Life's tangles work themselves out if you just give them enough time," she said, and went away to let that bit of homespun philosophy sink in.

Janie was unconvinced. Her tangles were bad ones. Maybe her new job would keep Leo out of her thoughts. At least she'd never have to worry about running into him at Shea's, she told herself. After Saturday night, he was probably off hard liquor for life.

BY SATURDAY NIGHT, Janie had four days of work under her belt and she was getting used to the routine. Shea's opened at lunchtime and closed at eleven. Shea's served

pizza and sandwiches and chips, as well as any sort of
liquor a customer could ask for. Janie often had to serve
drinks in between cooking chores. She got to recognize
some of the customers on sight, but she didn't make a
habit of speaking to them. She didn't want any trouble.

Her father had, inevitably, found out about her noc-
turnal activities. Saturday morning, he'd been raging
at her for lying to him.

"I do work in a restaurant," she'd defended herself.
"It's just sort of in a bar."

"You work in a bar, period!" he returned, furious. "I
want you to quit, right now!"

It was now or never, she told herself, as she faced
him bravely. "No," she replied quietly. "I'm not giving
notice. Mr. Duncan said I could work two weeks and
see if I could handle it, and that's just what I'm going
to do. And don't you dare talk to him behind my back,
Dad," she told him.

He looked tormented. "Girl, this isn't necessary!"

"It is, and not only because we need the money,"
she'd replied. "I need to feel independent."

He hadn't considered that angle. She was determined, and Duncan did have a good bouncer, a huge
man called, predictably, Tiny. "We'll see," he'd said
finally.

Janie had won her first adult argument with her parent. She felt good about it.

HARLEY SHOWED UP two of her five nights on the job,
just to check things out. He was back again tonight.
She grinned at him as she served him pizza and beer.

"How's it going?" he asked.

She looked around at the bare wood floors, the no-frills surroundings, the simple wooden tables and chairs and the long counter at which most of the customers— male customers—sat. There were two game machines and a jukebox. There were ceiling fans to circulate the heat, and to cool the place in summer. There was a huge dance floor, where people could dance to live music on Friday and Saturday night. The band was playing now, lazy Western tunes, and a couple was circling the dance floor alone.

"I really like it here," she told Harley with a smile. "I feel as if I'm standing on my own two feet for the first time in my life." She leaned closer. "And the tips are really nice!"

He chuckled. "Okay. No more arguments from me." He glanced toward Tiny, a huge man with tattoos on both arms and a bald head, who'd taken an immediate liking to Janie. He was reassuringly close whenever she spoke to customers or served food and drinks.

"Isn't he a doll?" Janie asked, smiling toward Tiny, who smiled back a little hesitantly, as if he were afraid his face might crack.

"That's not a question you should ask a man, Janie," he teased.

Grinning, she flipped her bar cloth at him, and went back to work.

LEO WENT LOOKING for Fred Brewster after lunch on Monday. He'd been out of town at a convention, and he'd lost touch with his friend.

Fred was in his study, balancing figures that didn't want to be balanced. He looked up as Hettie showed Leo in.

"Hello, stranger," Fred said with a grin. "Sit down. Want some coffee? Hettie, how about…!"

"No need to shout, Mr. Fred, it's already dripping," she interrupted him with a chuckle. "I'll bring it in when it's done."

"Cake, too!" he called.

There was a grumble.

"She thinks I eat too many sweets," Fred told Leo. "Maybe I do. How was the convention?"

"It was pretty good," Leo told him. "There's a lot of talk about beef exports to Japan and improved labeling of beef to show country of origin. Some discussion of artificial additives," he confided with a chuckle. "You can guess where that came from."

"J. D. Langley and the Tremayne brothers."

"Got it in one guess." Leo tossed his white Stetson into a nearby chair and sat down in the one beside it. He ran a hand through his thick gold-streaked brown hair and his dark eyes pinned Fred. "But aside from the convention, I've heard some rumors that bother me," he said, feeling his way.

"Oh?" Fred put aside his keyboard mouse and sat back. He'd heard about Janie's job, he thought, groaning inwardly. He drew in a long breath. "What rumors?" he asked innocently.

Leo leaned forward, his crossed arms on his knees. "That you're looking for partners here."

"Oh. That." Fred cleared his throat and looked past Leo. "Just a few little setbacks…"

"Why didn't you come to me?" Leo persisted, scowling. "I'd loan you anything you needed on the strength of your signature. You know that."

Fred swallowed. "I do…know that. But I wouldn't

dare. Under the circumstances." He avoided Leo's piercing stare.

"What circumstances?" Leo asked with resignation, when he realized that he was going to have to pry every scrap of information out of his friend.

"Janie."

Leo's breath expelled in a rush. He'd wondered if Fred knew about the friction between the two of them. It was apparent that he did. "I see."

Fred glanced at him and winced. "She won't hear your name mentioned," he said apologetically. "I couldn't go to you behind her back, and she'd find out anyway, sooner or later. Jacobsville is a small town."

"She wouldn't be likely to find out when she's away at college," Leo assured him. "She has gone back, hasn't she?"

There was going to be an explosion. Fred knew it without saying a word. "Uh, Leo, she hasn't gone back, exactly."

His eyebrows lifted. "She's not here. I asked Hettie. She flushed and almost dragged me in here without saying anything except Janie wasn't around. I assumed she'd gone back to school."

"No. She's, uh, got a job, Leo. A good job," he added, trying to reassure himself. "She likes it very much."

"Doing what, for God's sake?" Leo demanded. "She has no skills to speak of!"

"She's cooking. At a restaurant."

Leo felt his forehead. "No fever," he murmured to himself. It was a well-known fact that Janie could burn water in a pan. He pinned Fred with his eyes. "Would you like to repeat that?"

"She's cooking. She can cook," he added belligerently at Leo's frank astonishment. "Hettie spent two months with her in the kitchen. She can even make—" he started to say "biscuits" and thought better of it "—pizza."

Leo whistled softly. "Fred, I didn't know things were that bad. I'm sorry."

"The bull dying was nobody's fault," Fred said heavily. "But I used money I hoped to recoup to buy him, and there was no insurance. Very few small ranchers could take a loss like that and remain standing. He was a champion's offspring."

"I know that. I'd help, if you'd let me," Leo said earnestly.

"I appreciate it. But I can't."

There was a long, pregnant pause. "Janie told you about what happened at the ball, I suppose," Leo added curtly.

"No. She hasn't said a single word about that," Fred replied. He frowned. "Why?" He understood, belatedly, Leo's concerned stare. "She did tell me about what happened in the hardware store," he added slowly. "There's more?"

Leo glanced away. "There was some unpleasantness at the ball, as well. We had a major fight." He studied his big hands. "I've made some serious mistakes lately. I believed some gossip about Janie that I should never have credited. I know better now, but it's too late. She won't let me close enough to apologize."

That was news. "When did you see her?" Fred asked, playing for time.

"In town at the bank Friday," he said. "She snubbed me." He smiled faintly. It had actually hurt when she'd given him a harsh glare, followed by complete oblivion to his presence. "First time that's happened to me in my life."

"Janie isn't usually rude," Fred tried to justify her behavior. "Maybe it's just the new job…"

"It's what I said to her, Fred," the younger man replied heavily. "I really hurt her. Looking back, I don't know why I ever believed what I was told."

Fred was reading between the lines. "Marilee can be very convincing, Janie said. And she had a case on you."

"It wasn't mutual," Leo said surprisingly. "I didn't realize what was going on. Then she told me all these things Janie was telling people…" He stopped and cursed harshly. "I thought I could see through lies. I guess I'm more naive than I thought I was."

"Any man can be taken in," Fred reassured him. "It was just bad luck. Janie never said a word about you in public. She's shy, although you might not realize it. She'd never throw herself at a man. Well, not for real," he amended with a faint smile. "She did dress up and flirt with you. She told Hettie it was the hardest thing she'd ever done in her life, and she agonized over it for days afterward. Not the mark of a sophisticated woman, is it?"

Leo understood then how far he'd fallen. No wonder she'd been so upset when she overheard him running down her aggressive behavior. "No," he replied. "I wish I'd seen through it." He smiled wryly. "I don't like aggressive, sophisticated women," he confessed. "Call it a fatal flaw. I liked Janie the way she was."

"Harmless?" Fred mused.

Leo flushed. "I wouldn't say that."

"Wouldn't you?" Fred leaned back in his chair, smiling at the younger man's confusion. "I've sheltered Janie

too much. I wanted her to have a smooth, easy path
through life. But I did her no favors. She's not a dress-
up doll, Leo, she's a woman. She needs to learn inde-
pendence, self-sufficiency. She has a temper, and she's
learning to use that, too. Last week, she stood up to me
for the first time and told me what she was going to do."
He chuckled. "I must confess, it was pretty shocking to
realize that my daughter was a woman."

"She's going around with Harley," Leo said curtly.

"Why shouldn't she? Harley's a good man—young,
but steady and dependable. He, uh, did go up against
armed men and held his own, you know."

Leo did know. It made him furious to know. He
didn't hang out with professional soldiers. He'd been
in the service, and briefly in combat, but he'd never
fought drug dealers and been written up in newspapers as a local hero.

Fred deduced all that from the look on Leo's lean
face. "It's not like you think," he added. "She and Harley are friends. Just friends."

"Do I care?" came the impassioned reply. He grabbed
up his Stetson and got to his feet. He hesitated, turning back to Fred. "I won't insist, but Janie would never
have to know if I took an interest in the ranch," he
added firmly.

Fred was tempted. He sighed and stood up, too. "I've
worked double shifts for years, trying to keep it solvent.
I've survived bad markets, drought, unseasonable cold.
But this is the worst it's ever been. I could lose the property so easily."

"Then don't take the risk," Leo insisted. "I can loan
you what it takes to get you back in the black. And I
promise you, Janie will never know. It will be between

the two of us. Don't lose the ranch out of pride, Fred. It's been in your family for generations."

Fred grimaced. "Leo…"

The younger man leaned both hands on the desk and impaled Fred with dark eyes. "Let me help!"

Fred studied the determination, the genuine concern in that piercing stare. "It would have to be a secret," he said, weakening.

Leo's eyes softened. "It will be. You have my word. Blake Kemp's our family attorney. I'll make an appointment. We can sit down with him and work out the details."

Fred had to bite down hard on his lower lip to keep the brightness in his eyes in check. "You can't possibly know how much…" He choked.

Leo held up a hand, embarrassed by his friend's emotion. "I'm filthy rich," he said curtly. "What good is money if you can't use it to help out friends? You'd do the same for me in a heartbeat if our positions were reversed."

Fred swallowed noticeably. "That goes without saying." He drew in a shaky breath. "Thanks," he bit off.

"You're welcome." Leo slanted his hat across his eyes. "I'll phone you. By the way, which restaurant is Janie working at?" he added. "I might stop by for lunch one day."

"That wouldn't be a good idea just yet," Fred said, feeling guilty because Leo still didn't know what was going on.

Leo considered that. "You could be right," he had to agree. "I'll let it ride for a few days, then. Until she cools down a little, at least." He grinned. "She's got a hell of a temper, Fred. Who'd have guessed?"

Fred chuckled. "She's full of surprises lately."

"That she is. I'll be in touch."

Leo was gone and Fred let the emotion out. He hadn't realized how much his family ranch meant to him until he was faced with the horrible prospect of losing it. Now, it would pass to Janie and her family, her children. God bless Leo Hart for being a friend when he needed one so desperately. He grabbed at a tissue and wiped his eyes. Life was good. Life was very good!

FRED WAS STILL up when Janie got home from work. She was tired. It had been a long night. She stopped in the kitchen to say good-night to Hettie before she joined her father in his study.

"Hettie said Leo came by," she said without her usual greeting. She looked worried. "Why?"

"He wanted to check on his bull," he lied without meeting her eyes.

She hesitated. "Did he...ask about me?"

"Yes," he said. "I told him you had a job working in a restaurant."

She stared at her feet. "Did you tell him which one?"

He looked anxious. "No."

She met his eyes. "You don't have to worry, Dad. It's none of Leo Hart's business where I work, or whatever else I do."

"You're still angry," he noted. "I understand. But he wants to make peace."

She swallowed, hearing all over again his voice taunting her, baiting her. She clenched both hands at her sides. "He wants to bury the hatchet? Good. I know exactly where to bury it."

"Now, daughter, he's not a bad man."

"Of course he's not. He just doesn't like me," she bit off. "You can't blame him, not when he's got Marilee."

He winced. "I didn't think. You lost your only friend."

"Some friend," she scoffed. "She's gone to spend the holidays in Colorado," she added smugly. "A rushed trip, I heard."

"I imagine she's too ashamed to walk down the main street right now," her father replied. "People have been talking about her, and that's no lie. But she's not really a bad woman, Janie. She just made a mistake. People do."

"You don't," she said unexpectedly, and smiled at him. "You're the only person in the world who wouldn't stab me in the back."

He flushed. Guilt overwhelmed him. What would she say when she knew that he was going to let Leo Hart buy into the ranch, and behind her back? It was for a good cause, so that she could eventually inherit her birthright, but he felt suddenly like a traitor. He could only imagine how she'd look at him if she ever found out....

"Why are you brooding?" she teased. "You need to put away those books and go to bed."

He stared at the columns that wouldn't balance and thought about having enough money to fix fences, repair the barn, buy extra feed for the winter, buy replacement heifers, afford medicine for his sick cattle and veterinarian's fees. The temptation was just too much for him. He couldn't let the ranch go to strangers.

"Do you ever think about down the road," Fred murmured, "when your children grow up and take over the ranch?"

She blinked. "Well, yes, sometimes," she confessed.

"It's a wonderful legacy," she added with a soft smile. "We go back such a long way in Jacobsville. It was one of your great-uncles who was the first foreman of the Jacobs ranch properties when the founder of our town came here and bought cattle, after the Civil War. This ranch was really an offshoot of that one," she added. "There's so much history here!"

Fred swallowed. "Too much to let the ranch go down the tube, or end up in the hands of strangers, like the Jacobs place did." He shook his head. "That was sad, to see Shelby and Ty thrown off their own property. That ranch had been in their family over a hundred years."

"It wasn't much of a ranch anymore," she reminded him. "More of a horse farm. But I understand what you mean. I'm glad we'll have the ranch to hand down to our descendants." She gave him a long look. "You aren't thinking of giving it up without a fight?"

"Heavens, no!"

She relaxed. "Sorry. But the way you were talking…"

"I'd do almost anything to keep it in the family," Fred assured her. "You, uh, wouldn't have a problem with me taking on a partner or an investor?"

"Of course not," she assured him. "So you found someone in Colorado after all?" she added excitedly. "Somebody who's willing to back us?"

"Yes," he lied, "but I didn't hear until today."

"That's just great!" she exclaimed.

He gave her a narrow look. "I'm glad you think so. Then you can give up that job and go back to college…"

"No."

His eyebrows went up. "But, Janie…"

"Dad, even with an investor, we still have the day-to-day operation of the ranch to maintain," she reminded him gently. "How about groceries? Utilities? How about cattle feed and horse feed and salt blocks and fencing?"

He sighed. "You're right, of course. I'll need the investment for the big things."

"I like my job," she added. "I really do."

"It's a bad place on the weekends," he worried.

"Tiny likes me," she assured him. "And Harley comes in at least two or three times a week, mostly on Fridays and Saturdays, to make sure I'm doing all right. I feel as safe at Shea's as I do right here with you."

"It's not that I mind you working," he said, trying to explain.

"I know that. You're just worried that I might get in over my head. Tiny doesn't let anybody have too much to drink before he makes them leave. Mr. Duncan is emphatic about not having drunks in the place."

Fred sighed. "I know when I'm licked. I may show up for pizza one Saturday night, though."

She grinned. "You'd be welcome! I could show you off to my customers."

"Leo wanted to know where you were working," he said abruptly. "He wanted to come by and see you."

Her face tautened. "I don't want to see him."

"So I heard. He was, uh, pretty vocal about the way you snubbed him."

She tossed back her hair. "He deserved it. I'm nobody's doormat. He isn't going to walk all over me and get away with it!"

"He won't like you working at Shea's, no matter what you think."

"Why do you care?" she asked suspiciously.

He couldn't tell her that Leo might renege on the loan if he knew Fred was letting her work in such a dive.

He felt guilty as sin for not coming clean. But he was so afraid of losing the ranch. It was Janie's inheritance. He had to do everything he could to keep it solvent.

"He's my friend," he said finally.

"I used to think he was mine, too," she replied. "But friends don't talk about each other the way he was talking about me. As if I'd ever gossip about him!"

"I think he knows that now, Janie."

She forced the anger to the back of her mind. "I guess if he knew what I was doing, he'd faint. He doesn't think I can cook at all."

"I did tell him you had a cooking job," he confided.

Her eyes lit up. "You did? What did he say?"

"He was...surprised."

"He was astonished," she translated.

"It bothered him that you snubbed him. He said he felt really bad about the things he said, that you overheard. He, uh, told me about the fight you had at the ball, too."

Her face colored. "What did he tell you?"

"That you'd had a bad argument. Seemed to tickle him that you had a temper," he added with a chuckle.

"He'll find out I have a temper if he comes near me again." She turned. "I'm going to bed, Dad. You sleep good."

"You, too, sweetheart. Good night."

He watched her walk away with a silent sigh of relief. So far, he thought, so good.

CHAPTER SIX

THE FOLLOWING WEDNESDAY, Leo met with Blake Kemp and Fred Brewster in Kemp's office, to draw up the instrument of partnership.

"I'll never be able to thank you enough for this, Leo," Fred said as they finished a rough draft of the agreement.

"You'd have done it for me," Leo said simply. "How long will it take until those papers are ready to sign?" he asked Kemp.

"We'll have them by Monday," Kemp assured him.

"I'll make an appointment with your receptionist on the way out," Leo said, rising. "Thanks, Blake."

The attorney shook his outstretched hand, and then Fred's. "All in a day's work. I wish most of my business was concluded this easily, and amiably," he added wryly.

Leo checked his watch. "Why don't we go out to Shea's and have a beer and some pizza, Fred?" he asked the other man, who, curiously, seemed paler.

Fred was scrambling for a reason that Leo couldn't go to Shea's. "Well, because, uh, because Hettie made chili!" he remembered suddenly. "So why don't you come home and eat with me? We've got Mexican corn bread to go with it!"

Leo hesitated. "That does sound pretty good," he had

to admit. Then he remembered. Janie would be there. He was uncomfortable with the idea of rushing in on her unexpectedly, especially in light of recent circumstances. He was still a little embarrassed about his own behavior. He searched for a reason to refuse, and found one. "Oh, for Pete's sake, I almost forgot!" he added, slapping his forehead. "I'm supposed to have supper with Cag and Tess tonight. We're going in together on two new Santa Gertrudis bulls. How could I have forgotten…got to run, Fred, or I'll never make it on time!"

"Sure, of course," Fred said, and looked relieved. "Have a good time!"

Leo chuckled. "I get to play with my nephew. That's fun, all right. I like kids."

"You never seemed the type," Fred had to admit.

"I'm not talking about having any of my own right away," Leo assured him. "I don't want to get married. But I like all my nephews, not to mention my niece."

Fred only smiled.

"Thanks for the offer of supper, anyway," he told the older man with a smile. "Sorry I can't come."

Fred relaxed. "That's okay, Leo. More for me," he teased. "Well, I'll go home and have my chili. Thanks again. If I can ever do anything for you, anything at all, you only have to ask."

Leo smiled. "I know that, Fred. See you."

They parted in the parking lot. Leo got in his double-cabbed pickup and gunned the engine.

Fred got into his own truck and relaxed. At least, he thought, he didn't have to face Leo's indignation today. With luck, Leo might never realize what was going on.

Leo, honest to the core, phoned Cag and caged an invitation to supper to discuss the two new bulls the brothers were buying. But he had some time before he was due at his brother's house. He brooded over Fred's dead bull, and Christabel's, and he began to wonder. He had a bull from that same lot, a new lineage of Salers bulls that came from a Victoria breeder. Two related bulls dying in a month's time seemed just a bit too much for coincidence. He picked up the phone and called information.

CAG AND TESS were still like newlyweds, Leo noted as he carried their toddler around the living room after supper, grinning from ear to ear as the little boy, barely a year old, smiled up at him and tried to grab his nose. They sat close together on the sofa and seemed to radiate love. They were watching him with equal interest.

"You do that like a natural," Cag teased.

Leo shifted the little boy. "Lots of practice," he chuckled. "Simon's two boys, then Corrigan's boy and their new girl, and now your son." He lifted an eyebrow. "Rey and Meredith are finally expecting, too, I hear."

"They are," Cag said with a sigh. He eyed his brother mischievously. "When are you planning to throw in the towel and join up?"

"Me? Never," Leo said confidently. "I've got a big house to myself, all the women I can attract, no responsibilities and plenty of little kids to spoil as they grow." He gave them an innocent glance. "Why should I want to tie myself down?"

"Just a thought," Cag replied. "You'll soon get tired of going all the way to town every morning for a fresh biscuit." Cag handed the baby back to Tess.

"I'm thinking of taking a cooking course," Leo remarked.

Cag roared.

"I could cook if I wanted to!" Leo said indignantly.

Tess didn't speak, but her eyes did.

Leo stuffed his hands in his pockets. "Well, I don't really want to," he conceded. "And it is a long way to town. But I can manage." He sprawled in an easy chair. "There's something I want to talk to you about—besides our new bulls."

"What?" Cag asked, sensing concern.

"Fred's big Salers bull that died mysteriously," Leo said. "Christabel and Judd Dunn lost one, too, a young bull."

"Judd says it died of bloat."

"I saw the carcass, he didn't. He thinks Christabel made it up, God knows why. He wouldn't even come down from Victoria to take a look at it. It wasn't bloat. But she didn't call a vet out, and they didn't find any marks on Fred's bull." He sighed. "Cag, I've done a little checking. The bulls are related. The young herd sire of these bulls died recently as well, and the only champion Salers bull left that's still walking is our two-year-old bull that I loaned to Fred, although it's not related to the dead ones."

Cag sat up straight, scowling. "You're kidding."

Leo shook his head. "It's suspicious, isn't it?"

"You might talk to Jack Handley in Victoria, the rancher we bought our bull from."

"I did." He leaned forward intently. "Handley said he fired two men earlier this year for stealing from him. They're brothers, John and Jack Clark. One of them is a thief, the other has a reputation for vengeance that boggles the mind. When one former employer fired Jack Clark, he lost his prize bull and all four young bulls he'd got from it. No apparent cause of death. Handley checked and found a pattern of theft and retribution with those brothers going back two years. At least four employers reported similar problems with theft and firing. There's a pattern of bull deaths, too. The brothers were suspects in a recent case in Victoria, but there was never enough evidence to convict anyone. Until now, I don't imagine anyone's connected the dots."

"How the hell do they keep getting away with it?" Cag wanted to know.

"There's no proof. And they're brawlers," Leo said. "They intimidate people."

"They wouldn't intimidate us," Cag remarked.

"They wouldn't. But do you see the common thread here? Handley crossed the brothers. He had a new, expensive Salers bull that he bred to some heifers, and he sold all the young bulls this year, except for his seed bull. His seed bull, and all its offspring, which isn't many, have died. Christabel Gaines's young bull was one of Handley's, like Fred's. And Jack Clark was fired by Judd Dunn for stealing, too."

Cag was scowling. "Where are the brothers now?"

"I asked Handley. He says John Clark is working on a ranch near Victoria. We know that Jack, the one with a reputation for getting even, is right here in Jacobsville, driving a cattle truck for Duke Wright," Leo said. "I called Wright and told him what I know. He's going to keep an eye on the man. I called Judd Dunn, too, but he was too preoccupied to listen. He's smitten with that redheaded supermodel who's in the movie they're making on Christabel's ranch—Tippy Moore, the 'Georgia Firefly.'"

"He'll land hard, if I make my guess," Cag said. "She's playing. He isn't."

"He's married, too," Leo said curtly. "Something he doesn't seem to remember."

"He only married Christabel because she was going to lose the ranch after her father beat her nearly to death in a drunken rage. Her mother was an invalid. No way could the two of them have kept it solvent," Cag added. "That's not a real marriage. I'm sure he's already looked into annulling it when she turns twenty-one."

"She was twenty-one this month," Leo said. "Poor kid. She's got a real case on him, and she's fairly plain except for those soulful brown eyes and a nice figure. She couldn't compete with the Georgia Firefly."

"So ask yourself what does a supermodel worth millions want with a little bitty Texas Ranger?" Cag grinned.

Tess gave him a speaking look. "As a happily married woman, I can tell you that if I wasn't hung up on you, Judd Dunn would make my mouth water."

Cag whistled.

Leo shrugged. "Whatever. But I think we should keep a close eye on our Salers bull, as well as Wright's new cattle-truck driver. Handley says Clark likes to drink, so it wouldn't hurt to keep an eye out at Shea's, as well."

Cag frowned thoughtfully. "You might have a word with Janie..."

"Janie?"

"Janie Brewster," his brother said impatiently. "Tell her what the man looks like and have her watch him if he ever shows up out there."

Leo stared at his brother. "Will you make sense?

Why would Janie be at Shea's roadhouse in the first place?"

Realization dawned. Cag looked stunned, and then uncomfortable.

Tess grimaced. "He doesn't know. I guess you'd better tell him."

"Tell me what?" Leo grumbled.

"Well, it's like this," Cag said. "Janie's been working at Shea's for a couple of weeks..."

"She's working in a bar?" Leo exploded violently.

Cag winced. "Now, Leo, she's a grown woman," he began calmly.

"She's barely twenty-one!" he continued, unabashed. "She's got no business working around drunks! What the hell is Fred thinking, to let her get a job in a place like that?"

Cag sighed. "Talk is that Fred's in the hole and can hardly make ends meet," he told Leo. "I guess Janie insisted on helping out."

Leo got to his feet and grabbed up his white Stetson, his lips in a thin line, his dark eyes sparking.

"Don't go over there and start trouble," Cag warned. "Don't embarrass the girl with her boss!"

Leo didn't answer him. He kept walking. His footsteps, quick and hard, described the temper he was in. He even slammed the door on the way out, without realizing he had.

Cag looked at Tess worriedly as Leo's car careened down the driveway. "Should I warn her?" he asked Tess.

She nodded. "At least she'll be prepared."

Cag thought privately that it was unlikely that anybody could prepare for Leo in a temper, but he picked up the phone just the same.

SHEA'S WASN'T CROWDED when Leo jerked to a stop in the parking lot. He walked into the roadhouse with blood in his eye. Three men at a table near the door stopped talking when they saw him enter. Apparently they thought he looked dangerous.

Janie was thinking the same thing. She'd assured Cag that she wasn't afraid of Leo, but it was a little different when the man was walking toward her with his eyes narrow and his lips compressed like that.

He stopped at the counter. He noted her long apron, her hands with a dusting of flour, a pencil behind her ear. She looked busy. There were three cowboys at the counter drinking beers and apparently waiting for pizzas. A teenage boy was pulling a pizza on a long paddle out of a big oven behind her.

"Get your things," he told Janie in a tone he hadn't used with her since she was ten and had gotten into a truck with a cowboy who offered her a trip to the visiting carnival. He'd busted up that cowboy pretty bad, and for reasons Janie only learned later. She'd had a very close call. Leo had saved her. But she didn't need saving right now.

She lifted her chin and glared at him. The night of the ball came back to her vividly. "How's your foot?" she asked with sarcasm.

"My foot is fine. Get your things," he repeated curtly.

"I work here."

"Not anymore."

She crossed her arms. "You planning to carry me out kicking and screaming? Because that's the only way I'm leaving."

"Suits me." He started around the counter.

She picked up a pitcher of beer and dumped the contents on him. "Now you listen to me... Leo!"

The beer didn't even slow him down. He had her up in his arms and he turned, carrying her toward the door. She was kicking and screaming for all she was worth.

That attracted Tiny, the bouncer. He was usually on the job by six, but he'd arrived late today. To give him credit, the minute he saw Janie, he turned and went toward the big man bullying her.

He stepped in front of Leo. "Put her down, Leo," he drawled.

"You tell him, Tiny!" Janie sputtered.

"I'm taking her home where she'll be safe," Leo replied. He knew Tiny. The man was sweet-natured, but about a beer short of a six-pack on intelligence. He was also as big as a house. It didn't hurt to be polite. "She shouldn't be working in a bar."

"It isn't a bar," Tiny said reasonably. "It's a roadhouse. It's a nice roadhouse. Mr. Duncan don't allow no drunks. You put Miss Janie down, Leo, or I'll have to hit you."

"He'll do it," Janie warned. "I've seen him do it. He's hit men even bigger than you. Haven't you, Tiny?" she encouraged.

"I sure have, Miss Janie."

Leo wasn't backing down. He glared at Tiny. "I said," he replied, his voice dangerously soft, "I'm taking her home."

"I don't think she wants to go, Mr. Hart," came a new source of interference from the doorway behind him.

He swung around with Janie in his big arms. It was Harley Fowler, leaning against the doorjamb, looking intimidating. It would have been a joke a year ago. The new Harley made it look good.

"You tell him, Harley!" Janie said enthusiastically.

"You keep still," Leo told her angrily. "You've got no business working in a rough joint like this!"

"You have no right to tell me where I can work," Janie shot right back, red-faced and furious. "Won't Marilee mind that you're here pestering me?" she added viciously.

His cheeks went red. "I haven't seen Marilee in two weeks. I don't give a damn if I never see her again, either."

That was news. Janie looked as interested as Harley seemed to.

Tiny was still hovering. "I said, put her down," he persisted.

"Do you really think you can take on Tiny and me both?" Harley asked softly.

Leo was getting mad. His face tautened. "I don't know about Tiny," he said honestly, putting Janie back on her feet without taking his eyes off Harley. "But you're a piece of cake, son."

As he said it, he stepped forward and threw a quick punch that Harley wasn't expecting. With his mouth open, Harley tumbled backward over a table. Leo glared at Janie.

"You want this job, keep it," he said, ice-cold except for the glitter in those dark eyes. "But if you get slugged during a brawl or hassled by amorous drunks, don't come crying to me!"

"As...as if I ever...would!" she stammered, shocked by his behavior.

He turned around and stalked out the door without giving Harley a single glance.

Janie rushed to Harley and helped him back to his feet. "Oh, Harley, are you hurt?" she asked miserably.

He rubbed his jaw. "Only my pride, darlin'," he murmured with a rough chuckle. "Damn, that man can throw a punch! I wasn't really expecting him to do it." His eyes twinkled. "I guess you're a little more important to him than any of us realized."

She flushed. "He's just trying to run my life."

Tiny came over and inspected Harley's jaw. "Gonna have a bruise, Mr. Fowler," he said politely.

Harley grinned. He was a good sport, and he knew a jealous man when he saw one. Leo had wanted to deck him at the ball over Janie, but he'd restrained himself. Now, maybe, he felt vindicated. But Harley wished there had been a gentler way of doing it. His jaw was really sore.

"The beast," Janie muttered. "Come on, Harley, I'll clean you up in the bathroom before it gets crowded. Okay, guys, fun's over. Drink your beer and eat your pizzas."

"Yes, mother," one of the men drawled.

She gave him a wicked grin and led Harley to the back. She was not going to admit the thrill it had given her that Leo was worried about her job, or that people thought he was jealous of Harley. But she felt it all the way to her bones.

LEO WAS LUCKY not to get arrested for speeding on his way to Fred's house. He had the sports car flat-out on the four lane that turned onto the Victoria road, and he burned rubber when he left the tarmac and turned into Fred's graveled driveway.

Fred heard him coming and knew without a doubt what was wrong.

He stood on the porch with his hands in his jean pockets as he studied the darkening sky behind Leo, who was already out of the car and headed for the porch. His Stetson was pulled down right over his eyes, cocked as they said in cowboy vernacular, and Fred had never seen Leo look so much like a Hart. The brothers had a reputation for being tough customers. Leo looked it right now.

"I want her out of that damned bar," Leo told Fred flatly, without even a conventional greeting. "You can consider it a term of the loan, if you like, but you get her home."

Fred grimaced. "I did try to talk her out of it, when I found out where she was working," he said in his own defense. "Leo, she stood right up to me and said she was old enough to make her own decisions. What do I say to that? She's twenty-one and she told me she wasn't giving up her job."

Leo cursed furiously.

"What happened to your shirt?" Fred asked suddenly. He leaned closer and made a face. "Man, you reek of beer!"

"Of course I do! Your daughter baptized me in front of a crowd of cowboys with a whole pitcher of the damned stuff!" Leo said indignantly.

Fred's eyes opened wide. "Janie? My Janie?"

Leo looked disgusted. "She flung the pitcher at me. And then she set the bouncer on me and appealed to Harley Fowler for aid."

"Why did she need aid?" Fred asked hesitantly.

"Oh, she was kicking and screaming, and they thought she was in trouble, I guess."

"Kicking...?"

Leo's lips compressed. "All right, if you have to know, I tried to carry her out of the bar and bring her home. She resisted."

Fred whistled. "I'd say she resisted." He was trying very hard not to laugh. He looked at Leo's clenched fists. One, the right one, was bleeding. "Hit somebody, did you?"

"Harley," he returned uncomfortably. "Well, he shouldn't have interfered! He doesn't own Janie, she's not his private stock. If he were any sort of a man, he'd have insisted that she go home right then. Instead, he stands there calmly ordering me to put her down. Ordering me. Hell! He's lucky it was only one punch!"

"Oh, boy," Fred said, burying his face in his hand. Gossip was going to run for a month on this mixer.

"It wasn't my fault," Leo argued, waving his hands. "I went in there to save her from being insulted and harassed by drunk men, and look at the thanks I get? Drenched in beer, threatened by ogres, giggled at..."

"Who giggled?"

Leo shifted. "This little brunette who was sitting with one of the Tremayne brothers' cowboys."

Fred cleared his throat. He didn't dare laugh. "I guess it was a sight to see."

Grimacing, Leo flexed his hand. "Damned near broke my fingers on Harley's jaw. He needs to learn to keep his mouth shut. Just because he's not afraid of drug lords, he shouldn't think he can take me on and win."

"I'm sure he knows that now, Leo."

Leo took a deep breath. "You tell her I said she's going to give up that job, one way or the other!"

"I'll tell her." It won't matter though, he thought privately. Janie was more than likely to dig her heels in big time after Leo's visit to Shea's.

Leo gave him a long, hard stare. "I'm not mean with money, I don't begrudge you that loan. But I'm not kidding around with you, Fred. Janie's got no business in Shea's, even with a bouncer on duty. It's a rough place. I've been there on nights when the bouncer didn't have time for a cup of coffee, and there's been at least one shooting. It's dangerous. Even more dangerous right now."

Something in the younger man's tone made Fred uneasy. "Why?"

"Fred, you don't breathe a word of this, even to Janie, understand?"

Fred nodded, curious.

Leo told him what he'd learned from Handley about the Clark brothers, and the loss of the related Salers bulls.

Fred's jaw flew open. "You think my bull was killed deliberately?"

"Yes, I do," Leo admitted solemnly. "I'm sorry to tell you that, because I can't prove it and neither can you. Clark is shrewd. He's never been caught in the act. If you can't prove it, you can't prosecute."

Fred let out an angry breath. "Of all the damned mean, low things to do!"

"I agree, and it's why I'm putting two men over here to watch my bull," he added firmly. "No sorry cattle-killer is going to murder my bull and get away with it.

I'm having video cameras installed, too. If he comes near that bull, I'll have his hide in jail!"

Fred chuckled. "Don't I wish he'd try," he said thoughtfully.

"So do I, but I don't hold out a lot of hope," Leo returned. He moved his shoulders restlessly. The muscles were stretched, probably from Janie's violent squirming. He remembered without wanting to the feel of her soft breasts pressed hard against his chest, and he ached.

"Uh, about Janie," Fred continued worriedly.

Leo stared at him without speaking.

"Okay," the older man said wearily. "I'll try to talk some sense into her." He pursed his lips and peered up at Leo. "Of course, she could be a lot of help where she is right now," he murmured thoughtfully. "With the Clark man roaming around loose, that is. She could keep an eye on him if he comes into Shea's. If he's a drinking man, that's the only joint around that sells liquor by the drink."

"She doesn't know what he looks like," Leo said.

"Can't you find out and tell her?"

Leo sighed. "I don't like her being in the line of fire."

"Neither do I." Fred gave the other man a curious scrutiny. "You and Harley and I could arrange to drop in from time to time, just to keep an eye on her."

"She'll have to ask Harley. I won't."

"You're thinking about it, aren't you?" Fred persisted.

Leo was. His eyes narrowed. "My brothers could drop in occasionally, and so could our ranch hands. The Tremaynes would help us out. I know Harden. I'll talk to him. And most of our cowhands go into Shea's on the weekend. I'll talk to our cattle foreman."

"I know Cy Parks and Eb Scott," Fred told him. "They'd help, too."

Leo perked up. With so many willing spies, Janie would be looked after constantly, and she'd never know it. He smiled.

"It's a good idea, isn't it?"

Leo glared at him. "You just don't want to have to make Janie quit that job. You're scared of her, aren't you? What's the matter, think she'd try to drown you in cheap beer, too?"

Fred burst out laughing. "You have to admit, it's a shock to think of Janie throwing beer at anybody."

"I guess it is, at that," Leo seconded, remembering how shy Janie had been. It was only after Marilee had caused so much trouble with her lies that Leo had considered Janie's lack of aggression.

In the past, that was, he amended, because he'd never seen such aggression as he'd encountered in little Janie Brewster just an hour ago.

He shook his head. "It was all I could do not to get thrown on the floor. She's a handful when she's mad. I don't think I've ever seen her lose her temper before."

"There's a lot about her you don't know," Fred said enigmatically.

"Okay, she can stay," Leo said at once. "But I'll find out what Clark looks like. I'll get a picture if I can manage it. Maybe Grier at the police station would have an idea. He's sweet on Christabel Gaines, and she lost a bull to this dude, so he might be willing to assist."

"Don't get Judd Dunn mad," Fred warned.

Leo shrugged. "He's too stuck on his pretty model to care much about Christabel right now, or Grier, either. I don't want any more bulls killed, and I want that man out of the way before he really hurts somebody."

"Have you talked to his boss?"

"Duke Wright didn't have a clue that his new truck driver was such an unsavory character," Leo said, "and he was keen to fire him on the spot. I persuaded him not to. He needs to be where we can watch him. If he puts a foot wrong, we can put him away. I love animals," Leo said in an uncharacteristically tender mood. "Especially bulls. The kind we keep are gentle creatures. They follow us around like big dogs and eat out of our hands." His face hardened visibly. "A man who could cold-bloodedly kill an animal like that could kill a man just as easily. I want Clark out of here. Whatever it takes. But Janie's going to be watched, all the time she's working," Leo added firmly. "Nobody's going to hurt her."

Fred looked at the other man, sensing emotions under the surface that Leo might not even realize were there.

"Thanks, Leo," he said.

The younger man squared his shoulders and shrugged. "I've got to go home and change my shirt." He looked down at himself and smiled ruefully. "Damn. I may never drink another beer."

"It tastes better than it wears," Fred said, deadpan.

Leo gave him a haughty look and went home.

CHAPTER SEVEN

LEO STOPPED BY Cash Grier's office at the police station in Jacobsville, catching the new assistant chief of police on his lunch hour.

"Come on in," Grier invited. He indicated his big desk, which contained a scattering of white boxes with metal handles. "Like Chinese food? That's moo goo gai pan, that's sweet-and-sour pork, and that's fried rice. Help yourself to a plate."

"Thanks, but I had barbecue at Barbara's Café," Leo replied, sitting down. He noted with little surprise that the man was adept with chopsticks. "I saw Toshiro Mifune catch flies with those things in one of the 'Samurai Trilogy' films," he commented.

Grier chuckled. "Don't believe everything you see, and only half of what you hear," he replied. He gave Leo a dark-eyed appraisal over his paper plate. "You're here about Clark, I guess."

Leo's eyebrows jumped.

"Oh, I'm psychic," Grier told him straight-faced. "I learned that when I was in the CIA knocking off enemy government agents from black helicopters with a sniper kit."

Leo didn't say a word.

Grier just shook his head. "You wouldn't believe the stuff I've done, to hear people talk."

"You're mysterious," Leo commented. "You keep to yourself."

Grier shrugged. "I have to. I don't want people to notice the aliens spying on me." He leaned forward confidentially. "You see them, too, don't you?" he asked in a hushed tone.

Leo began to get it. He started laughing and was secretly relieved when Grier joined him. The other man leaned back in his chair, with his booted feet propped on his desk. He was as fit as Leo, probably in even better condition, if the muscles outlined under that uniform shirt were any indication. Grier was said to move like lightning, although Leo had never seen him fight. The man was an enigma, with his black hair in a rawhide ponytail and his scarred face giving away nothing— unless he wanted it to.

"That's more like it," Grier said as he finished his lunch. "I thought I'd move to a small town and fit in." He smiled wryly. "But people are all the same. Only the scenery changes."

"It was the same for Cy Parks when he first moved here," Leo commented.

Grier gave him a narrow look. "Are you asking a question?"

"Making a comment," Leo told him. "One of our local guys was in the military during a conflict a few years back, in a special forces unit," he added deliberately, recounting something Cy Parks had told him about Harley Fowler. "He saw you on a plane, out of uniform and armed to the teeth."

Grier began to nod. "It's a small world, isn't it?" he asked pleasantly. He put down his plate and the chopsticks with deliberate preciseness. "I did a stint with military intelligence. And with a few…government agencies." He met Leo's curious eyes. "How far has that gossip traveled?"

"It got to Cy Parks and stopped abruptly," Leo replied, recalling what Cy had said to Harley about loose lips. "Jacobsville is a small town. We consider people who live here family, whether or not we're related to them. Gossip isn't encouraged."

Grier was surprised. He actually smiled. "If you asked Parks, or Steele, or Scott why they moved here," he said after a minute, "I imagine you'd learn that what they wanted most was an end to sitting with their backs to the wall and sleeping armed."

"Isn't that why you're here?" Leo wanted to know.

Grier met his eyes levelly. "I don't really know why I'm here, or if I can stay here," he said honestly. "I think I might eventually fit in. I'm going to give it a good try for six months," he added, "no matter how many rubber-necked yahoos stand outside my office trying to hear every damned word I say!" he raised his voice.

There were sudden, sharp footfalls and the sound of scurrying.

Leo chuckled. Grier hadn't even looked at the door when he raised his voice. He shrugged and smiled sheepishly. "I don't have eyes in the back of my head, but I love to keep people guessing about what I know."

"I think that may be part of the problem," Leo advised.

"Well, it doesn't hurt to keep your senses honed. Now. What do you want to know about Clark?"

"I'd like some way to get a photo of him," Leo confessed. "A friend of mine is working at Shea's. I'm going to ask her if she'll keep an eye on who he talks to, what he does, if he comes in there. She'll need to know what he looks like."

Grier sobered at once. "That's dangerous," he said. "Clark's brother almost killed a man he suspected of spying on him, up in Victoria. He made some threats, too."

Leo frowned. "Why are guys like that on the streets?"

"You can't shoot people or even lock them up without due process here in the States," Grier said with a wistful smile. "Pity."

"Listen, do they give you real bullets to go with that gun?" Leo asked, indicating the .45 caliber automatic in a shoulder holster that the man was wearing.

"I haven't shot anybody in months," Grier assured him. "I was a cyber crime specialist in the D.A.'s office San Antonio. I didn't really beat up that guy I was accused of harassing, I just told him I'd keep flies off him if he didn't level with me about his boss's illegal money laundering. I had access to his computerized financial records," he added with a twinkle in his dark eyes.

"I heard about that," Leo chuckled. "Apparently you used some access codes that weren't in the book."

"They let me off with a warning. When they checked my ID, I still had my old 'company' card."

Leo just shook his head. He couldn't imagine Grier being in trouble for very long. He knew too much. "All that specialized background, and you're handing out speeding tickets in Jacobsville, Texas."

"Don't knock it. Nobody's shot at me since I've been here." He got up and opened his filing cabinet with a key. "I have to keep it locked," he explained. "I have copies of documents about alien technology in here." He glanced at Leo to see if he was buying it and grinned.

"Did you read that book by the Air Force guy who discovered night vision at a flying saucer crash?" He turned back to the files. "Hell, I should write a book. With what I know, governments might topple." He hesitated, frowned, with a file folder in his hand. "Our government might topple!"

"Clark?" Leo prompted.

"Clark. Right." He took a paper from the file, replaced it, closed the cabinet and locked it again. "Here. You don't have a clue where this photo came from, and I never saw you."

Leo was looking at a photograph of two men, obviously brothers, in, of all things, a newspaper clipping. Incredibly, they'd been honored with a good citizen award in another Texas town for getting a herd of escaped cattle out of the path of traffic and back into a fenced pasture with broken electric fencing.

"Neat trick," Grier said. "They cut the wire to steal the cattle, and then were seen rounding them up. Everybody thought they were saving the cattle. They had a tractor trailer truck just down the road and told people they were truck drivers who saw the cattle out and stopped to help." He laughed wholeheartedly. "Can you believe it?"

"Can you copy this for me?"

"That's a copy of the original. You can have it," Grier told him. "I've got two more."

"You were expecting trouble, I gather," Leo continued.

"Two expensive bulls in less than a month, both from the same herd sire, is a little too much coincidence even for me," Grier said as he sat back down. "When I heard

Clark was working for Duke Wright, I put two and two together."

"There's no proof," Leo said.

"Not yet. We'll give him a little time and see if he'll oblige us by hanging himself." He laced his lean, strong hands together on the desk in front of him. "But you warn your friend not to be obvious. These are dangerous men."

"I'll tell her."

"And stop knocking men over tables in Shea's. It's outside the city limits, so I can't arrest you. But I can have the sheriff pick you up for brawling," Grier said abruptly, and he was serious. "You can't abduct women in plain sight of the public."

"I wasn't abducting her, I was trying to save her!"

"From what?"

"Fistfights!"

Grier lost it. He got up from his desk. "Get out," he invited through helpless laughter. "I have real work to do here."

"If Harley Fowler said I hit him without provocation, he's lying," Leo continued doggedly. "He never should have ordered me to put her down, and leave my hands free to hit him!"

"You should just tell the woman how you feel," Grier advised. "It's simpler." He glanced at Leo's swollen hand. "And less painful."

Leo didn't really know how he felt. That was the problem. He gave Grier a sardonic look and left.

HE WORRIED ABOUT letting Janie get involved, even from the sidelines, with Clark. Of course, the man might not even come near Shea's. He might buy a bottle and drink on the ranch, in the bunkhouse. But it wasn't a long shot to think he might frequent Shea's if he wanted company while he drank.

He disliked anything that might threaten Janie, and he didn't understand why he hated Harley all of a sudden. But she was in a great position to notice a man without being obvious, and for everyone's sake, Clark had to be watched. A man who would kill helpless animals was capable of worse.

He went looking for her Sunday afternoon, in a misting rain. She wasn't at home. Fred said that she was out, in the cold rain no less, wandering around the pecan trees in her raincoat. Brooding, was how Fred put it. Leo climbed back into his pickup and went after her.

Janie was oblivious to the sound of an approaching truck. She had her hands in her pockets, her eyes on the ground ahead of her, lost in thought.

It had been a revelation that Leo was concerned about her working at Shea's, and it had secretly thrilled her that he tried to make her quit. But he'd washed his hands of her when she wouldn't leave willingly, and he'd hurt her feelings with his comment that she shouldn't complain if she got in trouble. She didn't know what to make of his odd behavior. He'd given her a hard time, thanks to Marilee. But she hadn't been chasing him lately, so she couldn't understand why he was so bossy about her life. And she did feel guilty that he'd slugged poor Harley, who was only trying to help her.

The truck was almost on top of her before she finally heard the engine and jumped to the side of the ranch trail.

Leo pulled up and leaned over to open the passenger door. "Get in before you drown out there," he said.

She hesitated. She wasn't sure if it was safe to get that close to him.

He grimaced. "I'm not armed and dangerous," he drawled. "I just want to talk."

She moved closer to the open door. "You're in a very strange mood lately," she commented. "Maybe the lack of biscuits in your life has affected your mind."

Both eyebrows went up under his hat.

She flushed, thinking she'd been too forward. But she got into the truck and closed the door, removing the hood of her raincoat from her long, damp hair.

"You'll catch cold," he murmured, turning up the heat.

"It's not that wet, and I've got a lined raincoat."

He drove down the road without speaking, made a turn, and ended up in a field on the Hart ranch, a place where they could be completely alone. He put the truck in Park, cut off the engine, and leaned back against his door to study her from under the wide brim of his Stetson. "Your father says you won't give up the job."

"He's right," she replied, ready to do battle.

His fingers tapped rhythmically on the steering wheel. "I've been talking to Grier," he began.

"Now listen here, you can't have me arrested because I won't quit my job!" she interrupted.

He held up a big, lean hand. "Not about that," he corrected. "We've got a man in town who may be involved in some cattle losses. I want you to look at this picture and tell me if you've ever seen him in Shea's."

He took the newspaper clipping out of his shirt pocket, unfolded it, and handed it to her.

She took it gingerly and studied the two faces surrounded by columns of newsprint. "I don't know the man on the left," she replied. "But the one on the right comes in Saturday nights and drinks straight whiskey," she said uneasily. "He's loud and foul-mouthed, and Tiny had to ask him to leave last night."

Leo's face tightened. "He's vindictive," he told her.

"I'll say he is," she agreed at once. "When Tiny went out to get into his car, all his tires were slashed."

That was disturbing. "Did he report it to the sheriff?"

"He did," she replied. "They're going to look into it, but I don't know how they'll prove anything."

Leo traced an absent pattern on the seat behind her head. They were silent while the rain slowly increased, the sound of it loud on the hood and cab of the truck. "The man we're watching is Jack Clark," he told her, "the man you recognize in that photo." He took it back from her, refolded it, and replaced it in his pocket. "If he comes back in, we'd like you to see who he talks to. Don't be obvious about it. Tell Tiny to let it slide about his tires, I'll see that they're replaced."

"That's nice of you," she replied.

He shrugged. "He's protective of you. I like that."

His eyes were narrow and dark and very intent on her face. She felt nervous with him all at once and folded her hands in her lap to try and keep him from noticing. It was like another world, closed up with him in a truck in a rainstorm. It outmatched her most fervent dreams of close contact.

"What sort of cattle deaths do you suspect him of?" she asked curiously.

"Your father's bull, for one."

Her intake of breath was audible. "Why would he kill Dad's bull?" she wanted to know.

"It was one of the offspring of a bull he killed in Victoria. He worked for the owner, who fired him. Apparently his idea of proper revenge is far-reaching."

"He's nuts!" she exclaimed.

He nodded. "That's why you have to be careful if he comes back in. Don't antagonize him. Don't stare at him. Don't be obvious when you look at him." He sighed angrily. "I hate the whole idea of having you that close to a lunatic. I should have decked Tiny as well as Fowler and carried you out of there anyway."

His level, penetrating gaze made her heart race. "I'm not your responsibility," she challenged.

"Aren't you?" His dark eyes slid over her from head to toe. His head tilted back at a faintly arrogant angle.

She swallowed. He looked much more formidable now than he had at Shea's. "I should go," she began.

He leaned forward abruptly, caught her under the arms, and pulled her on top of him. He was sprawled over the front seat, with one long, powerful leg braced against the passenger floorboard and the other on the seat. Janie landed squarely between his denim-clad legs, pressed intimately to him.

"Leo!" she exclaimed, horribly embarrassed at the intimate proximity and trying to get up.

He looped an arm around her waist and held her there, studying her flushed face with almost clinical scrutiny. "If you keep moving like that, you're going to discover the major difference between men and women in a vivid way, any minute."

She stilled at once. She knew what he meant. She'd felt that difference with appalling starkness at the ball. In fact, she was already feeling it again. She looked at him and her face colored violently.

"I told you," he replied, pursing his lips as he surveyed the damage. "My, my, didn't we know that men are easily aroused when we're lying full length on top of them?" he drawled. "We do now, don't we?"

She hit his shoulder, trying to hold on to her dignity as well as her temper. "You let go of me!"

"Spoilsport," he chided. He shifted her so that her head fell onto his shoulder and he could look down into her wide, startled eyes. "Relax," he coaxed. "What are you so afraid of?"

She swallowed. The closeness was like a drug. She felt swollen. Her legs trembled inside the powerful cage his legs made for them. Her breasts were hard against his chest, and they felt uncomfortably tight as well.

He looked down at them with keen insight, even moving her back slightly so that he could see the hard tips pressing against his shirt.

"You stop...looking at that!" she exclaimed without thinking.

He lifted an eyebrow and his smile was worldly. "A man likes to know that he's making an impression," he said outrageously.

She bit her lower lip, still blushing. "You're making too much of an impression already," she choked.

He leaned close and brushed his mouth lazily over her parted lips. "My body likes you," he whispered huskily. "It's making very emphatic statements about what it wants to do."

"You need...to speak...firmly to it," she said. She was trying to sound adult and firm, but her voice shook. It was hard to think, with his mouth hovering like that.

"It doesn't listen to reason," he murmured. He nibbled tenderly at her upper lip, parting it insistently from its companion. His free hand came up to tease around

the corners of her mouth and down her chin to the opening her v-necked blouse made inside her raincoat.

His mouth worked on her lips while his hands freed
her from the raincoat and slowly, absently, from her
blouse as well. She was hardly aware of it. His mouth
was doing impossibly erotic things to her lips, and one
of his lean, strong hands was inside her blouse, teasing
around the lacy edges of her brassiere.

The whole time, one long, powerful leg was sliding against the inside of her thigh, in a way so arousing that she didn't care what he did to her, as long as
he didn't try to get up.

Her hands had worked their way into his thick, soft
hair, and she was lifting up, trying to get closer to those
slow, maddening fingers that were brushing against
the soft flesh inside her bra. She'd never dreamed that
a man could arouse her so quickly with nothing more
invasive than a light brushing stroke of his hand. But
she was on fire with hunger, need, aching need, to have
him thrust those fingers down inside her frilly bra and
close on her breast. It was torture to have him tease her
like this. He was watching her face, too, watching the
hunger grow with a dark arrogance that was going to
make her squirm later in memory.

Right now, of course, she didn't care how he looked
at her. If he would just slide that hand…down a…cou-
ple of…inches!

She was squirming in another way now, twisting her
body ardently, pushing up against his stroking fingers
while his mouth nibbled and nipped at her parted lips
and his warm breath went into her mouth.

The rain was falling harder. It banged on the hood,
and on top of the cab, with tempestuous fury. Inside,

Janie could hear the tormented sound of her own breathing, feel her heartbeat shaking her madly, while Leo's practiced caresses grew slower and lazier on her taut body.

"Will you…please…!" she sputtered, gripping his arms.

"Will I please, what?" he whispered into her mouth.

"T-t-touch me!" she cried.

He nipped her upper lip ardently. "Touch you where?" he tormented.

Tears of frustration stung her eyes as they opened, meeting his. "You…know…where!"

He lifted his head. His face was taut, his eyes dark and glittery. He watched her eyes as his hand slowly moved down to where she ached to have it. She ground her teeth together to keep from crying out when she felt that big, warm, strong hand curl around her breast.

She actually shuddered, hiding her face in his throat as the tiny culmination racked her slender body and made it helpless.

"You are," he breathed, "the most surprising little trea-sure…"

His mouth searched for hers and suddenly ravished it while his hand moved on her soft flesh, molding it, tracing it, exploring it, in a hot, explosive silence. He kissed her until her mouth felt bruised and then she felt his hand move again, lifting free of her blouse, around to her back, unhooking the bra.

She didn't mind. She lifted up to help him free the catch. She looked up at him with wild, unsatisfied longing, shivering with reaction to the force of the desire he was teaching her.

"It will change everything," he whispered as he

began to move the fabric away from her body. "You know that."

"Yes." She shivered.

Both hands slid against her rib cage, carrying the fabric up with them until he uncovered her firm, tip-tilted little breasts. He looked at them with pure pleasure and delight. His thumbs edged out and traced the wide, soft nipples until they drew into hard, dusky peaks. His mouth ached to taste them.

She shifted urgently in his arms, feeling him turn toward her, feeling his leg insinuate itself even more intimately against her. He looked into her dazed eyes as his hand pressed hard against the lowest part of her spine and moved her right in against the fierce arousal she'd only sensed before.

She gasped, but he didn't relent. If anything, he brought her even closer, so that he was pressed intimately to her and the sensations exploded like sensual fire in her limbs.

"Leo!" she cried out, shivering.

"You turn me on so hard that I can't even think," he ground out as he bent to her open mouth. "I didn't mean for this to happen, Janie," he groaned into her mouth as he turned her under him on the seat and pressed his hips down roughly against hers. "Feel me," he whispered. "Feel me wanting you!"

She was lost, helpless, utterly without hope. She clung to him with no thought for her virtue or the future. She was drowning in the most delicious erotic pleasure she'd ever dreamed of experiencing. She could feel him, feel the rough, thrusting rhythm of his big body as he buffeted her against the seat. Something hit her arm. She was twisted in his embrace, and one leg was almost bent backward as he crushed her under him. Any minute, limbs were going to start breaking, she thought, and even that didn't matter. She wanted him...! She didn't realize she'd said it aloud until she heard his voice, deep and strained.

"I want you, too," he whispered back.

She felt his hand between them, working at her jeans. His hand was unfastening them. She felt it, warm and strong, against her belly. It was sliding down. She moved to make it easier for him, her mouth savage under the devouring pressure of his lips...

Leo heard the loud roar of an approaching engine in his last lucid second before he went in over his head. He froze against Janie's warm, welcoming body. His head lifted. He could barely breathe.

He looked down into her wide, misty eyes. It only then occurred to him that they were cramped together on the seat, his body completely covering hers, her bra and blouse crumpled at her collarbone, her jeans halfway down over her hips.

"What the hell are we doing?!" he burst out, shocked.

"You mean you don't know?" she gasped with unconscious humor.

He looked at the windows, so fogged up that nothing was visible outside them. He looked down at Janie, lying drowsy and submissive under the heavy crush of him.

He drew his hand away from her jeans and whipped onto his back so that he could help her sit up. He slid back into his own seat, watching her fumble her clothes back on while he listened, shell-shocked, to the loud tone of a horn from the other vehicle.

Janie was a mess. Her lips were swollen. Her cheeks were flushed. Her clothes were wrinkled beyond belief. Her hair stood out all around from the pressure of his hands in it.

He was rumpled, too, his hair as much as hers. His hat was on the floorboard somewhere, streaked with water from her raincoat and dirt from the floor mats. His shirt had obvious finger marks and lipstick stains on it.

He just stared at her for a long moment while the other vehicle came to a stop beside his truck. He couldn't see anything. All the windows were thickly fogged. Absently, he dug in the side pocket of the door for the red rag he always carried. He wiped the fog from the driver's window and scowled as he saw his brother Cag sitting in another ranch truck, with Tess beside him. They were trying not to stare and failing miserably!

CHAPTER EIGHT

BELATEDLY, LEO ROLLED the window down and glared at his brother and sister-in-law. "Well?" he asked belligerently.

"We just wondered if you were all right," Cag said, clearing his throat and trying very hard not to look at Janie. "The truck was sitting out here in the middle of nowhere, but we didn't see anybody inside."

"That's right," Tess said at once. "We didn't see anybody. At all. Or anything."

"Not anything." Cag nodded vigorously.

"I was showing Janie a photo of the Clark man," Leo said curtly. He pulled it out of his pocket. It was crumpled and slightly torn. He glared at it, trying to straighten it. "See?"

Cag cleared his throat and averted his eyes. "You, uh, should have taken it out of your pocket before you showed it to her... I'm going!"

Cag powered his window up with a knowing grin and gunned the engine, taking off in a spray of mud. Leo let his own window back up with flattened lips.

Janie was turned away from him, her shoulders shaking. Odd little noises that she was trying to smother kept slipping out. She was about to burst trying not to laugh.

He leaned back against the seat and threw the clipping at her.

"It's not my fault," she protested. "I was sitting here minding my own business when you got amorous."

He pursed his swollen lips and gave her a look that would have melted butter. "Amorous. That's a good word for it."

She was coming down from the heights and feeling self-conscious. She picked up the clipping and handed it back to him, belatedly noticing his white Stetson at her feet. She picked it up, too, and grimaced. "Your poor hat."

He took it from her and tossed it into the small back seat of the double cab. "It will clean," he said impatiently.

She folded her hands in her lap, toying with the streaked raincoat that she'd propped over her legs.

"Marilee caused a lot of trouble between us," he said after a minute, surprising her into meeting his somber gaze. "I'm sorry about that."

"You mean I don't really make you sick?" she asked in a thin voice.

He winced. "I was furious about what I thought you'd done," he confessed. "It was a lie, Janie, like all the other terrible things I said. I'm sorry for every one of them, if it does any good."

She toyed with a button on her raincoat and stared out the window at the rain. It did help, but she couldn't stop wondering if he hadn't meant it. Maybe guilt brought the apology out of him, rather than any real remorse. She knew he didn't like hurting people.

A long sigh came from the other side of the pickup. "I'll drive you back home," he said after a minute, and put the truck in gear. "Fasten your seat belt, honey."

The endearment made her feel warm all over, but she didn't let it show. She didn't really trust Leo Hart.

He turned back onto the main road. "Fred and I are going to mob you with company at Shea's," he said conversationally. "Between us, we know most of the ranchers around Jacobsville. You can ask Harley to keep dropping in from time to time, and Fred and I will talk to the others."

She gave him a quick glance. "Harley's jaw was really bruised."

His eyes darkened. "He had no business interfering. You don't belong to damned Harley!"

She didn't know what to say. That sounded very much like jealousy. It couldn't be, of course.

His dark eyes glanced off hers. "Do you sit around in parked trucks with him and let him take your blouse off?" he asked suddenly, furiously.

"I do *not!*" she exploded.

He calmed down at once. He shifted in the seat, still uncomfortable from the keen hunger she'd kindled in his powerful body. "Okay."

Her long fingers clenched on the fabric of the coat. "You have no right to be jealous of me!" she accused angrily.

"After what we just did?" he asked pleasantly. "In your dreams, Janie."

"I don't belong to you, either," she persisted.

"You almost did," he replied, chuckling softly. "You have no idea what a close call that was. Cag and Tess saved you."

"Excuse me?"

He gave her a rueful glance. "Janie, I had your jeans half off, or have you forgotten already?"

"Leo!"

"I'm not sure I could have stopped," he continued, slowing to make a turn. "And you were no damned help at all," he added with affectionate irony, "twisting your hips against me and begging me not to stop."

She gasped. Her face went scarlet. "Of all the blatant…!"

"That's how it was, all right," he agreed. "Blatant. For the record, when a man gets that hard, it's time to call a halt any way you can, before you get in over your head. I can tell you haven't had much practice at it, but now is a good time to listen to advice."

"I don't need advice!"

"Like hell you don't. Once I got my mouth on your soft belly, you'd never have been able to make me stop."

She stared at him with slowly dawning realization. She remembered the hot, exquisite pleasure of his mouth on her breasts. She could only imagine how it would feel to let him kiss her there, on her hips, on her long legs….

"You know far too much about women," she gritted.

"You know absolutely nothing about men," he countered. He smiled helplessly. "I love it. You were in over your head the minute I touched you with intent. You'd have let me do anything I wanted." He whistled softly. "You can't imagine how I felt, knowing that. You were the sweetest candy I've ever had."

He was confounding her. She didn't know what to make of the remarks. He'd been standoffish, insulting, offensive and furious with her. Now he'd done a complete about-face. He was acting more like a lover than a big brother.

His dark eyes cut around sideways and sized up her expression. "Do you think things can just go back to the way they were before?" he asked softly. "I remember telling you that it was going to change everything."

She swallowed. "I remember."

"It already has. I look at you and get aroused, all over again," he said bluntly. "It will only get worse."

Her face flamed. "I will not have an affair with you."

"Great. I'm glad to know you have that much self-control. You can teach it to me."

"I won't get in a truck with you again," she muttered.

"I'll bring the car next time," he said agreeably. "Of course, we'll have to open both doors. I'll never be able to stretch out in the front seat the way I did in the cab of this truck."

Her fingers clenched on the raincoat. "That won't happen again."

"It will if I touch you."

She glared at him. "You listen here…!"

He pulled the truck onto a dirt road that led through one of Fred's pastures, threw it out of gear, switched off the engine and reached for Janie with an economy of motion that left her gasping.

He had her over his lap, and his mouth hit hers with the force of a gust of wind. He burrowed into her parted lips while one lean hand went to her spine, grinding her into the fierce arousal that just the touch of her had provoked.

"Feel that?" he muttered against her lips. "Now try to stop me."

She went under in a daze of pleasure. She couldn't even pretend to protest, not even when his big hand found her breast and caressed it hungrily right through the cloth of her blouse.

Her arms went around his neck. She lifted closer,

shivering, as she felt the aching hunger of his body echo in her own. She moaned helplessly.

"Of all the stupid things I've done lately…" He groaned, too, his big arms wrapping her up tight as the kiss went on and on and on.

He moved out from under the steering wheel and shifted her until she was straddling his hips, her belly lying against his aroused body so blatantly that she should have been shocked. She wasn't. He felt familiar to her, beloved to her. She wanted him. Her body yielded submissively to the insistent pressure of both his hands on her hips, dragging them against his in a fever of desire.

The approaching roar of a truck engine for the second time in less than an hour brought his head up. He looked down into Janie's heated face, at the position they were in. His dazed eyes went out the windshield in time to see Fred's old pickup coming down the long pasture road about a quarter mile ahead of them.

He let out a word Janie had only heard Tiny use during heated arguments with patrons, and abruptly put her back in her own seat, pausing to forcefully strap her into her seat belt.

She felt shaky all over. Her eyes met his and then went involuntarily to what she'd felt so starkly against her hungry body. She flushed.

"Next time you'll get a better look," he said harshly. "I wish I could explain to you how it feels."

She wrapped her arms around her body. "I know… how it feels," she whispered unsteadily. "I ache all over."

The bad temper left him at once. He scowled as he watched her, half-oblivious to Fred's rapid approach. He couldn't take his eyes off her. She was delicious.

She managed to meet his wide, shocked eyes. "I'm sorry."

"For what?" he asked huskily. "You went in head-first, just like I did."

She searched his eyes hungrily. Her body was on fire for him. "If you used something…" she said absently.

He actually flushed. He got back under the steering wheel and avoided looking at her. He couldn't believe what she was saying.

Fred roared up beside them and pulled onto the hard ground to let his window down.

"Rain's stopped," he told Leo. "I thought I'd run over to Eb Scott's place and have a talk with him about getting his cowboys to frequent Shea's at night."

"Good idea," Leo said, still flushed and disheveled.

Fred wisely didn't look too closely at either of them, but he had a pretty good idea of what he'd interrupted. "I won't be long, sweetheart," he told Janie.

"Okay, Dad. Be careful," she said in a husky voice.

He nodded, grinned, and took off.

Leo started the engine. He was still trying to get his breath. He stared at the dirt path ahead instead of at Janie. "I could use something," he said after a minute. "But lovemaking is addictive, Janie. One time would be a beginning, not a cure, do you understand?"

She shook her head, embarrassed now that her blood was cooling.

He reached out and caught one of her cold hands in his, intertwining their fingers. "You can't imagine how flattered I am," he said quietly. "You're a virgin, and you'd give yourself to me…"

She swallowed hard. "Please. Don't."

His hand contracted. "I'll drive you home. If you

weren't working next Saturday, we could take in a movie and have dinner somewhere."

Her heart jumped up into her throat. "M-me?"

He looked down at her with the beginnings of possession. "You could wear that lacy white thing you wore to the ball," he added softly. "I like your shoulders bare. You have beautiful skin." His eyes fell to her bodice and darkened. "Beautiful breasts, too, with nice nipples…"

"Leo Hart!" she exclaimed, horrified.

He leaned over and kissed her hungrily. "I'll let you look at me next time," he whispered passionately. "Then you won't be so embarrassed when we compare notes."

She thought of seeing him without clothes and her whole face colored.

"I know what I said, but…" she protested.

He stopped the truck, bent, and kissed her again with breathless tenderness. "You've known me half your life, Janie," he said, and he was serious. He searched her worried eyes. "Am I the kind of man who takes advantage of a green girl?"

She was worried, too. "No," she had to admit.

His breathing was uneven as he studied her flushed face. "I never would," he agreed. "You were special to me even before I kissed you the first time, in your own kitchen." His head bent again. His mouth trailed across hers in soft, biting little kisses that made her moan. "But now, after the taste of you I've just had, I'm going to be your shadow. You don't even realize what's happened, do you?"

"You want me," she said huskily.

His teeth nibbled her upper lip. "It's a little more complicated than sex." He kissed her again, hard, and lifted his head with flattering reluctance. "Look up addiction in the dictionary," he mused. "It's an eye-opener."

"Addiction?"

His nose brushed hers. "Do you remember how you moaned when I put my hands inside your blouse?"

She swallowed. "Yes."

"Now think how it would feel if I'd put my mouth on your breast, right over the nipple."

She shivered.

He nodded slowly. "Next time," he promised, his voice taut and hungry. "You have that to look forward to. Meanwhile, you keep your eyes and ears open, and don't do anything at work that gives Clark a hint that you're watching him," he added firmly.

"I'll be careful," she promised unsteadily.

His eyes were possessive on her soft face. "If he touches you, I'll kill him."

It sounded like a joke. It wasn't. She'd never seen that look in a man's eyes before. In fact, the way he was watching her was a little scary.

His big hand slid under her nape and brought her mouth just under his. "You belong to me, Janie," he whispered as his head moved down. "Your first man is going to be me. Believe it!"

The kiss was as arousing as it was tender, but it didn't last long. He forced himself to let her go, to move away. He started the truck again, put it in gear, and went back down the farm road. But his hand reached for hers involuntarily, his fingers curling into hers, as if he couldn't bear to lose contact with her. She didn't know it, but he'd reached a decision in those few seconds. There was no going back now.

JACK CLARK DID show up in the bar, on the following Friday night.

Janie hadn't told any of the people she worked with about him, feeling that any mention of what she knew about him might jeopardize her safety.

But she did keep a close eye on him. The man was rangy and uncouth. He sat alone at a corner table, looking around as if he expected trouble and was impatient for it to arrive.

A cowboy from Cy Parks's spread, one of Harley Fowler's men, walked to the counter and sat down, ordering a beer and a pizza.

"Hey, Miss Janie," he said with a grin that showed a missing front tooth. "Harley said to tell you he'd be in soon to see you."

"That's sweet of him," she said with a grin. "I'll just put your order in, Ned."

She scribbled the order on a slip of green paper and put it up on the long string for Nick, the teenage cook, with a clothespin.

"Where's my damned whiskey?" Clark shouted. "I been sitting here five minutes waiting for it!"

Janie winced as Nick glanced at her and shrugged, indicating the pizza list he was far behind on. He'd taken the order and got busy all of a sudden. Tiny was nowhere in sight. He was probably out back having a cigarette. Nick was up to his elbows in dough and pizza sauce. Janie had to get Clark's order, there was nobody else to do it.

She got down a shot glass, poured whiskey into it, and put it on one of the small serving trays.

She took it to Clark's table and forced a smile to her

lips. "Here you are, sir," she said, placing the shot glass in front of him. "I'm sorry it took so long."

Clark glared up at her from watery blue eyes. "Don't let that happen again. I don't like to be kept waiting."

"Yes, sir," she agreed.

She turned away, but he caught her apron strings and jerked her back. She caught her breath as his hand slid to the ones tied at her waist.

"You're kind of cute. Why don't you sit on my lap and help me drink this?" he drawled.

He was already half-lit, she surmised. She would have refused him the whiskey, if Tiny had been close by, despite the trouble he'd already caused. But now she was caught and she didn't know how to get away. All her worst fears were coming to haunt her.

"I have to get that man's drink," she pointed to Harley's cowboy. "I'll come right back, okay?"

"That boy can get his drink."

"He's making pizza," she protested. "Please."

That was a mistake. He liked it when women begged. He smiled at her. It wasn't a pleasant smile. "I said, come here!"

He jerked her down on his thin, bony legs and she screamed.

In a flash, two cowboys were on their feet and heading toward Clark, both of them dangerous looking.

"Well, looky, looky, you've got guardian angels in cowboy boots!" Clark chuckled. He stood up, dragging Janie with him. "Stay back," he warned, catching her hair in its braid. "Or else." He slapped her, hard, across the face, making her cry out, and his hand went into his pocket and came out with a knife. He flicked it and a blade appeared. He caught her around the shoulders from behind and brandished the knife. "Stay back, boys," he said again. "Or I'll cut her!"

The knife pressed against her throat. She was shaking. She remembered all the nice self-defense moves she'd ever learned in her life from watching television or listening to her father talk. Now, she knew how useless they were. Clark would cut her throat if those men tried to help her. She had visions of him dragging her outside and assaulting her. He could do anything. There was nobody around to stop him. These cowboys weren't going to rush him and risk her life. If only Leo were here!

She was vaguely aware of Nick sliding out of sight toward the telephones. If he could just call the sheriff, the police, anybody!

Her hands went to Clark's wrist, trying to get him to release the press of the blade.

"You're hurting," she choked.

"Really?" He pressed harder.

Janie felt his arm cutting off the blood to her head. Then she remembered something she'd heard of a female victim doing during an attack. If she fainted, he might turn her loose.

"Can't...breathe..." she gasped, and closed her eyes. He might drop her if she sagged, he might cut her throat. She could die. But they'd get him. That would almost be worth it....

She let her body sag just as she heard a shout from the doorway. She pretended to lose consciousness. In the next few hectic seconds, Clark threw her to the floor so hard that she hit right on her elbow and her head, and groaned aloud with the pain of impact.

At the same moment, Leo Hart and Harley Fowler exploded into the room from the front door and went right for Clark, knife and all. They'd been in the parking lot, talking about Janie's situation, and had come running when they heard the commotion.

Harley aimed a kick at the knife and knocked it out of Clark's hands, but Clark was good with his feet, too. He landed a roundhouse kick in Harley's stomach and put him over a table. Leo slugged him, but he twisted around, got Leo's arm behind him and sent him over a table, too.

The two cowboys held back, aware of Leo's size and Harley's capability, and the fact that Clark had easily put both of them down.

There was a sudden silence. Janie dragged herself into a sitting position in time to watch Cash Grier come through the doorway and approach Clark.

Clark dived for the knife, rolled, and got to his feet. He lunged at Grier with the blade. The assistant police chief waited patiently for the attack, and he smiled. It was the coldest, most dangerous smile Janie had ever seen in her life.

Clark lunged confidently. Grier moved so fast that he was like a blur.

Seconds later, the knife was in Grier's hand. He threw it, slamming it into the wall next to the counter so deep that it would take Tiny quite some time, after the brawl, to pull it out again. He turned back to Clark even as the knife hit, fell into a relaxed stance, and waited.

Clark rushed him, tipsy and furious at the way the older man had taken his knife away. Grier easily sidestepped the intended punch, did a spinning heel kick that would have made Chuck Norris proud, and proceeded to beat the living hell out of the man with lightning punches and kicks that quickly put him on the floor, breathless and drained of will. It was over in less than three minutes. Clark held his ribs and groaned. Grier stood over him, not even breathing hard, his hand going to the handcuffs on his belt. He didn't even look winded.

Leo had picked himself up and rushed to Janie, propping her against his chest while she nursed her elbow.

"Is it broken?" he asked worriedly.

She shook her head. "Just bruised. Is my mouth bleeding?" she asked, still dazed from the confrontation.

He nodded. His face was white. He cursed his own helplessness. Between them, he and Harley should have been able to wipe the floor with Clark. He pulled out a white linen handkerchief and mopped up the bleeding lip and the cut on her cheek from Clark's nails. A big, bad bruise was already coming out on the left side of her face.

By now, Grier had Clark against a wall with a minimum of fuss. He spread the man's legs with a quick movement of his booted feet and nimbly cuffed him.

"I'll need a willing volunteer to see the magistrate and file a complaint," Grier asked.

"Right here," Harley said, wiping his mouth with a handkerchief. "I expect Mr. Hart will do the same."

"You bet," Leo agreed. "But I've got to get Janie home first."

"No rush," Grier said, with Clark by the neck. "Harley, you know where magistrate Burr Wiley lives, don't you? I'm taking Clark by there now."

"Yes, sir, I do, I'll drive right over there and swear out a complaint so you can hold that...gentleman," Harley agreed, substituting for the word he really meant to use. "Janie, you going to be okay?" he added worriedly.

She was wobbly, but she got to her feet, with Leo's support. "Sure," she said. She managed a smile. "I'll be fine."

"I'll get you!" Clark raged at Janie and Leo. "I'll get both of you!"

"Not right away," Grier said comfortably. "I'll have the judge set bail as high as it's possible to put it, and we'll see how many assault charges we can press."

"Count on me for two of them!" Janie volunteered fearlessly, wincing as her jaw protested.

"But not tonight," Leo said, curling his arm around her. "Come on, honey," he said gently. "I'll take you home."

They followed Grier with his prisoner and Harley out the door and over to Leo's big double-cabbed pickup truck.

He put her inside gently and moved around to the driver's seat. She noticed then, for the first time, that he was in working clothes.

"You must have come right from work," she commented.

"We were moving livestock to a new pasture," he replied. "One of the bulls got out and we had to chase him through the brush. Doesn't it show?" he added with a nod toward his scarred batwing chaps and his muddy boots. "I meant to be here an hour ago. Harley and I arrived together. Just in the nick of time, too."

"Two of Cy Parks's guys were at the counter," she said, "but when Clark threatened to cut me, they were afraid to rush him."

He caught her hand in his and held it tight, his eyes

going to the blood on her face, her blouse, her forearm. She was going to have a bruise on her pretty face. The sight of those marks made him furious.

"I'll be all right, thanks to all of you," she managed to say.

"We weren't a hell of a lot of help," he said with a rueful smile. "Even Harley didn't fare well. Clark must have a military background of some sort. But he was no match for Grier." He shook his head. "It was like watching a martial arts movie. I never even saw Grier move."

She studied him while he started the truck and put their seat belts on. "Did he hurt you?"

"Hurt my pride," he replied, smiling gently. "I've never been put across a table so fast."

"At least you tried," she pointed out. "Thank you."

"I should never have let you stay in there," he said. "It's my fault."

"It was my choice."

He kissed her eyelids shut. "My poor baby," he said softly. "I'm not taking you to your father in this condition," he added firmly, noting the blood on her blouse and face. "I'll take you home with me and clean you up, first. We'll phone him and tell him there was a little trouble and you'll be late."

"Okay," she said. "But he's no wimp."

"I know that." He put the truck in gear. "Humor me. I want to make sure you're all right."

"I'm fine," she argued, but then she smiled. "You can clean me up, anyway."

He pursed his lips and smiled wickedly. "Best offer I've had all night," he replied as he pulled out of the parking lot.

CHAPTER NINE

THE HOUSE WAS QUIET, deserted. The only light was the one in the living room. Leo led Janie down the hall to his own big bedroom, closed the door firmly, and led her into his spacious blue-tiled bathroom.

The towels were luxurious, sea-blue and white-striped blue towels, facecloths and hand towels. There were soaps of all sorts, a huge heated towel rack, and a whirlpool bath.

He tugged her to the medicine cabinet and turned her so that he could see her face. "You've got a bad scratch here," he remarked. He tilted her chin up, and found another smaller cut on the side of her throat, thankfully not close enough to an artery to have done much damage.

His hands went to her blouse. She caught them.

"It's all right," he said gently.

She let go.

He unfastened the blouse and tossed it onto the floor, looking her over for other marks. He found a nasty bruise on her shoulder that was just coming out. He unfastened the bra and let it fall, too, ignoring her efforts to catch it. There was a bruise right on her breast, where Clark had held her in front of him.

"The bastard," he exclaimed, furious, as he touched the bruise.

"He got a few bruises, too, from Grier," she said, trying to comfort him. He looked devastated.

"He'd have gotten more from me, if I hadn't walked right into that punch," he said with self-contempt. "I can't remember the last time I took a stupid hit like that."

She reached up and touched his lean face gently. "It's all right, Leo."

He looked down at her bare breasts and his eyes narrowed hotly. "I don't like that bruise."

"I got a worse one when my horse threw me last month," she told him. "It will heal."

"It's in a bad place."

She smiled. "So was the other one."

He unzipped her jeans and she panicked.

He didn't take any notice. He bent and removed her shoes and socks and then stripped the jeans off her. She was wearing little lacy white briefs and his hands lingered on them.

"Leo!" she screeched.

He grimaced. "I knew it was going to be a fight all the way, and you're in no condition for another one." He unbraided her hair and let it tangle down her shoulders. He turned and started the shower.

"I can do this!" she began.

His hands were already stripping off the briefs. He stopped with his hands on her waist and looked at her with barely contained passion. "I thought you'd be in a class of your own," he said huskily. "You're a knockout, baby." He lifted her and stood her up in the shower, putting a washcloth in her hand before he closed the sliding glass door. "I'll get your things in the wash."

She was too shell-shocked to ask if he knew how to

use a washing machine. *Well, you fool,* she told her-self, *you stood there like a statue and let him take your clothes off and stare at you! What are you complaining about?*

She bathed and used the shampoo on the shelf in the shower stall, scrubbing until she felt less tainted by Clark's filthy touch.

She turned off the shower and climbed out, wrapping herself in one of the sea-blue towels. It was soft and huge, big enough for Leo, who was a giant of a man. It swallowed her up whole.

Before she could wonder what she was going to do about something to wear, he opened the door and walked right in with a black velvet robe.

"Here," he said, jerking the towel away from her and holding out the robe.

She scurried into it, red-faced and embarrassed.

He drew her back against him and she realized that she wasn't the only one who'd just had a shower. He was wearing a robe, too. But his was open, and the only thing under it was a pair of black silk boxer shorts that left his powerful legs bare. His chest was broad and covered with thick, curling hair. He turned her until she was facing him, and his eyes were slow and curious.

"You'll have bruises. Right now, I want to treat those cuts with antibiotic cream. Then we'll dry your hair and brush it out." He smiled. "It's long and thick and glossy. I love your hair."

She smiled shyly. "It takes a lot of drying."

"I'm not in a hurry. Neither are you. I phoned your dad and told him as little as I could get away with."

"Was he worried?"

He lifted an eyebrow as he dug in the cabinet for the

antibiotic cream. "About your virtue, maybe," he teased. "He thinks I've got you here so I can make love to you."

She felt breathless. "Have you?" she asked daringly.

He turned back to her with the cream in one big hand. His eyes went over her like hands. "If you want it, yes. But it's up to you."

That was a little surprising. She stood docilely while he applied the cream to her cuts and then put it away. He hooked a hair dryer to a plug on the wall and linked his fingers through her thick light brown hair while he blew it dry. There was something very intimate about standing so close to him while he dried her hair. She thought she'd never get over the delight of it, as long as she lived. Every time she washed her hair from now on, she'd feel Leo's big hands against her scalp. She smiled, her head back, her eyes closed blissfully.

"Don't go to sleep," he teased as he put the hair dryer down.

"I'm not."

She felt his lips in her hair at the same moment she felt his hands go down over her shoulders and into the gap left by the robe.

If she'd been able to protest, that would have been the time to do it. But she hesitated, entranced by the feel of his hands so blatantly invading the robe, smoothing down over her high, taut breasts as if he had every right to touch her intimately whenever he felt like it.

Seconds later, the robe was gone, she was turned against him, his robe was on the floor, and she was experiencing her first adult embrace without clothing.

She whimpered at the fierce pleasure of feeling his bare, hair-roughened chest against her naked breasts.

Her nails bit into the huge muscles of his upper arms as she sucked in a harsh breath and tried to stay on her feet.

"You like that, do you?" he whispered at her lips. "I know something that's even more exciting."

He picked her up in his arms and started kissing her hungrily. She responded with no thought of denying him whatever he wanted.

He carried her to the bed, paused to whip the covers and the pillows out of the way, and placed her at the center of it. His hands went to the waistband of his boxer shorts, but he hesitated, grinding his teeth together as he looked at her nudity with aching need.

He managed to control his first impulse, which was to strip and bury himself in her. He eased onto the bed beside her, his chest pressing her down into the mattress while his mouth opened on her soft lips and pressed them wide apart.

"I've ached for this," he ground out, moving his hands from her breasts down her hips to the soft inside of her thighs. "I've never wanted anything so much!"

She tried to speak, but one of his hands invaded her in the most intimate touch she'd ever experienced. Her eyes flew open and she gaped up at him.

"You're old enough, Janie," he whispered, moving his hand just enough to make her tense.

As he spoke, he touched her delicately and when she protested, he eased down to cover her mouth with his. His fingers traced her, probed, explored her until she began to whimper and move with him. It was incredible. She was lying here, naked, in his bed, letting him explore her body as if it belonged to him. And she was...enjoying it. Glorying in it. Her back arched and she moaned as he found a pressure and a rhythm that lifted her off the bed on a wave of pleasure.

One of his long, powerful legs hooked over one of hers. She felt him at her hip, aroused and not hiding it. Through the thin silk, she was as aware of him as if he'd been naked.

"Touch me," he groaned. "Don't make me do it all. Help me."

She didn't understand what he wanted. Her hands went to his chest and began to draw through the thick hair there.

"No, baby," he whispered into her mouth. He caught one of her hands and tugged it down to the shorts he was wearing. "Don't be afraid. It's all right."

He coaxed her hand onto that part of him that was blatantly male. She gasped. He lifted his head and looked into her eyes, but he wouldn't let her hand withdraw. He spread her fingers against him, grimacing as the waves of pleasure hit him and closed his eyes on a shudder.

His reaction fascinated her. She knew so little. "Does it...hurt?"

"What?" he asked huskily. "Your hand, or what it's doing?"

"Both. Either."

He pressed her hand closer, looking down. "Look," he whispered, coaxing her eyes to follow his. It was intimate. But not intimate enough for him.

"Don't panic, baby," he whispered, levering onto his back. He ripped off the shorts and tossed them onto the carpet. He rolled onto his side and caught one of her hands, insistent now, drawing it to him.

She made a sound as she looked, for the first time,

at an aroused male without a thing to conceal him except her hand.

"Don't be embarrassed," he whispered roughly. "I wouldn't want any other woman to see me like this."

"You wouldn't?"

He shook his head. It was difficult not to lose control. But he eased her fingers back to him and held them there. "I'm vulnerable."

Her eyes brightened. "Oh." She hadn't considered that he was as helpless as she was to resist the pleasure of what they were doing.

His own hand went back to her body. He touched her, as she was touching him, and he smiled at her fascination.

She couldn't believe it was happening at all. She stared up at him with all her untried longings in her eyes, on her rapt face. She belonged to him. He belonged to her. It was incredible.

"Are you going to?" she whispered.

He kissed her eyelids lazily. "Going to what?"

"Take me," she whispered back.

He chuckled, deep in his throat. "What a primitive description. It's a mutual thing, you know. Wouldn't you take me, as well?"

Her eyes widened. "I suppose I would," she conceded. She stiffened and shivered. "Oh!"

His eyes darkened. There was no more humor on his face as his touch became slowly invasive. "Will you let me satisfy you?" he asked.

"I don't...understand."

"I know. That's what makes it so delicious." He bent slowly, but not to her mouth. His lips hovered just above her wide nipple. "This is the most beautiful thing I've ever done with a woman," he whispered. His lips parted. "I want nothing, except to please you."

His mouth went down over the taut nipple in a slow, exquisite motion that eventually all but swallowed her breast. She felt his tongue moving against the nipple, felt the faint suction of his mouth. All the while, his hand was becoming more insistent, and far more intimate, on her body. He felt her acceptance, even as she opened her legs for him and began to moan rhythmically with every movement of his hands.

"Yes," he whispered against her breast when he felt the pulsing of her body. "Let me, baby." He lifted his head and looked down into her eyes as she moaned piteously.

She was pulsating. She felt her body clench. She was slowly drifting up into a glorious, rhythmic heat that filled her veins, her arteries, the very cells of her body with exquisite pleasure. She'd never dreamed there was such pleasure.

"Janie, touch me, here," he whispered unsteadily.

She felt his hand curling around her fingers, teaching her, insistent, his breath jerky and violent as he twisted against her.

"Baby," he choked, kissing her hungrily. "Baby, baby!"

He moved, his big body levering slowly between her long legs. He knelt over her, his eyes wild, his body shuddering, powerfully male, and she looked up at him with total submission, still shivering from the taste of pleasure he'd already given her. It would be explosive, ecstatic. She could barely breathe for the anticipation. She was lost. He was going to have her now. She loved him. She was going to give herself. There was nothing that could stop them, nothing in all the world!

"Mr. Hart! Oh, Mr. Hart! Are you in here?"

Leo stiffened, his body kneeling between her thighs, his powerful hands clenching on them. He looked blindly down into her wide, dazed eyes. He shuddered violently and his eyes closed on a harsh muffled curse.

He threw himself onto the bed beside her, on his belly. He couldn't stop shaking. He gasped at a jerky breath and clutched the sheet beside his head as he fought for control.

"Mr. Hart!" the voice came again.

He suddenly remembered that he hadn't locked the bedroom door, and the cowboy didn't know that he wasn't alone. Even as he thought it, he heard the doorknob turn. "Open that door…and you're fired!" he shouted hoarsely. Beside him, Janie actually gasped as she belatedly realized what was about to happen.

The doorknob was released at once. "Sorry, sir, but I need you to come out here and look at this bull. I think there's something wrong with him, Mr. Hart! We got him loaded into one of the trailers and put him in the barn, but…"

"Call the vet!" he shouted. "I'll be there directly!"

"Yes, sir!"

Footsteps went back down the carpeted hall. Leo lifted his head. Beside him, Janie looked as shattered as he felt. Tears were swimming in her eyes.

He groaned softly, and pulled her to him, gently. "It's all right," he whispered, kissing her eyelids shut. "Don't cry, baby. Nothing happened."

"Nothing!" she choked.

His hands smoothed down the long line of her back. "Almost nothing," he murmured dryly.

She was horrified, not only at her own behavior, but

at what had almost happened. "If he hadn't called to you," she began in a high-pitched whisper.

His hands tangled in her long hair and he brought her mouth under his, tenderly. He nibbled her upper lip. "Yes, I know," he replied gently. "But he did." He pulled away from her and got to his feet, stretching hugely, facing her. He watched her try not to look at him with amused indulgence. But eventually, she couldn't resist it. Her eyes were huge, shocked...delighted.

"Now, when we compare notes, you'll have ammunition," he teased.

She flushed and averted her eyes, belatedly noticing that she wasn't wearing clothes, either. She tugged the sheet up over her breasts, but it was difficult to feel regrets when she looked at him.

He was smiling. His eyes were soft, tender. He looked down at what he could see of her body above the sheet with pride, loving the faint love marks on her breasts that his mouth had made.

"Greenhorn," he chided at her scarlet blush. "Well, you know a lot more about men now than you did this morning, don't you?"

She swallowed hard. Her eyes slid down him. She didn't look away, but she was very flushed, and not only because of what she was seeing. Her body throbbed in the most delicious way.

"I think I'd better take you home. Now," he added with a rueful chuckle. "From this point on, it only gets worse."

He was still passionately aroused. He wondered if she realized what it meant. He chuckled at her lack of comprehension. "I could have you three times and I'd still be like this," he said huskily. "I'm not easily satisfied."

She shivered as she looked at him, her body yielded, submissive.

"You want to, don't you?" he asked quietly, reading her expression. "So do I. More than you know. But we're not going that far together tonight. You've had enough trauma for a Friday night."

He caught her hand and pulled her up, free of the sheet and open to his eyes as he led her back into the bathroom. He turned on the shower and climbed in with her, bathing both of them quickly and efficiently, to her raging embarrassment.

He dried her and then himself before he put his shorts back on and left her to get her things. He'd washed them while she was in the shower the first time and put them in the dryer. They were clean and sweet-smelling, and the bloodstains were gone.

But when she went to take them from him, he shook his head. "One of the perks," he said softly. "I get to dress you."

And he did, completely. Then he led her to the dresser, and ran his own brush through her long, soft hair, easing it back from her face. The look in his eyes was new, fascinating, incomprehensible. She looked back at him with awe.

"Now you know something about what sex feels like, even though you're still very much a virgin," he said matter-of-factly. "And you won't be afraid of the real thing anymore, when it happens, will you?"

She shook her head, dazed.

He put the brush down and framed her face in his big, lean hands. He wasn't smiling. "You belong to me now," he said huskily. "I belong to you. Don't agonize over what you let me do to you tonight. It's as natural as breathing. Don't lie awake feeling shame or embarrassment. You saw me as helpless as I saw you. There won't be any jokes about it, any gossiping about it. I'll never tell another living soul what you let me do."

She relaxed. She hadn't really known what to expect. But he sounded more solemn than he'd ever been. He was looking at her with a strange expression.

"Are you sorry?" she asked in a hushed whisper.

"No," he replied quietly. "It was unavoidable. I was afraid for you tonight. I couldn't stop Clark. Neither could Harley. Until Grier walked in, I thought you'd had it. What happened in here was a symptom of the fear, that's all. I wanted to hold you, make you part of me." He drew in a shaky breath and actually shivered. "I wanted to go right inside you, Janie," he whispered bluntly. "But we'll save that pleasure for the right time and place. This isn't it."

She colored and averted her eyes.

He turned her face back to his. "Meanwhile," he said slowly, searching her eyes, "we'll have no more secrets, of any kind, between us."

She stood quietly against him, watching his face. "Nobody's seen me without my clothes since I was a little kid," she whispered, as if it was a fearful secret.

"Not that many women have seen me without mine," he replied unexpectedly. He smiled tenderly.

Her eyebrows arched.

"Shocked?" he mused, moving away to pull clothes out of his closet and socks out of his drawers. He sat down to pull on the socks, glancing at her wryly. "I'm not a playboy. I'm not without experience, but there was always a limit I wouldn't cross with women I only

knew slightly. It gives people power over you when they
know intimate things about you."

"Yes," she said, moving to sit beside him on the bed,
with her hands folded in her lap. "Thanks."

"For what?"

She smiled. "For making it feel all right. That I…let
you touch me that way, I mean."

He finished pulling on his socks and tilted her face
up to his. He kissed her softly. "I won't ever touch another woman like that," he whispered into her mouth.
"It would be like committing adultery, after what we
did on this bed."

Her heart flew up into the clouds. Her wide, fascinated eyes searched his. "Really?"

He chuckled. "Are you anxious to rush out and ex-
periment with another man?"

She shook her head.

"Why?"

She smiled shyly. "It would be like committing adultery," she repeated what he'd said.

He stood up and looked down at her with possession. "It was a near thing," he murmured. "I don't know
whether to punch that cowboy or give him a raise for
interrupting us. I lost it, in those last few seconds. I
couldn't have stopped."

"Neither could I." She lifted her mouth for his soft
kiss. She searched his eyes, remembering what he'd told
her. "But the books say a man can only do it once," she
blurted out, "and then he has to rest."

He laughed softly. "I know. But a handful of men
can go all night. I'm one of them."

"Oh!"

He pulled up his slacks and fastened them before

he shouldered into a knit shirt. He turned back to her, smoothing his disheveled hair. "I was contemplating even much more explosive pleasures when someone started shouting my name."

This was interesting. "More explosive pleasures?" she prompted.

He drew her up against him and held her close. "What we did and what we didn't do, is the difference between licking an ice-cream cone and eating a banana split," he teased. "What you had was only a small taste of what we can have together."

"Wow," she said softly.

"Wow," he echoed, bending to kiss her hungrily. He sighed into her mouth. "I was almost willing to risk getting you pregnant, I was so far gone." He lifted his head and looked at her. "How do you feel about kids, Janie?"

"I love children," she said honestly. "How about you?"

"Me too. I'm beginning to rethink my position on having them." His lean hand touched her belly. "You've got nice wide hips," he commented, testing them.

She felt odd. Her body seemed to contract. She searched his eyes because she didn't understand what was happening to her.

"You can tell Shea's you're through," he said abruptly. "I'm not risking you again. If we can't keep Clark in jail for the foreseeable future, we have to make plans to keep you safe."

Her lips parted. She'd all but forgotten her horrible experience. She touched her throat and felt again the prick of the knife. "You said he was vindictive."

"He'll have to get through me," he said. "And with a gun, I'm every bit his equal," he added.

She reached up and touched his hard mouth. "I don't want you to get hurt."

"I don't want you to get hurt," he seconded. His face twisted. "Baby, you are the very breath in my body," he whispered, and reached for her.

She felt boneless as he kissed her with such passion and fire that she trembled.

"I wish I didn't have to take you home," he groaned at her lips. "I want to make love to you completely. I want to lie against you and over you, and inside you!"

She moaned at his mouth as it became deep and insistent, devouring her parted lips.

He was shivering. He had to drag his mouth away from hers. He looked shattered. He touched her long hair with a hand that had a faint tremor. "Amazing," he whispered gruffly. "That I couldn't see it, before it happened."

"See what?" she asked drowsily.

His eyes fell to her swollen, parted lips. "Never mind," he whispered. He bent and kissed her with breathless tenderness. "I'm taking you home. Then I'll see about my bull. Tomorrow morning, I'll come and get you and we'll see about swearing out more warrants against Clark."

"You don't think Clark will get out on bond?" she asked worriedly.

"Not if Grier can prevent it." He reached for his truck keys and took her by the arm. "We'll go out the back," he said. "I don't want anyone to know you were here with me tonight. It wouldn't look good, even under the circumstances."

"Don't worry, nobody will know," she assured him.

THE NEXT MORNING, Fred Brewster came into the dining room looking like a thunderstorm.

"What were you doing in Leo Hart's bedroom last night when you were supposed to be working, Janie?" he asked bluntly.

She gaped at him with her mouth open. He was furious.

"How in the world...?" she exclaimed.

"One of the Harts' cowboys went to get him about a sick bull. He saw Leo sneaking you out the back door!" He scowled and leaned closer. "And what the hell happened to your face? Leo said you had a troublesome customer and he was bringing you home! What the hell's going on, Janie?"

She was scrambling for an answer that wouldn't get her in even more trouble when they heard a pickup truck roar up the driveway and stop at the back door. A minute later there was a hard rap, and the door opened by itself.

Leo came in, wearing dressy boots and slacks, a white shirt with a tie, and a sports coat. His white Stetson had been cleaned and looked as if it had never been introduced to a muddy truck mat. He took off the hat and tossed it onto the counter, moving past Fred to look at Janie's face.

"Damn!" he muttered, turning her cheek so that the violet bruise was very noticeable. "I didn't realize he hit you that hard, baby!"

"Hit her?!" Fred burst out. "Who hit her, and what was she doing in your bedroom last night?!"

Leo turned toward him, his face contemplative, his dark eyes quiet and somber. "Did she tell you?" he asked.

"I never!" Janie burst out, flushing.

"One of your cowboys mentioned it to one of my cowboys," Fred began.

Leo's eyes flashed fire. "He'll be drawing his pay at the end of the day. Nobody, but nobody, tells tales about Janie!"

Father and daughter exchanged puzzled glances.

"Why are you so shocked?" he asked her, when he saw her face. "Do you think I take women to my house, ever?"

She hadn't considered that. Her lips parted on a shocked breath.

He glanced at Fred, who was still unconvinced. "All right, you might as well know it all. Jack Clark made a pass at her in Shea's and when she protested, he pulled a knife on her." He waited for that to sink in, and for Fred to sit down, hard, before he continued. "Harley and I got there about the same time and heard yelling. We went inside to find Janie with a knife at her throat. We rushed Clark, but he put both of us over a table. Janie's co-worker had phoned the sheriff, but none of the deputies were within quick reach, so they radioed Grier and he took Clark down and put him in jail." He grimaced, looking at Janie's face. "She was covered with blood and so upset that she could hardly stand. I couldn't bring myself to take her home in that condition, so I took her home with me and cleaned her up and calmed her down first."

Fred caught Janie's hand in his and held it hard. "Oh, daughter, I'm sorry!"

"It's okay. We were trying to spare you, that's all," she faltered.

Leo pulled a cell phone from his pocket, dialed a number, and got his foreman. "You tell Carl Turley that he's fired. You get him the hell out of there before I get home, or he'll need first aid to get off the ranch. Yes. Yes." His face was frightening. "It was true. Clark's in jail now, on assault charges. Of course nothing was going on, and you can repeat that, with my blessing! Just get Turley out of there! Right."

He hung up and put the phone away. He was vibrating with suppressed fury, that one of his own men would gossip about him and Janie, under the circumstances. "So much for gossip," he gritted.

"Thanks, Leo," Fred said tersely. "And I'm sorry I jumped to the wrong conclusion. It's just that, normally, a man wouldn't take a woman home with him late at night unless he was...well..."

"...planning to seduce her?" Leo said for him. He looked at Janie and his eyes darkened.

She flushed.

"Yes," Fred admitted uncomfortably.

Leo's dark eyes began to twinkle as they wandered over Janie like loving hands. "Would this be a bad time to tell you that I have every intention of seducing her at some future time?"

CHAPTER TEN

FRED LOOKED AS if he'd swallowed a chicken, whole. He flushed, trying to forget that Leo had loaned him the money to save his ranch, thinking only of his daughter's welfare. "Now, look here, Leo…" he began.

Leo chuckled. "I was teasing. She's perfectly safe with me, Fred," he replied. He caught Janie's hand and tugged her to her feet. "We have to go see the magistrate about warrants," he said, sobering. "I want him to see these bruises on her face," he added coldly. "I don't think we'll have any problem with assault charges."

Janie moved closer to Leo. He made her feel safe, protected. He bent toward her, his whole expression one of utter tenderness. Belatedly, Fred began to understand what he was seeing. Leo's face, to him, was an open book. He was shocked. At the same time, he realized that Janie didn't understand what was going on. Probably she thought he was being brotherly.

"Don't you want breakfast first?" Fred offered, trying to get his bearings again.

For the first time, Leo seemed to notice the table. His hand, holding Janie's, contracted involuntarily. Bacon, scrambled eggs, and…biscuits? Biscuits! He scowled, letting go of Janie's fingers to approach the bread basket. He reached down, expecting a concretelike substance, remembering that he and Rey had secretly sailed some of Janie's earlier efforts at biscuit-making over the target range for each other and used them for skeet targets. But these weren't hard. They were flaky, delicate. He opened one. It was soft inside. It smelled delicious.

He was barely aware of sitting down, dragging Janie's plate under his hands. He buttered a biscuit and put strawberry jam on it. He bit into it and sighed with pure ecstasy.

"I forgot about the biscuits," Janie told her father worriedly.

Fred glanced at their guest and grimaced. "Maybe we should have saved it for a surprise."

Leo was sighing, his eyes closed as he chewed.

"We'll never get to the magistrate's now," Janie thought aloud.

"He'll run out of biscuits in about ten minutes, at that rate," Fred said with a grin.

"I'll get another plate. We can split the eggs and bacon," Janie told her father, inwardly beaming with pride at Leo's obvious enjoyment of her efforts. Now, finally, the difficulty of learning to cook seemed worth every minute.

Leo went right on chewing, oblivious to movement around him.

The last biscuit was gone with a wistful sigh when he became aware of his two companions again.

"Who made the biscuits?" Leo asked Janie.

She grimaced. "I did."

"But you can't cook, honey," he said gently, trying to soften the accusation.

"Marilee said you didn't like me because I couldn't make biscuits or cook anything edible," she confessed without looking at him. "So I learned how."

He caught her fingers tightly in his. "She lied. But those were wonderful biscuits," he said. "Flaky and soft inside, delicately browned. Absolutely delicious."

She smiled shyly. "I can make them anytime you like."

He was looking at her with pure possession. "Every morning," he coaxed. "I'll stop by for coffee. If Fred doesn't mind," he added belatedly.

Fred chuckled. "Fred doesn't mind," he murmured dryly.

Leo scowled. "You look like a cat with a mouse."

Fred shrugged. "Just a stray thought. Nothing to worry about."

Leo held the older man's reluctant gaze and understood the odd statement. He nodded slowly. He smiled sheepishly as he realized that Fred wasn't blind at all.

Fred got up. "Well, I've got cattle to move. How's your bull, by the way?" he added abruptly, worried.

"Colic," Leo said with a cool smile. "Easily treated and nothing to get upset over."

"I'm glad. I had visions of you losing yours to Clark as well."

"He isn't from the same herd as yours was, Fred," Leo told him. "But even so, I think we'll manage to keep Clark penned up for a while. Which reminds me," he added, glancing at Janie. "We'd better get going."

"Okay. I'll just get the breakfast things cleared away first."

Leo sat and watched her work with a smitten expression on his face. Fred didn't linger. He knew a hooked fish when he saw one.

THEY SWORE OUT warrants and presented them to the sheriff. Clark had already been transferred to the county lockup, after a trip to the hospital emergency room the night before, and Leo and Janie stopped in to see Grier at the police station.

Grier had just finished talking to the mayor, a pleasant older man named Tarleton Connor, newly elected to his position. Connor and Grier had a mutual cousin, as did Grier and Chet Blake, the police chief. Chet was out of town on police business, so Grier was nominally in charge of things.

"Have a seat," Grier invited, his eyes narrow and angry on Janie's bruised face. "If it's any consolation, Miss Brewster, Clark's got bruised ribs and a black eye."

She smiled. It was uncomfortable, because it irritated the bruise. "Thanks, Mr. Grier," she said with genuine appreciation.

"That goes double for me," Leo told him. "He put Harley and me over a table so fast it's embarrassing to admit it."

"Why?" Grier asked, sitting down behind his desk. "The man was a martial artist," he elaborated. "He had a studio up in Victoria for a while, until the authorities realized that he was teaching killing techniques to ex-cons."

Leo's jaw fell.

Grier shrugged. "He was the equivalent of a black belt, too. Harley's not bad, but he needs a lot more training from Eb Scott before he could take on Clark." He pursed his lips and his eyes twinkled as he studied Leo's expression. "Feel better now?"

Leo chuckled. "Yes. Thanks."

Grier glanced at Janie's curious expression. "Men don't like to be overpowered by other men. It's a guy thing," he explained.

"Anybody ever overpower you?" Leo asked curiously.

"Judd Dunn almost did, once. But then, I taught him everything he knows."

"You know a lot," Janie said. "I never saw anybody move that fast."

"I was taught by a guy up in Tarrant County," Grier told her with a smile. "He's on television every week. Plays a Texas Ranger."

Janie gasped.

"Nice guy," Grier added. "And a hell of a martial artist."

Leo was watching him with a twinkle in his own eyes. "I did think the spinning heel kick looked familiar."

Grier smiled. He sat up. "About Clark," he added. "His brother came to see him at the county lockup this morning and got the bad news. With only one charge so far, Harley's, he's only got a misdemeanor…"

"We took out a warrant for aggravated assault and battery," Leo interrupted. "Janie had a knife at her throat just before you walked in."

"So I was told." Grier's dark eyes narrowed on Janie's throat. The nick was red and noticeable this morning. "An inch deeper and we'd be visiting you at the funeral home this morning."

"I know," Janie replied.

"You kept your head," he said with a smile. "It probably saved your life."

"Can you keep Clark in jail?" she asked worriedly.

"I'll ask Judge Barnett to set bail as high as he can. But Clark's brother isn't going to settle for a public defender. He said he'd get Jack the best attorney he could find, and he'd pay for it." He shrugged. "God knows what he'll pay for it with," he added coldly. "John Clark owes everybody, up to and including his boss. So does our local Clark brother."

"He may have to have a public defender."

"We'll see. But meanwhile, he's out of everybody's way, and he'll stay put."

"What about his brother?" Leo wanted to know. "Is Janie in any danger?"

Grier shook his head. "John Clark went back to Victoria after he saw his brother. I had him followed, by one of my off-duty guys, just to make sure he really left. But I'd keep my eyes open, if I were you, just the same. These boys are bad news."

"We'll do that," Leo said.

HE DROVE JANIE back to his own ranch and took her around with him while he checked on the various projects he'd initiated. He pulled up at the barn and told her to stay in the truck.

She was curious until she remembered that he'd fired the man who'd interrupted them the night before. She was glad about the interruption, in retrospect, but uneasy about the gossip that man had started about her and Leo.

He was back in less than five minutes, his face hard, his eyes blazing. He got into the truck and glanced at her, forcibly wiping the anger out of his expression.

"He's gone," he told her gently. "Quit without his check," he added with a rueful smile. "I guess Charles told him what I said." He shrugged. "He wasn't much of a cowboy, at that, if he couldn't tell colic from bloat."

She reached out and put her nervous fingers over his

big hand on the steering wheel. He flinched and she jerked her hand back.

"No!" He caught her fingers in his and held them tight. "I'm sorry," he said at once, scowling. "You've never touched me voluntarily before. It surprised me. I like it," he added, smiling.

She was flushed and nervous. "Oh. Okay." She smiled shyly.

He searched her eyes with his for so long that her heart began to race. His face tautened. "This won't do," he said in a husky, deep tone. He started the truck with a violent motion and drove back the way they'd come, turning onto a rutted path that led into the woods and, far beyond, to a pasture. But he stopped the truck halfway to the pasture, threw it out of gear, and cut off the engine.

He had Janie out of her seat belt and into his big arms in seconds, and his hungry mouth was on her lips before she could react.

She didn't have any instincts for self-preservation left. She melted into his aroused body, not even protesting the intimate way he was pressing her hips against his. Her arms curled around his neck and she kissed him back with enthusiasm.

She felt his hands going under her blouse, against her breasts. That felt wonderful. It was perfectly all right, because she belonged to him.

He lifted his mouth from hers, breathing hard, and watched her eyes while his hands caressed her. She winced and he caught his breath.

"I'm sorry!" he said at once, soothing the bruise he'd forgotten about. "I didn't mean to hurt you," he whispered.

She reached up to kiss his eyelids shut, feeling the shock that ran through him at the soft caress. His hands moved to her waist and rested there while he held his breath, waiting. She felt the hunger in him, like a living thing. Delighted by his unexpected submission to her mouth, she kissed his face softly, tenderly, drawing her lips over his thick eyebrows, his eyelids, his cheeks and nose and chin. They moved to his strong throat and lingered in the pulsating hollow.

One lean hand went between them to the buttons of his cotton shirt. He unfastened them quickly, jerking the fabric out of her way, inviting her mouth inside.

Her hands spread on the thick mat of hair that covered the warm, strong muscles of his chest. Her mouth touched it, lightly, and then not lightly. She moved to where his heart beat roughly, and then over the flat male nipple that was a counterpart to her own. But the reaction she got when she put her mouth over it was shocking.

He groaned so harshly that she was sure she'd hurt him. She drew back, surprising a look of anguish on his lean face.

"Leo?" she whispered uneasily.

"It arouses me," he ground out, then he shivered.

She didn't know what to do next. He looked as if he ached to have her repeat the caress, but his body was as taut as a rope against her.

"You'll have to tell me what to do," she faltered. "I don't want to make it worse."

"Whatever I do is going to shock you speechless," he choked out. "But, what the hell…!"

He dragged her face back to his nipple and pressed it there, hard. "You know what I want."

She did, at some level. Her mouth eased down against him with a soft, gentle suction that lifted him back against the seat with a harsh little cry of pleasure. His hands at the back of her head were rough and insistent. She gave in and did what he was silently asking her for. She felt him shudder and gasp, his body vibrating as if it was overwhelmed by pleasure. He bit off a harsh word and trembled violently for a few seconds before he turned her mouth away from him and pressed her unblemished cheek against his chest. His hands in her hair trembled as they caressed her scalp. His heartbeat was raging under her mouth.

He fought to breathe normally. "Wow," he whispered unsteadily.

Her fingers tangled in the thick hair under them. "Did you really like it?" she whispered back.

He actually laughed, a little unsteadily. "Didn't you feel what was happening to me?"

"You were shaking."

"Yes. I was, wasn't I? Just the way you were shaking last night when I touched you..."

Her cheek slid back onto his shoulder so that she could look up into his soft eyes. "I didn't know a man would be sensitive, there, like a woman is."

He bent and drew his lips over her eyelids. "I'm sensitive, all right." His lips moved over her mouth and pressed there hungrily. "It isn't enough, Janie. I've got to have you. All the way."

"Right now?" she stammered.

He lifted his head and looked down at her in his arms. He was solemn, unsmiling, as he met her wide eyes. His body was still vibrating with unsatisfied de-

sire. Deliberately, he drew her hips closer against his
and let her feel him there.

She didn't protest. If anything, her body melted even
closer.

One lean hand went to her belly and rested there, between them, while he searched her eyes. "I want...to
make you pregnant," he said in a rough whisper.

Her lips fell open. She stared at him, not knowing
what to say.

He looked worried. "I've never wanted that with
a woman," he continued, as if he was discussing the
weather. His fingers moved lightly on her body. "Not
with anyone."

He was saying something profound. She hadn't believed it at first, but the expression on his face was hard
to explain away.

"My father would shoot you," she managed to say
weakly.

"My brothers would shoot me, too," he agreed, nodding.

She was frowning. She didn't understand.

He bent and kissed her, with an odd tenderness. He
laughed to himself. "Just my luck," he breathed against
her lips, "to get mixed up with a virgin who can cook."

"We aren't mixed up," she began.

His hand contracted against the base of her spine,
grinding her into him, and one eyebrow went up over
a worldly smile as she blushed.

She cleared her throat. "We aren't very mixed up,"
she corrected.

He nibbled at her upper lip. "I look at you and get
turned on so hard I can hardly walk around without
bending over double. I touch you and I hurt all over. I

dream of you every single night of my life and wake
up vibrating." He lifted his head and looked down into
her misty eyes. He wasn't smiling. He wasn't kidding.
"Never like this, Janie. Either we have each other, or
we stop it, right now."

Her fingers touched his face lovingly. "You can do
whatever you like to me," she whispered unsteadily.

His jaw tautened. "Anything?"

She nodded. She loved him with all her heart.

His eyes closed. His arms brought her gently against
him, and his mouth buried itself in her throat, pressing
there hot and hard for a few aching seconds. Then he
dragged in a harsh breath and sat up, putting her back
in her seat and fastening her seat belt.

He didn't look at her as he fastened his own belt
and started the truck. She sat beside him as he pulled
out onto the highway, a little surprised that he didn't
turn into the road that led to his house. She'd expected
him to take her there. She swallowed hard, remembering the way they'd pleasured each other on his big bed
the night before, remembering the look of his powerful body without clothes. She flushed with anticipated
delight. She was out of her mind. Her father was going
to kill her. She looked at Leo with an ache that curled
her toes up inside her shoes, and didn't care if he did.
Some things were worth dying for.

Leo drove right into town and pulled into a parking
spot in front of the drugstore. Right, she thought nervously, he was going inside to buy...protection...for
what they were going to do. He wanted a child, though,
he'd said. She flushed as he got out of the truck and
came around to open her door.

He had to unfasten her seat belt first. She didn't even have the presence of mind to accomplish that.

He helped her out of the truck and looked down at her with an expression she couldn't decipher. He touched her cheek gently, and then her hair, and her soft mouth. His eyes were full of turmoil.

He tugged her away from the truck and closed her door, leading her to the sidewalk with one small hand tightly held in his fingers.

She started toward the drugstore.

"Wrong way, sweetheart," he said tenderly, and led her right into a jewelry store.

The clerk was talking to another clerk, but he came forward, smiling, when they entered the shop.

"May I help you find something?" he asked Leo.

"Yes," Leo said somberly. "We want to look at wedding bands."

Janie felt all the blood draining out of her face. It felt numb. She hoped she wasn't going to pass out.

Leo's hand tightened around her fingers, and slowly linked them together as he positioned her in front of the case that held engagement rings and wedding rings.

The clerk took out the tray that Leo indicated. Leo looked down at Janie with quiet, tender eyes.

"You can have anything you want," he said huskily, and he wasn't talking solely of rings.

She met his searching gaze with tears glistening on her lashes. He bent and kissed the wetness away.

The clerk averted his eyes. It was like peering through a private window. He couldn't remember ever seeing such an expression on a man's face before.

"Look at the rings, Janie," Leo said gently.

She managed to focus on them belatedly. She didn't

care about flashy things, like huge diamonds. She was a country girl, for all her sophistication. Her eyes kept coming back to a set of rings that had a grape leaf pattern. The wedding band was wide, yellow gold with a white gold rim, the pattern embossed on the gold surface. The matching engagement ring had a diamond, but not a flashy one, and it contained the same grape leaf pattern on its circumference.

"I like this one," she said finally, touching it.

There was a matching masculine-looking wedding band. She looked up at Leo.

He smiled. "Do you want me to wear one, too?" he teased.

Her eyes were breathless with love. She couldn't manage words. She only nodded.

He turned his attention back to the clerk. "We'll take all three," he said.

"They'll need to be sized. Let me get my measuring rod," the clerk said with a big grin. The rings were expensive, fourteen karat, and that diamond was the highest quality the store sold. The commission was going to be tasty.

"It isn't too expensive?" Janie worried.

Leo bent and kissed the tip of her nose. "They're going to last a long time," he told her. "They're not too expensive."

She couldn't believe what was happening. She wanted to tell him so, but the clerk came back and they were immediately involved in having their fingers sized and the paperwork filled out.

Leo produced a gold card and paid for them while Janie looked on, still shell-shocked.

Leo held her hand tight when they went back to

the truck. "Next stop, city hall," he murmured dryly. "Rather, the fire station—they take the license applications when city hall is closed. I forgot it was Saturday." He lifted both eyebrows at her stunned expression. "Might as well get it all done in one day. Which reminds me." He pulled out his cell phone after he'd put her in the truck and phoned the office of the doctors Coltrain. While Janie listened, spellbound, he made an appointment for blood tests for that afternoon. The doctors Coltrain had a Saturday clinic.

He hung up and slipped the phone back into his pocket with a grin. "Marriage license next, blood tests later, and about next Wednesday, we'll have a nice and quiet small wedding followed by," he added huskily, "one hell of a long passionate wedding night."

She caught her breath at the passion in his eyes. "Leo, are you sure?" she wanted to know.

He dragged her into his arms and kissed her so hungrily that a familiar couple walking past the truck actually stared amusedly at them for a few seconds before hurrying on past.

"I'm sorry, baby. I can't...wait...any longer," he ground out into her eager mouth. "It's marriage or I'm leaving the state!" He lifted his head, and his eyes were tortured. He could barely breathe. "Oh, God, I want you, Janie!"

She felt the tremor in his big body. She understood what he felt, because it was the same with her. She drew in a slow breath. It was desire. She thought, maybe, there was some affection as well, but he was dying to have her, and that was what prompted marriage plans. He'd said often enough that he was never going to get married.

He saw all those thoughts in her eyes, even through the most painful desire he'd ever known. "I'll make you glad you said yes," he told her gruffly. "I won't ever cheat on you, or hurt you. I'll take care of you all my life. All of yours."

It was enough, she thought, to take a chance on. "All right," she said tenderly. She reached up and touched his hard, swollen mouth. "I'll marry you."

It was profound, to hear her say it. He caught his breath at the raging arousal the words produced in his already-tortured body. He groaned as he pressed his mouth hard into the palm of her hand.

She wasn't confident enough to tease him about his desire for her. But it pleased her that he was, at least, fiercely hungry for her in that way, if no other.

He caught her close and fought for control. "We'd better go and get a marriage license," he bit off. "We've already given Evan and Anna Tremayne an eyeful."

"What?" she asked drowsily.

"They were walking past when I kissed you," he said with a rueful smile.

"They've been married for years," she pointed out.

He rubbed his nose against hers. "Wait until we've been married for years," he whispered. "We'll still be fogging up windows in parked trucks."

"Think so?" she asked, smiling.

"Wait and see."

He let go of her, with obvious reluctance, and moved back under the steering wheel. "Here we go."

THEY APPLIED FOR the marriage license, had the blood tests, and then went to round up their families to tell them the news.

Janie's aunt Lydia had gone to Europe over the holidays on an impromptu sightseeing trip, Fred Brewster told them when they gave him the news. "She'll be livid if she misses the wedding," he said worriedly.

"She can be here for the first christening," Leo said with a grin at Janie's blush. "You can bring Hettie with you, and come over to the ranch for supper tomorrow night," he added, amused at Fred's lack of surprise at the announcement. "I've invited my brothers to supper and phoned Barbara to have it catered. I wanted to break the news to all of them at once."

"Hettie won't be surprised," Fred told them, tongue-in-cheek. "But she'll enjoy a night out. We'll be along about six."

"Fine," Leo said, and didn't offer to leave Janie at home. He waited until she changed into a royal-blue pantsuit with a beige top, and carried her with him to the ranch.

He did chores and paperwork with Janie right beside him, although he didn't touch her.

"A man only has so much self-control," he told her with a wistful sigh. "So we'll keep our hands off each other, until the wedding. Fair enough?"

She grinned at him. "Fair enough!"

He took her home after they had supper at a local restaurant. "I'd love to have taken you up to Houston for a night on the town," he said when he walked her to her door. "But not with your face like that." He touched it somberly. "Here in Jacobsville, everybody already knows what happened out at Shea's last night. In Houston, people might think I did this, or allowed it to happen." He bent and kissed the painful bruise. "Nobody will ever hurt you again as long as I live," he swore huskily.

She closed her eyes, savoring the soft touch of his mouth. "Are you sure you want to marry me?" she asked.

"I'm sure. I'll be along about ten-thirty," he added.

She looked up at him, puzzled. "Ten-thirty?"

He nodded. "Church," he said with a wicked grin. "We have to set a good example for the kids."

She laughed, delighted. "Okay."

"See you in the morning, pretty girl," he said, and brushed his mouth lightly over hers before he bounded back down the steps to his car and drove off with a wave of his hand.

FRED WAS AMAZED that Leo did take her to church, and then came back to the house with her for a lunch of cold cuts. He and Fred talked cattle while Janie lounged at Leo's side, still astounded at the unexpected turn of events. Fred couldn't be happier about the upcoming nuptials. He was amused that Hettie had the weekend off and didn't know what had happened. She had a shock coming when she arrived later in the day.

Leo took Janie with him when he went home, approving her choice of a silky beige dress and matching high heels, pearls in her ears and around her throat, and her hair long and luxurious down her back.

"Your brothers will be surprised," Janie said worriedly on the way there.

Leo lifted an eyebrow. "After the Cattleman's Ball? Probably not," he said. Then he told her about Corrigan offering to drive him home so that he could pump him for information to report back to the others.

"You were very intoxicated," she recalled, embarrassed when she recalled the fierce argument they'd had.

"I'd just found out that Marilee had lied about you," he confided. "And seeing you with damned Harley didn't help."

"You were jealous," she realized.

"Murderously jealous," he confessed at once. "That only got worse, when you took the job at Shea's." He glanced at her. "I'm not having you work there any longer. I don't care what compromises I have to make to get you to agree."

She smiled to herself. "Oh, I don't mind quitting," she confessed. "I'll have enough to do at the ranch, after we're married, getting settled in."

"Let's try not to talk about that right now, okay?"

She stared at him, worriedly. "Are you getting cold feet?" she asked.

"I'll tell you what I'm getting," he said, turning dark eyes to hers. And he did tell her, bluntly, and starkly. He nodded curtly at her scarlet flush and directed his attention back at the road. "Just for the record, the word 'marriage' reminds me of the words 'wedding night,' and I go nuts."

She whistled softly.

"So let's think about food and coffee and my brothers and try not to start something noticeable," he added in a deep tone. "Because all three of them are going to be looking for obvious signs and they'll laugh the place down if they see any."

"We can recite multiplication tables together," she agreed.

He glanced at her with narrow eyes. "Great idea,"

he replied sarcastically. "That reminds me of rabbits, and guess what rabbits remind me of?"

"I know the Gettysburg Address by heart," she countered. "I'll teach it to you."

"That will put me to sleep."

"I'll make biscuits for supper."

He sat up straight. "Biscuits? For supper? To go with Barbara's nice barbecue, potato salad and apple pie. Now that's an idea that just makes my mouth water! And here I am poking along!" He pushed down on the accelerator. "Honey, you just said the magic word!"

She chuckled to herself. Marriage, she thought, was going to be a real adventure.

CHAPTER ELEVEN

NOT ONLY DID CORRIGAN, Rey, and Cag show up for supper with their wives, Dorie, Meredith and Tess, but Simon and Tira came all the way from Austin on a chartered jet. Janie had just taken off her apron after producing a large pan of biscuits, adding them to the deliciously spread table that Barbara and her assistant had arranged before they left.

All four couples arrived together, the others having picked up Simon and Tira at the Jacobsville airport on the way.

Leo and Janie met them at the door. Leo looked unprepared.

"All of you?" he exclaimed.

Simon shrugged. "I didn't believe them," he said, pointing at the other three brothers. "I had to come see for myself."

"We didn't believe him, either," Rey agreed, pointing at Leo.

They all looked at Janie, who moved closer to Leo and blushed.

"If she's pregnant, you're dead," Cag told Leo pointedly when he saw the look on Janie's face. He leaned closer before Leo could recover enough to protest. "Have you been beating her?"

"She is most certainly not pregnant!" Leo said, offended. "And you four ought to know that I have never hit a woman in my life!"

"But he hit the guy who did this to me," Janie said with pride, smiling up at him as she curled her fingers into his big ones.

"Not very effectively, I'm afraid," Leo confessed.

"That's just because the guy had a black belt," Janie said, defending Leo. "Nobody but our assistant police chief had the experience to bring him down."

"Yes, I know Grier," Simon said solemnly. "He's something of a legend in law enforcement circles, even in Austin."

"He has alien artifacts in his filing cabinet, and he was a government assassin," Janie volunteered with a straight face.

Everybody stared at her.

"He was kidding!" Leo chuckled.

She grinned at him. He wrinkled his nose at her. They exchanged looks that made the others suddenly observant. All at once, they became serious.

"We can do wedding invitations if we e-mail them tonight," Cag said offhand. He pulled a list from his pocket. "This is a list of the people we need to invite."

"I can get the symphony orchestra to play," Rey said, nodding. "I've got their conductor's home phone number in my pocket computer." He pulled it out.

"We can buy the gown online and have it overnighted here from Neiman-Marcus in Dallas," Corrigan volunteered. "All we need is her dress size. What are you, a size ten?"

Janie balked visibly, but nodded. "Here comes her father," Dorie said enthusiastically, noting the new arrival.

"I'll e-mail the announcement to the newspaper,"

Tess said. "They have a Tuesday edition, we can just make it. We'll need a photo."

There was a flash. Tira changed the setting on her digital camera. "How's this?" she asked, showing it to Tess and Meredith.

"Great!" Meredith said. "We can use Leo's computer to download it and e-mail it straight to the paper, so they'll have it first thing tomorrow. We can e-mail it to the local television station as well. Come on!"

"Wait for me! I'll write the announcement," Dorie called to Corrigan, following along behind the women.

"Hey!" Janie exclaimed.

"What?" Tira asked, hesitating. "Oh, yes, the reception. It can be held here. But the cake! We need a caterer!"

"Cag can call the caterer," Simon volunteered his brother.

"It's my wedding!" Janie protested.

"Of course it is, dear," Tira said soothingly. "Let's go, girls."

The women vanished into Leo's study. The men went into a huddle. Janie's father and Hettie came in the open door, looking shell-shocked.

"Never mind them," Leo said, drawing Janie to meet her parent and her housekeeper. "They're taking care of the arrangements," he added, waving his hand in the general direction of his brothers and sisters-in-law. "Apparently, it's going to be a big wedding, with a formal gown and caterers and newspaper coverage." He grinned. "You can come, of course."

Janie hit him. "We were going to have a nice, quiet little wedding!"

"You go tell them what you want, honey," he told Janie. "Just don't expect them to listen."

Hettie started giggling. Janie glared at her.

"You don't remember, do you?" the housekeeper asked Janie. "Leo helped them do the same thing to Dorie, and Tira, and Tess, and even Meredith. It's payback time. They're getting even."

"I'm afraid so," Leo told Janie with a smug grin. "But look at the bright side, you can just sit back and relax and not have to worry about a single detail."

"But, my dress…" she protested.

He patted her on the shoulder. "They have wonderful taste," he assured her.

Fred was grinning from ear to ear. He never would have believed one man could move so fast, but he'd seen the way Leo looked at Janie just the morning before. It was no surprise to him that a wedding was forthcoming. He knew a man who was head over heels when he saw one.

BY THE END of the evening, Janie had approved the wedding gown, provided the statistics and details of her family background and education, and climbed into the car with Leo to let him take her home.

"The rings will be ready Tuesday, they promised," he told her at her father's door. He smiled tenderly. "You'll be a beautiful bride."

"I can't believe it," she said softly, searching his lean face.

He drew her close. "Wednesday night, you'll believe it," he said huskily, and bent to kiss her with obvious restraint. "Now, good night!"

He walked to the car. She drifted inside, wrapped in dreams.

IT WAS A honey of a society wedding. For something so hastily concocted, especially with Christmas approaching, it went off perfectly. Even the rings were ready on time, the dress arrived by special overnight delivery, the blood tests and marriage license were promptly produced, the minister engaged, press coverage assured, the caterer on time—nothing, absolutely nothing, went wrong.

Janie stood beside Leo at the Hart ranch at a makeshift arch latticed with pink and white roses while they spoke their vows. Janie had a veil, because Leo had insisted. And after the last words of the marriage ceremony were spoken, he lifted the veil from Janie's soft eyes and looked at her with smoldering possession. He bent and kissed her tenderly, his lips barely brushing hers. She had a yellowing bruise on one cheek and she was careful to keep that side away from the camera, but Leo didn't seem to notice the blemish.

"You are the most beautiful bride who ever spoke her vows," he whispered as he kissed her. "And I will cherish you until they lay me down in the dark!"

She reached up and kissed him back, triggering a burst of enthusiastic ardor that he was only able to curb belatedly. He drew away from her, smiling sheepishly at their audience, caught her hand, and led her back to the house through a shower of rice.

The brothers were on the job even then. The press was delicately prompted to leave after the cake and punch were consumed, the symphony orchestra was coaxed to load their instruments. The guests were delicately led to the door and thanked. Then the brothers carried their wives away in a flurry of good wishes and, at last, the newlyweds were alone, in their own home.

Leo looked at Janie with eyes that made her heart race. "Alone," he whispered, approaching her slowly, "at last."

He bent and lifted her, tenderly, and carried her down the hall to the bedroom. He locked the door. He took the phone off the hook. He closed the curtains. He came back to her, where she stood, a little apprehensive, just inside the closed door.

"I'm not going to hurt you," he said softly. "You're a priceless treasure. I'm going to be slow, and tender, and I'm going to give you all the time you need. Don't be afraid of me."

"I'm not, really," she said huskily, watching him divest her of the veil and the hairpins that held her elaborate coiffure in place with sprigs of lily of the valley. "But you want me so much," she tried to explain. "What if I can't satisfy you?"

He laughed. "You underestimate yourself."

"Are you sure?"

He turned her around so that he could undo the delicate hooks and snaps of her gown. "I'm sure."

She let him strip her down to her lacy camisole, white stockings and lacy white garter belt, her eyes feeding on the delighted expression that claimed his lean face.

"Beautiful," he said huskily. "I love you in white lace."

"You're not bad in a morning coat," she teased, liking the vested gray ceremonial rig he was wearing.

"How am I without it?" he teased.

"Let's find out." She unbuttoned his coat and then the vest under it. He obligingly stripped them off for her, along with his tie, and left the shirt buttons to her hands. "You've got cuff links," she murmured, trying to release them.

"I'll do it." He moved to the chest of drawers and put his cuff links in a small box, along with his pocket change and keys. He paused to remove his shirt and slacks, shoes and socks before he came back to her, in silky gray boxer shorts like the ones he'd worn the night they were almost intimate.

"You are…magnificent," she whispered, running her hands over his chest.

"You have no idea how magnificent, yet." He unsnapped the shorts and let them fall, coaxing her eyes to him. He shivered at the expression on her face, because he was far more potent than he'd been the one time she'd looked at him like this.

While she was gaping, he unfastened the camisole with a delicate flick of his fingers and unhooked the garter belt. He stripped the whole of it down her slender body and tipped her back onto the bed while he pulled the stockings off with the remainder of her clothing.

He pulled back the cover and tossed the pillows off to the side before he arranged her on the crisp white sheets and stood over her, vibrating with desire, his eyes eating her nude body, from her taut nipples to the visible trembling of her long, parted legs.

She watched him come down to her with faint apprehension that suddenly vanished when he pressed his open mouth down, hard, right on her soft belly.

He'd never touched her like that, and in the next few feverish minutes, she went from shock to greater shock as he displayed his knowledge of women.

"No, you can't, you can't!" she sobbed, but he was, he did, he had!

She arched up toward his mouth with tears of tortured ecstasy raining down her cheeks in a firestorm of sensation, sobbing as the pleasure stretched her tight as a rope under the warm, expert motions of his lips.

She gasped as the wave began to hit her. Her eyes opened, and his face was there, his body suddenly right over hers, his hips thrusting down. She felt him, and then looked and saw him, even as she felt the small stabbing pain of his invasion. The sight of what was happening numbed the pain, and then it was gone altogether as he shifted roughly, dragging his hips against hers as he enforced his possession of her innocence.

Her nails bit into his long back as he moved on her, insisting, demanding. His face, above her, was strained, intent.

"Am I hurting you?" he ground out.

"N-no!" she gasped, lifting toward him, her eyes wide, shocked, fascinated.

He looked down, lifting himself so that he could watch her body absorb him. "Look," he coaxed through his teeth. "Look, Janie. Look at us."

She glanced down and her breath caught at the intimate sight that met her eyes. She gasped.

"And we've barely begun," he breathed, shifting suddenly, fiercely, against her.

She sobbed, shivering.

He did it again, watching her face, assessing her reaction. "I can feel you, all around me, like a soft, warm glove," he whispered, his lips compressing as pleasure shot through him with every deepening motion of his hips. "Take me, baby. Take me inside you. Take all of me. Make me scream, baby," he murmured.

She was out of her mind with the pleasure he was

giving her. She writhed under him, arching her hips, pushing against him, watching his face. She shifted and he groaned harshly. She laughed, through her own torment, and suddenly cried out as the pleasure became more and more unbearable. Her hands went between them, in a fever of desire.

"Yes," he moaned as he felt her trembling touch. "Yes. Oh… God…baby…do it, do it! Do it!"

She was going to die. She opened her eyes and looked at him, feeling her body pulse as he shortened and deepened his movements, watching her with his mouth compressed, his eyes feverish.

"Do it…harder," she choked.

He groaned in anguish and his hips ground into hers suddenly, his hands catching her wrists and slamming them over her head as he moved fiercely above her, his eyes holding hers prisoner as his body enforced its possession violently.

She felt her body strain to accommodate him and in the last few mad seconds, she wondered if she would be able to…

He blurred in her sight. She was shaking. Her whole body rippled in a shuddering parody of convulsions, whipping against his while her mouth opened, gasping at air, and her voice uttered sounds she'd never heard from it in her entire life.

"Get it," he groaned. "Yes. Get it…!"

He cried out and then his body, too, began to shudder rhythmically. A sound like a harsh sob tore from his throat. He groaned endlessly as his body shivered into completion. Seconds, minutes, hours, an eternity of pleasure later, he collapsed on her.

They both shivered in the aftermath. She felt tears

on her face, in her mouth. She couldn't breathe. Her body ached, even inside, and when she moved, she felt pleasure stab her in the most secret places, where she could still feel him.

She sobbed, her nails biting into the hands pinning her wrists.

He lifted his head. "Look at me," he whispered, and when she did, he began to move again.

She sobbed harder, her legs parting, her hips lifting for him, her whole body shivering in a maelstrom of unbelievable delight.

"I can go again, right now," he whispered huskily, holding her eyes. "Can you? Or will it hurt?"

"I can't...feel pain," she whimpered. Her eyes closed on a shiver and then opened again, right into his. "Oh, please," she whispered brokenly. "Please, please...!"

He began to move, very slowly. "I love watching you," he whispered breathlessly. "Your face is beautiful, like this. Your body..." He looked down at it, watching its sensuous movements in response to his own. "I could eat you with a spoon right now, Mrs. Hart," he added shakily. "You are every dream of perfection that I've ever had."

"And you...are mine," she whispered. She lifted up to him, initiating the rhythm, whimpering softly as the pleasure began to climb all over again. "I love you...so much," she sobbed.

His body clenched. He groaned, arched, his face going into her throat as his body took over from his mind and buffeted her violently.

She went over the edge almost at once, holding on for dear life while he took what he wanted from her. It was feverish, ardent, overwhelming. She thought she might

faint from the ecstasy when it throbbed into endless sa-
tiation. He went with her, every second of the way. She
felt him when his body gave up the pleasure he sought,
felt the rigor, heard the helpless throb of his voice at her
ear when he shuddered and then relaxed completely.

She held him close, drinking in the intimate sound
and feel and scent of his big body over hers in the damp
bed. It had been a long, wild loving. She'd never imag-
ined, even in their most passionate encounters, that
lovemaking would be like this.

She told him so, in shy whispers.

He didn't answer her. He was still, and quiet, for such
a long time that she became worried.

"Are you all right?" she whispered at his ear. Over
her, she could hear and feel the beat of his heart as it
slowly calmed.

His head lifted, very slowly. He looked into her wide
eyes. "I lost consciousness for a few seconds," he said
quietly. He touched her lower lip, swollen from the
fierce pressure of his mouth just at the last. "I thought…
I might die, trying to get deep enough to satisfy us
both."

She flushed.

He put his finger over her lips. He wasn't smiling.
He moved deliberately, letting her feel him. "You aren't
on the Pill," he said. "And I was too hot to even think
of any sort of birth control. Janie," he added, hesitantly,
"I think I made you pregnant."

Her eyes searched his. "You said you wanted to," she
reminded him in a whisper.

"I do. But it should have been your choice, too," he
continued, sounding worried.

She traced his long, elegant nose and smiled with

delicious exhaustion. "Did you hear me shouting, Leo, stop and run to the pharmacy to buy protection!"

He laughed despite the gravity of the situation. "Was that about the time I was yelling, 'get it, baby'?"

She hit his chest, flushed, and then laughed.

"You did, too, didn't you?" he asked with a smug grin. "So did I. Repeatedly." He groaned as he moved slowly away from her and flopped onto his back, stretching his sore muscles. "Damn, I'm sore! And I told you I could go all night, didn't I?"

She sat up, torn between shock and amusement as she met his playful eyes. "Sore? Men get sore?"

"When they go at it like that, they do," he replied sardonically. "What a wedding night," he said, whistling through his lips as he studied her nude body appreciatively. "If they gave medals, you could have two."

Her eyebrows arched. "Really? I was… I was all right?"

He tugged her down to him. "Women have egos, too, don't they?" he asked tenderly. He pushed her damp hair away from her cheeks and mouth. "You were delicious. I've never enjoyed a woman so much."

"I didn't know anything at all."

He brought her head down and kissed her eyelids. "It isn't a matter of knowledge."

She searched his eyes. "You had enough of that for both of us," she murmured.

"Bodies in the dark," he said, making it sound unimportant. "I wanted to have you in the light, Janie," he said solemnly. "I wanted to look at you while I was taking you."

"That's a sexist remark," she teased.

"You took me as well," he conceded. He touched her

mouth with a long forefinger. "I've never seen anything so beautiful," he whispered, and sounded breathless. "Your face, your body…" His face clenched. "And the pleasure." His eyes closed and he shivered. "I've never known anything like it." His eyes opened again. "It was love," he whispered to her, scowling. "Making love. Really making love."

Her breath caught in her throat. She traced his sideburn to his ear. "Yes."

"Do you know what I'm trying to tell you?" he asked quietly.

She looked down into his eyes and saw it there. Her heart jumped into her throat. "You're telling me that you love me," she said.

He nodded. "I love you. I knew it when Clark assaulted you, and I went at him. It hurt my pride that I couldn't make him beg for forgiveness. I cleaned you up and dried your hair, and knew that I loved you, all at once. It was a very small step from there to a wedding ring." He brought hers to his lips and kissed it tenderly. "I couldn't bear the thought of losing you. Not after that."

She smiled dreamily. "I loved you two years ago, when you brought me a wilted old daisy you'd picked out in the meadow, and teased me about it being a bouquet. You didn't know it, but to me, it was."

"I've given you a hard time," he told her, with obvious regret. "I'm sorry."

She leaned down and kissed him tenderly. "You made up for it." She moved her breasts gently against his chest. "I really can go all night," she whispered. "When you've recovered, I'll show you."

He chuckled under the soft press of her mouth, and

his big arms swallowed her. "When *you're* recovered, I'll let you. I love you, Mrs. Hart. I love you with all my heart."

"I love you with all mine." She kissed him again, and thought how dreams did, sometimes, actually come true.

A WEEK LATER, they celebrated their first Christmas together at a family party, to which Janie's father, Aunt Lydia and Hettie were also invited. After kissing her with exquisite tenderness beneath the mistletoe, Leo gave Janie an emerald necklace, to match her eyes, he said, and she gave him an expensive pocket watch, with his name and hers engraved inside the case.

ON NEW YEAR'S EVE, the family gathered with other families at the Jacobsville Civic Center for the first annual celebration. A live band played favorites and couples danced on the polished wood floor. Calhoun Ballenger had mused aloud that since Jacobsville's economy was based on cattle and agriculture, they should drop a pair of horns instead of a ball to mark the new year. He was red-faced at the celebration, when the city fathers took him seriously and did that very thing.

While Leo and Janie stood close together on the patio of the second floor ballroom to watch the neon set of longhorns go down to the count, a surprising flurry of snow came tumbling from the sky to dust the heads of the crowd.

"It's snowing!" Janie exclaimed, holding out a hand to catch the fluffy precipitation. "But it never snows in Jacobsville! Well, almost never."

Leo caught her close as the horns went to the bottom

of the courthouse tower across the street and bent to her mouth, smiling. "One more wish come true," he teased, because he knew how much she loved snow. "Happy New Year, my darling," he whispered.

"Happy New Year," she whispered back, and met his kiss with loving enthusiasm, to the amused glances of the other guests. They were, after all, newlyweds.

The new year came and soon brought with it unexpected tragedy. John Clark went back to Victoria to get his jailed brother a famous attorney, but he didn't have any money. So he tried to rob a bank to get the money. He was caught in the act by a security guard and a Texas Ranger who was working on a case locally. Judd Dunn was one of the two men who exchanged shots with Clark in front of the Victoria Bank and Trust. Clark missed. Judd and the security guard didn't. Ballistics tests were required to pinpoint who fired the fatal bullet.

Jack Clark, still in jail in Victoria, was let out long enough to attend his brother's funeral in Victoria. He escaped from the kindly sheriff's deputy who was bringing him back in only handcuffs instead of handcuffs and leg chains. After all, Jack Clark had been so docile and polite, and even cried at his brother's grave. The deputy was rewarded for his compassion by being knocked over the head twice with the butt of his own .38 caliber service revolver and left for dead in a driving rain in the grass next to the Victoria road. Later that day, his squad car was found deserted a few miles outside Victoria.

It was the talk of the town for several days, and Leo and Janie stayed close to home, because they knew Clark had scores to settle all around Jacobsville. They were in their own little world, filled with love. They barely heard all the buzz and gossip. But what they did hear was about Tippy Moore and Cash Grier.

"Tippy's not Grier's sort," Janie murmured sleepily. They didn't do a lot of sleeping at night, even now. She cuddled up in her husband's lap and nuzzled close. "He needs someone who is gentle and sweet. Not a harpy."

He wrapped her up close and kissed the top of her head. "What would you know about harpies?" he teased. "You're the single sweetest human being I've ever known."

She smiled.

"Well, except for me, of course," he added.

"Leo Hart!" she exclaimed, drawing back.

"You said I was sweet," he murmured, bending his head. "You said it at least six times. You were clawing my back raw at the time, and swearing that you were never going to live through what I was doing to you…"

She tugged his head down and kissed him hungrily. "You're sweet, all right," she whispered raggedly. "Do it again…!"

He groaned. They were never going to make it to the bed. But the doors were locked…what the hell.

An hour later, he carried her down the hall to their bedroom and tucked her up next to him, exhausted and still smiling.

"At least," he said wearily, "hopefully Clark will go to prison for a long, long time when he's caught. He won't be in a position to threaten you again."

"Or you." She curled closer. "Did I tell you that Marilee phoned me yesterday?"

He stiffened. "No."

She smiled. "It's okay. She only wanted to apologize.

She's going to Europe to visit her grandmother in London. I told her to have a nice trip."

"London's almost far enough away."

She sighed, wrapping her arms around him. "Be generous. She'll never know what it is to be as happy as we are."

"Who will?" he teased, but the look he gave her was serious. He touched her hair, watching her succumb to sleep.

He lay awake for a long time, his eyes intent on her slender, sleeping body. She made wonderful biscuits, she could shoot a shotgun, she made love like a fairy. He wondered what he'd ever done in his life to deserve her.

"Dreams," she whispered, shocking him.

"What, honey?"

She nuzzled her face into his throat and melted into him. "Dreams come true," she whispered, falling asleep again.

He touched her lips with his and smoothed back her long hair. "Yes, my darling," he whispered with a long, sweet smile. "Dreams come true."

* * * * *

JORDAN

CHAPTER ONE

LIBBY COLLINS COULDN'T figure out why her stepmother, Janet, had called a real estate agent out to the house. Her father had only been dead for a few weeks. The funeral was so fresh in her mind that she cried herself to sleep at night. Her brother, Curt, was equally devastated. Riddle Collins had been a strong, happy, intelligent man who'd never had a serious illness. He had no history of heart trouble. So his death of a massive heart attack had been a real shock. In fact, the Collinses' nearest neighbor, rancher Jordan Powell, said it was suspicious. But then, Jordan thought everything was suspicious. He thought the government was building cloned soldiers in some underground lab.

Libby ran a small hand through her wavy black hair, her light green eyes scanning the horizon for a sight of her brother. But Curt was probably up to his ears in watching over the births of early spring cattle, far in the northern pasture of the Powell ranch. It was almost April and the heifers, the two-year-old first-time mothers, were beginning to drop their calves right on schedule. There was little hope that Curt would show up before the real estate agent left.

Around the corner of the house, Libby heard the real estate agent speaking. She moved closer, careful to keep out of sight, to see what was going on. Her father had

loved his small ranch, as his children did. It had been
in their family almost as long as Jordan Powell's family had owned the Bar P.

"How long will it take to find a buyer?" Janet was
asking.

"I can't really say, Mrs. Collins," the man replied.
"But Jacobsville is growing by leaps and bounds. There
are plenty of new families looking for reasonable housing. I think a subdivision here would be perfectly situ-
ated and I can guarantee you that any developer would
pay top dollar for it."

Subdivision? Surely she must be hearing things!

But Janet's next statement put an end to any such
suspicion. "I want to sell it as soon as possible," Janet
continued firmly. "I have the insurance money in hand.
As soon as this sale is made, I'm moving out of the
country."

Another shattering revelation! Why was her stepmother in such a hurry? Her husband of barely nine
months had just died, for heaven's sake!

"I'll do what I can, Mrs. Collins," the real estate
agent assured her. "But you must understand that the
housing market is depressed right now and I can't guarantee a sale—as much as I'd like to."

"Very well," Janet said curtly. "But keep me informed of your progress, please."

"Certainly."

Libby ran for it, careful not to let herself be seen. Her
heart was beating her half to death. She'd wondered at
Janet's lack of emotion when her father died. Now her
mind was forming unpleasant associations.

She stood in the shadows of the front porch until she

heard the real estate agent drive away. Janet left immediately thereafter in her Mercedes.

Libby's mind was whirling. She needed help. Fortunately, she knew exactly where to go to get it.

She walked down the road toward Jordan Powell's big Spanish-style ranch house. The only transportation Libby had was a pickup truck, which was in the shop today having a water pump replaced. It was a long walk to the Powell ranch, but Libby needed fortifying to tackle her stepmother. Jordan was just the person to put steel in her backbone.

It took ten minutes to walk to the paved driveway that led through white fences to the ranch house. But it took another ten minutes to walk from the end of the driveway to the house. On either side of the fence were dark red-coated Santa Gertrudis cattle, purebred seed stock, which were the only cattle Jordan kept. One of his bulls was worth over a million dollars. He had a whole separate division that involved artificial insemination and the care of a special unit where sperm were kept. Libby had been fascinated to know that a single straw of bull semen could sell for a thousand dollars, or much more if it came from a prize bull who was dead. Jordan sold those straws to cattle ranchers all over the world. He frequently had visitors from other countries who came to tour his mammoth cattle operation. Like the Tremayne brothers, Cy Parks, and a number of other local ranchers, he was heavily into organic ranching. He used no hormones or dangerous pesticides or unnecessary antibiotics on his seed stock, even though they were never sold for beef. The herd sires he kept on the ranch lived in a huge breeding barn—as luxurious as a modern hotel—that was on property just adjacent to the Collinses' land. It was so close that they could hear the bulls bellowing from time to time.

Jordan was a local success story, the sort men liked to tell their young sons about. He started out as a cowboy long before he ever had cattle of his own. He'd grown up the only child of a former debutante and a hobby farmer. His father had married the only child of wealthy parents, who cut her off immediately when she announced her marriage. They left her only the property that Jordan now owned. His father's drinking cost him almost everything. When he wasn't drinking, he made a modest living with a few head of cattle, but after the sudden death of Jordan's mother, he withdrew from the world. Jordan was left with a hard decision to make. He took a job as a ranch hand on Duke Wright's palatial ranch and in his free time he went the rounds of the professional rodeo circuit. He was a champion bull rider, with the belt buckles and the cash to prove it.

But instead of spending that cash on good times, he'd paid off the mortgage that his father had taken on the ranch. Over the years he'd added a purebred Santa Gertrudis bull and a barn, followed by purebred heifers. He'd studied genetics with the help of a nearby retired rancher and he'd learned how to buy straws of bull semen and have his heifers artificially inseminated. His breeding program gave him the opportunity to enter his progeny in competition, which he did. Awards starting coming his way and so did stud fees for his bull. It had been a long road to prosperity, but he'd managed it, despite having to cope with an alcoholic father who eventually got behind the wheel of a truck and plowed it into a telephone pole. Jordan was left alone in the world.

Well, except for women. He sure seemed to have plenty of those, to hear her brother, Curt, talk.

Libby loved the big dusty-yellow adobe ranch house Jordan had built two years ago, with its graceful arches and black wrought-iron grillwork. There was a big fountain in the front courtyard, where Jordan kept goldfish and huge koi that came right up out of the water to look at visitors. It even had a pond heater, to keep the fish alive all winter. It was a dream of a place. It would have been just right for a family. But everybody said that Jordan Powell would never get married. He liked his freedom too much.

She went up to the front door and rang the doorbell. She knew how she must look in her mud-stained jeans and faded T-shirt, her boots caked in mud, like her denim jacket. She'd been helping the lone part-time worker on their small property pull a calf. It was a dirty business, something her pristine stepmother would never have done. Libby still missed her father. His unexpected death had been a horrible blow to Curt and Libby, who were only just getting used to Riddle Collins's new wife.

No sooner was Riddle buried than Janet fought to get her hands on the quarter-of-a-million-dollar insurance policy he'd left behind, of which she alone was listed as beneficiary. She'd started spending money the day the check had arrived, with no thought for unpaid bills and Riddle's children. They were healthy and able to work, she reasoned. Besides, they had a roof over their heads. Temporarily, at least. Janet's long talk with the real estate agent today was disquieting. Riddle's new will, which his children knew nothing about, had given Janet complete and sole ownership of the house as well as Riddle's comfortable but not excessive savings account. Or so Janet said. Curt was furious. Libby hadn't said anything. She missed her father so much. She felt as if she were still walking around in a daze and it was almost April. A windy, cold almost-April, at that, she thought, feeling the chill.

She was frowning when the door opened. She jumped involuntarily when instead of the maid, Jordan Powell himself opened it.

"What the hell do you want?" he asked coldly. "Your brother's not here. He's supervising some new fencing up on the north property.

"Well?" he asked impatiently when she didn't speak immediately. "I've got things to do and I'm late already!"

He was so dashing, she thought privately. He was thirty-two, very tall, lean and muscular, with liquid black eyes and dark, wavy hair. He had a strong, masculine face that was dark from exposure to the sun and big ears and big feet. But he was handsome. Too handsome.

"Are you mute?" he persisted, scowling.

She shook her head, sighing. "I'm just speechless. You really are a dish, Jordan," she drawled.

"Will you please tell me what you want?" he grumbled. "And if it's a date, you can go right back home. I don't like being chased by women. I know you can't keep your eyes off me, but that's no excuse to come sashaying up to my front door looking for attention."

"Fat chance," she drawled, her green eyes twinkling up at him. "If I want a man, I'll try someone accessible, like a movie star or a billionaire...."

"I said I'm in a hurry," he prompted.

"Okay. If you don't want to talk to me..." she began.

He let out an impatient sigh. "Come in, then," he muttered, looking past her. "Hurry, before you get trampled by the other hopeful women chasing me."

"That would be a short list," she told him as she went in and waited until he closed the door behind him. "You're famous for your bad manners. You aren't even housebroken."

"I beg your pardon?" he said curtly.

She grinned at him. "Your boots are full of red mud and so's that fabulously expensive wool rug you brought back from Morocco," she pointed out. "Amie's going to kill you when she sees that."

"My aunt only lives here when she hasn't got someplace else to go," he pointed out.

"Translated, that means that she's in hiding. Why are you mad at her this time?" she asked.

He gave her a long-suffering stare and sighed. "Well, she wanted to redo my bedroom. Put yellow curtains at the windows. With ruffles." He spat out the word. "She thinks it's too depressing because I like dark wood and beige curtains."

She lifted both eyebrows over laughing eyes. "You could paint the room red…."

He glared down at her. "I said women chased me, not that I brought them home in buckets," he replied.

"My mistake. Who was it last week, Senator Merrill's daughter, and before her, the current Miss Jacobs County…?"

"That wasn't my fault," he said haughtily. "She stood in the middle of the parking lot at that new Japanese place and refused to move unless I let her come home with me." Then he grinned.

She shook her head. "You're impossible."

"Come on, come on, what do you want?" He looked at his watch. "I've got to meet your brother at the old line cabin in thirty minutes to help look over those pregnant heifers." He lifted an eyebrow and his eyes began to shimmer. They ran up and down her slender figure. "Maybe I could do you justice in fifteen minutes...."

She struck a pose. "Nobody's sticking me in between roundup and supper," she informed him. "Besides, I'm abstaining indefinitely."

He put a hand over his heart. "As God is my witness, I never asked your brother to tell you that Bill Paine had a social disease..."

"I am not sweet on Bill Paine!" she retorted.

"You were going to Houston with him to a concert that wasn't being given that night and I knew that Bill had an apartment and a bad reputation with women," he replied with clenched lips. "So I just happened to mention to one of my cowhands, who was standing beside your brother, that Bill Paine had a social disease."

She was aghast, just standing there gaping at his insolence. Curt had been very angry about her accepting a date with rich, blond Bill, who was far above them in social rank. Bill had been a client of Blake Kemp's, where he noticed Libby and started flirting with her. After Curt had told her what he overheard about Bill, she'd cancelled the date. She was glad she did. Later she'd learned that Bill had made a bet with one of his pals that he could get Libby anytime he wanted her, despite her standoffish pose.

"Of course, I don't have any social diseases," Jordan said, his deep voice dropping an octave. He checked his watch again. "Now it's down to ten minutes, if we hurry."

She threw up her hands. "Listen, I can't possibly be seduced today, I've got to go to the grocery store. What I came to tell you is that Janet's selling the property to a developer. He wants to put a subdivision on it," she added miserably.

"A what?" he exploded. "A subdivision? Next door to my breeding barn?" His eyes began to burn. "Like hell she will!"

"Great. You want to stop her, too. Do you have some strong rope?"

"This is serious," he replied gravely. "What the hell is she doing, selling your home out from under you? Surely Riddle didn't leave her the works! What about you and Curt?"

"She says we're young and can support ourselves," she said, fighting back frustration and fury.

He didn't say anything. His silence was as eloquent as shouting. "She's not evicting you. You go talk to Kemp."

"I work for Mr. Kemp," she reminded him.

He frowned. "Which begs the question, why aren't you at work?"

She sighed. "Mr. Kemp's gone to a bar association conference in Florida," she explained. "He said I could have two vacation days while he's gone, since Mabel and Violet were going to be there in case the attorney covering his practice needed anything." She glowered at him. "I don't get much time off."

"Indeed you don't," he agreed. "Blake Kemp is a busy attorney, for a town the size of Jacobsville. You do a lot of legwork for him, don't you?"

She nodded. "It's part of a paralegal's job. I've learned a lot."

"Enough to tempt you to go to law school?"

She laughed. "No. Not that much. A history degree is enough, not to mention the paralegal training. I've had all the education I want." She frowned thoughtfully. "You know, I did think about teaching adult education classes at night...."

"Your father was well-to-do," he pointed out. "He had coin collections worth half a million, didn't he?"

"We thought so, but we couldn't find them. I suppose he sold them to buy that Mercedes Janet is driving," she said somberly.

"He loved you and Curt."

She had to fight tears. "He wrote a new will just after he married her, leaving everything to her," she said simply. "She said she had it all in his safe-deposit box, along with the passbook to his big savings account, which her name was on as well as his. The way it was set up, that account belonged to her, so there was no legal problem with it," she had to admit. "Daddy didn't leave us a penny."

"There's something fishy going on here," he said, thinking out loud.

"It sounds like it, I guess. But Daddy gave everything to her. That was his decision to make, not ours. He was crazy about her."

Jordan looked murderous. "Has the will gone through probate yet?"

She shook her head. "She said she's given it to an attorney. It's pending."

"You know the law, even better than I do. This isn't right. You should get a lawyer," he repeated. "Get Kemp, in fact, and have him investigate her. There's something not right about this, Libby. Your father was the healthiest man I ever knew. He never had any symptoms of heart trouble."

"Well, I thought that, too, and so did Curt." She sighed, glancing down at the elegant blue-and-rose carpet, and her eyes grew misty. "He was really crazy about her, though. Maybe he just didn't think we'd need much. I know he loved us...." She choked back a sob. It was still fresh, the grief.

Jordan sighed and pulled her close against his tall, powerful body. His arms were warm and comforting as they enfolded her. "Why don't you just cry, Libby?" he asked gently. "It does help."

She sniffed into his shoulder. It smelled nice. His shirt had a pleasant detergent smell to it. "Do you ever cry?"

"Bite your tongue, woman," he said at her temple. "What would happen to the ranch if I sat down and bawled every time something went wrong? Tears won't come out of Persian carpet, you just ask my aunt!"

She laughed softly, even through the tears. He was a comforting sort of man and it was surprising, because he had a quick temper and an arrogance that put most people's backs up at first meeting.

"So that's why you yell at your cowboys? So you won't cry?"

"Works for me," he chuckled. He patted her shoulder. "Feel better?"

She nodded, smiling through tears. She wiped them away with a paper towel she'd tucked into her jeans. "Thanks."

"What are prospective lovers for?" he asked, smiling wickedly, and laughing out loud when she flushed.

"You stop corrupting me, you bad influence!"

"I said nothing corrupting, I just gave advance notice of bad intentions." He laughed at her expression. "At least it stopped the cascading waterfalls," he added, tongue in cheek, as he glanced at the tear tracks down her cheeks.

"Those weren't tears," she mumbled. "It was dew." She held up a hand. "I feel it falling again!"

"Talk to Kemp," he reiterated, not adding that he was going to do the same. "If she's got a new will and a codicil, signed, make her prove it. Don't let her shove you off your own land without a fight."

"I guess I could ask to see it," she agreed. Then she winced. "I hate arguments. I hate fights."

"I'll remember that the next time you come chasing after me," he promised.

She shook her head impotently, turning to go.

"Hey."

She glanced at him over her shoulder.

"Let me know what you find out," he said. "I'm in this, too. I can't manage a subdivision right near my barn. I can't have a lot of commotion around those beautiful Santa Gerts, it stresses them out too much. It would cost a fortune to tear down that barn and stick it closer to the house. A lawsuit would be cheaper."

"There's an idea," she said brightly. "Take her to court."

"For what, trying to sell property? That's rich."

"Just trying to help us both out," she said.

He glanced at his watch again. "Five minutes left and even I'm not that good," he added. "Pity. If you hadn't kept running your mouth, by now we could have…"

"You hush, Jordan Powell!" she shot at him. "Honestly, of all the blatant, arrogant, sex-crazed ranchers in Texas…!"

She was still mumbling as she went out the door. But when she was out of sight, she grinned. He was a tonic.

THAT NIGHT, JANET DIDN'T say a word about any real estate deals. She ate a light supper that Libby had prepared, as usual without any compliments about it.

"When are you going back to work?" she asked Libby irritably, her dyed blond hair in an expensive hairdo, her trendy silk shell and embroidered jeans marking her new wealth. "It can't be good for you to lie around here all day."

Curt, who was almost the mirror image of his sister, except for his height and powerful frame, glared at the woman. "Excuse me, since when did you do any housework or cooking around here? Libby's done both since she turned thirteen!"

"Don't you speak to me that way," Janet said haughtily. "I can throw you out anytime I like. I own everything!"

"You don't own the property until that will goes through probate," Libby replied sweetly, shocked at her own boldness. She'd never talked that way to the woman before. "You can produce it, I hope, because you're going to have to. You don't get the property yet. Maybe not even later, if everything isn't in perfect order."

"You've been talking to that rancher again, haven't you?" Janet demanded. "That damned Powell man! He's so suspicious about everything! Your father had a heart attack. He's dead. He left everything to me. What else do you want?" she raged, standing.

Libby stood, too, her face flushed. "Proof. I want proof. And you'd better have it before you start making any deals with developers about selling Daddy's land!"

Janet started. "De...developers?"

"I heard you this afternoon with that real estate agent," Libby said, with an apologetic glance at her brother, who looked shocked. She hadn't told him. "You're trying to sell our ranch and Daddy hasn't even been dead a month!"

Curt stood up. He looked even more formidable than Libby. "Before you make any attempt to sell this land, you're going to need a lawyer, Janet," he said in that slow, cold drawl that made cowhands move faster.

"How are you going to afford one, Curt, dear?" she asked sarcastically. "You just work for wages."

"Oh, Jordan will loan us the money," Libby said confidently.

Janet's haughty expression fluttered. She threw down her napkin. "You need cooking lessons," she said spitefully. "This food is terrible! I've got to make some phone calls."

She stormed out of the room.

Libby and Curt sat back down, both angry. Libby explained about the real estate agent's visit and what she'd overheard. Curt had only just come in when Libby had put the spaghetti and garlic bread on the table. It was Curt's favorite food and his sister made it very well, he thought, despite Janet's snippy comment.

"She's not selling this place while there's a breath left in my body," he told his sister. "Anyway, she can't do that until the will is probated. And she'd better have a legitimate will."

"Jordan said we needed to get Mr. Kemp to take a look at it," she said. "And I think we're going to need a handwriting expert to take a look, too."

He nodded.

"But what are we going to do about money to file suit?" she asked. "I was bluffing about Jordan loaning us the money. I don't know if he would."

"He's not going to want a subdivision on his doorstep, I'll tell you that," Curt said. "I'll talk to him."

"I already did," she said, surprising him. "He thinks there's something fishy going on, too."

"You can't get much past Jordan," he agreed. "I've been working myself to death trying not to think about losing Dad. I should have paid more attention to what was going on here."

"I've been grieving, too." She sighed and folded her small hands on the tablecloth. "Isn't it amazing how snippy she is, now that Daddy's not here? She was all over us like poison ivy before he died."

"She married him for what he had, Libby," he said bitterly.

"She seemed to love him…."

"She came on to me the night they came back from that Cancún honeymoon," he said bitterly.

Libby whistled. Her brother was a very attractive man. Their father, a sweet and charming man, had been overweight and balding. She could understand why Janet might have preferred Curt to his father.

"I slapped her down hard and Dad never knew." He shook his head. "How could he marry something like that?"

"He was flattered by all the attention she gave him, I guess," Libby said miserably. "And now here we are. I'll bet she sweet-talked him into changing that will. He would have done anything for her, you know that—he was crazy in love with her. He might have actually written us out of it, Curt. We have to accept that."

"Not until they can prove to me that it wasn't forged," he said stubbornly. "I'm not giving up our inheritance without a fight. Neither are you," he asserted.

She sighed. "Okay, big brother. What do you want to do?"

"When do you go back to work?"

"Monday. Mr. Kemp's out of town."

"Okay. Monday, you make an appointment for both of us to sit down with him and hash this out."

She felt better already. "Okay," she said brightly. "I'll do that very thing. Maybe we do have a chance of keeping Daddy's ranch."

He nodded. "There's always hope." He leaned back in his chair. "So you went to see Jordan." He smiled indulgently. "I can remember a time not so long ago when you ran and hid from him."

"He always seemed to be yelling at somebody," she recalled. "I was intimidated by him. Especially when I graduated from high school. I had a sort of crush on him. I was scared to death he'd notice. Not that he was ever around here that much," she added, laughing. "He and Daddy had a fight a week over water rights."

"Dad usually lost, too," Curt recalled. He studied his sister with affection. "You know, I thought maybe Jordan was sweet on you himself—he's only eight years older than you."

"He's never been sweet on me!" she flashed at him, blushing furiously. "He's hardly even smiled at me, in all the years we've lived here, until the past few months! If anything, he usually treats me like a contagious virus!"

Curt only smiled. He looked very much like her, with the same dark wavy hair and the same green eyes. "He picks at you. Teases you. Makes you laugh. You do the same thing to him. People besides me have noticed. He bristles if anyone says anything unkind about you."

Her eyes widened. "Who's been saying unkind things about me?" she asked.

"That assistant store manager over at Lord's Department Store."

"Oh. Sherry King." She leaned back in her chair. "She can't help it, you know. She was crazy about Duke Wright and he wanted to take me to the Cattleman's Ball. I wouldn't go and he didn't ask anybody else. I feel sorry for her."

"Duke's not your sort of man," he replied. "He's a mixer. Nobody in Jacobsville has been in more brawls," he said, pausing. "Well, maybe Leo Hart has."

"Leo Hart got married, he won't be brawling out at Shea's Roadhouse and Bar anymore."

"Duke's not likely to get married again. His wife took their five-year-old son to New York City, where her new job is. He says she doesn't even look after the little boy. She's too busy trying to get a promotion. The child stays with her sister while she jets all over the world closing real estate deals."

"It's a new world," Libby pointed out. "Women are competing with men for the choice jobs now. They have to move around to get a promotion."

Curt's eyes narrowed. "Maybe they should get promotion before they get pregnant," he said impatiently.

She shrugged. "Accidents happen."

"No child of mine is ever going to be an accident," Curt said firmly.

"Nice to be so superior," she teased, eyes twinkling. "Never to make mistakes…"

He swiped at her with a napkin. "You don't even stick your toes in the water, so don't lecture me about drowning."

She chuckled. "I'm sensible, I am," she retorted. "None of this angst for me. I'll just do my routine job and keep my nose out of emotional entanglements."

He studied her curiously. "You go through life avoiding any sort of risk, don't you, honey?" he mused.

She moved one shoulder restlessly. "Daddy and Mama fought all the time, remember?" she said. "I swore I'd never get myself into a fix like that. She told me that she and Daddy were so happy when they first met, when they first married. Then, six months later, she was pregnant with you and they couldn't manage one pleasant meal together without shouting." She shook her head. "That means you can't trust emotions. It's better to use your brain when you think about marrying somebody. Love is…sticky," she concluded. "And it causes insanity, I'm sure of it."

"Why don't you ask Kemp if that's why he's stayed single so long? He's in his middle thirties, isn't he, and never even been engaged."

"Who'd put up with him?" she asked honestly. "Now there's a mixer for you," she said enthusiastically. "He actually threw another lawyer out the front door and onto the sidewalk last month. Good thing there was a welcome mat there, it sort of broke the guy's fall."

"What did he want?" Curt asked.

She shook her head. "I have no idea. But I don't expect him to be a repeat client."

Curt chuckled. "I see what you mean."

LIBBY WENT TO bed early that night, without another word to Janet. She knew that anything she said would be too much. But she did miss her father and she couldn't believe that he wouldn't have mentioned Libby and Curt in his will. He did love them. She knew he did.

She thought about Jordan Powell, too, and about Curt's remark that he thought Jordan was sweet on her. She tingled all over at the thought. But that wasn't going to happen, she assured herself. Jordan was gorgeous and he could have his pick of pretty women. Libby Collins would be his last resort. The world wasn't ending yet, so she was out of the running.

She rolled over, closed her eyes, and went to sleep.

CHAPTER TWO

JANET WASN'T AT breakfast the next morning. Her new gold Mercedes was gone and she hadn't left a note. Libby saw it as a bad omen.

The weekend passed with nothing remarkable except for Janet's continued absence. The truck was ready Saturday and Curt picked it up in town, catching a lift with one of Jordan's cowboys. It wasn't as luxurious as a Mercedes, but it had a good engine and it was handy for hauling things like salt blocks and bales of hay. Libby tried to picture hauling hay in Janet's Mercedes and almost went hysterical with laughter.

Libby went back to work at Blake Kemp's office early Monday morning, dropped off by Curt on his way to the feed store for Jordan. She felt as if she hadn't really had a vacation at all.

Violet Hardy, Mr. Kemp's secretary, who was dark-haired, blue-eyed, pretty and somewhat overweight, smiled at her as she came in the door. "Hi! Did you have a nice vacation?"

"I spent it working," Libby confessed. "How did things go here?"

Violet groaned. "Don't even ask."

"That bad, huh?" Libby remarked.

Mabel, the blonde grandmother who worked at reception, turned in her chair after transferring a call into

Mr. Kemp's office. "Bad isn't the word, Libby," she said in a whisper, glancing down the hall to make sure the doors were all closed. "That lawyer Mr. Kemp got to fill in for him got two cases confused and sent the clients to the wrong courtrooms in different counties."

"Yes—" Violet nodded "—and one of them came in here and tried to punch Mr. Kemp."

Libby pursed her lips. "No. Did he have insurance?"

All three women chuckled.

"For an attorney who handles so many assault cases," Violet whispered, "he doesn't practice what he preaches. Mr. Kemp punched the guy back and they wound up out on the street. Our police chief, Cash Grier, broke it up and almost arrested Mr. Kemp."

"What about the other guy? Didn't he start it?" Libby exclaimed.

"The other guy was Duke Wright," Violet confessed, watching Libby color. "And Chief Grier said that instead of blaming Mr. Kemp for handling Mrs. Wright's divorce, he should thank him for not bankrupting Mr. Wright in the process!"

"Then what?" Libby asked.

All three women glanced quickly down the hall.

"Mr. Wright threw a punch at Chief Grier."

"Well, that was smart thinking. Duke's in the hospital, then?" Libby asked facetiously.

"Nope," Violet said, her blue eyes twinkling. "But he was in jail briefly until he made bail." She shook her head. "I don't expect he'll try that twice."

"Crime has fallen about fifty percent since we got Cash Grier as chief," Violet sighed, smiling.

"And Judd Dunn as assistant chief," Libby reminded her.

"Poor Mr. Wright," Mabel said. "He does have the worst

luck. Remember that Jack Clark who worked for him, who was convicted of murdering that woman in Victoria? Mr. Wright sure hated the publicity. It came just when he was trying to get custody of his son."

"Mr. Wright would have a lot less trouble if he didn't spend so much time out looking for it," came a deep, gruff voice from behind them.

They all jumped. Blake Kemp was standing just at the entrance to the hallway with a brief in one hand and a coffee cup in the other. He was as much a dish as Jordan Powell. He had wavy dark hair and blue eyes and the most placid, friendly face—until he got in front of a jury. Nobody wanted to be across the courtroom from Kemp when a trial began. There was some yellow and purple discoloration on one high cheekbone, where a fist had apparently landed a blow. Duke Wright, Libby theorized silently.

"Libby, before you do anything else, would you make a pot of coffee, please?" he asked in a long-suffering tone. He impaled a wincing Violet with his pale blue eyes. "I don't give a damn what some study says is best for me, I want caffeine. C-A-F-F-E-I-N-E," he added, spelling it letter by letter for Violet's benefit.

Violet lifted her chin and her own blue eyes glared right back at him. "Mr. Kemp, if you drank less of it, you might not be so bad-tempered. I mean, really, that's the second person you've thrown out of our office in a month! Chief Grier said that was a new city record...."

Kemp's eyes were blazing now, narrow and intent. "Miss Hardy, do you want to still be employed here tomorrow?"

Violet looked as if she was giving that question a lot of deliberation. "But, sir..." she began.

"I like caffeine. I'm not giving it up," Kemp said curtly. "You don't change my routine in this office. Is that clear?"

"But, Mr. Kemp—!" she argued.

"I don't remember suggesting anything so personal to you, Miss Hardy," he shot back, clearly angry. "I could, however," he added, and his cold blue eyes made insinuations about her figure, which was at least two dress sizes beyond what it should have been.

All three women gasped at the outrageous insinuation and then glared at their boss.

Violet flushed and stood up, as angry as he was, but not intimidated one bit by the stare. "My...my father always said that a woman should look like a woman and not a skeleton encased in skin. I may be a little overweight, Mr. Kemp, but at least I'm doing something about it!"

He glanced pointedly at a cake in a box on her desk.

She colored. "I live out near the Hart Ranch. I promised Tess Hart I'd pick that up at the bakery for her before I came to work and drop it by her house when I go home for lunch. It's for a charity tea party this afternoon." She was fuming. "I do not eat cake! Not anymore."

He stared at her until she went red and sat back down. She averted her eyes and went back to work. Her hands on the computer keyboard were trembling.

"You fire me if you want to, Mr. Kemp, but nothing I said to you was as mean as what you were insinuating to me with that look," Violet choked. "I know I weigh too much. You don't have to rub it in. I was only trying to help you."

Mabel and Libby were still glaring at him. He shifted uncomfortably and put the brief down on Violet's desk with a slap. "There are six spelling errors in that. You'll have to redo it. You can buzz me when the coffee's ready," he added shortly. He turned on his heel and took his coffee cup back into his office. As an afterthought, he slammed the door.

"Oh, and like anybody short of a druggist could read those chicken scratches on paper that you call hand-writing!" Violet muttered, staring daggers after him.

Libby let out the breath she'd been holding and gaped at sweet, biddable Violet, who'd never talked back to Mr. Kemp in the eight months she'd worked for him. So did Mabel.

"Well, it's about time!" Mabel said, laughing de-lightedly. "Good for you, Violet. It's no good, letting a man walk all over you, no matter how crazy you are about him!"

"Hush!" Violet exclaimed, glancing quickly down the hall. "He'll hear you!"

"He doesn't know," Libby said comfortingly, putting an arm around Violet. "And we'll never tell. I'm proud of you, Violet."

"Me, too," Mabel grinned.

Violet sighed. "I guess he'll fire me. It might not be a bad thing. I spend too much time trying to take care of him and he hates it." Her blue eyes were wistful under their long, thick lashes. "You know, I've lost fifteen pounds," she murmured. "And I'm down a dress size."

"A new diet?" Libby asked absently as she checked her "in" tray.

"A new gym, just for women," Violet confessed with a grin. "I love it!"

Libby looked at the other woman with admiration. "You're really serious about this, aren't you?"

Violet's shoulder moved gently. She was wearing a

purple dress with a high collar and lots of frills on the bodice and a very straight skirt that clung to her hips. It was the worst sort of dress for a woman who had a big bust and wide hips, but nobody had the heart to tell Violet. "I had to do something. I mean, look at me! I'm so big!"

"You're not that big. But I think it's great that you're trying so hard, Violet," Libby said gently. "And to keep you on track, Mabel and I are giving up dessert when you eat lunch with us."

"I have to go home and see about Mother most every day at lunchtime," Violet confessed. "She hates that. She said I was wasting my whole life worrying about her, when I should be out having fun. But she's already had two light strokes in the past year since Daddy died. I can't leave her alone."

"Honey, people like you are why there's a heaven," Mabel murmured softly. "You're one in a million."

Violet waved her away. "Everybody's got problems," she laughed. "For all we know, Mr. Kemp has much bigger ones than we do. He's such a good person. When Mother had that last stroke, the bad one, he even drove me to the hospital after I got the call."

"He is a good person," Libby agreed. "But so are you."

"You'd better make that coffee, I guess," Violet said wistfully. "I really thought I could make it half and half and he wouldn't be able to taste the difference. He's so uptight lately. He's always in a hurry, always under pressure. He drinks caffeine like water and it's so bad for his heart. I know about hearts. My dad died of a heart attack last year. I was just trying to help."

"It's hard to help a rattlesnake across the road, Violet," Mabel said, tongue in cheek.

Libby was curious about the coincidence of Violet's father dying of a heart attack, like her father, such a short time ago. "Violet could find one nice thing to say about a serial killer," Libby agreed affectionately. "Even worse, she could find one nice thing to say about my stepmother."

"Ouch," Mabel groaned. "Now there's a hard case if I ever saw one." She shook her head. "People in Branntville are still talking about her and old man Darby."

Libby, who'd just finished filling the coffeepot, started it brewing and turned jerkily. "Excuse me?"

"Didn't I ever tell you?" Mabel asked absently. "Just a sec. Good morning, Kemp Law Offices," she said. "Yes, sir, I'll connect you." She started to push the intercom button when she saw with shock that it was already depressed. The light was on the switch. She and Libby, who'd also seen it, exchanged agonized glances. Quickly, without telling Violet, she pushed it off and then on again. "Mr. Kemp, it's Mrs. Lawson for you on line two." She waited, hung up, and swung her chair around. She didn't dare tell poor Violet that Mr. Kemp had probably heard every single word she'd said about him.

"Your stepmother, Janet," Mabel told Libby, "was working at a nursing home over in Branntville. She sweet-talked an old man who was a patient there into leaving everything he had to her." She shook her head. "They said that Janet didn't even give him a proper funeral. She had him cremated and put in an urn and there was a graveside service. They said she bought a designer suit to wear to it."

Libby was getting cold chills. There were too many similarities there to be a coincidence. Janet had wanted to have Riddle Collins cremated, too, but Curt and Libby had talked to the funeral director and threatened a lawsuit if he complied with Janet's request. They went home and told Janet the same thing and also insisted on a church funeral at the Presbyterian church where Riddle had been a member since childhood. Janet had been furious, but in the end, she reluctantly agreed.

Violet wasn't saying anything, but she had a funny look on her face and she seemed pale. She turned away before the others saw. But Libby's expression was thought-provoking.

"You're thinking something. What?" Mabel asked Libby.

Fortunately, the phone rang again while Libby was deciding if it was wise to share her thoughts.

Violet got up from her desk and went close to Libby. "She wanted to cremate your father, too, didn't she?"

Libby nodded.

"You should go talk to Mr. Kemp."

Libby smiled. "You know, Violet, I think you're right." She hugged the other girl and went back to Mabel. "When he gets off the phone, I need to talk to him."

Mabel grinned. "Now you're talking." She checked the board. "He's free. Just a sec." She pushed a button. "Mr. Kemp, Libby needs to speak to you, if it's convenient."

"Send her in, Mrs. Jones."

"Good luck," Mabel said, crossing her fingers.

Libby grinned back.

"COME IN," KEMP SAID, opening the door for Libby and closing it behind her. "Have a seat. I don't need ESP to know what's on your mind. I had a call from Jordan Powell at home last night."

Her eyebrows arched. "Well, he jumped the gun!"

"He's concerned. Probably with good reason," he added. "I went ahead on my own and had a private detective I know run a check on Janet's background. This isn't the first time she's become a widow."

"I know," Libby said. "Mabel says an elderly man in a nursing home left her everything he had. She had him sent off to be cremated immediately after they got him to the funeral home."

He nodded. "And I understand from Don Hedgely at our funeral home here that she tried to have the same thing done with your father, but you and your brother threatened a lawsuit."

"We did," Libby said. "Daddy didn't believe in cremation. He would have been horrified."

Kemp leaned back in his desk chair and crossed his long legs, with his hands behind his head. He pursed his lips and narrowed his blue eyes, deep in thought. "There's another thing," he said. "Janet was fired from that nursing home for being too friendly with their wealthiest patients. One of whom—the one you know about—was an elderly widower with no children. He died of suspicious causes and left her his estate."

Libby folded her arms. She felt chilled all over now. "Wasn't it enough for her?" she wondered out loud.

"Actually, it took the entire estate to settle his gambling debts," he murmured. "Apparently, he liked the horses a little too much."

"Then there was our father." She anticipated his next thought.

He shook his head. "That was after Mr. Hardy in San Antonio."

Libby actually gasped. It couldn't be!

Kemp leaned forward quickly. "Do you think Violet is happy having to live in a rented firetrap with her invalid mother? Her parents were wealthy. But a waitress at Mr. Hardy's favorite restaurant apparently began a hot affair with him and talked him into making her a loan of a quarter of a million dollars to save her parents from bankruptcy and her father from suicide. He gave her a check and had a heart attack before he could stop payment on it—which he planned to do. He told his wife and begged forgiveness of her and his daughter before he died." His eyes narrowed. "He died shortly after he was seen with a pretty blonde at a San Antonio motel downtown."

"You think it was Janet? That it wasn't a heart attack at all—that she killed him?"

"I think there are too many coincidences for comfort in her past," Kemp said flatly. "But the one eyewitness who saw her with Hardy at that motel was unable to pick her out of a lineup. She'd had her hair color changed just the day before the lineup. She remained a brunette for about a week and then changed back to blond."

Libby's face tightened. "She might have killed my father," she bit off.

"That is a possibility," Kemp agreed. "It's early days yet, Libby. I can't promise you anything. But if she's guilty and I can get her on a witness stand, in a court of law, I can break her," he said with frightening confidence. "She'll tell me everything she knows."

She swallowed. "I don't want her to get away with it," she began. "But Curt and I work for wages…"

He flapped his hand in her direction. "Every lawyer takes a pro bono case occasionally. I haven't done it in months. You and Curt can be my public service for the year," he added, and he actually smiled. It made him look younger, much less dangerous than he really was.

"I don't know what to say," she said, shaking her head in disbelief.

He leaned forward. "Say you'll be careful," he replied. "I can't find any suspicion that she ever helped a young person have a heart attack, but I don't doubt for a minute that she knows how. I'm working with Micah Steele on that aspect of it. There isn't much he doesn't know about the darker side of medicine, even if he is a doctor. And what he doesn't know about black ops and untimely death, Cash Grier does."

"I thought Daddy died of a heart condition nobody knew he had." She took a deep breath. "When I tell Curt, he'll go crazy."

"Let me tell him," Kemp said quietly. "It will be easier."

"Okay."

"Meanwhile, you have to go back home and pretend that nothing's wrong, that your stepmother is innocent of any foul play. That's imperative. If you give her a reason to think she's being suspected of anything, she'll bolt, and we may never find her."

"We'd get our place back without a fight," Libby commented wistfully.

"And a woman who may have murdered your father, among others, would go free," Kemp replied. "Is that really what you want?"

Libby shook her head. "Of course not. I'll do whatever you say."

"We'll be working in the background. The most important thing is to keep the pressure on, a little at a time, so that she doesn't get suspicious. Tell her you've spoken to an attorney about the will, but nothing more."

"Okay," she agreed.

He got up. "And don't tell Violet I said anything to you about her father," he added. His broad shoulders moved restlessly under his expensive beige suit, as if he were carrying some difficult burden. "She's…sensitive."

What a surprising comment from such an insensitive man, she thought, but she didn't dare say it. She only smiled. "Certainly."

She was reaching for the doorknob when he called her back. "Yes, sir?"

"When you make another pot of coffee," he said hesitantly, "I guess we could use some of that half and half."

Her dropped jaw told its own story.

"She means well," he said abruptly, and turned back to his desk. "But for now, I want it strong and black and straight up. Call me when it's made and I'll bring my cup."

"It should be ready right now," she faltered. Even in modern times, few bosses went to get their own coffee. But Mr. Kemp was something of a puzzle. Perhaps, Libby thought wickedly as she followed him down the hall, even to himself.

He glanced at Violet strangely, but he didn't make any more comments. Violet sat with her eyes glued to her computer screen until he poured his coffee and went back to his office.

Libby wanted so badly to say something to her, but she didn't know what. In the end, she just smiled and

made a list of the legal precedents she would have to
look up for Mr. Kemp at the law library in the county
courthouse. Thank God, she thought, for computers.

SHE WAS ON her way home in the pickup truck after a
long day when she saw Jordan on horseback, watching several men drive the pregnant heifers into pastures close to the barn. He had a lot of money invested
in those purebred calves and he wasn't risking them
to predators or difficult births. He looked so good on
horseback, she thought dreamily. He was arrow-straight
and his head, covered by that wide-brimmed creamy
Stetson he favored, was tilted in a way that was partic-
ularly his. She could have picked him out of any crowd
at a distance just by the way he carried himself.

He turned his head when he heard the truck coming
down the long dirt road and he motioned Libby over
to the side.

She parked the truck, cut off the engine, and stood
on the running board to talk to him over the top of the
old vehicle. "I wish I had a camera," she called. "Mama
Powell, protecting his babies…"

"You watch it!" he retorted, shaking a finger at her.

She laughed. "What are you going to do, jump the
fence and run me down?"

"Poor old George here couldn't jump a fence. He's
twenty-four," he added, patting the old horse's withers.
"He hates his corral. I thought I'd give him a change of
scenery, since I wasn't going far."

"Everything gets old, I guess. Most everything, anyway," she added with a faraway, wistful look in her eyes.
She had an elderly horse of her own, that she might yet

have to give away because it was hard to feed and keep him on her salary.

He dismounted and left George's reins on the ground to jump the fence and talk to her. "Did you see Kemp?" he asked.

"Yes. He said you phoned him."

"I asked a few questions and got some uncomfortable answers," he said, coming around the truck to stand beside her. His big lean hands went to her waist and he lifted her down close to him. Too close. She could smell his shaving lotion and feel the heat off his body under the Western cut long-sleeved shirt. In her simple, jacketed suit, she felt overly dressed.

"You don't look too bad when you fix up," he commented, approving her light makeup and the gray suit that made her eyes look greener than they were.

"You don't look too bad when you don't," she replied. "What uncomfortable answers are you getting?"

His eyes were solemn. "I think you can guess. I don't like the idea of you and Curt alone in that house with her."

"We have a shotgun somewhere. I'll make a point of buying some shells for it."

He shook her by the waist gently. "I'm not teasing. Can you lock your bedroom door? Can Curt?"

"It's an old house, Jordan," she faltered. "None of the bedroom doors have locks."

"Tell Curt I said to get bolts and put them on. Do it when she's not home. In the meantime, put a chair under the doorknob."

"But why?" she asked uncertainly.

He drew a long breath. His eyes went to her soft bow of a mouth and he studied it for several seconds before he spoke. "There's one very simple way to cause a heart attack. You can do it with a hypodermic syringe filled with nothing but air."

She couldn't speak for a moment. "Could they...tell that if they did an autopsy on my father?"

"I'm not a forensic specialist, despite the fact that there are half a dozen shows on TV that can teach you how to think you are. I'll ask somebody who knows," he added.

She hated the thought of disinterring her father. But it would be terrible if he'd met with foul play and it never came out.

He tilted her face up to his narrow dark eyes. "You're worrying. Don't. I'm as close as your phone, night or day."

She smiled gently. "Thanks, Jordan."

His thumbs moved on her waist while he looked down at her. His face hardened. His eyes were suddenly on her soft mouth, with real hunger.

The world stopped. It seemed like that. She met his searching gaze and couldn't breathe. Her body felt achy. Hungry. Feverish. She swallowed, hoping it didn't show.

"If you play your cards right, I might let you kiss me," he murmured.

Her heart skipped. "Excuse me?"

One big shoulder lifted and fell. "Where else are you going to get any practical experience?" he asked. "Duke Wright is a candidate for the local nursing home, after all..."

"He's thirty-six!" she exclaimed. "That isn't old!"

"I'm thirty-two," he pointed out. "I have all my own teeth." He grinned to display them. "And I can still out-run at least two of my horses."

"That's an incentive to kiss you?" she asked blankly.

"Think of the advantages if you kiss me during a stampede," he pointed out.

She laughed. He was a case. Her eyes adored him. "I'll keep you in mind," she promised. "But you mustn't get your hopes up. This town is full of lonely bachelors who can't get women to kiss them. You'll have to take a number and wait."

"Wait until what?" he asked, tweaking her waist with his thumbs.

"I don't know. Christmas? I could kiss you as part of your present."

His eyebrows arched. "What's the other part?"

"It's not Christmas. Listen, I have to get home and make supper."

"I'll send Curt on down," he said.

She was seeing a new pattern. "To make sure I'm not left alone with Janet, is that right?"

"For my peace of mind," he corrected. "I've gotten…used to you," he added slowly. "As a neighbor," he added deliberately. "Think how hard it would be to break in another one, at my age."

"You just said you weren't old," she reminded him.

"Maybe I am, just a little," he confessed. He drew her up until she was standing completely against him, so close that she could feel the hard press of his muscular legs against her own. "Come on," he taunted, bending his head with a mischievous little smile. "You know you're dying to kiss me."

"I am?" she whispered dreamily as she studied the long, wide, firm curve of his lips.

"Desperately."

She felt his nose brushing against hers. Somewhere,

a horse was neighing. A jet flew over. The wind ruffled leaves in a small tree nearby. She was deaf to any
sound other than the throb of her own heartbeat. There
was nothing in the world except Jordan's mouth, a scant
inch from her own. He'd never kissed her. She wanted
him to. She ached for him to.

His hands tightened on her waist, lifting her closer.
"Come on, chicken. Give it all you've got."

Her hands were flat against his chest, feeling the
warm muscles under his cotton shirt. She tasted his
breath. Her arms slid up to his shoulders. He had her
hypnotized. She wanted nothing more than to drown
in him.

"That's it," he whispered.

She closed her eyes and lifted up on her tiptoes as
she felt the slow, soft press of her own lips against his
for the first time.

Her knees were weak. She didn't think they were
going to support her. And still Jordan didn't move,
didn't respond.

Frustrated, she tried to lift up higher, her arms cir-
cled his neck and pulled, trying to make his mouth firm
and deepen above hers. But she couldn't budge him.

"Oh, you arro…!"

It was the opening he'd been waiting for. His mouth
crushed down against her open lips and his arms contracted hungrily. Libby moaned sharply at the rush of
sensation it caused in her body. It had never been like
this in her life. She was burning alive. She ached. She
longed. She couldn't get close enough….

"Hey, Jordan!"

The distant shout broke the spell. Jordan jerked his
head around to see one of his men waving a wide-

brimmed hat and gesturing toward a pickup truck that was driving right out into the pasture where Jordan was putting those pregnant heifers.

"It's the feed supplement I ordered," he murmured, letting her go slowly. "Damn his timing."

He didn't smile when he said that. She couldn't manage even a word.

He touched her softly swollen mouth with his fingertips. "Maybe you could take me on a date and we could get lost on some deserted country road," he suggested.

She took a breath and shook her head to clear it. "I do not seduce men in parked cars," she pointed out.

He snapped his fingers. "Damn!"

"He's waving at you again," she noted, looking over his shoulder.

"All right, I'll go to work. But I'll send Curt on home." He touched her cheek. "Be careful, okay?"

She managed a weak smile. "Okay."

He turned and vaulted the fence, mounting George with the ease of years of practice as a horseman. "See you."

She nodded and watched him ride away. Her life had just changed course, in the most unexpected way.

CHAPTER THREE

BUT ALL JORDAN'S WORRY—and Libby's unease—was
for nothing. When she got home, Janet's Mercedes was
gone. There was a terse little note on the hall table that
read, Gone to Houston shopping, back tomorrow.

Even as she was reading it, Curt came in the back
door, bareheaded and sweaty.

"She's gone?" he asked.

She nodded. "Left a note. She's gone to Houston and
won't be back until tomorrow."

"Great. It'll give me time to put locks on the bedroom doors," he said.

She sighed. "Jordan's been talking to you, hasn't he?"
she asked.

"Yes, and he's been kissing you, apparently," he murmured, grinning. "Old Harry had to yell himself hoarse
to get Jordan's attention when they brought those feed
supplements out."

She flushed. She couldn't think of a single defense.
But she hadn't heard Harry yelling, except one time.
No wonder people were talking.

"Interested in you, is he?" Curt asked softly.

"He wanted me to ask him out on a date and get him
lost on a dirt road," she said.

"And you said…?"

She moved restively. "I said that I didn't seduce men

in parked cars on deserted roads, of course," she assured him.

He looked solemn. "Sis, we've never really talked about Jordan...."

"And we really don't need to, now," she interrupted. "I'm a big girl and I know all about Jordan. He's only teasing. I'm older and he's doing it in a different way, that's all."

Curt wasn't smiling. "He isn't."

She cleared her throat. "Well, it doesn't matter. He's not a marrying man and I'm not a frivolous woman. Besides, his tastes run to beauty queens and state senators' daughters."

He hesitated.

She smiled before he could say anything else. "Let it drop. We've got enough on our minds now without adding more to them. Let's rush to the hardware store and buy locks before she gets back."

He shrugged and let it go. There would be another time to discuss Jordan Powell.

WHEN LIBBY GOT home from work Tuesday evening she was still reeling from the shocking news that a fed-up Violet had quit her job and gone to work for Duke Wright. Blake Kemp had not taken the news well. Her mood lifted when she found Jordan's big burgundy double-cabbed pickup truck sitting in her front yard. He was sitting on the side of the truck bed, whittling a piece of wood with a pocket knife, his broad-brimmed hat pushed way back on his head. He looked up at her approach and jumped down to meet her.

"You're late," he complained.

She got out of her car, grabbing her purse on the

way. "I had to stay late and type up some notes for Mr. Kemp."

He scowled. "That's Violet's job."

"Violet's leaving," she said on a sigh. "She's going to work for Duke Wright."

"But she's crazy for Kemp, isn't she?" Jordan wondered.

She scowled at him. "You aren't supposed to know that," she pointed out.

"Everybody knows that." He looked around the yard. "Janet hasn't shown up. Curt said she'd gone to Houston."

"That's what the note said," she agreed, walking beside him to the front porch. "Curt put the locks on last night."

"I know. I asked him."

She unlocked the door and pushed it open. "Want some coffee?"

"I'd love some. Eggs? Bacon? Cinnamon toast?" he added.

"Oh, I see," she mused with a grin. "Amie's gone and you're starving, huh?"

He shrugged nonchalantly. "She didn't have to leave. I only yelled a little."

"You shouldn't scare her. She's old."

"Dirt's old. Amie's a spring chicken." He chuckled. "Anyway, she was shopping for antique furniture on the Internet and she found a side table she couldn't live without in San Antonio. She drove up to look at it. She said she'd see me in a couple of days."

"And you're starving."

"You make the nicest scrambled eggs, Libby," he coaxed. "Nice crisp bacon. Delicious cinnamon toast. Strong coffee."

"It isn't the time of day for breakfast."

"No law that you can't have breakfast for supper," he pointed out.

She sighed. "I was planning a beef casserole."

"It won't go with scrambled eggs."

She put her hands on her hips and gave him a considering look. "You really are a pain, Jordan."

He moved a step closer and caught her by the waist with two big lean hands. "If you want me to marry you, you have to prove that you're a good cook."

"Marry...?"

Before she could get another word out, his mouth crushed down over her parted lips. He kissed her slowly, tenderly, his big hands steely at her waist, as if he were keeping them there by sheer will when he wanted to pull her body much closer to his own.

Her hands rested on his clean shirt while she tried to decide if he was kidding. He had to be. Certainly he didn't want to marry anybody. He'd said so often enough.

He lifted his head scant inches. "Stop doing that."

She blinked. "Doing what?"

"Thinking. You can't kiss a man and do analytical formulae in your head at the same time."

"You said you'd never marry anybody...."

His eyes were oddly solemn. "Maybe I changed my mind."

Before she could answer him, he bent his head and kissed her again. This time it wasn't a soft, teasing sample of a kiss. It was bold, brash, invasive and possessive. He enveloped her in his hard arms and crushed her down the length of his powerful body. She felt a husky groan go into her mouth as he grew more insistent.

Against her hips, she felt the sudden hardness of his body. As if he realized that and didn't like having her feel it, he moved away a breath. Slowly, he lifted his hard mouth from her swollen lips and looked down at her quietly, curiously.

"This is getting to be a habit," she said breathlessly. Her body was throbbing, like her heart. She wondered if he could hear it.

His dark eyes fell to the soft, quick pulsing of her heart, visible where her loose blouse bounced in time with it. Beneath it, two hard little peaks were blatant. He saw them and his eyes began to glitter.

"Don't look at me like that," she whispered gruffly.

His eyes shot up to catch hers. "You want me," he said curtly. "I can see it. Feel it."

Her breath was audible. "You conceited…!"

His hands caught her hips and pushed them against his own. "It's mutual."

"I noticed!" she burst out, jerking away from him, red-faced.

"Don't be such a child," he chided, but gently. "You're old enough to know what desire feels like."

Her face grew redder. "I will not be seduced by you in my own kitchen over scrambled eggs!"

His eyebrows arched. "You're making them, then?" he asked brightly.

"Oh!" She pushed away from him. "You just won't take no for an answer!"

He smiled speculatively. "You can put butter on that," he agreed. His eyes went up and down her slender figure while she walked through to the kitchen, leaving her purse on the hall table as she went. "Not going to change before you start cooking?" he drawled, following her in. "I don't mind helping."

She shot him a dark glare.

He held up both hands. "Just offering to be helpful, that's all."

She laughed helplessly. "I can dress myself, thanks."

"I was offering to help you undress," he pointed out.

She had to fight down another blush. She was a modern, independent woman. It was just that the thought of Jordan's dark eyes on her naked body had an odd, pleasurable effect on her. Especially after that bone-shaking kiss.

"You shouldn't go around kissing women like that unless you mean business," she pointed out as she got out a big iron skillet to cook the bacon in.

"What makes you think I didn't mean it?" he probed, straddling a kitchen chair to watch her work.

"You? Mr. I'll-Never-Marry?"

"I didn't say that. I said I didn't want to get married."

"Well, what's the difference?" she asked, exasperated.

His dark eyes slid down to her breasts with a boldness that made her uncomfortable. "There's always the one woman you can't walk away from."

"There's no such woman in your life."

"Think so?" He frowned. "What are you doing with that?" he asked as she put the skillet on the burner.

"You're the one who wanted bacon!" she exclaimed.

"Bacon, yes, not liquid fat!" He got up from the chair, pulled a couple of paper towels from the roll and pulled a plate from the cabinet. "Don't you know how to cook bacon?"

He proceeded to show her, layering several strips of bacon on a paper-towel-coated plate and putting another paper towel on top of it.

She was watching with growing amusement. "And it's going to cook like that," she agreed. "Uh-huh."

"It goes in the microwave," he said with exaggerated patience. "You cook it for…"

"What's wrong?"

He was looking around, frowning, with the plate in one big hand. He opened cupboards and checked in the china cabinet. "All right, I'll bite. Where is it?"

"Where is what?"

"Your microwave oven!"

She sighed. "Jordan, we don't have a microwave oven."

"You're kidding." He scowled at her. "Everybody's got a microwave oven!"

"We haven't got one."

He studied her kitchen and slowly he put the plate back on the counter with a frown. The stove was at least ten years old. It was one of the old-fashioned ones that still had knobs instead of buttons. She didn't even have a dishwasher. Everything in the kitchen was old, like the cast-iron skillet she used for most every meal.

"I didn't realize how hard things were for you and Curt," he said after a minute. "I thought your father had all kinds of money."

"He did, until he married Janet," she replied. "She wanted to eat out all the time. The stove was worn-out and so was the dishwasher. He was going to replace them, but she had him buy her a diamond ring she wanted, instead."

He scowled angrily. "I'm sorry. I'm really sorry."

His apology was unexpected and very touching. "It's all right," she said gently. "I'm used to doing things the hard way. Really I am."

He moved close, framing her oval face in his big warm hands. "You never complain."

She smiled. "Why should I? I'm healthy and strong and able to do anything that needs doing around here."

"You make me ashamed, Libby," he said softly. He bent and kissed her with aching tenderness.

"Why?" she whispered at his firm mouth.

"I'm not really sure. Do that again."

He nibbled her upper lip, coaxing her body to lean heavily against his. "This is even better than dessert," he murmured as he deepened the pressure of his mouth. "Come here!"

He lifted her against him and kissed her hungrily, until her mouth felt faintly bruised from the slow, insistent pressure. It was like flying. She loved kissing Jordan. She hoped he was never going to stop!

But all at once, he did, with a jerky breath. "This won't do," he murmured a little huskily. "Curt will be home any minute. I don't want him to find us on the kitchen table."

Her mouth flew open. "Jordan!"

He shrugged and looked sheepish. "It was heading that way. Here." He handed her the plate of bacon. "I guess you'd better fry it. I don't think it's going to cook by itself."

She smiled up at him. "I'll drain it on paper towels and get rid of some of the grease after it's cooked."

"Why are you throwing those away?" he asked when she put the bacon on to fry and threw away the paper towels it had laid on.

"Bacteria," she told him. "You never put meat back on a plate where it's been lying, raw."

"They teach you that in school these days, I guess?"

She nodded. "And lots of other stuff."

"Like how to use a prophylactic...?" he probed wickedly.

She flushed. "They did not! And I'll wash your mouth out with soap if you say that again!" she threatened.

"Never mind. I'll teach you how to use it, when the time comes," he added outrageously.

"I am not using a prophylactic!"

"You want kids right away, then?" he persisted.

"I am not having sex with you on my kitchen table!"

There was a sudden stunned silence. Jordan was staring over her shoulder and his expression was priceless. Grimacing, she turned to find her older brother standing there with his mouth open.

"Oh, shut your mouth, Curt," she grumbled. "It was a hypothetical discussion!"

"Except for the part about the prophylactic," Jordan said with a howling mad grin. "Did you know that they don't teach people how to use them in school?"

Curt lost it. He almost doubled over laughing.

Libby threw a dish towel at him. "Both of you, out of my kitchen! I'll call you when it's ready. Go on, out!"

They left the room obediently, still laughing.

Libby shook her head and started turning the bacon.

"HASN'T JANET EVEN phoned to say if she was coming back today?" Jordan asked the two siblings when they were seated at the kitchen table having supper.

"There wasn't anything on the answering machine," Libby said. "I checked it while the bacon was cooking. Maybe she thinks we're on to something and she's running for it."

"No, I don't think so," Curt replied at once. "She's

not about to leave this property to us. Not considering what it would be worth to a developer."

"I agree," Jordan said. "I've given Kemp the phone number of a private detective I know in San Antonio," he added. "He's going to look into the case for me."

"We'll pay you back," Curt promised, and Libby nodded.

"Let's cross our bridges one at a time," Jordan replied. "First order of business is to see if we can find any proof that she's committed a crime in the past."

"Mabel said she was suspected in a death at a nursing home in Branntville," she volunteered.

"So Kemp told me," Jordan said. "This is good bacon," he added.

"Thanks," she said with a smile.

"Violet's father was another one of her victims," Libby added.

Jordan nodded while Curt scowled curiously at both of them. "But they can't prove that. Not unless there's enough evidence to order an exhumation. And, considering the physical condition of Violet's mother," he added, "I'm afraid she'd never be able to agree to it. The shock would probably kill her mother."

Libby sighed. "Poor Violet. She's had such a hard life. And now to have to change jobs…"

"She works for Kemp, doesn't she?" Curt asked.

"She did. She quit today," Libby replied. "She's going to work for Duke Wright."

"Oh, Sherry King's going to love that," Curt chuckled.

"She doesn't own Duke," Libby said. "He doesn't even like her."

"She's very possessive about men she wants."

"More power to her if she can put a net over him and lock him in her closet."

Jordan chuckled. "He's not keen on the thought of a second wife."

"He's still trying to get custody of his son, isn't he?" Curt asked. "Poor guy."

"He won't be the first man who lost a woman to a career," Jordan reminded him. "Although it's usually the other way around." He glanced at Libby. "Just for the record, I think you're more important than a new bull, no matter what his ancestry is."

"Gee, thanks," she replied, tongue in cheek.

"It never hurts to clear up these little details before they become issues," he said wryly. "On the other hand, it would be nice if you'd tell me if you have plans to go to law school and move to a big city to practice law?"

"Not me, thanks," she replied. "I'm very happy where I am."

"You don't know any other life except this one," he persisted. "What if you regret not spreading your wings further on down the road?"

"We can't see into the future, Jordan," she replied thoughtfully. "But I don't like cities, although I'm sure they're exciting for some people. I don't like parties or business and I wouldn't trade jobs with Kemp for anything on earth. I'm happy looking up case precedents and researching options. I wouldn't like having to stand up in a courtroom and argue a case."

"You don't know that," he mused, and a shadow crossed his face. "What if you got a taste of it one day and couldn't live without it, but it was too late?"

"Too late?"

"What if you had kids and a husband?" he prompted.

"You're thinking about Duke Wright," she said slowly.

He drew in a hard breath, aware that Curt was watching him curiously. "Yes," he told her. "Duke's wife was a secretary. She took night courses to get her law degree and then got pregnant just before she started practice. While Duke was giving bottles and changing diapers, she was climbing the ladder at a prestigious San Antonio law firm, living there during the week and coming home on weekends. Then they offered her a job in New York City."

Libby couldn't quite figure out the look on his face. He was taking it all quite seriously and she'd thought he was teasing.

"So you see," he continued, "she didn't know she wanted a career until it was too late. Now she's making a six-figure annual income and their little boy's in her way. She doesn't want to give him up, but she doesn't have time to take care of him properly. And Duke's caught in the middle."

"I hadn't realized it was that bad," she confessed. "Poor Duke."

"He had a choice," he told her. "He married her thinking she wanted what he did, a nice home and a comfortable living, and kids." He drew a breath. "But she was very young," he added, his eyes studying her covertly. "Maybe she didn't really know what she wanted. Then."

"I suppose some women don't," she replied. "It's a new world. Maybe it took her a long time to realize the opportunities and then it was too late to go back."

He lowered his eyes to his boots. "That's very possible."

"But it's Duke's problem," she added, smiling. "Want some pie? I've got a cherry one that I made yesterday in the refrigerator."

He shook his head. "Thanks. But I won't stay." He got to his feet. "I'll tell Kemp to let you know what the private detective finds out. Meanwhile," he added, glancing at Curt, "not a word to Janet. Okay?"

They both nodded.

"Thanks, Jordan," Curt added.

"What are neighbors for?" he replied, and he chuckled. But his eyes didn't quite meet Libby's.

"JORDAN WAS ACTING very oddly tonight, wasn't he?" Libby asked her brother after they'd washed the dishes and put them away.

"He's a man with a lot on his mind," he replied. "Calhoun Ballenger's making a very powerful bid for that senate seat that old man Merrill's had for so many years. They say old man Merrill's worried and so's his daughter, Julie. You remember, she's been pursuing Jordan lately."

"But he and Calhoun have been friendly for years," she said.

"So they have. There's more. Old man Merrill got pulled over for drunk driving by a couple of our local cops. Now Merrill's pulling strings at city hall to try and make the officers withdraw the charges. Merrill doesn't have a lot of capital. Jordan does."

"Surely you don't think Jordan would go against Cash Grier, even for Julie?" she wondered, concerned.

He started to speak and then thought better of it. "I'm not sure I really know," he said.

She rubbed at a clean plate thoughtfully. "Do you suppose he's serious about her? She and her father are very big socially and they have a house here that they stay in from time to time. She has a college degree. In fact, they say she may try her hand at politics. He was talking about marriage and children to us—like he was serious about it." She frowned. "Does that kind of woman settle down? Or was that what he meant, when he said some women don't know what they want until they find it?"

"I don't know that he's got marriage on his mind," Curt replied slowly. "But he's spent a good deal of time with Julie and the senator just lately."

That hurt. She bit her lower lip, hard, and forced her mind away from the heat and power of Jordan's kisses. "We've got a problem of our own. What are we going to do about Janet?"

"Kemp's working on that, isn't he? And Jordan's private detective will be working with him. They'll turn up something. She isn't going to put us out on the street, Libby," he said gently. "I promise you she isn't."

She smiled up at him. "You're sort of nice, for a brother."

He grinned. "Glad you noticed!"

She didn't sleep all night, though, wondering about Jordan's odd remarks and the way he'd looked at her when he asked if she had ambitions toward law practice. She really didn't, but he seemed to think she was too young to know her own mind.

Well, it wasn't really anything to worry about, she assured herself. Jordan had no idea of marrying her, regardless of her ambition or lack thereof. But Curt had said he was seeing a lot of Julie Merrill. For some unfathomable reason, the thought made her sad.

CHAPTER FOUR

IT WAS LATE afternoon before Janet came back, looking out of sorts. She threw herself onto the sofa in the living room and lit a cigarette.

"You'll stink up the place," Libby muttered, hunting for an ashtray. She put it on the table.

"Well, then, you'll have to invest in some more air freshener, won't you, darling?" the older woman asked coldly.

Libby stared at her angrily. "Where have you been for three days?"

Janet avoided looking at her. "I had some business to settle."

"It had better not have been any sales concerning this property," Libby told her firmly.

"And who's going to stop me?" the other woman demanded hotly.

"Mr. Kemp."

Janet crushed out the cigarette. "Let him try. You try, too! I own everything here and I'm not letting you take it away from me! No matter what I have to do," she added darkly. "I earned what I'm getting, putting up with your father handling me like a live doll. The repulsive old fool made my skin crawl!"

"My father loved you," Libby bit off, furious that

the awful woman could make such a remark about her
father, the kindest man she'd ever known.

"He loved showing me off, you mean," Janet muttered. "If he'd really loved me, he'd have given me the
things I asked him for. But he was so cheap! Well, I'm
not being cheated out of what's mine," she added, with
a cold glare at Libby. "Not by you or your brother. I
have a lawyer, too, now."

Libby felt sick. But she managed a calm smile. "We
have locks on our bedroom doors, by the way," she said
out of the blue. "And Mr. Kemp is having a private detective check you out."

Janet looked shocked. "W-what?"

"Violet who works in my office thinks you might
have known her father— Mr. Hardy from San Antonio?" she added deliberately. "He had a heart attack,
just like Daddy…?"

Janet actually went pale. She jumped to her feet as
if she'd been stung.

"Where are you going?" Libby asked seconds later,
when the older woman rushed from the room.

Janet went into her bedroom and slammed the door.
The sound of objects bouncing off walls followed in a
furious staccato.

Libby bit her lip. She'd been warned not to do anything to make Janet panic and make a run for it, but the
woman had pricked her temper. She wished she hadn't
opened her mouth.

With dark thoughts, she finished baking a ham and
made potato salad to go with it, along with homemade
rolls. It gave her something to do besides worry.

But when Curt came home to eat, he was met by
Janet with a suitcase, going out the door.

"Where are you off to?" he asked her coolly.

She threw a furious glance at the kitchen. "Anywhere I don't have to put up with your sister!" she snarled. "I'll get a motel room in town. You'll be hearing from my attorney in a day or so."

Curt's eyebrows lifted. "Funny. I was just about to tell you the same thing. I had a phone call from Kemp while I was at work. His private investigator has turned up some very interesting information about your former employment at a nursing home in Branntville...?"

Janet brushed by him in a mad rush toward her Mercedes. She threw her case in and jumped in behind it, spraying dirt as she spun out of the driveway.

"Well, that's clinched it," Curt mused as he joined his troubled sister in the kitchen. "She won't be back, or I'll miss my bet."

"I don't think it was a good idea to run her off," she commented as she set the table. "I'd already opened my big mouth and mentioned the locks on our bedroom doors and Violet's father to her."

"It's okay," Curt said gently. "I'm doing what Kemp told me to. I put her on the run."

"Mr. Kemp said to do that?"

He nodded, tossing his hat onto a side table and pulling out a chair. "Any coffee going? We've been mucking out line cabins all day. I'm beat!"

"Mucking out line cabins, not stables?"

"The river ran out of its banks right into that cabin on the north border," he said heavily. "We've been shoveling mud all afternoon. Crazy, isn't it? We had drought for four years, now it's floods. God must really be mad at somebody!"

"Don't look at me, I haven't done a single thing out of line."

He smiled. "When have you ever?" He studied her as she put food on the table. "Jordan says he's taking you out to a movie next week...watch it!"

Her hands almost let go of the potato salad bowl. She caught it and put it down carefully, gaping at her brother. "Jordan's taking me to a movie?"

"It's what usually happens when men start kissing women," he said philosophically, leaning back in his chair with a wicked grin. "They get addicted."

"How did you know he was kissing me last night?"

He grinned wickedly. "I didn't."

She cleared her throat and turned away, reddening as she remembered the passionate kiss she and Jordan had shared before the supper he'd coaxed her to cook for him. She hadn't slept well all night thinking about it. Or about what Curt had said, that Jordan was spending a lot of time with Julie Merrill. But he couldn't be interested in the woman, if he wanted to take Libby out!

"You never got addicted to any women," she pointed out.

He shrugged. "My day will come. It just hasn't yet."

"What were you telling Janet about a private investigator and the nursing home?"

"Oh, yes." He waited until she sat down and they said grace before he continued, while piling ham on his plate. "I'm not sure how much Kemp told you already but it seems that Janet has changed her legal identity since she worked in the nursing home. Also her hair color. She was under suspicion for the death of that elderly patient who liked to play the horses. She was making off with his bank account when it seems she was paid a visit by a gentleman representing a rather shadowy figure who was owed a great deal of money by the deceased. She left everything and ran for her life." He smiled complacently. "You see, there were more debts than money left in the elderly gentleman's entire estate!"

Libby was listening intently.

"There's more." He took a bite of ham. "This is nice!" he exclaimed when he tasted it.

"Isn't it?" She smiled. "I got it from Duke Wright. He's sidelining into a pork products shop and he's marketing on the Internet. He's doing organic bacon and ham."

"Smart guy."

She nodded. "There's more, you said?"

"Yes. They've just managed to convince Violet's mother that her husband might have been murdered. She's agreed to an exhumation."

"But they said the shock might be fatal!"

"Mrs. Hardy loved her husband. She never believed it was a heart attack. He'd had an echocardiogram that was misread, leading to a heart catheterization. They found nothing that would indicate grounds for a heart attack."

"Poor Violet," Libby said sadly. "It's going to be hard on her, too." She glanced up at her brother. "I still can't believe she quit and is going to work for Duke Wright."

"I know," he said. "She was crazy about Kemp!"

She nodded sadly. "Serves him right. He's been unpleasant to her lately. Violet's tired of eating her heart out for him. And who knows. It might prompt Mr. Kemp to do some soul-searching."

"More than likely he'll just hire somebody else and forget all about her. If he wanted to be married, he could be," he added.

"He doesn't date anybody, does he?" she asked curiously.

He shook his head. "But he's not gay."

"I never thought he was. I just wondered why he keeps so much to himself."

"Maybe he's like a lot of other bachelors in Jacobsville, he's got a secret past that he doesn't want to share!"

"We're running out of bachelors," she retorted. "The Hart boys were the last to go and nobody ever thought they'd end up with families."

"Biscuits were their downfall," he pointed out.

"Jordan doesn't like biscuits," she mused. "I did ask, you know."

He chuckled. "Jordan doesn't have a weakness and he's never lacked dates when he wanted them." He eyed her over his coffee cup. "But he may be at the end of his own rope."

"Don't look at me," she said, having spent too much time lately thinking about Jordan's intentions toward her. "I may be the flavor of the week, but Jordan isn't going to want to marry down, if you see what I mean."

His eyes narrowed. "We may not be high society, but our people go back a long way in Jacobs County."

"That doesn't put us in monied circles, either," she reminded him. Her eyes were dreamy and faraway. "He's got a big, fancy house and he likes to keep company with high society. Maybe that's why he's been taking Senator Merrill's daughter around. It gets him into places he was never invited to before. We'd never fit. Especially me," she added in a more wistful tone than she realized.

"That wouldn't matter."

She smiled sadly. "It would and you know it. He'll need a wife who can entertain and throw parties, ar-

range sales, things like that. Most of all, he'll want a
woman who's beautiful and intelligent, someone he'll
be proud to show off. He might take me to a movie. But
believe me, he won't take me to a minister."

"You're sure of that?"

She looked up at him. "You said it yourself—Jordan
has been spending a lot of time with the state senator's
daughter. He's running for reelection and the latest polls
say that Calhoun Ballenger is almost tied with him. He
needs all the support he can get, financial and otherwise.
I think Jordan's going to help him, because of Julie."

"Then why is he kissing you?"

"To make her jealous?" she pondered. "Maybe to
convince himself that he's still attractive to women. But
it's not serious. Not with him." She looked up. "And I
don't have affairs, whether it's politically correct or not."

He sighed. "I suppose we all have our pipe dreams."

"What's yours, while we're on the subject?"

He smiled. "I'd like to start a ranch supply company.
The last one left belonged to Ted Regan's father-in-law.
When he died, the store went bust, and then his daughter Corrie married Ted Regan and didn't need to make
her own living. The hardware store can order most sup-
plies, but not cattle feed or horse feed. Stuff like that."

She hadn't realized her brother had such ambitions.
"If we weren't in such a financial mess, I'd be more than
willing to cosign a loan with the house as collateral."

He stared at her intently. "You'd do that for me?"

"Of course. You're my brother. I love you."

He reached out and caught her hand. "I love you,
too, sis."

"Pipe dreams are nice. Don't you give yours up.
Eventually we'll settle this inheritance question and

we might have a little capital to work with." She studied him with pride. "I think you'd make a great success of it. You've kept us solvent, up until Janet's unexpected arrival."

"She'll be out for blood. I should probably call Kemp and update him on what's happened."

"That might not be a bad idea. Maybe we should get a dog," she added slowly.

"Bad idea. We can hardly afford to feed old Bailey, your horse. We'd have to buy food for a dog, too, and it would break us."

She saw his eyes twinkle and she burst out laughing, too.

JANET'S ATTORNEY NEVER showed up and two days later, Janet vanished, leaving a trail of charges to the Collinses for everything from clothes to the motel bill.

"You won't have to pay that," Kemp told Libby when he'd related the latest news to her. "I've already alerted the merchants that she had no authority to charge anything to you or Curt, or the estate."

"Thanks," she said with relief. "What do we do now?"

"I've got the state police out looking for her," he replied, his hands deep in his slacks' pockets. "On suspicion of murder. You won't like what's coming next."

"What?"

"I want to have your father exhumed."

She ground her teeth together. "I was afraid of that."

"We'll be discreet. But we need to have the crime lab check for trace evidence of poisoning. You see, we know what killed the old man at the nursing home where she worked. I believe she did kill him. Poisoners tend to stick to the same routine."

"Poor Daddy," she said, feeling sick. Now she wondered if they might have saved him, if they'd only realized sooner that Janet was dangerous.

"Don't play mind games with yourself, Libby," Kemp said quietly. "It does no good."

"What a terrible way to go."

"The poison she used was quick," he replied. "Some can cause symptoms for months and the victim dies a painfully slow death. That wasn't the case here. It's the only good news I have for you, I'm afraid. But after they autopsy Mr. Hardy, there may be more forensic evidence to make a case against her. We've found a source for the poison."

"But the doctor said that Daddy died of a heart attack," she began.

"He might have," Kemp had to admit. "But he could as easily have died of poison or an air embolism."

"Jordan mentioned that," she recalled.

He smiled secretively. "Jordan doesn't miss a trick."

"But Janet's gone. What if they discover that Daddy's death was foul play and then they can't find her?" Libby pointed out. "She's gotten away with it at least two times, by being cagey."

"Every criminal eventually makes a mistake," he said absently. "She'll make one. Mark my words."

She only nodded. She glanced at Violet's empty desk and winced.

"I have an ad in the paper for a new secretary," he said coldly. "Meanwhile, Mabel's going to do double duty," he added, nodding toward Mabel, who was on the phone taking notes.

"It's going to be lonely without her," she said without thinking.

Kemp actually ground his teeth, turned on his heel and went back into his office. As an afterthought, he slammed the door.

Libby lost it. She laughed helplessly. Mabel, off the phone now and aware of Kemp's shocking attitude, laughed, too.

"It won't last long," Mabel whispered. "Violet was the only secretary he's ever had who could make and break appointments without hurting people's feelings. She was the fastest typist, too. He's not going to find somebody to replace her overnight."

Libby agreed silently. But it promised to be an interesting working environment for the foreseeable future.

Libby didn't even notice there was a message on the answering machine until after supper, when she'd had a lonely sandwich after Curt had phoned and said he was eating pizza with the other cowboys over at the Regan place for their weekly card game.

Curious, Libby punched the answer key and listened to the message. In a silken tone, the caller identified himself as an attorney named Smith and said that Mrs. Collins had hired him to do the probate on her late husband's will. He added that the children of Riddle Collins would have two weeks to vacate the premises.

Libby went through the roof. Her hands trembled as she tried to call Kemp and failing to reach him, she punched in Jordan's number.

It took a long time for him to answer the phone and when he finally did, there was conversation and music in the background.

"Yes?" he asked curtly.

Libby faltered. "Am I interrupting? I can call you another time..."

"Libby?" His voice softened. "Wait a minute." She heard muffled conversation, an angry reply, and the sound of a door closing. "Okay," he said. "What's wrong?"

"I can't get Mr. Kemp," she began urgently, "and Janet's attorney just called and said we had two weeks to get out of the house before they did the probate!"

"Libby," he said softly, "just sit down and use your mind. Think. When has anybody ever been asked to vacate a house just so that probate papers could be filed?"

She took a deep breath and then another. Her hands were still cold and trembling but she was beginning to remember bits and pieces of court documents. She was a paralegal. For God's sake, she knew about probate!

She sighed heavily. "Thanks. I just lost it. I was so shocked and so scared!"

"Is Curt there?"

"No, he went to his weekly card game with the cowboys over at Ted Regan's ranch," she said.

"I'm sorry I can't come over and talk to you. I'm having a fundraising party for Senator Merrill tonight."

Merrill. His daughter Julie was the socialite. She was beautiful and rich and…socially acceptable. Certainly, she'd be at the party, too.

"Libby?" he prompted, when she didn't answer him.

"That's…that's okay, Jordan, I don't need company, honest," she said at once. "I just lost my mind for a minute. I'm sorry I bothered you. Really!"

"You don't have to apologize," he said, as if her statement unsettled him.

"I'll hang up now. Thanks, Jordan!"

He was still talking when she put the receiver down, very quickly, and put the answering machine back on. If he called back, she wasn't answering him. Janet's vicious tactics had unsettled her. She knew Janet had gotten someone to make that phone call deliberately, to upset Riddle's children.

It was her way of getting even, no doubt, for what Libby and Curt had said to her. She wondered if there was any way they could trace a call off an answering machine? A flash of inspiration hit her. Before Jordan would have time to call and foul the connection, she jerked up the phone and pressed the *69 keys. It gave her the number of the party who'd just phoned and she wrote it down at once, delighted to see that it was not a local number. She'd give it to Kemp the next morning and let his private investigator look into it.

Feeling more confident, she went back to the kitchen and finished washing up the few dishes. She couldn't forget Jordan's deep voice on the phone and the sound of a woman's voice arguing angrily when he went into another room to talk to Libby. It must be that senator's daughter. Obviously she felt possessive of Jordan and was wary of any potential rival. But Libby was no rival, she told herself. Jordan had just kissed her. That was all.

If only she could forget how it had felt. Then she remembered something else: Jordan's odd statements about Duke Wright's wife, and how young she was, and how she didn't quite know she wanted a career until she was already married and pregnant. He'd given Libby an odd, searching look when he said that.

The senator's daughter, Julie Merrill, was twenty-six, she recalled, with a degree in political science. Obviously she already knew what she wanted. She wanted Jordan. She was at his house tonight, probably hostessing the party there. Libby looked down at her worn jeans and faded blouse and then around her at the shabby but

useful furniture in the old house. She laughed mirthlessly. What in the world would Jordan want with her,
anyway? She'd been daydreaming. She'd better wake
up, before she had her heart torn out.

SHE DIDN'T PHONE Jordan again and he didn't call her
back. She did give the telephone number of the so-
called attorney to Mr. Kemp, who passed it along to
his investigator.

Several days later, he paused by Libby's desk while
she was writing up a precedent for a libel case, and he
looked smug.

"That was quick thinking on your part," he remarked
with a smile. "We traced the number to San Antonio.
The man isn't an attorney, though. He's a waiter in a
high-class restaurant who thinks Janet is his meal ticket
to the easy life. We, uh, disabused him of the idea and
told him one of her possible futures. We understand that
he quit his job and left town on the next bus to make
sure he wasn't involved in anything she did."

She laughed softly. "Thank goodness! Then Curt
and I don't have to move!"

Kemp glared at her. "As if I'd stand by and let any
so-called attorney toss you out of your home!"

"Thanks, boss," she said with genuine gratitude.

He shrugged. "Paralegals are thin on the ground,"
he said with twinkling blue eyes.

"Callie Kirby and I are the only ones that I know of
in town right now," she agreed.

"And Callie's got a child," he said, nodding. "I don't
think Micah's going to want her to come back to work
until their kids are in school."

"I expect not. She's got Micah's father to help take care of, too," she added, "after his latest stroke."

"People die," he said, and his eyes seemed distant and troubled.

"Mabel called in sick," she said reluctantly. "She's got some sort of stomach virus."

"They go around every spring," he agreed with a sigh. "Can you handle everything, or do you want to get a temp? If you do, call the agency. Ask if they've got somebody who can type."

She gave him her most innocent look. "Of course I can do the work of three women, sir, and even make coffee…"

He laughed. "Call the agency."

"Yes, sir."

He glowered. "It's Violet's fault," he muttered, turning. "I'll bet she's cursed us. We'll have sick help from now on."

"I'm sure she'd never do that, Mr. Kemp," she assured him. "She's a nice person."

"Imagine taking offense at a look and throwing in the towel. Hell, I look at people all the time and they don't quit!"

She cleared her throat and nodded toward the door, which was just opening.

A lovely young woman with a briefcase and long blond hair came in. "I'm Julie Merrill," she said with a haughty smile. "Senator Merrill's daughter? You advertised for a secretary, I believe."

Libby could not believe her eyes. Jordan's latest love and she turned up here looking for work! Of all the horrible bad luck…

Kemp stared at the young woman without speaking.

"Oh, not me!" Julie laughed, clearing her throat.

"Heavens, I don't need a job! No, it's my friend Lydia. She's just out of secretarial school and she can't find anything suitable."

"Can she type?"

"Yes! Sixty words a minute. And she can take shorthand, if you don't dictate too fast."

"Can she speak?"

Julie blinked. "I beg your pardon?"

Kemp gave her a scrutiny that would have stopped traffic. His eyes became a wintry blue, which Libby knew from experience meant that his temper was just beginning to kindle.

"I don't give jobs through third persons, Miss Merrill, and I don't give a damn who your father is," he said with a cool smile.

She colored hotly and gaped at him. "I… I…just thought… I mean, I could ask…!"

"Tell your friend she can come in and fill out an application, but not to expect much," he added shortly. "I have no respect for a woman who has to be helped into a job through favoritism. And in case it's escaped your attention," he added, moving a step closer to her, "nobody works for me unless they're qualified."

Julie shot a cold glare at Libby, who was watching intently. "I guess you think she's qualified," she said angrily.

"I have a diploma as a trained paralegal," Libby replied coolly. "It's on the wall behind you, at my desk."

Kemp only smiled. It wasn't a nice smile.

Julie set her teeth together so hard that they almost clicked. "I don't think Lydia would like this job, anyway!"

Kemp's right eyebrow arched. "Was there anything else, Miss Merrill?"

She turned, jerking open the door. "My father will not be happy when I tell him how you've spoken to me."

"By all means, tell him, with my blessing," Kemp said. "One of his faults is a shameful lack of discipline with his children. I understand you've recently expressed interest in running for public office in Jacobs County, Miss Merrill. Let me give you a piece of advice. Don't."

Her mouth fell open. "How dare you…!"

"It's your father's money, of course. If he wants to throw it away, that's his concern."

"I could win an election!"

Kemp smiled. "Perhaps you could. But not in Jacobs County," he said pleasantly. His eyes narrowed and became cold and his voice grew deceptively soft. "Closet skeletons become visible baggage in an election. And no one here has forgotten your high-school party. Especially not the Culbertsons."

Julie's face went pale. Her fingers on the briefcase tightened until the knuckles showed. She actually looked frightened.

"That was…a terrible accident."

"Shannon Culbertson is still dead."

Julie's lower lip trembled. She turned and went out the door so quickly that she forgot to close it.

Kemp did it for her, his face cold and hard, full of repressed fury.

Libby wondered what was going on, but she didn't dare ask.

Later, of course, when Curt got home from work, she couldn't resist asking the question.

He scowled. "What the hell did Julie want in Kemp's

office? Lydia doesn't need a job, she already has a job—a good one—at the courthouse over in Bexar County!"

"She said Lydia wanted to work for Mr. Kemp, but she was giving me the evil eye for all she was worth."

"She wants Jordan. You're in the way."

"Sure I am," she laughed coldly. "What about that girl, Shannon Culbertson?"

Curt hesitated. "That was eight years ago."

"What happened?"

"Somebody put something in her drink—which she wasn't supposed to have had in the first place. It was a forerunner of the date-rape drug. She had a hidden heart condition. It killed her."

"Who did it?"

"Nobody knows, but Julie tried to cover it up, to save her father's senate seat. Kemp dug out the truth and gave it to the newspapers." He shook his head. "A vindictive man, Kemp."

"Why?" she asked.

"They say Kemp was in love with the girl. He never got over it."

"But Julie's father won the election," she pointed out.

"Only because the leading lights of the town supported him and contributed to his reelection campaign. Most of those old-timers are dead or in nursing homes and the gossip around town is that Senator Merrill is already over his ears in debt from his campaign. Besides which, he's up against formidable opposition for the first time in recent years."

CHAPTER FIVE

So THAT WAS Kemp's secret, Libby thought. A lost love. "Yes, I know," she said. "Calhoun Ballenger has really shaken up the district politically. A lot of people think he's going to win the nomination right out from under Merrill."

"I'm almost sure he will," Curt replied. "The powers that be in the county have changed over the past few years. The Harts have come up in the world. So have the Tremaynes, the Ballengers, Ted Regan, and a few other families. The power structure now isn't in the hands of the old elite. If you don't believe that, notice what's going on at city hall. Chief Grier is making a record number of drug busts and I don't need to remind you that Senator Merrill was arrested for drunk driving."

"That never was in the paper, you know," she said with a wry smile.

"The publisher is one of his cronies—he refused to run the story. But Merrill's up to his ears in legal trouble. So he's trying to get the mayor and two councilmen who owe him favors to fire the two police officers who made the arrest and discredit them. The primary election is the first week of May, you know."

"Poor police," she murmured.

"Mark my words, they'll never lose their jobs. Grier has contacts everywhere and despite his personal problems, he's not going to let his officers go down without a fight. I'd bet everything I have on him."

She grinned. "I like him."

Curt chuckled. "I like him, too."

"Mr. Kemp said they traced the lawyer's call to San Antonio," she added, and told him what was said. "Why would she want us out of the house?"

"Maybe she thinks there's something in it that she hasn't gotten yet," he mused. "Dad's coin collection, for instance."

"I haven't seen that in months," she said.

"Neither have I. She probably sold it already," he said with cold disgust. "But Janet's going to hang herself before she quits." He gave his sister a sad look. "I'm sorry about the exhumation. But we really need to know the truth about how Dad died."

"I know," she replied. The pain was still fresh and she had to fight tears. She managed a smile for him. "Daddy wouldn't mind."

"No. I don't think he would."

"I wish we'd paid more attention to what was going on."

"He thought he loved her, Libby," he said. "Maybe he did. He wouldn't have listened to us, no matter what we said, if it was something bad about her. You know how he was."

"Loving her blindly may have cost him his life."

"Try to remember that he died happy. He didn't know what Janet was. He didn't know that she was cheating him."

"It doesn't help much."

He nodded. "Nothing will bring him back. But

maybe we can save somebody else's father. That would make it all worthwhile."

"Yes," she agreed. "It would."

THAT EVENING WHILE they were watching television, a truck drove up. A minute later, there was a hard knock on the door.

"I've got it," Curt said, leaving Libby with her embroidery.

There were muffled voices and then heavy footsteps coming into the room.

Jordan stared at Libby curiously. "Julie came to your office today," he said.

"She was looking for a job for her friend Lydia," Libby said in a matter-of-fact tone.

"That's not what she said," Jordan replied tersely. "She told me that you treated her so rudely that Kemp made her leave the office."

Libby lifted both eyebrows. "Wow. Imagine that."

"I'm not joking with you, Libby," Jordan said, and his tone chilled. "That was a petty thing to do."

"It would have been," she agreed, growing angry herself, "if I'd done it. She came into the office in a temper, glared at me, made some rude remarks to Mr. Kemp and got herself thrown out."

"That's not what she told me," he repeated.

Libby got to her feet, motioning to Curt, who was about to protest on her behalf. "I don't need help, Curt. Stay out of it, that's a nice brother." She moved closer to Jordan. "Miss Merrill insinuated that Mr. Kemp had better offer Lydia a job because of her father's position in the community. And he reminded her about her high-school graduation party where a girl died."

"He what?" he exploded.

"Mr. Kemp doesn't take threats lying down," she said, uneasy because of Jordan's overt hostility. "Miss Merrill was very haughty and very rude. And neither of us can understand why she'd try to get Lydia a job at Kemp's office, because she's already got one in San Antonio!"

Jordan didn't say anything. He just stood there, silent.

"She was with you when I phoned your house, I guess, and she got the idea that I was chasing you," she said, gratified by the sudden blinking of his eyelids. "You can tell her, for me," she added with saccharine sweetness, "that I would not have you on a hot dog bun with uptown relish. If she thinks I'm the competition, all she has to do is look where I live." Her face tautened. "Go ahead, Jordan, look around you. I'm not even in your league, whatever your high-class girlfriend thinks. You're a kind neighbor whom I asked for advice and that's all you ever were. Period," she lied, trying to save face.

He still wasn't moving or speaking. But his eyes were taking on a nasty glitter. Beside his lean hips, one of his hands was clenched until the knuckles went white. "Ever?" he prodded, his tone insinuating things.

She knew what he meant. She swallowed hard, trying not to remember the heat and power of the kisses they'd shared. Obviously, they'd meant nothing to him!

"Ever," she repeated. "I certainly wasn't trying to tie you down, Jordan. I'm not at all sure that I want to spend the rest of my life in Jacobsville working for a lawyer, anyway," she added deliberately, but without looking at him. "I've thought about that a lot, about what you said. Maybe I do have ambitions."

He didn't speak for several seconds. His eyes became narrow and cold.

"If you'd like to show your Julie that I'm no competition, you can bring her down here and show her how we live," she offered with a smile. "That would really open her eyes, wouldn't it?"

"Libby," Curt warned. "Don't talk like that."

"How should I talk?" she demanded, her throat tightening. "Our father is dead and it looks like our stepmother killed him right under our noses! She's trying to take away everything we have, getting her friends to call and threaten and harass us, and now here's Jordan's Goody-two-shoes girlfriend making me out to be a man-stealer, or somebody. How the hell should I talk?"

Jordan let out a long breath. "I thought you knew what you wanted," he said after a minute.

"I'm young. Like you said," she said cynically. "Sorry I ever asked you for help, Jordan, and made your girlfriend mad. You can bet I'll never make that mistake twice."

She turned and went into the kitchen and slammed the door behind her. She was learning really bad habits from Mr. Kemp, she decided, as she wiped tears away with a paper towel.

She heard the door open behind her and close again, firmly. It was Curt, she supposed, coming to check on her.

"I guess I handled that badly," she said, choking on tears. "Has he gone?"

Big, warm hands caught her shoulders and turned

her around. Jordan's eyes glittered down into hers. "No, he hasn't gone," he bit off.

He looked ferocious like that. She should have been intimidated, but she wasn't. He was handsome, even bristling with temper.

"I've said all I have to say," she began.

"Well, I haven't," he shot back, goaded. "I've never looked down on you for what you've got and you know it."

"Julie Merrill does," she muttered.

His hands tightened and relaxed. He looked vaguely embarrassed. His dark eyes slid past her to the worn calendar on the wall. "You know how I grew up," he said heavily. "We had nothing. I was never invited to parties. My parents were glorified servants in the eyes of the town's social set."

She drew in a short breath. "And now Julie's opening the doors and inviting you in and you like it."

He seemed shocked by the statement. His eyes dropped to meet hers. "Maybe."

"Can't you see why?" she asked quietly. "You're rich now. You made something out of nothing. You have confidence, and power, and you know how to behave in company. But there's more to it than that, where the Merrills are concerned."

"That's not your business," he said shortly.

She smiled sadly. "They need financial backing. Their old friends aren't as wealthy as they used to be. Calhoun Ballenger has the support of the newer wealthy people in Jacobsville and they don't deal in 'good old boy' politics."

"In other words, Julie only wants me for money to run her father's reelection campaign."

"You know better than that," she replied, searching his hard face hungrily. "You're handsome and sexy. Women adore you."

One eyebrow lifted. "Even you?"

She wanted to deny it, but she couldn't. "Even me," she confessed. "But I'm no more in your class, really, than you're in Julie's. They're old money. It doesn't really matter to them how rich you get, you'll never be one of them."

His eyes narrowed angrily. "I am one of them," he retorted. "I'm hobnobbing with New York society, with Kentucky Thoroughbred breeders, with presidential staff members—even with Hollywood producers and actors!"

"You could do that on your own," she said. "You don't need the Merrills to make you socially acceptable. And in case you've forgotten, Christabel and Judd Dunn have been hobnobbing with Hollywood people for a year. They're not rich. Not really."

He was losing the argument and he didn't like it. He glared down at her with more riotous feelings than he'd entertained in years. "Julie wants to marry me," he said, producing the flat statement like a weapon.

She managed not to react to the retort, barely. Her heart was sinking like lead in her chest as she pictured Julie in a designer wedding gown flashing diamonds like pennies on her way to the altar.

"She doesn't want a career," he added, smiling coldly.

Neither did Libby, really. She liked having a job, but she also liked living in Jacobsville and working around the ranch. She'd have liked being Jordan's wife more than anything else she could think of. But that wasn't going to happen. He didn't want her.

She tried to pull away from Jordan's strong hands, but he wasn't budging.

"Let me go," she muttered. "I'm sure Julie wouldn't like this!"

"Wouldn't like what?" he drawled. "Being in my arms, or having you in them?"

"Are you having fun?" she challenged.

"Not yet," he murmured, dropping his gaze to her full lips. "But I expect to be pretty soon…"

"You can't…!"

But he could. And he was. She felt the warm, soft, coaxing pressure of his hard mouth before she could finish the protest. Her eyes closed. She was aware of his size and strength, of the warmth of his powerful body against hers. She could feel his heartbeat, feel the rough sigh of his breath as he deepened the kiss.

He hadn't really meant to do this. But when he had her so close that he could feel her heart beating like a wild thing against him, nothing else seemed to matter except pleasing her, as she was pleasing him.

He drew her up closer, so that he could feel the soft, warm imprint of her body on the length of his. He traced her soft mouth with his lips, with the tip of his tongue. He felt her stiffen and then lift up to him. He gathered her completely against him and forgot Julie, forgot the argument, forgot everything.

She felt the sudden ardor of his embrace grow unmanageable in a space of seconds. His mouth was insistent on hers, demanding. His hands had gone to her hips. They were pressing her against the sudden rigidity of his powerful body. Even as she registered his urgent hunger for her, she felt one of his big, lean hands seeking between them for the soft, rounded curve of her breast...

She pulled away from him abruptly, her mouth swollen, her eyes wild. "N-no," she choked.

He tried to pull her back into his arms. "Why not?" he murmured, his eyes on her mouth.

"Curt," she whispered.

"Curt." He spoke the name as if he didn't recognize it. He blinked. He took a deep breath and suddenly realized where they were and what he'd been doing.

He drew in a harsh, deep breath.

"You have to go home," she said huskily.

He stood up straight and stared down his nose at her. "If you keep throwing yourself into my arms, what do you expect?" he asked outrageously.

She gaped at him.

"It's no use trying to look innocent," he added as he moved back another step. "And don't start taking off your blouse, it won't work."

"I am not...!" she choked, crossing her arms quickly.

He made a rough sound in his throat. "A likely story. Don't follow me home, either, because I lock my doors at night."

She wanted to react to that teasing banter that she'd enjoyed so much before, but she couldn't forget that he'd taken Julie's side against her.

She stared at him coldly. "I won't follow you home. Not while you're spending all your free time defending Julie Merrill, when I'm the one who was insulted."

He froze over. "The way Julie tells it, you started on her first."

"And you believe her, of course. She's beautiful and rich and sophisticated."

"Something no man in his right mind could accuse you of," he shot back. With a cold glare, he turned and went out the door.

He didn't pause to speak to Curt, who was just coming in the front door. He shot him a look bare of courtesy and stormed outside. He was boiling over with emotion, the strongest of which was frustrated desire.

LIBBY DIDN'T EXPLAIN anything to her brother, but she knew he wasn't blind or stupid. He didn't ask questions, either. He just hugged her and smiled.

She went to bed feeling totally at sea. How could an argument lead to something so tempestuous that she'd almost passed out at Jordan's feet? And if he really wanted Julie, then how could he kiss Libby with such frustrated desire? And why had he started another fight before he left?

She was still trying to figure out why she hadn't slapped his arrogant face when she fell asleep.

THE TENSION BETWEEN Jordan and his neighbors was suddenly visible even to onlookers. He never set foot on their place. When he had a barbecue for his ranch hands in April, to celebrate the impressive calf sale he'd held, Curt wasn't invited. When Libby had a small birthday party to mark her twenty-fourth birthday, Jordan wasn't on the guest list. Jacobsville being the small town it was, people noticed.

"Have you and Jordan had some sort of falling out?" Mr. Kemp asked while his new secretary, a sweet little brunette fresh out of high school named Jessie, was out to lunch.

Libby looked up at him with wide-eyed innocence. "Falling out?"

"Julie Merrill has been telling people that she and Jordan have marriage plans," he said. "I don't believe it. Her father's in financial hot water and Jordan's rich. Old man Merrill is going to need a lot of support in today's political climate. He made some bad calls on the budget and education and the voters are out to get him."

"So I've heard. They say Calhoun Ballenger's just pulled ahead in the polls."

"He'll win," Kemp replied. "It's no contest. Regardless of Jordan's backing."

"Mr. Kemp, would they really use what happened at Julie's party as a weapon against her father?" she asked carefully.

"Of course they would!" he said shortly. "Even in Jacobs County, dirty laundry has a value. There are other skeletons in that closet, too. Plenty of them. Merrill has already lost the election. His way of doing business, under the table, is obsolete. He's trying to make Cash Grier fire those arresting officers and swear they lied. It won't happen. He and his daughter just don't know it and she refuses to face defeat."

"She's at Jordan's house every day now," she said on a sigh that was more wistful than she knew. "She's very beautiful."

"She's a tarantula," Kemp said coldly. "She's got her finger in a pie I can't tell you about, but it's about to hit the tabloids. When it does, her father can kiss his career goodbye."

"Sir?"

He lifted both eyebrows. "Can you keep a secret?"

"If I can't, why am I working for you?" she asked pertly.

"Those two officers Grier's backing, who caught the senator driving drunk—" he said. "They've also been investigating a house out on the Victoria road where drugs are bought and sold. That's the real reason they're facing dismissal. Merrill's nephew is our mayor."

"And he's in it up to his neck, I guess?" she fished.

He nodded. "The nephew and Miss Merrill herself. That's where her new Porsche came from."

Libby whistled. "But if Jordan's connected with her..." she said worriedly.

"That's right," he replied. "He'll be right in hot water with her, even though he's not doing anything illegal. Mud not only sticks, it rubs off."

She chewed her lower lip. "You couldn't warn him, I guess?"

He shook his head. "We aren't speaking."

She stared at him. "But you're friends."

"Not anymore. You see, he thinks I took your side unjustly against Miss Merrill."

She frowned. "I'm sorry."

He chuckled. "It will all blow over in a few weeks. You'll see."

She wasn't so confident. She didn't think it would and she hated the thought of seeing Jordan connected with such an unsavory business.

SHE WALKED DOWN to Barbara's Café for lunch and ran right into Julie Merrill and Jordan Powell, who were waiting in line together.

"Oh, look, it's the little secretary," Julie drawled

when she saw Libby in line behind them. "Still telling lies about me, Miss Collins?" she asked with a laugh.

Jordan was looking at Libby with an expression that was hard to classify.

Libby ignored her, turning instead to speak to one of the girls from the county clerk's office, who was in line behind her.

"Don't you turn your back on me, you little creep!" Julie raged, attracting attention as she walked right up to Libby. Her eyes were glazed, furious. "You told Jordan that I tried to throw my weight around in Kemp's office and it was a lie! You were just trying to make yourself look good, weren't you?"

Libby felt sick at her stomach. She was no good at dealing with angry people, despite the fact that she had to watch Kemp's secretaries do it every day. She wasn't really afraid of the other girl, but she was keenly aware of their differences on the social ladder. Julie was rich and well-known and sophisticated. Libby was little more than a rancher's daughter turned legal apprentice.

"Jordan can't stand you, in case you wondered, so it's no use calling him up all the time for help, and standing at his door trying to make him notice you!" Julie continued haughtily. "He wouldn't demean himself by going out with a dirty little nobody like you!"

Libby pulled herself up and stared at the older girl, keenly aware of curious eyes watching and people listening in the crowded lunch traffic. "Jordan is our neighbor, Miss Merrill," she said in a strained tone. Her legs were shaking, but she didn't let it show. "Nothing more. I don't want Jordan."

"Good. I'm glad you realize that Jordan's nothing

more than a neighbor, because you're a nuisance! No man in his right mind would look at you twice!"

"Oh, I don't know about that," Harley Fowler said suddenly, moving up the line to look down at Julie Merrill with cold eyes. "I'd say her manners are a damned sight better than yours and your mouth wouldn't get you into any decent man's house in Jacobsville!"

Julie's mouth fell open.

"I wouldn't have her on toast!" one of the Tremaynes' cowboys ventured from his table.

"Hey, Julie, how about a dime bag?" some anonymous voice called. "I need a fix!"

Julie went pale. "Who said that?" she demanded shakily.

"Julie, let's go," Jordan said curtly, taking her by the arm.

"I'm hungry!" she protested, fighting his hold.

Libby didn't look up as he passed her with Julie firmly at his side. He didn't look at her, either, and his face was white with rage.

As she went out the door, there was a skirl of belligerent applause from the patrons of the café. Julie made a rude gesture toward them, which was followed by equally rude laughter.

"Isn't she a pain?" The girl from the clerk's office laughed. "Honestly, Libby, you were such a lady! I'd have laid a chair across her thick skull!"

"Me, too," said another girl. "Nobody can stand her. She thinks she's such a debutante."

Libby listened to the talk with a raging heartbeat. She was sick to her stomach from the unexpected confrontation and glad that Jordan had gotten the girl out of the room before things got ugly. But it ruined her lunch. It ruined her whole day.

IT DIDN'T OCCUR to Libby that Jordan would be upset about the things that Julie had said in the café, especially since he hadn't said a word to Libby at the time. But he actually came by Kemp's office the next day, hat in hand, to apologize for Julie's behavior.

He looked disappointed when Kemp was sitting perched on the edge of Libby's desk, as if he'd hoped to find her alone. But he recovered quickly.

He gave Kemp a quick glare, his gaze returning at once to Libby. "I wanted to apologize for Julie," he said curtly. "She's sorry she caused a scene yesterday. She's been upset about her father facing drunk-driving charges."

"I don't receive absentee apologies," Libby said coldly. "And you'll never convince me that she would apologize."

Kemp's eyebrows collided. "What's that?"

"Julie made some harsh remarks about me in Barbara's Café yesterday," Libby told him, "in front of half the town."

"Why didn't you come and get me?" Kemp asked. "I'd have settled her hash for her," he added, with a dangerous look at Jordan.

"Harley Fowler defended me," Libby said with a quiet smile. "So did several other gentlemen in the crowd," she added deliberately.

"She's not as bad as you think she is," Jordan said grimly.

"The hell she's not," Kemp replied softly. He got up. "I know things about her that you're going to wish you did and very soon. Libby, don't be long. We've got a case first thing tomorrow. I'll need those notes," he added, nodding toward the computer screen. He went to his office and closed the door.

"What was Kemp talking about?" Jordan asked Libby curiously.

"I could tell you, but you wouldn't believe me," she said sadly, remembering how warm their relationship had been before Julie Merrill clouded the horizon.

He drew in a long breath and moved a little closer, pushing his hat back over his dark hair. He looked down at her with barely contained hunger. Mabel was busy in the back with the photocopier and the girl who was filling in for Violet had gone to a dental appointment. Mr. Kemp was shut up in his office. Libby kept hoping the phone would ring, or someone would come in the front door and save her from Jordan. It was all she could do not to throw herself into his arms, even after the fights they'd had. She couldn't stop being attracted to him.

"Look," he said quietly, "I'm not trying to make an enemy of you. I like Julie. Her father is a good man and he's had some hard knocks lately. They really need my help, Libby. They haven't got anybody else."

She could just imagine Julie crying prettily, lavishing praise on Jordan for being so useful, dressing up in her best—which was considerably better than Libby's best—and making a play for him. She might be snippy and aggressive toward other women, but Julie Merrill was a practiced seducer. She knew how to wind men around her finger. She was young and beautiful and cultured and rich. She knew tricks that most men—even Jordan—wouldn't be able to resist.

"Why are you so attracted to her?" Libby wondered aloud.

Jordan gave her an enigmatic look. "She's mature," he said without thinking. "She knows exactly what she wants and she goes after it wholeheartedly. Besides that, she's a woman who could have anybody."

"And she wants you," she said for him.

He shrugged. "Yes. She does."

She studied his lean, hard face, surprising a curious rigidity there before he concealed it. "I suppose you're flattered," she murmured.

"She draws every man's eye when she walks into a room," he said slowly. "She can play the piano like a professional. She speaks three languages. She's been around the world several times. She's dated some of the most famous actors in Hollywood. She's even been presented to the queen in England." He sighed. "Most men would have a hard time turning up their noses at a woman like that."

"In other words, she's like a trophy."

He studied her arrogantly. "You could say that. But there's something more, too. She needs me. She said everyone in town had turned their backs on her father. Calhoun Ballenger is drawing financial support from some of the richest families in town, the same people who promised Senator Merrill their support and then withdrew it. Julie was in tears when she told me how he'd been sold out by his best friends. Until I came along, he actually considered dropping out of the race."

And pigs fly, Libby thought privately, but she didn't say it. The Merrills were dangling their celebrity in front of Jordan, a man who'd been shut out of high society even though he was now filthy rich. They were

offering him entry into a closed community. All that
and beautiful Julie, as well.

"Did you hear what she said to me in Barbara's
Café?" she wondered aloud.

"What do you mean?" he asked curiously.

"You stood there and let her attack me, without saying a word."

He scowled. "I was talking to Brad Henry while we
stood in line, about a bull he wanted to sell. I didn't realize what was going on until Julie raised her voice. By
then, Harley Fowler and several other men were making catcalls at her. I thought the best thing to do would
be to get her outside before things escalated."

"Did you hear her accuse me of chasing you? Did
you hear her warn me off you?"

He cocked his head. "I heard that part," he admitted.
"She's very possessive and more jealous of me than I
realized. But I didn't like having her insult you, if that's
what you mean," he said quietly. "I told her so later. She
said she'd apologize, but I thought it might come easier
from me. She's insecure, Libby. You wouldn't think so,
but she really takes things to heart."

A revelation a minute, Libby was thinking. Jordan
actually believed what he was saying. Julie had really
done a job on him.

"She said that you wouldn't waste your time on a
nobody like me," she persisted.

"Women say things they don't mean all the time." He
shrugged it off. "You take things to heart, too, Libby,"
he added gently. "You're still very young."

"You keep saying that," she replied, exasperated.
"How old do I have to be for you to think of me as an
adult?"

He moved closer, one lean hand going to her slender throat, slowly caressing it. "I've thought of you like that for a long time," he said deeply. "But you're an addiction I can't afford. You said it yourself—you're ambitious. You won't be satisfied in a small town. Like the old-timers used to say, you want to go and see the elephant."

She was caught in his dark eyes, spellbound. She'd said that, yes, because of the way he'd behaved about Julie's insults. She'd wanted to sting him. But she didn't mean it. She wasn't ambitious. All she wanted was Jordan. Her eyes were lost in his.

"The elephant?" she parroted, her gaze on his hard mouth.

"You want to see the world," he translated. But he was moving closer as he said it and his head was bending, even against his will. This was stupid. He couldn't afford to let himself be drawn into this sweet trap. Libby wanted a career. She was young and ambitious. He'd go in headfirst and she'd take off and leave him, just as Duke Wright's young wife had left him in search of fame and fortune. He'd deliberately drawn back from Libby and let himself be vamped by Julie Merrill, to show this little firecracker that he hadn't been serious about those kisses they'd exchanged. He wasn't going to risk his heart on a gamble this big. Libby was in love with love. She was attracted to him. But that wasn't love. She was too young to know the difference. He wasn't. He'd grabbed at Julie the way a drowning man reaches for a life jacket. Libby didn't know that. He couldn't admit it.

While he was thinking, he was parting her lips with his. He forgot where they were, who they were. He forgot the arguments and all the reasons he shouldn't do this.

"Libby," he growled against her soft lips.

She barely heard him. Her blood was singing in her veins like a throbbing chorus. Her arms went around his neck in a stranglehold. She pushed up against him, forcing into his mouth in urgency.

His arms swallowed her up whole. The kiss was slow, deep, hungry. It was invasive. Her whole body began to throb with delight. It began to swell. Their earlier kisses had been almost chaste. These were erotic. They were…narcotic.

A soft little cry of pleasure went from her mouth into his and managed to penetrate the fog of desire she was drowning him in.

He jerked back from her as if he'd been stung. He fought to keep his inner turmoil from showing, his weakness from being visible to her. His big hands caught her waist and pushed her firmly away.

"I know," she said breathlessly. "You think I've had snakebite on my lip and you were only trying to draw out the poison."

He burst out laughing in spite of himself.

She swallowed hard and backed away another step. "Just think how Julie Merrill would react if she saw you kissing me."

That wiped the smile off his face. "That wasn't a kiss," he said.

"No kidding?" She touched her swollen mouth ironically. "I'll bet Julie could even give you lessons."

"Don't talk about her like that," he warned.

"You think she's honest and forthright, because you are," she said, a little breathless. "You're forgetting that her father is a career politician. They both know how to bend the truth without breaking it, how to influence public opinion."

"Politics is a science," he retorted.

"It can be a horrible corruption, as well," she reminded him. "Calhoun Ballenger has taken a lot of heat from them, even a sexual harassment charge that had no basis in fact. Fortunately, people around here know better, and it backfired. It only made Senator Merrill look bad."

His eyes began to glitter. "That wasn't fiction. The woman swore it happened."

"She was one of Julie's cousins," she said with disgust.

He looked as if he hadn't known that. He scowled, but he didn't answer her.

"Julie thinks my brother and I are so far beneath her that we aren't even worth mentioning," she continued, folding her arms over her chest. "She chooses her friends by their social status and bank accounts. Curt and I are losers in her book and she doesn't think we're fit to associate with you. She'll find a way to push you right out of our lives."

"I don't have social status, but I'm welcome in their home," he said flatly.

"There's an election coming up, they don't have enough money to win it, but you do. They'll take your money and make you feel like an equal until you're not needed anymore. Then you'll be out on your ear. You don't come from old money, Jordan, even if you're rich now…"

"You don't know a damned thing about what I come from," he snapped.

The furious statement caught her off guard. She

knew Jordan had made his own fortune, but he never spoke about his childhood. His mother worked as a housekeeper. Everybody knew it. He sounded as if he couldn't bear to admit his people were only laborers.

"I didn't mean to be insulting," she began slowly.

"Hell! You're doing your best to turn me against Julie. She said you would," he added. "She said something else, too—that you're involved with Harley Fowler."

She refused to react to that. "Harley's sweet. He defended me when Julie was insulting me."

That was a sore spot, because Jordan hadn't really heard what Julie was saying until it was too late. He didn't like Harley, anyway.

"Harley's a nobody."

"Just like me," she retorted. "I'd much rather have Harley than you, Jordan," she added. "He may be just a working stiff, but he's got more class than you'll ever have, even if you hang out with the Merrills for the next fifty years!"

That did it. He gave her a furious glare, spit out a word that would have insulted Satan himself and marched right out the door.

"And stay out!" she called after it slammed.

Kemp stuck his head out of his office door and stared at her. "Are you that same shy, introverted girl who came to work here last year?"

She grinned at him through her heartbreak. "You're rubbing off on me, Mr. Kemp," she remarked.

He laughed curtly and went back into his office.

LATER, LIBBY WAS MISERABLE. They'd exhumed her father's body and taken it up to the state crime lab in Austin for tests.

Curt was furious when she told him that Jordan had been to her office to apologize for the Merrill girl.

"As if she'd ever apologize to the likes of us," he said angrily. "And Jordan just stood by and let her insult you in the café without saying a word!"

She gaped at him. "How did you know that?"

"Harley Fowler came by where I was working this morning to tell me about it. He figured, rightly, that you'd try to keep it to yourself." He sank down into a chair. "I gave Jordan notice this afternoon. In two weeks, I'm out of there."

She grimaced. "But, Curt, where will you go?"

"Right over to Duke Wright's place," he replied with a smile. "I already lined up a job and I'll get a raise, to boot."

"That's great," she said, and meant it.

"We'll be fine. Don't worry about it." He sighed. "It's so much lately, isn't it, sis? But we'll survive. We will!"

"I know that, Curt. I'm not worried."

BUT SHE WAS. She hated being enemies with Jordan, who was basically a kind and generous man. She was furious with the Merrills for coming between them for such a selfish reason. They only wanted Jordan's money for the old man's reelection campaign. They didn't care about Jordan. But perhaps he was flattered to be included in such high society, to be asked to hang out with their friends and acquaintances.

But Libby knew something about the people the Merrills associated with that, perhaps, Jordan didn't. Many of them were addicts, either to liquor or drugs. They did nothing for the community; only for themselves. They wanted to know the right people, be seen in the right places, have money that showed when people looked. But to Libby, who loved her little house and little ranch, it seemed terribly artificial.

She didn't have much but she was happy with her life. She enjoyed planting things and watching them grow. She liked teaching Vacation Bible School in the summer and working in the church nursery with little children. She liked cooking food to carry to bereaved families when relatives died. She liked helping out with church bazaars, donating time to the local soup kitchen. She didn't put on airs, but people seemed to like her just the way she was.

Certainly Harley Fowler did. He'd come over to see her the day after Julie's attack in the café, to make sure she was all right. He'd asked her out to eat the following Saturday night.

"Only to Shea's," he chuckled. "I just paid off a new transmission for my truck and I'm broke."

She'd grinned at him. "That's okay. I'm broke, too!"

He shook his head, his eyes sparkling as he looked down at her with appreciation. "Libby, you're my kind of people."

"Thanks, Harley."

"Say, can you dance?"

She blinked. "Well, I can do a two-step."

"That's good enough." He chuckled. "I've been taking these dance courses on the side."

"I know. I heard about the famous waltz with Janie Brewster at the Cattleman's Ball last year."

He smiled sheepishly. "Well, now I'm working on the jitterbug and I hear that Shea's live band can play that sort of thing."

"You can teach me to jitterbug, Harley," she agreed at once. "I'd love to go dancing with you."

He looked odd. "Really?"

She nodded and smiled. "Really."

"Then I'll see you Saturday about six. We can eat there, too."

"Suits me. I'll leave supper for Curt in the refrigerator. That was really nice of you to go to bat for him with your boss, Harley," she added seriously. "Thanks."

He shrugged. "Mr. Parks wasn't too pleased with the way Powell's sucking up to the Merrills, either," he said. "He knows things about them."

"So do I," she replied. "But Jordan doesn't take wellmeant advice."

"His problem," Harley said sharply.

She nodded. "Yes, Harley. It's his problem. I'll see you Saturday!" she added, laughing.

When she told Curt about the upcoming date, he seemed pleased. "It's about time you went out and had some fun for a change."

"I like Harley a lot," she told her brother.

He searched her eyes knowingly. "But he's not Jordan."

She turned away. "Jordan made his choice. I'm making mine." She smiled philosophically. "I dare say we'll both be happy!"

CHAPTER SIX

LIBBY AND HARLEY raised eyebrows at Shea's Roadhouse and Bar with their impromptu rendition of the jitterbug. It was a full house, too, on a Saturday night. At least two of the Tremayne brothers were there with their wives, and Calhoun Ballenger and his wife, Abby, were sitting at a table nearby with Leo Hart and his wife, Janie.

"I'm absolutely sure that Calhoun's going to win the state senate seat," Harley said in Libby's ear when they were seated again, drinking iced tea and eating hamburgers. "It looks like he's going to get some support from the Harts."

"Is Mr. Parks in his corner, too?" she asked.

He nodded. "All the way. The political landscape has been changing steadily for the past few years, but old man Merrill just keeps going with his old agenda. He hasn't got a clue what the voters want anymore. And, more important, he doesn't control them through his powerful friends."

"You'd think his daughter would be forward thinking," she pointed out.

He didn't say anything. But his face was eloquent.

"Somebody said she was thinking of running for public office in Jacobsville," she began.

"No name identification," Harley said at once. "You

have to have it to win an office. Without it, all the money in the world won't get you elected."

"You seem to know something about politics," she commented.

He averted his eyes. "Do I?" he mused.

Harley never talked about his family, or his past. He'd shown up at Cy Parks's place one day and proved himself to be an exceptional cowboy, but nobody knew much about him. He'd gone on a gigantic drug bust with Jacobsville's ex-mercenaries and he had a reputation for being a tough customer. But he was as mysterious in his way as the town's police chief, Cash Grier.

"Wouldn't you just know they'd show up and spoil everything?" Harley said suddenly, glaring toward the door.

Sure enough, there was Jordan Powell in an expensive Western-cut sports coat and Stetson and boots, escorting pretty Julie Merrill in a blue silk dress that looked simple and probably cost the earth.

"Doesn't she look expensive?" Harley mused.

"She probably is," Libby said, trying not to look and sound as hurt as she really was. It killed her to see Jordan there with that terrible woman.

"She's going to find out, pretty soon, that she's the equivalent of three-day-old fish with this crowd," Harley predicted coolly, watching her stick her nose up at the Ballengers as she passed them.

"I just hope she doesn't drag Jordan down with her," Libby said softly. "He started out like us, Harley," she added. "He was just a working cowboy with ambition."

Jordan seated Julie and shot a cool glance in Harley and Libby's direction, without even acknowledging them. He sat down, placing his Stetson on a vacant chair and motioned a waiter.

"Did you want something stronger to drink?" Harley asked her.

She grinned at him. "I don't have a head for liquor, Harley. I'd rather stick to iced tea, if you don't mind."

"So would I," he confided, motioning for a waiter.

The waiter, with a fine sense of irony, walked right past Jordan to take Harley's order. Julie Merrill was sputtering like a stepped-on garden hose.

"Two more iced teas, Charlie," Harley told the waiter. "And thanks for giving us preference."

"Oh, I know who the best people are, Harley," the boy said with a wicked grin. And he walked right past Jordan and Julie again, without even looking at them. A minute later, Jordan got up and stalked over to the counter to order their drinks.

"He'll smolder for the rest of the night over that," Harley mused. "So will she, unless I miss my guess. Isn't it amazing," he added thoughtfully, "that a man with as much sense as Jordan Powell can't see right through that debutante?"

"How is it that you can?" Libby asked him curiously.

He shrugged. "I know politicians all too well," he said, and for a moment, his expression was distant. "Old man Merrill has been hitting the bottle pretty hard lately," he said. "It isn't going to sit well with his constituents that he got pulled over and charged with drunk driving by Jacobsville's finest."

"Do you think they'll convict him?" she wondered aloud.

"You can bet money on it," Harley replied. "The world has shifted ten degrees. Local politicians don't meet in parked cars and make policy anymore. The sun-shine laws mean that the media get wind of anything crooked and they report it. Senator Merrill has been living in the past. He's going to get a hell of a wake-up call at the primary election, when Calhoun Ballenger knocks him off the Democratic ballot as a contender."

"Mr. Ballenger looks like a gentleman," Libby commented, noticing the closeness of Calhoun and his brunette wife, Abby. "He and his wife have been married a long time, haven't they?"

"Years," Harley said. "He and Justin are honest and hardworking men. They came up from nothing, too, although Justin's wife, Shelby, was a Jacobs before she married him," he reminded her. "A direct descendant of Big John Jacobs. But don't you think either of the Ballenger brothers would have been taken in by Julie Merrill, even when they were still single."

She paused to thank the waiter, who brought their two glasses of tall, cold iced tea. Jordan was still waiting for his order at the counter, while Julie glared at Libby and Harley.

"She's not quite normal, is she?" Libby said quietly. "I mean, that outburst in Barbara's Café was so… violent."

"People on drugs usually are violent," Harley replied. "And irrational." He looked right into Libby's eyes. "She's involved in some pretty nasty stuff, Libby. I can't tell you what I know, but Jordan is damaging himself just by being seen in public with her. The campaigns will get hot and heavy later this month and some dirty linen is about to be exposed to God and the general public."

Libby was concerned. "Jordan's a good man," she

said quietly, her eyes going like homing pigeons to his lean, handsome face.

He caught her looking at him and glared. Julie, seeing his attention diverted, looked, too.

Once he returned to the table Julie leaned over and whispered something to Jordan that made him give Libby a killing glare before he started ignoring her completely.

"Watch your back," Harley told Libby as he sipped his iced tea. "She considers you a danger to her plans with Jordan. She'll sell you down the river if she can."

She sighed miserably. "First my stepmother, now Julie," she murmured. "I feel like I've got a target painted on my forehead."

"We all have bad times," Harley told her gently, and slid a big hand over one of hers where it lay on the table. "We get through them."

"You, too?" she wondered aloud.

"Yeah. Me, too," he replied, and he smiled at her.

Neither of them saw the furious look on Jordan Powell's face, or the calculating look on Julie's.

THE FOLLOWING WEEK, when Libby went to Barbara's Café for lunch, she walked right into Jordan Powell on the sidewalk. He was alone, as she was, and his expression made her feel cold all over.

"What's this about you going up to San Antonio for the night with Harley last Wednesday?" he asked bluntly.

Libby couldn't even formulate a reply for the shock. She'd driven Curt over to Duke Wright's place early Wednesday afternoon and from there she'd driven up to San Antonio to obtain some legal documents from the county clerk's office for Mr. Kemp. She hadn't even seen Harley there.

"I thought you were pure as the driven snow," Jordan continued icily. His dark eyes narrowed on her shocked face. "You put on a good act, don't you, Libby? I don't need to be a mind reader to know why, either. I'm rich and you and your brother are about to lose your ranch."

"Janet hasn't started probate yet," she faltered.

"That's not what I hear."

"I don't care what you hear," she told him flatly. "Neither Curt nor I care very much what you think, either, Jordan. But you're going to run into serious problems if you hang out with Julie Merrill until her father loses the election."

He glared down at her. "He isn't going to lose," he assured her.

She hated seeing him be so stubborn, especially when she had at least some idea of what Julie was going to drag him down into. She moved a step closer, her green eyes soft and beseeching. "Jordan, you're an intelligent man," she began slowly. "Surely you can see what Julie wants you for..."

A worldly look narrowed his eyes as they searched over her figure without any reaction at all. "Julie wants me, all right," he replied, coolly. "That's what's driving you to make these wild comments, isn't it? You're jealous because I'm spending so much time with her."

She didn't dare let on what she was feeling. She forced a careless smile. "Am I? You think I don't know when a man is teasing me?"

"You know more than I ever gave you credit for and that's the truth," he said flatly. "You and Harley Fowler." He made it sound like an insult.

"Harley is a fine man," she said, defending him.

"Obviously you think so, or you wouldn't be shacking up with him," he accused. "Does your brother know?"

"I'm a big girl now," she said, furious at the insinuation.

"Both of you had better remember that I make a bad enemy," he told her. "Whatever happens with your ranch, I don't want to have a subdivision full of people on my border."

He didn't know that Libby and Curt had already discussed how they were going to manage without their father's life insurance policy to pay the mortgage payments that were still owed. Riddle had taken out a mortgage on the ranch to buy Janet's Mercedes. Janet had waltzed off with the money and the private detective Jordan had recommended to Mr. Kemp had drawn a blank when he tried to dig into Janet's past. The will hadn't been probated, either, so there was no way Riddle Collins's children could claim any of their inheritance with which to pay bills or make that huge mortgage payment. They'd had to let their only helper—their part-time cowboy—go, for lack of funds to pay him. They only had one horse left and they'd had to sell off most of their cattle. The only money coming in right now was what Curt and Libby earned in their respective jobs, and it wasn't much.

Of course, Libby wasn't going to share that information with a hostile Jordan Powell. Things were so bad that she and Curt might have to move off the ranch anyway because they couldn't make that mortgage payment at the end of the month. It was over eight hundred dollars. Their collective take-home pay wouldn't amount to that much and there were still other bills owing. Janet had run up huge bills while Riddle was still alive.

Jordan felt sick at what he was saying to Libby. He was jealous of Harley Fowler, furiously jealous. He couldn't bear the thought of Libby in bed with the other man. She wasn't even denying what Julie had assured him had happened between them. Libby, in Harley's arms, kissing him with such hunger that his toes tingled. Libby, loving Harley...

Jordan ached to have her for himself. He dreamed of her every night. But Libby was with Harley now. He'd lost his chance. He couldn't bear it!

"Is Harley going to loan you enough money to keep the ranch going until Janet's found?" he wondered aloud. He smiled coldly. "He hasn't got two dimes to rub together, from what I hear."

Libby remembered the mortgage payments she couldn't make. Once, she might have bent her pride enough to ask Jordan to loan it to her. Not anymore. Not after what he'd said to her.

She lifted her chin. "That's not your business, Jordan," she said proudly.

"Don't expect me to lend it to you," he said for spite.

"Jordan, I wouldn't ask you for a loan if the house burned down," she assured him, unflinching. "Now, if you'll excuse me, I'm using up my lunch hour."

She started to go around him, but he caught her arm and marched her down the little alley between her office and the town square. It was an alcove, away from traffic, with no prying eyes.

While she was wondering what was on his mind, he backed her up against the cold brick and brought his mouth down on her lips.

He lifted his head a bare inch and looked into her wide green eyes with possession and desire. It never stopped. He couldn't get within arm's length of her without giving in to temptation. Did she realize? No. She had no idea. She thought it was a punishment for her harsh words. It was more. It was anguish.

"You still want me," he ground out. "Do you think I don't know?"

"What?" she murmured, her eyes on his mouth. She could barely think at all. She felt his body so close that when he breathed, her chest deflated. Her breasts ached at the warm pressure of his broad chest. It was heaven to be so close to him. And she didn't dare let it show.

"Are you trying to prove something?" she murmured, forcing her hands to push instead of pull at his shoulders.

"Only that Harley isn't in my league," he said in a husky, arrogant tone, as he bent again and forced her mouth open under the slow, exquisite skill of his kisses. "In fact," he bit off against her lips, "neither are you, cupcake."

She wanted to come back with some snappy reply. She really did. But the sensations he was arousing were hypnotic, drugging. She felt him move one long, powerful jean-clad leg in between both of hers. It was broad daylight, in the middle of town. He was making love to her against a wall. And she didn't care.

She moved against him, her lips welcoming, her hands spreading, caressing, against his rib cage, his chest. There was no tomorrow. There was only Jordan, wanting her.

Her body throbbed in time with her frantic heartbeat.

She was hot all over, swelling, aching. She wanted relief. Anything…!

Voices coming close pushed them apart when she would have said that nothing could. Jordan stepped back, his face a rigid mask. She looked up at him, her crushed mouth red from the ardent pressure, her eyes soft and misty and dazed.

Her pocketbook was on the ground. He reached down and handed it back to her, watching as she put the strap over her shoulder and stared up at him, still bemused.

She wanted to tell him that Harley was a better lover, to make some flip remark that would sting him. But she couldn't.

He was in pretty much the same shape. He hated the very thought of Harley. But even through the jealousy, he realized that Libby's responses weren't those of any experienced woman. When Julie kissed him, it was with her whole body. She was more than willing to do anything he liked. But he couldn't take Julie to bed because he didn't want her that way. It was a source of irritation and amazement to him. And to Julie, who made sarcastic remarks about his prowess.

It wasn't a lack of ability. It was just a lack of desire. But he raged with it when he looked at Libby. He'd never wanted a woman to the point of madness until now and she was the one woman he couldn't have.

"Women and their damned ambitions," he said under his breath. "Damn Harley. And damn you, Libby!"

"Damn you, too, Jordan," she said breathlessly. "And don't expect me to drag you into any more alleys and make love to you, if that's going to be your attitude!"

She turned and walked away before he had time to realize what she'd said. He had to bite back a laugh. This was no laughing matter. He had to get a grip on himself before Libby realized what was wrong with him.

AFTER THEIR DISTURBING ENCOUNTER, she wondered if she and Curt wouldn't do better to just move off their property and live somewhere else. In fact, she told herself, that might not be a bad idea.

Mr. Kemp didn't agree.

"You have to maintain a presence on the property," he told Libby firmly. "If you move out, Janet might use that against you in court."

"You don't understand," she groaned. "Jordan is driving me crazy. And every time I look out the window, Julie's speeding down the road to Jordan's house."

"Jordan's being conned," he ventured.

"I know that, but he won't listen," Libby said, sitting down heavily behind her desk. "Julie's got him convinced that I'm running wild with Harley Fowler."

"That woman is big trouble," he said. "I'd give a lot to see her forced to admit what she did to the Culbertson girl at that party."

"You think it was her?" she asked, shocked.

He shrugged. "Nobody else had a motive," he said, his eyes narrow and cold. "Shannon Culbertson was running against her for class president and Julie wanted to win. I don't think she planned to kill her. She was going to set her up with one of the boys she was dating and ruin Shannon's reputation. But it backfired. At least, that's my theory. If this gets out it's going to disgrace her father even further."

"Isn't he already disgraced enough because of the drunk-driving charges?" she asked.

"He and his cronies at city hall are trying desperately to get those charges dropped, before they get into some newspaper whose publisher doesn't owe him a favor," Kemp replied, perching on the edge of her desk. "There's a disciplinary hearing at city hall next month for the officers involved. Grier says the council is going to try to have the police officers fired."

She smiled. "I can just see Chief Grier letting that happen."

Kemp chuckled. "I think the city council is going to be in for a big surprise. Our former police chief, Chet Blake, never would buck the council, or stand up for any officer who did something politically incorrect with the city fathers. Grier isn't like his cousin."

"What if they fire him, too?" she asked.

He stood up. "If they even try, there will be a recall of the city council and the mayor," Kemp said simply. "I can almost guarantee it. A lot of people locally are fed up with city management. Solid waste is backing up, there's no provision for water conservation, the fire department hasn't got one piece of modern equipment, and we're losing revenue hand over fist because nobody wants to mention raising taxes."

"I didn't realize that."

"Grier did." He smiled to himself. "He's going to shake up this town. It won't be a bad thing, either."

"Do you think he'll stay?"

Kemp nodded. "He's put down deep roots already, although I don't think he realizes how deep they go just yet."

Like everyone else in Jacobsville, Libby knew what was going on in Cash Grier's private life. After all, it had been in most of the tabloids. Exactly what the situation was between him and his houseguest, Tippy

Moore, was anybody's guess. The couple were equally tight-lipped in public.

"Could I ask you to do something for me, sir?" she asked suddenly.

"Of course."

"Could you find out if they've learned anything about... Daddy at the state crime lab and how much longer it's going to be before they have a report?" she asked.

He frowned. "Good Lord, I didn't realize how long it had been since the exhumation," he said. "Certainly. I'll get right on it, in fact."

"Thanks," she said.

He shrugged. "No problem." He got to his feet and hesitated. "Have you talked to Violet lately?" he asked reluctantly.

"She's lost weight and she's having her hair frosted," she began.

His lips made a thin line. "I don't want to know about her appearance. I only wondered how she likes her new job."

"A lot," she replied. She pursed her lips. "In fact, she and my brother are going out on a date Saturday night."

"Your brother knows her?" he asked.

She nodded. "He's working for Duke Wright, too..."

"Since when?" he exclaimed. "He was Jordan's right-hand man!"

She averted her eyes. "Not anymore. Jordan said some pretty bad things about me and Curt quit."

Kemp cursed. "I don't understand how a man who was so concerned for both of you has suddenly become an enemy. However," he added, "I imagine Julie Merrill has something to do with his change of heart."

"He's crazy about her, from what we hear."

"He's crazy, all right," he said, turning back toward his office. "He'll go right down the tubes with her and her father if he isn't careful."

"I tried to tell him. He accused me of being jealous."

He glanced back at her. "And you aren't?" he probed softly.

Her face closed up. "What good would it do, Mr. Kemp? Either people like you or they don't."

Kemp had thought, privately, that it was more than liking on Jordan's part. But apparently, he'd been wrong right down the line.

"Bring your pad, if you don't mind, Libby," he said. "I want you to look up a case for me at the courthouse law library."

"Yes, sir," she said, picking up her pad. It was always better to stay busy. That way she didn't have so much time to think.

SHE WAS WALKING into the courthouse when she met Calhoun Ballenger coming out of it. He stopped and grinned at her.

"Just the woman I was looking for," he said. "On the assumption that I win this primary election for the Democratic candidate, how would you like to join my campaign staff in your spare time?"

She caught her breath. "Mr. Ballenger, I'm very flattered!"

"Duke Wright tells me that you have some formidable language skills," he continued. "Not that my secretaries don't, but they've got their hands full right now trying to get people to go to the polls and vote for me in May. I need someone to write publicity for me. Are you interested?"

"You bet!" she said at once.

"Great! Come by the ranch Saturday about one. I've invited a few other people, as well."

"Not...the Merrills or Jordan Powell?" she asked worriedly.

He glowered at her. "I do not invite the political competition to staff meetings," he said with mock hauteur. He grinned. "Besides, Jordan and I aren't speaking."

"That's a relief," she said honestly.

"You're on the wrong side of him, too, I gather?"

She nodded. "Me and half the town."

"More than half, if I read the situation right," he said with a sigh. "A handful of very prominent Democrats have changed sides and they're now promoting me." He smiled. "More for our side."

She smiled back. "Exactly! Well, then, I'll see you Saturday."

"I've already invited your boss and Duke Wright, but Duke won't come," he added heavily. "I invited Grier, and Duke's still browned off about the altercation he had with our police chief."

"He shouldn't have swung on him," she pointed out.

"I'm sure he knows that now," he agreed, his eyes twinkling. "See you."

She gave him a wave and walked into the courthouse lobby. Jordan Powell was standing there with a receipt for his automobile tag and glaring daggers at Libby.

"You're on a friendly basis with Calhoun Ballenger, I gather?" he asked.

"I'm going to work on his campaign staff," she replied with a haughty smile.

"He's going to lose," he told her firmly. "He doesn't have name identification."

She smiled at him. "He hasn't been arrested for drunk driving, to my knowledge," she pointed out.

His eyes flashed fire. "That's a frame," he returned. "Grier's officers planted evidence against him."

She glared back. "Chief Grier is honest and open-handed," she told him. "And his officers would never be asked to do any such thing!"

"They'll be out of work after that hearing," he predicted.

"You swallow everything Julie tells you, don't you, Jordan?" she asked quietly. "Maybe you should take a look at the makeup of our city council. Those were people who once owned big businesses in Jacobsville and had tons of money. But their companies are all going downhill and they're short of ready cash. They aren't the people who have the power today. And if you think Chief Grier is going to stand by and let them railroad his employees, you're way off base."

Jordan didn't reply at once. He stared at Libby until her face colored.

"I never thought you'd go against me, after all I've done for you and Curt," he said.

She was thinking the same thing. It made her ashamed to recall how he'd tried to help them both when Janet was first under suspicion of murder and fraud. But he'd behaved differently since he'd gotten mixed up with Senator Merrill's daughter. He'd changed, drastically.

"You have done a lot for us," she had to agree. "We'll always be grateful for it. But you took sides against us first, Jordan. You stood by with your mouth closed in Barbara's Café and let Julie humiliate me."

Jordan's eyes flashed. It almost looked like guilt. "You had enough support."

"Yes, from Harley Fowler. At least someone spoke up for me."

He looked ice-cold. "You were rude to Julie first, in your own office."

"Why don't you ask Mr. Kemp who started it?" she replied.

"Kemp hates her," he said bluntly. "He'd back your story. I'm working for Senator Merrill and I'm going to get him reelected. You just side with the troublemakers and do what you please. But don't expect me to come around with my hat in my hand."

"I never did, Jordan," she said calmly. "I'm just a nobody around Jacobsville and I'm very aware of it. I'm not sophisticated or polished or rich, and I have no manners. On the other hand, I have no aspirations to high society, in case you wondered."

"Good thing. You'd never fit in," he bit off.

She smiled sadly. "And you think you will?" she challenged softly. "You may have better table manners than I do—and more money—but your father was poor. None of your new high-class friends is ever going to forget that. Even if you do."

He said something nasty. She colored a little, but she didn't back down.

"Don't worry, I know my place, Mr. Powell," she replied, just to irritate him. "I'm a minor problem that you've put out beside the road. I won't forget."

She was making him feel small. He didn't like it.

"Thank you for being there when we needed you most," she added quietly. "We aren't going to sell our land to developers."

"If you ever get title to it," he said coldly.

She shrugged. "That's out of our hands."

"Kemp will do what he can for you," he said, feeling guilty, because he knew that she and Curt had no money for attorneys. He'd heard that Janet was still missing and that Kemp's private detective had drawn a blank when he looked into her past. Libby and Curt must be worried sick about money.

"Yes, Mr. Kemp will do what he can for us." She studied his face, so hard and uncompromising, and wondered what had happened to make them so distant after the heated promises of those kisses they'd exchanged only weeks before.

"Curt likes working for Wright, I suppose?" he asked reluctantly.

She nodded. "He's very happy there."

"Julie had a cousin who trains horses. He's won trophies in steeplechase competition. He's working in Curt's place now, with my two new Thoroughbreds."

"I suppose Julie wants to keep it all in the family," she replied.

He glared down at her. "Keep all what in the family?"

"Your money, Jordan," she said sweetly.

"You wouldn't have turned it down, if I'd given you the chance," he accused sarcastically. "You were laying it on thick."

"Who was kissing whom in the alley?" she returned huskily.

He didn't like remembering that. He jerked his wide-brimmed hat down over his eyes. "A moment of weakness. Shouldn't have happened. I'm not free anymore."

Insinuating that he and Julie were much more than

friends, Libby thought correctly. She looked past Jordan to Julie, who was just coming out of the courthouse looking elegant and cold as ice. She saw Libby standing with Jordan and her lips collided furiously.

"Jordan! Let's go!" she called to him angrily.

"I was only passing the time of day with him, Julie," Libby told the older woman with a vacant smile.

"You keep your sticky hands to yourself, you little liar," Julie told her as she passed on the steps. "Jordan is mine!"

"No doubt you mean his money is yours, right?" Libby ventured.

Julie drew back her hand and slapped Libby across the cheek as hard as she could. "Damn you!" she raged.

Libby was shocked at the unexpected physical reply, but she didn't retaliate. She just stood there, straight and dignified, with as much pride as she could muster. Around the two women, several citizens stopped and looked on with keen disapproval.

One of them was Officer Dana Hall, one of the two police officers who had arrested Senator Merrill for drunk driving.

She walked right up to Libby. "That was assault, Miss Collins," she told Libby. "If you want to press charges, I can arrest Miss Merrill on the spot."

"Arrest!" Julie exploded. "You can't arrest me!"

"I most certainly can," Officer Hall replied. "Miss Collins, do you want to press charges?"

Libby stared at Julie Merrill with cold pleasure, wondering how it would look on the front page of Jacobsville's newspaper.

"Wouldn't that put another kink in your father's re-election campaign?" Libby ventured softly.

Julie looked past Libby and suddenly burst into tears. She threw herself into Jordan Powell's arms. "Oh, Jordan, she's going to have me arrested!"

"No, she's not," Jordan said curtly. He glanced at Libby. "She wouldn't dare."

Libby cocked her head. "I wouldn't?" She glared at him. "Look at my cheek, Jordan."

It was red. There was a very obvious handprint on it.

"She insulted me," Julie wailed. "I had every right to hit her back!"

"She never struck you, Miss Merrill," Officer Hall replied coldly. "Striking another person is against the law, regardless of the provocation."

"I never meant to do it!" Julie wailed. She was sobbing, but there wasn't a speck of moisture under her eyes. "Please, Jordan, don't let them put me in jail!"

Libby and Officer Hall exchanged disgusted looks.

"Men are so damned gullible," Libby remarked with a glare at Jordan, who looked outraged. "All right, Julie, have it your way. But you'd better learn to produce tears as well as broken sobs if you want to convince another woman that you're crying."

"Jordan, could we go now?" Julie sobbed. "I'm just sick…!"

"Not half as sick as you'll be when your father loses the election, Julie," Libby drawled sweetly, and walked up the steps with Officer Hall at her side. She didn't even look at Jordan as she went into the courthouse.

CHAPTER SEVEN

CALHOUN BALLENGER'S MEETING with his volunteer staff
was a cheerful riot of surprises. Libby found herself
working with women she'd known only by name a few
months earlier. Now she was suddenly in the cream of
society, but with women who didn't snub her or look
down their noses at her social position.

Libby was delighted to find herself working with Violet, who'd come straight from her job at Duke Wright's
ranch for the meeting.

"This is great!" Violet exclaimed, hugging Libby.
"I've missed working with you!"

"I've missed you, too, Violet," Libby assured her.
She shook her head as she looked at the other woman.
"You look great!"

Violet grinned. She'd dropped at least two dress sizes.
She was well-rounded, but no longer obese even to the
most critical eye. She'd had her brown hair frosted and
it was waving around her face and shoulders. She was
wearing a low-cut dress that emphasized the size of her
pretty breasts, and her small waist and voluptuous hips,
along with high heels that arched her small feet nicely.

"I've worked hard at the gym," Violet confessed. She
was still laughing when her eyes collided with Blake
Kemp's across the room. The expression left her face.
She averted her eyes quickly. "Excuse me, won't you,

Libby? I came with Curt. You, uh, don't mind, do you?" she added worriedly.

"Don't be silly," Libby said with a genuine smile. "Curt's nice. So are you. I think you'd make a lovely couple…"

"Still happy with Duke Wright, Miss Hardy?" came a cold, biting comment from Libby's back.

Blake Kemp moved into view, his pale eyes expressive on Violet's pretty figure and the changes in the way she dressed.

"I'm…very happy with him, Mr. Kemp," Violet said, clasping her hands together tightly. "If you'll excuse me…"

"You've lost weight," Kemp said gruffly.

Violet's eyes widened. "And you actually noticed?"

The muscles in his face tautened. "You look…nice."

Violet's jaw dropped. She was literally at a loss for words. Her eyes lifted to Kemp's and they stood staring at each other for longer than was polite, neither speaking or moving.

Kemp shifted restlessly on his long legs. "How's your mother?"

Violet swallowed hard. "She's not doing very well, I'm afraid. You know…about the exhumation?"

Kemp nodded. "They're still in the process of evaluating Curt and Libby's father's remains, as well, at the crime lab. So far, they have nothing to report."

Violet looked beside him at Libby and winced. "I didn't know, Libby. I'm so sorry."

"So am I, for you," Libby replied. "We didn't want to do it, but we had to know for sure."

"Will they really be able to tell anything, after all

this time?" Violet asked Kemp, and she actually moved a step closer to him.

He seemed to catch his breath. He was looking at her oddly. "I assume so." His voice was deeper, too. Involuntarily, his lean fingers reached out and touched Violet's long hair. "I like the frosting," he said reluctantly. "It makes your eyes look...bluer."

"Does it?" Violet asked, but her eyes were staring into his as if she'd found treasure there.

With an amused smile, Libby excused herself and joined her brother, who was talking to the police chief.

Cash Grier noticed her approach and smiled. He looked older somehow and there were new lines around his dark eyes.

"Hi, Chief," she greeted him. "How's it going?"

"Don't ask," Curt chuckled. "He's in the middle of a controversy."

"So are we," Libby replied. "We're on the wrong side of the election and Jordan Powell is furious at us."

"We're on the right side," Cash said carelessly. "The city fathers are in for a rude awakening." He leaned down. "I have friends in high places." He paused. "I also have friends in low places." He grinned.

Libby and Curt burst out laughing, because they recognized the lines from a country song they'd all loved.

Calhoun Ballenger joined them, clapping Cash on the back affectionately. "Thanks for coming," he said. "Even if it is putting another nail in your coffin with the mayor."

"The mayor can kiss my..." Cash glanced at Libby and grinned. "Never mind."

They all laughed.

"She's lived with me all her life," Curt remarked. "She's practically unshockable."

"How's Tippy?" Calhoun asked.

Cash smiled. "Doing better, thanks. She'd have come, too, but she's still having a bad time."

"No wonder," Calhoun replied, recalling the ordeal Tippy had been through in the hands of kidnappers. It had been in all the tabloids. "Good thing they caught the culprits who kidnapped her."

"Isn't it?" Cash said, not giving away that he'd caught them, with the help of an old colleague. "Nice turnout, Calhoun," he added, looking around them. "I thought you invited Judd."

"I did," Calhoun said at once, "but the twins have a cold."

"Damn!" Cash grimaced. "I told Judd that he and Crissy needed to stop running that air conditioner all night!"

"It wasn't that," Calhoun confided. "They went to the Coltrains' birthday party for their son—his second birthday—and that's where they got the colds."

Cash sighed. "Poor babies."

"He's their godfather," Calhoun told Libby and Curt. "But he thinks Jessamina belongs to him."

"She does," Cash replied haughtily.

Nobody mentioned what the tabloids had said—that Tippy had been pregnant with Cash's child a few weeks earlier and lost it just before her ordeal with the kidnapping.

Libby diplomatically changed the subject. "Mr. Kemp said that you can put up campaign posters in our office windows," she told Calhoun, "and Barbara's willing to let you put up as many as you like in her café," she added with a grin. "She said she's never going to forgive Julie Merrill for making a scene there."

Calhoun chuckled. "I've had that sort of offer all

week," he replied. "Nobody wants Senator Merrill back in office, but the city fathers have thrown their support behind him and he thinks he's unbeatable. What we really need is a change in city government, as well. We're on our second mayor in eight months and this one is afraid of his own shadow."

"He's also Senator Merrill's nephew," Curt added.

"Which is why he's trying to make my officers back down on those DWI charges," Cash Grier interposed.

"I'd like to see it. Carlos Garcia wouldn't back down from anybody," Calhoun mused. "Or Officer Dana Hall, either."

"Ms. Hall came to my assistance at the courthouse this week," Libby volunteered. "Julie Merrill slapped me. Officer Hall was more than willing to arrest her, if I'd agreed to press charges."

"Good for Dana," Cash returned. "You be careful, Ms. Collins," he added firmly. "That woman has poor impulse control. I wouldn't put it past her to try and run somebody down."

"Neither would I," Curt added worriedly. "She's already told Jordan some furious lies about us and he believes her."

"She can be very convincing," Libby said, not wanting to verbally attack Jordan even now.

"It may get worse now, with all of you backing me," Calhoun told the small group. "I won't have any hard feelings if you want to withdraw your support."

"Do I look like the sort of man who backs away from trouble?" Cash asked lazily, with a grin.

"Speaking of Duke Wright," Libby murmured dryly, "he's throwing his support to Mr. Ballenger, too. But he had, uh, reservations about coming to the meeting."

Cash chuckled. "I don't hold grudges."

"Yes, but he does," Calhoun said on a chuckle. "He'll get over it. He's got some personal problems right now."

"Don't we all?" Cash replied wistfully, and his dark eyes were troubled.

Libby and Curt didn't add their two cents' worth, but they exchanged quiet looks.

THE CAMPAIGN WAS winding down for the primary, but all the polls gave Calhoun a huge lead over Merrill. Printed materials were ordered, along with buttons, pencils, bumper stickers and key chains. There was enough promotional matter to blanket the town and in the days that followed, Calhoun's supporters did exactly that in Jacobs County and the surrounding area in the state senatorial district that Merrill represented.

Julie Merrill was acting as her father's campaign manager and she was coordinating efforts for promotion with a group of teenagers she'd hired. Some of them were delinquents and there was a rash of vandalisms pertaining to the destruction of Calhoun's campaign posters.

Cash Grier, predictably, went after the culprits and rounded them up. He got one to talk and the newspapers revealed that Miss Merrill had paid the young man to destroy Calhoun's campaign literature. Julie denied it. But the vandalism stopped.

Meanwhile, acting mayor Ben Brady was mounting a fervent defense for Senator Merrill on the drunk-driving charges and trying to make things hot for the two officers. He ordered them suspended and tried to get the city council to back him up.

Cash got wind of it and phoned Simon Hart, the state's attorney general. Simon phoned the city attor-

ney and they had a long talk. Soon afterward, the officers were notified that they could stay on the job until
the hearing the following month.

Meanwhile, the state crime lab revealed the results
of its report to Blake Kemp. He walked up to Libby's
desk while she was on the phone and waited impatiently
for her to hang up.

"They can't find any evidence of foul play, Libby,"
he said at once.

"And if there was any, they would?" she asked quickly.

He nodded. "I'm almost certain of it. The crime lab
verified our medical examiner's diagnosis of myocardial
infarction. So Janet's off the hook for that one, at least."

Libby sat back with a long sigh and closed her eyes.
"Thank God. I couldn't have lived with it if she'd poisoned Daddy and we never knew."

He nodded. "On the other hand, they hit pay dirt with
Violet's father," he added.

She sat up straight. "Poison?"

"Yes," he said heavily. "I'm not going to phone her.
I'm going over to Duke Wright's place to tell her in
person. Then I'll take her home to talk to her mother.
She'll need someone with her."

Yes, she would, and Libby was secretly relieved that
Kemp was going to be the person. Violet would need a
shoulder to cry on.

"I'll phone Curt and tell him," she said.

"Libby, give me half an hour first," he asked quietly.
"I don't want him to tell Violet."

She wondered why, but she wasn't going to pry. "Okay."

He managed a brief smile. "Thanks."

"What about Janet?" she wondered miserably. "They
still haven't found her."

"They will. Now all we need is a witness who can place her with Mr. Hardy the night of his death, and we can have her arrested and charged with murder," he replied.

"Chance would be a fine thing, Mr. Kemp," she said heavily.

"Don't give up hope," he instructed. "She's not going to get away with your inheritance. I promise."

She managed a smile. "Thanks."

BUT SHE WASN'T really convinced. She went home that afternoon feeling lost and alone. She'd told Curt the good news after Violet had gone home with Kemp. Curt had been as relieved as she had, but there was still the problem of probate. Everything was in Janet's name, as their father had instructed. Janet had the insurance money. Nobody could do anything with the estate until the will was probated and Janet had to sign the papers for that. It was a financial nightmare.

There was a message on the answering machine when Libby got home. She pushed the Play button and her heart sank right to her ankles.

"This is the loan officer at Jacobsville Savings and Loan," came the pleasant voice. "We just wanted to remind you that your loan payment was due three days ago. Please call us if there's a problem." The caller gave her name and position and her telephone number. The line went dead.

Libby sat down beside the phone and just stared at it. Curt had told her already that they weren't going to be able to make the payment. Jordan had assured her that he wasn't going to loan her the money to pay it. There was nobody else they would feel comfortable asking.

She put her face in her hands and let the tears fall. The financial establishment would repossess the ranch. It wouldn't matter where Janet was or what state the probate action was in. They were going to lose their home.

SHE WENT OUT to the barn and ran the currycomb over Bailey, her father's horse. He was the last horse they had.

The barn leaked. It was starting to rain and Libby felt raindrops falling on her shoulder through a rip in the tin roof from a small tornado that had torn through a month earlier. The straw on the floor of the barn needed changing, but the hay crop had drowned in the flooding. They'd have to buy some. Libby looked down at her worn jeans, at the small hand resting on them. The tiger's-eye ring her father had given her looked ominous in the darkened barn. She sighed and turned back to the horse.

"Bailey, I don't know what we're going to do," she told the old horse, who neighed as if he were answering her.

The sound of a vehicle pulling up in the yard diverted her. She looked down the long aisle of the barn to see Jordan's pickup truck sitting at the entrance. Her heart skipped as he got out and came striding through the dirty straw, his cotton shirt speckled with raindrops that had escaped the wide brim of his white straw hat.

"What do you want?" she asked, trying to ignore him to finish her grooming job on the horse.

"My two new Thoroughbreds are missing."

She turned, the currycomb suspended in her small hand. "And you think we took them?" she asked incredulously. "You honestly think we'd steal from you, even if we were starving?"

He averted his face, as if the question had wounded him.

"Please leave," she said through her teeth.

He rammed his hands into his pockets and moved a step closer, looking past her to Bailey. "That horse is useless for ranch work. He's all of twenty."

"He's my horse," she replied. "I'm not getting rid of him, whatever happens."

She felt his lean, powerful body at her back. "Libby," he began. "About that bank loan…"

"Curt and I are managing just fine, thanks," she said without turning.

His big, strong hands came down heavily on her shoulders, making her jump. "The bank president is a good friend of the Merrills."

She pulled away from him and looked up, her unspoken fears in her green eyes. "They can't do anything to us without Janet," she told him. "She has legal power of attorney."

"Damn it, I know that!" he muttered. "But it's not going to stop the bank from foreclosing, don't you see? You can't make the loan payment!"

"What business is that of yours?" she asked bitterly.

He drew in a slow breath. "I can talk to the president of the Jacobsville Merchant Bank for you," he said. "He might be willing to work out something for the land. You and Curt can't work it, anyway, and you don't have the capital to invest in it. The best you could do is sell off your remaining cattle and give it up."

She couldn't even manage words. She had no options at all and he had to know it. She could almost hate him.

"We can't sell anything," she said harshly. "I told you, Janet has power of attorney. And she was named in Daddy's will as the sole holder of the property. We can't even sell a stick of furniture. We're going to have to watch the bank foreclose, Jordan, because Janet has our hands tied. We're going to lose everything Daddy worked for, all his life…"

Her lower lip trembled. She couldn't even finish the sentence.

Jordan stepped forward and wrapped her up tight in his arms, holding her while she cried. "Damn, what a mess!"

She beat a small fist against his massive chest. "Why?" she moaned. "Why?"

His arms tightened. "I don't know, baby," he whispered at her ear, his voice deep and soothing. "I wish I did."

She nuzzled closer, drowning in the pleasure of being close to him. It had been so long since he'd held her.

His chest rose and fell heavily. "Kemp's detective hasn't tracked her down yet?"

"Not yet. But she didn't…kill Daddy. The autopsy showed that he died of a heart attack."

"That's something, I guess," he murmured.

"But Violet's daddy was poisoned," she added quietly, her eyes open as they stared past Jordan's broad chest toward his truck parked at the front of the barn. "So they'll still get her for murder, if they can ever find her."

"Poor Violet," he said.

"Yes."

His hand smoothed her hair. It tangled in the wavy soft strands. "You smell of roses, Libby," he murmured deeply, and the pressure of his arms changed in some subtle way.

She could feel the sudden tautness of his lean body against her, the increasing warmth of his embrace. But he'd taken Julie's side against her and she wasn't comfortable being in his arms anymore.

She tried to pull away, but he wouldn't let her.

"Don't fight me," he said gruffly. "You know you don't want to."

"I don't?"

He lifted his head and looked down into her misty and wet green eyes. His voice was deep with feeling. "You haven't stopped wanting me."

"I want hot chocolate, too, Jordan, but it still gives me migraine, so I don't drink it," she said emphatically.

His dark eyebrows lifted. "That's cute. You think you convinced me?"

"Sure," she lied.

He laughed mirthlessly, letting his dark eyes fall to her lips. "Let's see."

He bent, drawing his lips slowly, tenderly, across her mouth in a teasing impression of a kiss. He was lazy and gentle and after a few seconds of imitating a plank of wood, her traitorous body betrayed her.

She relaxed into the heat of his body with a shaky little sigh and found herself enveloped in his arms. He kissed her again, hungrily this time, without the tenderness of that first brief exchange.

"Yes," he groaned. His long leg slid lazily against hers, and between them, while his big, warm hands smoothed blatantly over her rib cage, his thumbs sliding boldly right over her breasts. "Don't think," he whispered against her parted lips. "Just give in. I won't hurt you."

"I know that," she whispered. "But…"

He nibbled on her lower lip. His thumbs edged out gently and found her nipples. They moved lazily, back and forth, coaxing the tips into hard little nubs. She shivered with unexpected pleasure.

He lifted his head and looked into her eyes while he did it again. If she was used to this sort of love play, it certainly didn't show. She was pliable, yielded, absolutely fascinated with what he was doing to her body. She liked it.

That was all he needed to know. His leg became insistent between hers, coaxing them to move apart, to admit the slow, exquisite imprint of his hips between her long legs. It was like that day in the alley beyond her office, when she hadn't cared if all of Jacobsville walked by while he was pressing her aching body against the brick wall. She was drowning in pleasure.

Surely, she thought blindly, it couldn't be wrong to give in to something so sweet! His hands on her body were producing undreamed of sensations. He was giving her pleasure in hot, sweeping waves. He touched her and she ached for more. He kissed her and she lifted against him to find his mouth and coax it into ardor. One of her legs curled helplessly around his powerful thigh and she moaned when he accepted the silent invitation and moved into near intimacy with her.

He was aroused. He was powerful. She felt the hard thrust of him against her body and she wanted to rip off her clothes and invite his hands, his eyes, his body, into complete surrender with her. She wanted to feel the ecstasy she knew he could give her. He was skilled, masterful. He knew what she needed, what she wanted. He could give her pleasure beyond bearing, she knew it.

His lean hands moved under her blouse, searching for closeness, unfastening buttons, invading lace. She felt his fingers brush tenderly, lovingly, over her bare breasts in an intimacy she'd never shared with anyone.

Her dreams of him had been this explicit, but she'd never thought she would live them in such urgent passion. As he touched her, she arched to help him, moved to encourage him. Her mouth opened wide under his. She felt his tongue suddenly thrust into it with violent need.

She moaned loudly, her fingertips gripping the hard muscle of his upper arms as he thrust her blouse and bra up to her throat and bent at once to put his mouth on her breasts.

The warm, moist contact was shattering. She stiffened with the shock of pleasure it produced. He tasted her in a hot, feverish silence, broken only by his urgent breathing and the rough sigh of her own voice in his ear.

"Yes," he groaned, opening his mouth. "Yes, Libby. Here. Right here. You and me. I can give you more pleasure than damned Harley ever dreamed of giving you!"

Harley. Harley. She felt her body growing cold. "Harley?" she whispered.

He lifted his head and looked down at her breasts with grinding urgency. "He's had you."

"He has not!" she exclaimed, shocked.

He scowled, in limbo, caught between his insane need to possess her and his jealousy of the other man.

She took advantage of his indecision by jerking out of his arms and pulling her blouse down as she dragged herself out of the stall. She groped for fastenings while she flushed with embarrassment at what she'd just let him do to her.

She looked devastated. Her hair was full of straw, like her clothes. Her green eyes were wild, her face flushed, her mouth swollen.

He got to his feet, still in the grip of passion, and started toward her. His hat was off. His hair was wild, from her searching fingers, and his shirt was half-open over hair-matted muscle.

"Come back here," he said huskily, moving forward.

"No!" she said firmly, shivering. "I'm not standing in for Julie Merrill!"

The words stopped him in his tracks. He hesitated, his brows meeting over turbulent dark eyes.

"Remember Julie? Your girlfriend?" she persisted shakily. Throwing his lover in his face was a way to cover her hurt for the insinuation he'd made about her and Harley. "What in the world would she think if she could see you now?"

He straightened, but with an effort. His body was raging. He wanted Libby. He'd never wanted anyone, anything, as much as he wanted her.

"Julie has nothing to do with this," he ground out. "I want you!"

"For how long, Jordan?" she asked bitingly. "Ten minutes? Thirty?"

He blinked. His mind wasn't working.

"I am nobody's one-night stand," she flashed at him. "Not even yours!"

He took a deep breath, then another one. He stared at her blankly while he tried to stop thinking about how sweet it was to feel her body under his hands.

"I want you to leave, now," she repeated, folding her

arms over her loose bra. She could feel the swollen contours of her breasts and remembered with pure shame how it felt to have him touching and kissing them.

"That isn't what you wanted five minutes ago," he reminded her flatly.

She closed her eyes. "I'm grass-green and stupid," she said curtly. "It wouldn't be the first time an experienced man seduced an innocent girl."

"Don't make stupid jokes," he said icily. "You're no innocent."

"You believe what you like about me, Jordan, it doesn't matter anymore," she interrupted him. "I've got work to do. Why don't you go home?"

He glared at her, frustrated desire riding him hard. He cursed himself for ruining everything by bringing up Harley Fowler. "You're a hard woman, Libby," he said. "Harder than I ever realized."

"Goodbye, Jordan," she said, and she turned away to pick up the curry comb she'd dropped.

He gave her a furious glare and stormed out of the barn to his truck. Bailey jumped as Jordan slammed the door and left skid marks getting out of the driveway. She relaxed then, grateful that she'd managed to save herself from that masterful seduction. She'd had a close call. She had to make sure that Jordan never got so close to her again. She couldn't trust him. Not now.

CHAPTER EIGHT

JANET WAS STILL in hiding before the primary election and probate hadn't begun. But plenty had changed in Jacobsville. Libby and Curt had been forced to move out of the farmhouse where they'd grown up, because the bank had foreclosed.

They hadn't said a word to Jordan about it. Curt moved into the bunkhouse at the Wright ranch where he worked. Libby moved into a boardinghouse where two other Jacobsville career women lived.

Bailey would have had to be boarded and Libby didn't have the money. But she worked out a deal with a dude ranch nearby. Bailey would be used for trail rides for people who were nervous of horses and Libby would help on the weekends. It wasn't the ideal solution, but it was the only one she had. It was a wrench to give up Bailey, even though it wasn't going to be forever.

Jordan and Julie Merrill were apparently engaged. Or so Julie was saying, and she was wearing a huge diamond on her ring finger. Her father was using every dirty trick in the book to gain his party's candidacy.

Julie Merrill was vehemently outspoken about some unnamed dirty tactics being used against her father in the primary election campaign, and she went on television to make accusations against Calhoun Ballenger.

The next morning, Blake Kemp had her served as the defendant in a defamation lawsuit.

"THEY'RE NOT GOING to win this case," Julie raged at Jordan. "I want you to get me the best attorney in Austin! We're going to put Calhoun Ballenger right in the gutter where he belongs, along with all these jump-up nouveau riche that think they own our county!"

Jordan, who was one of those jump-ups, gave her a curious look. "Excuse me?" he asked coolly.

"Well, I'm not standing by while Ballenger talks my father's constituents into deserting him!"

"You're the one who's been making allegations, Julie," Jordan said quietly. "To anyone who was willing to listen."

She waved that away. "You have to do that to win elections."

"I'm not going to be party to anything dishonest," Jordan said through his teeth.

Julie backed down. She curled against him and sighed. "Okay. I'll tone it down, for your sake. But you aren't going to let Calhoun Ballenger sue me, are you?"

Jordan didn't know what he was going to do. He felt uneasy at Julie's temperament and her tactics. He'd taken her side against Kemp when she told him that one of the boys at her graduation party had put something in the Culbertson girl's drink and she couldn't turn him in. She'd cried about Libby Collins making horrible statements against her. But Libby had never done such a thing before.

He'd liked being Julie's escort, being accepted by the social crowd she ran around with. But it was getting old and he was beginning to believe that Julie was only playing up to him for money to put into her father's campaign. Libby had tried to warn him and he'd jumped down her throat. He felt guilty about that, too. He felt guilty about a lot of things lately.

"Listen," he said. "I think you need to step back and take a good look at what you're doing. Calhoun Ballenger isn't some minor citizen. He and his brother own a feedlot that's nationally known. Besides that, he has the support of most of the people in Jacobsville with money."

"My father has the support of the social set," she began.

"Yes, but Julie, they're the old elite. The demographics have changed in Jacobs County in the past ten years. Look around you. The Harts are a political family from the roots up. Their brother is the state attorney general and he's already casting a serious eye on what's going on in the Jacobsville city council, about those police officers the mayor's trying to suspend."

"They can't do anything about that," she argued.

"Julie, the Harts are related to Chief Grier," he said shortly.

She hesitated. For the first time, she looked uncertain.

"Not only that, they're related to the governor and the vice president. And while it isn't well-known locally, Grier's people are very wealthy."

She sat down. She ran a hand through her blond hair. "Why didn't you say this before?"

"I tried to," he pointed out. "You refused to listen."

"But Daddy can't possibly lose the election," she said with a child's understanding of things. "He's been state senator from this district for years and years."

"And now the voters are looking for some new blood," he told her. "Not only in local government, but in state and national government. You and your father don't really move with the times, Julie."

"Surely, you don't think Calhoun can beat Daddy?" she asked huskily.

"I think he's going to," he replied honestly, ramming his hands into his pockets. "He's way ahead of your father in the polls. You know that. You and your father have made some bad enemies trying to have those police officers fired. You've gotten on the wrong side of not only Cash Grier, but the Harts, as well. There will be repercussions. I've already heard talk of a complete recall of the mayor and the city council."

"But the mayor is Daddy's nephew. How could they...?"

"Don't you know anything about small towns?" he ground out. "Julie, you've spent too much time in Austin with your father and not enough around here where the elections are decided."

"This is just a hick town," she said, surprised. "Why should I care what goes on here?"

Jordan's face hardened. "Because Jacobs County is the biggest county in your father's district. He can't get reelected without it. You've damaged his campaign by the way you've behaved to Libby Collins."

"That nobody?" she scoffed.

"Her father is a direct descendant of old John Jacobs," he pointed out. "They may not have money and they may not be socially acceptable to you and your father, but the Collinses are highly respected here. The reason Calhoun's got such support is because you've tried to hurt Libby."

"But that's absurd!"

"She's a good person," he said, averting his eyes as he recalled his unworthy treatment of her—and of Curt—on Julie's behalf. "She's had some hard knocks recently."

"So have I," Julie said hotly. "Most notably, having a lawsuit filed against me for defamation of character by that lawyer Kemp!" She turned to him. "Are you going to get me a lawyer, or do I have to find my own?"

Jordan was cutting his losses while there was still time. He felt like ten kinds of fool for the way he'd behaved in the past few weeks. "I think you'd better do that yourself," he replied. "I'm not going against Calhoun Ballenger."

She scoffed. "You'll never get that Collins woman to like you again, no matter what you do," she said haughtily. "Or didn't you know that she and her brother have forfeited the ranch to the bank?"

He was speechless. "They've what?"

"Nobody would loan them the money they needed to save it," she said with a cold smile. "So the bank president foreclosed. Daddy had a long talk with him."

He looked furious. His big fists clenched at his hips. "That was low, Julie."

"When you want to win, sometimes you have to fight dirty," she said simply. "You belong to me. I'm not letting some nobody of a little dirt rancher take you away from me. We need you."

"I don't belong to you," he returned, scooping up his hat. "In fact, I've never felt dirtier than I do right now."

She gaped at him. "I beg your pardon! You can't talk to me like that!"

"I just did." He started toward the door.

"You're no loss, Jordan," she yelled after him. "We

needed your money, but I never wanted you! You're one of those jump-ups with no decent background. I'm sorry I ever invited you here the first time. I'm ashamed that I told my friends I liked you!"

"That makes two of us," he murmured icily, and he went out the door without a backward glance.

KEMP WAS GOING over some notes with Libby when Jordan Powell walked into the office without bothering to knock.

"I'd like to talk to Libby for a minute," he said solemnly, hat in hand.

Libby stared at him blankly. "I can't think what you have to say," she replied. "I'm very busy."

"She is," Kemp replied. "I'm due in court in thirty minutes."

"Then I'll come back in thirty minutes," Jordan replied.

"Feel free, but I won't be here. I have nothing to say to you, Jordan," she told him bluntly. "You turned your back on me when I needed you the most. I don't need you now. I never will again."

"Listen," he began impatiently.

"No." She turned back to Kemp. "What were you saying, boss?"

Kemp hesitated. He could see the pain in Jordan's face and he had some idea that Jordan had just found out the truth about Julie Merrill. He checked his watch. "Listen, I can read your writing. Just give me the pad and I'll get to the courthouse. It's okay," he added when she looked as if he were deserting her to the enemy. "Really."

She bit her lower lip hard. "Okay."

"Thanks," Jordan said stiffly, as Kemp got up from the desk.

"You owe me one," he replied, as he passed the taciturn rancher on the way out the door.

MINUTES LATER, MABEL WENT into Kemp's office to put some notes on his desk, leaving Jordan and Libby alone.

"I've made some bad mistakes," he began stiffly. He hated apologies. Usually, he found ways not to make them. But he'd hurt Libby too badly not to try.

She was staring at her keyboard, trying not to listen.

"You have to understand what it's been like for me," he said hesitantly. He sat down in a chair next to her desk, with his wide-brimmed hat in his hands. "My people were like yours, poor. My mother had money, but her people disinherited her when she married my dad. I never had two nickels to rub together. I was that Powell kid, whose father worked for wages, whose mother was reduced to working as a housekeeper." He stared at the floor with his pride aching. "I wanted to be somebody, Libby. That's all I ever wanted. Just to have respect from the people who mattered in this town." He shrugged. "I thought going around with Julie would give me that."

"I don't suppose you noticed that her father belongs to a group of respectable people who no longer have any power around here," she said stiffly.

He sighed. "No, I didn't. I had my head turned. She was beautiful and rich and cultured, and she came at me like a hurricane. I was in over my head before I knew it."

Libby, who wasn't beautiful or rich or cultured, felt her heart breaking. She knew all this, but it hurt to hear him admit it. Because it meant that those hungry, sweet kisses she'd shared with him meant nothing at all. He wanted Julie.

"I've broken it off with her," he said bluntly.

Libby didn't say anything.

"Did you hear me?" he asked impatiently.

She looked up at him with disillusioned eyes. "You believed her. She said I was shacking up with Harley Fowler. She said I attacked her in this office and hurt her feelings. You believed all that, even though you knew me. And when she attacked me in Barbara's Café and on the courthouse steps, you didn't say a thing."

He winced.

"Words don't mean anything, Powell," she said bitterly. "You can sit there and apologize and try to smooth over what you did for the rest of your life, but I won't listen. When I needed you, you turned your back on me."

He drew in a long breath. "I guess I did."

"I can understand that you were flattered by her attention," she said. "But Curt and I have lost everything we had. Our father is dead and we don't even have a home anymore."

He moved his hat in his hands. "You could move in with me."

She laughed bitterly. "Thanks."

"No, listen," he said earnestly, leaning forward.

She held up a hand. "Don't. I've had all the hard knocks I can handle. I don't want anything from you, Jordan. Not anything at all."

He wanted to bite something. He felt furious at his own stupidity, at his blind allegiance to Julie Merrill and her father, at his naivete in letting them use him. He felt even worse about the way he'd turned on Libby.

But he was afraid of what he'd felt for her, afraid of her youth, her changeability. Now he only felt like a fool.

"Thanks for the offer and the apology," she added heavily. "Now, if you'll excuse me, I have to get back to work."

She turned on the computer, brought up her work screen and shut Jordan out of her sight and mind.

He got up slowly and moved toward the door. He hesitated at it, glancing back at her. "What about the autopsy?" he asked suddenly.

She swallowed hard. "Daddy died of a heart attack, just like the doctors said," she replied.

He sighed. "And Violet's father?"

"Was poisoned," she replied.

"Riddle had a lucky escape," he commented. "So did you and Curt."

She didn't look at him. "I just hope they can find her, before she kills some other poor old man."

He nodded. After a minute, he gave her one last soulful glance and went out the door.

LIFE WENT ON as usual. Calhoun's campaign staff cranked up the heat. Libby spent her free time helping to make up flyers and make telephone calls, offering to drive voters to the polls during the primary election if they didn't have a way to get to the polls.

"You know, I really think Calhoun's going to win," Curt told Libby while they were having a quick lunch together on Saturday, after she got off from work.

She smiled. "So do I. He's got all kinds of support."

He picked at his potato chips. "Heard from Jordan?"

She stiffened. "He came by the office to apologize a few days ago."

He drew in a long breath. "Rumor is that Julie Merrill's courting Duke Wright now."

"Good luck to her. He's still in love with his wife. And he's not quite as gullible as Jordan."

"Jordan wasn't so gullible," he defended his former boss. "When a woman that pretty turns up the heat, most normal men will follow her anywhere."

She lifted both eyebrows. "Even you?"

He grinned. "I'm not normal. I'm a cowboy."

She chuckled and sipped her iced tea. "They're still looking for Janet. I've had an idea," she said.

"Shoot."

"What if we advertise our property for sale in all the regional newspapers?"

"Whoa," he said. "We can't sell it. We don't have power of attorney and the will's not even in probate yet."

"She's a suspected murderess," she reminded him. "Felons can't inherit, did you know? If she's tried and convicted, we might be able to get her to return everything she got from Daddy's estate."

He frowned, thinking hard. "Do you remember Dad telling us about a new will he'd made?"

She blinked. "No."

"Maybe you weren't there. It was when he was in the hospital, just before he died. He could hardly talk for the pain and he was gasping for breath. But he said there was a will. He said he put it in his safest place." He frowned heavily. "I never thought about that until just now, but what if he meant a new will, Libby?"

"It wouldn't have been legal if it wasn't witnessed," she said sadly. "He might have written something down and she found it and threw it out. I doubt it would stand up in court."

"No. He went to San Antonio without Janet, about two days before he had the heart attack," he persisted.

"Who did he know in San Antonio?" she wondered aloud.

"Why don't you ask Mr. Kemp to see if his private detective could snoop around?" he queried softly.

She pursed her lips. "It would be a long shot. And we couldn't afford to pay him...."

"Dad had a coin collection that was worth half a million dollars, Libby," Curt said. "It's never turned up. I can't find any record that he ever sold it, either."

Her lips fell open. In the agony of the past few months, that had never occurred to her. "I assumed Janet cashed it in...."

"She had the insurance money," he reminded her, "and the property—or so she assumed. But when we were sorting out Dad's personal belongings, that case he kept the coins in was missing. What if—" he added eagerly "—he took it to San Antonio and left it with someone, along with an altered will?"

She was trying to think. It wasn't easy. If they had those coins, if nothing else, they could make the loan payment.

"I can ask Mr. Kemp if he'll look into it," she said. "He can take the money out of my salary."

"I can contribute some of mine," Curt added.

She felt lighter than she had in weeks. "I'll go ask him right now!"

"Finish your sandwich first," he coaxed. "You've lost weight, baby sister."

She grimaced. "I've been depressed since we had to leave home."

"Yeah. Me, too."

She smiled at him. "But things are looking up!"

SHE FOUND KEMP just about to leave for the day. She stopped him at the door and told him what she and Curt had been discussing.

He closed the door behind them, picked up the phone, and dialed a number. Libby listened while he outlined the case to someone, most likely the private detective he'd hired to look for Janet.

"That's right," he told the man. "One more thing, there's a substantial coin collection missing, as well. I'll ask." He put his hand over the receiver and asked Libby for a description of it, which he gave to the man. He added a few more comments and hung up, smiling.

"Considering the age of those coins and their value, it wouldn't be hard to trace them if they'd been sold. Good work, Libby!"

"Thank my brother," she replied, smiling. "He remembered it."

"You would have, too, I expect, in time," he said in a kindly tone. "Want me to have a talk with the bank president?" he added. "I think he might be more amenable to letting you and Curt back on the property with this new angle in mind. It might be to his advantage," he added in a satisfied tone.

"You mean, if we turn out to have that much money of our own, free and clear, it would make him very uncomfortable if we put it in the Jacobsville Municipal Bank and not his?"

"Exactly."

Her eyes blazed. "Which is exactly where we will put it, if we get it," she added.

He chuckled. "No need to tell him that just yet."

Her eyebrows lifted. "Mr. Kemp, you have a devious mind."

He smiled. "What else is new?"

LIBBY WAS FURIOUS at herself for not thinking of her father's impressive coin collection until now. She'd watched those coins come in the mail for years without really noticing them. But now they were important. They meant the difference between losing their home and getting it back again.

She sat on pins and needles over the weekend, until Kemp heard from the private detective the following Monday afternoon.

He buzzed Libby and told her to come into the office.

He was smiling when she got there. "We found them," he said, chuckling when she made a whoop loud enough to bring Mabel down the hall.

"It's okay," Libby told her coworker, "I've just had some good news for a change!"

Mabel grinned and went back to work.

Libby sat down in the chair in front of Kemp's big desk, smiling and leaning forward.

"Your father left the coins with a dealer who locked them in his safe. He was told not to let Janet have them under any circumstances," he added gently. "Besides that, there was a will. He's got that, too. It's not a self-made will, either. It was done by a lawyer in the dealer's office and witnessed by two people who work for him."

Libby's eyes filled with tears. "Daddy knew! He knew she was trying to cut us out of the will!"

"He must have," he conceded. "Apparently she'd made some comments about what she was going to do when he died. And she'd been harassing him about his health, making remarks about his heart being weak, as well." His jaw clenched. "Whatever the cause, he changed the will in your favor—yours and Curt's. This will is going to stand up in a court of law and it changes the entire financial situation. You and Curt can go home and I'll get the will into probate immediately."

"But the insurance…"

He nodded. "She was the beneficiary for one of his insurance policies." He smiled at her surprise. "There's another one, a half-a-million-dollar policy, that he left with the same dealer who has the will. You and Curt are co-beneficiaries."

"He didn't contact us!" she exclaimed suddenly.

"Yes, and that's the interesting part," he said. "He tried to contact you and Janet told him that you and Curt were out of the country on an extended vacation. She planned to go and talk to him the very day you made the remarks about Violet's father and having locks put on your bedroom doors. She ran for her life before she had time to try to get to the rest of your inheritance." He chuckled. "Maybe she had some idea of what the seller was guarding and decided that the insurance policy would hold her for a while without risking arrest."

"Oh, thank God," she whispered, shivering with delight. "Thank God! We can go home!"

"Apparently," he agreed, smiling. "I'm going to drive up to San Antonio today and get those documents and the coin collection."

She was suddenly concerned. "But what if Janet hears about it? She had that friend in San Antonio who called and tried to get us off the property…" She stopped abruptly. "That's why they were trying to get us out of the house! They knew about the coin collection!" She sat back heavily. "But they could be dangerous…."

"Cash Grier is going with me."

She pursed her lips amusedly. "Okay."

He chuckled. "Nobody is going to try to attack me with Grier in the car. Even if he isn't armed."

"Good point," she agreed.

"So call your brother and tell him the news," he said. "And stop worrying. You're going to land on your feet, Libby."

"How's Violet?" she asked without thinking.

He stood up, his hands deep in his pockets. "She and her mother are distraught, as you might imagine. They never realized that Mr. Hardy had been the victim of foul play. I've tried to keep it out of the papers, but when Janet's caught, it's going to be difficult."

"Is there anything I can do?"

He smiled. "Take them a pizza and let Violet talk to you about it," he suggested. "She misses working here."

"I miss her, too."

He shifted, averting his gaze. "I offered to let her come back to work here."

"You did?" she asked, enthused.

"She's going to think about it," he added. "You might, uh, tell her how shorthanded we are here, and that the temporary woman we got had to quit. Maybe she'll feel sorry for us and come back."

She smiled. "I'll do my best."

He looked odd. "Thanks," he said stiffly.

CHAPTER NINE

THE VERY NEXT DAY, Kemp came into the office grinning like a lottery winner. He was carrying a cardboard box, in which was a mahogany box full of rare gold coins, an insurance policy, a few personal items that had belonged to Riddle Collins and a fully executed new will.

Libby had to sit down when Kemp presented her with the hard evidence of her father's love for herself and Curt.

"The will is legal," he told her. "I'm going to take it right to the courthouse and file it. It will supersede the will that Janet probably still has in her possession. You should take the coins to the bank and put them in a safe-deposit box until you're ready to dispose of them. The dealer said he'll buy them from you at market value anytime you're ready to sell them."

"But I'll have to use them as collateral for a loan to make the loan payment…"

"Actually, no, you won't," Kemp said with a smile, drawing two green-covered passbooks out of the box and handing them to her.

"What are these?" she asked blankly.

"Your father had two other bank accounts, both in San Antonio." He smiled warmly. "There's more than enough there to pay off the mortgage completely so that the ranch is free and clear. You'll still have a small fortune left over. You and your brother are going to be rich, Libby. Congratulations."

She cried a little, both for her father's loving care of them even after death and for having come so close to losing everything.

She pulled a tissue out of the pocket of her slacks and wiped her red eyes. "I'll take these to the Jacobsville Municipal Bank right now," she said firmly, "and have the money transferred here from San Antonio. Then I'll have them issue a cashier's check to pay off the other bank," she added with glee.

"Good girl. You can phone the insurance company about the death benefit, too. How does it feel, not to have to worry about money?"

She chuckled. "Very good." She eyed him curiously. "Does this mean you're firing me?"

"Well, Libby, you won't really need to work for a living anymore," he began slowly.

"But I love my job!" she exclaimed, and had the pleasure of watching his high cheekbones go ruddy. "Can't I stay?"

He drew in a long breath. "I'd be delighted if you would," he confessed. "I can't seem to keep a paralegal these days."

She smiled, remembering that Callie Kirby had been one, until she'd married Micah Steele. There had been two others after her, but neither had stayed long.

"Then it's settled. I have to go and call Curt!"

"Go to the bank first, Libby," he instructed with a grin. "And I'll get to the courthouse. Mabel, we're going to be out of the office for thirty minutes!"

"Okay, boss!"

They went down the hall together and they stopped dead.

Violet was back at her desk, across from a grinning Mabel, looking radiant. "You said I could come back," she told Kemp at once, looking pretty and uncertain at the same time.

He drew in a sharp breath and his eyes lingered on her. "I certainly did," he agreed. "Are you staying?"

She nodded.

"How about making a fresh pot of coffee?" he asked.

"Regular?" she asked.

He averted his gaze to the door. "Half and half," he murmured. "Caffeine isn't good for me."

He went out the door, leaving Violet's jaw dropped.

"I told you he missed you," Libby whispered as she followed Kemp out the door and onto the sidewalk.

LIBBY AND CURT were able to go home the next morning. But their arrival was bittersweet. The house had been ransacked in their absence.

"We'd better call the sheriff's office," Curt said angrily, when they'd ascertained that the disorder was thorough. "We'll need to have a report filed on this for insurance purposes."

"Do we even have insurance?"

He nodded. "Dad had a homeowner's policy. I've been keeping up the payments, remember?"

She righted a chair that had been turned over next to the desk her father had used in his study. The filing cabinet had been emptied onto the floor, along with a lot of other documents pertaining to the ranch's business.

"They were looking for that coin collection," Curt guessed as he picked up the phone. "I'll bet anything Janet knew about it. She must be running short of cash already!"

"Thank God Mr. Kemp was able to track it down," she said.

"Sheriff's department?" Curt said into the telephone receiver. "I need you to send someone out to the Collins ranch. That's right, it's just past Jordan Powell's place. We've had a burglary. Yes. Okay. Thanks!" He hung up. "I talked to Hayes. He's going to come himself, along with his investigator."

"I thought he was overseas with his army unit in Iraq," she commented.

"He's back." He glanced at her amusedly. "You used to have a case on him, just before you went nuts over Jordan Powell."

She hated hearing Jordan's name mentioned. "Hayes is nice."

"So he is." He toyed with the telephone cord. "Libby, Jordan's having some bad times lately. His association with the Merrills has made him enemies."

"That was his choice," she reminded her brother.

"He was good to us, when Dad died."

She knew that. It didn't help. Her memories of Jordan's betrayal were too fresh. "Think I should do anything before they get here?"

"Make coffee," he suggested dryly. "Hayes's investigator is Mack Hughes, and he lives on caffeine."

"I'll do that."

SHERIFF HAYES CARSON pulled up at the front steps in his car, a brightly polished black vehicle with all sorts of antennae sticking out of it. The investigator, Mack Hughes, pulled up beside it in his black SUV with a deck of lights on the roof.

"Thanks for coming so quickly," Curt said, shaking hands with both men. "You remember my sister, Libby."

"Hello, Elizabeth," Hayes said with a grin, having always used her real first name instead of the nickname most people called her by. He was dashing, with blond hair and dark eyes, tall and muscular and big. He was in his mid-thirties; one tough customer, too. He and Cash Grier often went head-to-head in disputes, although they were good colleagues when there was an emergency.

"Hi, Hayes," she replied with a smile. "Hello, Mack."

Mack, tall and dark, nodded politely. "Let's see what you've got."

They ushered the law-enforcement officers inside and stood back while they went about searching for clues.

"Any idea who the perpetrators were?" Hayes murmured while Mack looked around.

"Someone connected to our stepmother, most likely," Libby commented. "Dad had a very expensive coin collection and some secret bank accounts that even we didn't know about. If that's what they were looking for, they're out of luck. Mr. Kemp tracked them to San Antonio. Everything's in the bank now and a new will we recovered is in the proper hands."

Hayes whistled softly. "Lucky for you."

There was a sudden commotion in the front yard, made by a truck skidding to a stop between the two law-enforcement vehicles. A dusty, tired Jordan Powell came up the steps, taking them two at a time, and stopped abruptly in the living room.

"What's happened?" he asked at once, his eyes homing to Libby with dark concern.

"The house was ransacked," Hayes told him. "Have you seen anything suspicious?"

"No. But I'll ask my men," Jordan assured them. He looked at Libby for a long time. "You okay?"

"Curt and I are fine, thanks," she said in a polite but reserved tone.

Jordan looked around at the jumble of furniture and paper on the floor, along with lamps and broken pieces of ceramic items that had been on the mantel over the fireplace.

"This wasn't necessary," Jordan said grimly. "Even if they were looking for something, they didn't have to break everything in the house."

"It was malicious, all right," Hayes agreed. He moved just in front of Libby. "I heard from Grier that you've had two confrontations with Julie Merrill, one of them physically violent. She's also been implicated in acts of vandalism. I want to know if you think she might have had any part in this."

Libby glanced at Jordan apprehensively.

"It could be a possibility," Jordan said, to her dismay. "She was jealous of Libby and I've just broken with Julie and her father. She didn't take it well."

"I'll add her to the list of suspects," Hayes said quietly. "But I have to tell you, she isn't going to like being accused."

"I don't care," Curt replied, answering for himself as well as Libby. "Nobody has a right to do something like this."

"Boss!" Mack called from the back porch. "Could you ask the Collinses to come out here, please?"

Curt stood aside to let Libby go first. On the small

back stoop, Mack was squatting down, looking at a big red gas can. "This yours?" he asked Curt.

Curt frowned. "We don't have one that big," he replied. "Ours is locked up in the outbuilding next to the barn."

Mack and Hayes exchanged curious looks.

"There's an insurance policy on the house," Libby remarked worriedly. "It's got Janet, our stepmother, listed as beneficiary."

"That narrows down the suspects," Hayes remarked.

"Surely she wouldn't…" Libby began.

"You've made a lot of trouble for her," Jordan said grimly. "And now she's missed out on two savings accounts and a will that she didn't even know existed."

"How did you know that?" Libby asked belligerently.

"My cousin owns the Municipal Bank," Jordan said nonchalantly.

"He had no business telling you anything!" Libby protested.

"He didn't, exactly," Jordan confessed. "I heard him talking to one of his clerks about opening the new account for you and setting up a safe-deposit box."

"Eavesdropping should be against the law," she muttered.

"I'll make a note of it," Hayes said with a grin.

She grinned back. "Thanks, Hayes."

He told Mack to start marking evidence to be collected. "We'll see if we can lift any latent prints," he told the small group. "If it was Janet, or someone she hired, they'll probably have been wearing gloves. If it was Julie Merrill, we might get lucky."

"I hope we can connect somebody to it," Libby said

wearily, looking around. "If for no other reason than to make them pay to help have this mess cleaned up!"

"I'll take care of that," Jordan said at once, and reached for his cell phone.

"We don't need—!" Libby began hotly.

But Jordan wasn't listening. He was talking to Amie at his ranch, instructing her to phone two housekeepers she knew who helped her with heavy tasks and send them over to the Collins place.

"You might as well give up," Hayes remarked dryly. "Once Jordan gets the bit between his teeth, it would take a shotgun to stop him. You know that."

She sighed angrily. "Yes. I know."

Hayes pushed his wide-brimmed hat back off his forehead and smiled down at Libby. "Are you doing anything Saturday night?" he asked. "They're having a campaign rally for Calhoun's supporters at Shea's."

"I know, I'm one of them," she replied, smiling. "Are you going to be there?"

He shrugged. "I might as well. Somebody'll have a beer too many and pick a fight, I don't doubt. Tiny the bouncer will have his hands full."

"Great!" she said enthusiastically.

Jordan was eavesdropping and not liking what he heard. He wanted to tell Hayes to back off. He wanted to tell Libby what he felt. But he couldn't get the words out.

"If you two are moving back in," Hayes added, "I think we'd better have somebody around overnight. I've got two volunteer deputies in the Sheriff's Posse who would be willing, I expect, if you'll keep them in coffee."

She smiled. "I'd be delighted. Thanks, Hayes. It

would make me feel secure. We've got a shotgun, but I don't even know where it is."

"You could both stay with me until Hayes gets a handle on who did this," Jordan volunteered.

"No, thanks," Libby said quietly, trying not to remember that Jordan had already asked her to do that. No matter how she felt about the big idiot, she wasn't going to step into Julie Merrill's place.

"This is our home," Curt added.

Jordan drew in a long, sad breath. "Okay. But if you need help…"

"We'll call Hayes, thanks," Libby said, turning back to the sheriff. "I need to tidy up the kitchen. Is it all right?"

Hayes went with her into the small room and looked around. There wasn't much damage in there and nothing was broken. "It looks okay. Go ahead, Libby. I'll see you Saturday, then?"

She grinned up at him. "Of course."

He grinned back and then rejoined the men in the living room. "I'm going to talk to my volunteers," he told Curt. "I'll be in touch."

"Thanks a lot, Hayes," Curt replied.

"Just doing my job. See you, Jordan."

"Yeah." Jordan didn't offer to shake hands. He glared after the other man as he went out the front door.

"I can clean my own house," Libby began impatiently.

Jordan met her eyes evenly. "I've made a lot of mistakes. I've done a lot of damage. I know I can't make it up to you in one fell swoop, but let me do what I can to make amends. Will you?"

Libby looked at her brother, who shrugged and walked away, leaving her to deal with Jordan alone.

"Some help you are," Libby muttered at his retreating back.

"I don't like the idea of that gas can," Jordan said, ignoring her statement. "You can't stay awake twenty-four hours a day. If Janet is really desperate enough to set fire to the house trying to get her hands on the insurance money, neither you nor Curt is going to be safe here."

"Hayes is getting us some protection," she replied coolly.

"I know that. But even deputies have to use the bathroom occasionally," he said flatly. "Why won't you come home with me?"

She lifted her chin. "This is my place, mine and Curt's. We're not running anymore."

He sighed. "I admire your courage, Libby. But it's misplaced this time."

She turned away. "I've got a lot to do, Jordan. Thanks anyway."

He caught her small waist from behind and held her just in front of him. His warm breath stirred the hair at the back of her head. "I was afraid."

"Of…what?" she asked, startled.

His big hands contracted. "You're very young, even for a woman your age," he said stiffly. "Young women are constantly changing."

She turned in his hold, curious. She looked up at him without understanding. "What has that got to do with anything?"

He reached out and traced her mouth with his thumb. He looked unusually solemn. "You really don't know, do you?" he asked quietly. "That's part of the problem."

"You aren't making any sense."

"I am. You're just not hearing what I'm saying." He bent and kissed her softly beside her ear, drawing away almost at once. "Never mind. You'll figure it out one day. Meanwhile, I'm going to do a better job of looking after you."

"I can—"

He interrupted at once. "If you say 'look after myself,' so help me, I'll…!"

She glared at him.

He glared back.

"You're up against someone formidable, whoever it is," he continued. "I'm not letting anything happen to you, Libby."

"Fat lot you cared before," she muttered.

He sighed heavily. "Yes, I know. I'll eat crow without catsup if it will help you trust me again."

"Julie's very pretty," she said reluctantly.

"She isn't a patch on you, butterfly," he said quietly.

She hesitated. But she wasn't giving in easily. He'd hurt her. No way was she going to run headfirst into his arms the first time he opened them.

She watched him suspiciously.

His broad chest rose and fell. "Okay. We'll do it your way. I'll see you at Shea's."

"You're the enemy," she pointed out. "You're not on Calhoun's team."

He shrugged. "A man can change sides, can't he?" he mused. "Meanwhile, if you need me, I'll be at the house. If you call, I'll come running."

She nodded slowly. "All right."

He smiled at her.

Curt came back in. He was as cool to Jordan as his

sister. The older man shrugged and left without another word.

"Now he's changed sides again," Libby told Curt when Jordan was gone.

"Jordan's feeling his age, Libby," Curt told her. "And some comments were made by his cowboys about that kiss they saw."

Her eyebrows arched. "What?"

He sighed. "I never had the heart to tell you. But one of the older hands said Jordan was trying to rob the cradle. It enraged Jordan. But it made him think, too. He knows how sheltered you've been. I think he was trying to protect you."

"From what?"

"Maybe from a relationship he didn't think you were ready for," he replied. "Julie was handy, he'd dated her a time or two, and she swarmed all over him just about the time he was drawing back from you. I expect he was flattered by her attention and being invited into that highbrow social set that shut out his mother after she was disinherited because she married his father. The local society women just turned their backs on her. She was never invited anywhere ever again. Jordan felt it keenly, that some of his playmates weren't allowed to invite him to their houses."

"I didn't know it was so hard on him. He's only told me bits and pieces about his upbringing."

"He doesn't advertise it," he added. "She gave up everything to marry his father. She worked as a housekeeper in one of the motels owned by her father's best friend. It was a rough upbringing for Jordan."

"I can imagine." She sighed, unable to prevent her heart from thawing.

SHEA'S WAS FILLED to capacity on Saturday evening. Cash Grier got a lot of attention because he brought Tippy with him. She looked good despite her ordeals, except for the small indications of healing cuts on her lovely face. She was weak and still not totally recovered and it showed. Nevertheless, she was still the most beautiful woman in the room. But she had eyes only for Cash and that showed, too.

When they got on the dance floor together, Libby was embarrassed to find herself staring wistfully at them. Tippy melted into Cash's tall body as if she'd found heaven. He looked that way, as well. They clung together to the sound of an old love song. And when she looked up at him, he actually stopped dancing and just stared at her.

"They make a nice couple," Jordan said from behind her.

She glanced up at him. He looked odd. His dark eyes were quiet, intent on her uplifted face.

"Yes, they do," she replied. "They seem to fit together very well."

He nodded. "Dance with me," he said in a deep voice, and drew her into his arms.

She hesitated, but only for a few seconds. She'd built dreams on those kisses they'd shared and she thought it was all over. But the way he was holding her made her knees weak. His big hand covered hers against his chest and pressed it hard into the warm muscle.

"I've been an idiot," he said at her ear.

"What do you mean?" she wondered aloud, drugged by his closeness.

"I shouldn't have backed off," he replied quietly. "I got cold feet at the very worst time."

"Jordan…"

"…mind if I cut in?" Hayes Carson asked with a grin.

Jordan stopped, his mind still in limbo. "We were talking," he began.

"Plenty of time for that later. Shall we, Libby?" he asked, and moved right in front of Jordan. He danced Libby away before she had a chance to stop him.

"Now that's what I call a jealous man," Hayes murmured dryly, glancing over her shoulder at Jordan. "No need to ask about the lay of the land."

"Jordan doesn't feel that way about me," Libby protested.

"He doesn't?"

She averted her eyes to the crowded dance floor. "He isn't a marrying man."

"Uh-huh."

She glanced up at Hayes, who was still grinning.

She flushed at the look in his eyes.

Across the room, Jordan Powell saw that flush and had to restrain himself from going over there and tearing Libby out of Hayes's embrace.

"What the devil are you doing here?" Calhoun Ballenger asked abruptly.

Jordan glanced at him wryly. "Not much," he murmured. "But I came to ask if you needed another willing ally. I've, uh, changed camps."

Calhoun's eyebrows went up almost to his blond hairline.

"I do like to be on the winning side," Jordan drawled.

Calhoun burst out laughing. "Well, you're not a bad diplomat, I guess," he confessed, holding out his hand. "Welcome aboard."

"My pleasure."

JORDAN CONTRIVED TO drive Libby and Curt home, but he was careful to let Curt go into the ranch house before he cut off the engine and turned to Libby.

"There's been some news," he said carefully.

"About Janet?" she exclaimed.

"About Julie," he corrected. He toyed with a strand of her hair in the dim light of the car interior. "One of Grier's men saw her with a known drug dealer earlier today. She's put her neck in a noose and she doesn't even know it."

"She uses, doesn't she?" she asked.

He shrugged. "Her behavior is erratic. She must."

"I'm sorry. You liked her…"

He bent and kissed her hungrily, pulling her across his lap to wrap her up in his warm, strong arms. "I like you," he whispered against her mouth. "More than I ever dreamed I could!"

She wanted to ask questions, but she couldn't kiss him and breathe at the same time. She gave up and ran her arms up around his neck. She relaxed into his close embrace and kissed him back until her mouth grew sore and swollen.

He sighed into her throat as he held her and rocked her in his arms in the warm darkness.

"Libby, I think we should start going out together."

She blinked. "You and me?"

He nodded. "You and me." He drew back and looked down at her possessively. "I could give up liver and on-ions, if I had to. But I can't give you up."

"Listen, I don't have affairs…"

He kissed her into silence. "Neither do I. So I guess maybe we won't sleep together after all."

"But if we go out together…" she said worriedly.

He grinned. "You have enough self-restraint for both of us, I'm sure," he drawled. "You can keep me honest."

She drew back a little and noted the position of his big lean hands under her blouse. She looked at him intently.

He cleared his throat and drew his hands out from under the blouse. "Every man is entitled to one little slip. Right?" His eyes were twinkling.

She laughed. "Okay."

He touched her mouth with his one last time. "In that case, you'd better rush inside before I forget to be honest."

"Thanks for bringing us home."

"My pleasure. Lock the doors," he added seriously. "And I'm only a phone call away if you need me. You call me," he emphasized. "Not Hayes Carson. Got that?"

"And since when did I become your personal property?" she asked haughtily.

"Since the minute you let me put my hands under your blouse," he shot right back, laughing. "Think about it."

She got out of the vehicle, dizzy and with her head swimming. In one night, everything had changed.

"Don't worry," he added gently, leaning out the window. "I have enough restraint for both of us!"

Before she could answer him, he gunned the engine and took off down the road.

CHAPTER TEN

FOR THE NEXT few days, Jordan was at Libby's house more than at his own. He smoothed over hard feelings with her brother and became a household fixture. Libby and Curt filed the insurance claim, paid off the mortgage, and started repurchasing cattle for the small ranch.

Janet was found a couple of days later at a motel just outside San Antonio, with a man. He turned out to be the so-called attorney who'd phoned and tried to get Libby and Curt out of their home. She was arrested and charged with murder in the death of Violet's father. There was DNA evidence taken from the dead man's clothing and the motel room that was directly linked to Janet. It placed her at the motel the night Mr. Hardy died. When she realized the trouble she was in, she tried to make a deal for a reduced sentence. She agreed to confess to the murder in return for a life sentence without hope of parole. But she denied having a gas can. She swore that she never had plans to burn down Riddle Collins's house with his children in it. Nobody paid her much attention. She'd told so many lies.

It was a different story for Julie Merrill. She continued to make trouble, and not only for Calhoun Ballenger. She was determined that Jordan wasn't going to desert her for little Libby Collins. She had a plan. Two days before the hearing to decide the fate of the police officers who'd arrested her father— Saturday, she put it into practice.

She phoned Libby at work and apologized profusely for all the trouble she'd caused.

"I never meant to be such a pain in the neck," she assured Libby. "I want to make it up to you. You get off at one on Saturdays, don't you? Suppose you come over here for lunch?"

"To your house?" Libby replied warily.

"Yes. I've had our cook make something special," she purred. "And I can tell you my side of the story. Will you?"

Dubious, Libby hesitated.

"Surely you aren't afraid of me?" Julie drawled. "I mean, what could I do to you, even if I had something terrible in mind?"

"You don't need to feed me," Libby replied cautiously. "I don't hold grudges."

"You'll come, then," Julie persisted. "Today at one. Will you?"

It was against her better judgment. But it was a bad idea to keep a feud going, especially now that Jordan seemed really interested in her.

"Okay," Libby said finally. "I'll be there at one."

"Thanks!" Julie said huskily. "You don't know how much I appreciate it! Uh, I don't guess you'd like to bring your brother, too?" she added suddenly.

Libby frowned. "Curt's driving a cattle truck for Duke Wright up to San Antonio today."

"Well, then, another time, perhaps! I'll see you at one." Julie hung up, with a bright and happy note in her voice.

Libby frowned. Was she stupid to go to the woman's home? But why would Julie risk harming her now, with the primary election so close? It was the following Tuesday.

She phoned Jordan. "Guess what just happened?" she asked.

"You've realized how irresistible I am and you're rushing over to seduce me?" he teased. "Shall I turn down the covers on my bed?"

"Stop that," she muttered. "I'm serious."

"So am I!"

"Jordan," she laughed. "Julie just called to apologize. She invited me to lunch."

"Did she?" he asked. "Are you going?"

"I thought I might." She hesitated. "Don't you think it's a good idea, to mend fences, I mean?"

"I don't know, Libby," he replied seriously. "She's been erratic and out of control lately. I don't think it's a good idea. I'd rather you didn't."

"Are you afraid she might tell me something about you that I don't know?" she returned, suspicious.

He sighed. "No. It's not that. She wasn't happy when I broke off with her. I don't trust her."

"What can she do to me in broad daylight?" she laughed. "Shoot me?"

"Of course not," he scoffed.

"Then stop worrying. She only wants to apologize."

"You be careful," he returned. "And phone me when you get home. Okay?"

"Okay."

"How about a movie tonight?" he added. "There's a new mystery at the theater. You can even have popcorn."

"That sounds nice," she said, feeling warm and secure.

"I'll pick you up about six."

"I'll be ready. See you then."

She hung up and pondered over his misgivings. Surely he was overreacting. He was probably afraid Julie might make up a convincing lie about how intimate they'd been. Or perhaps she might be telling the truth. She only knew that she had to find out why Julie wanted to see her in person. She was going.

BUT SOMETHING NIGGLED at the back of her mind when she drove toward Julie's palatial home on the Jacobs River. Julie might have wanted to invite Libby over to apologize, but why would she want Curt to come, too? She didn't even know Curt.

Libby's foot lifted off the accelerator. Her home was next door to Jordan's. Julie was furious that Jordan had broken off with her. If the house was gone, Libby and Curt would have to move away again, as they had before…!

Libby turned the truck around in the middle of the road and sped toward her house. She wished she had a cell phone. There was no way to call for help. But she was absolutely certain what was about to happen. And she knew immediately that her stepmother hadn't been responsible for that gas can on the porch.

The question was, who had Julie convinced to set that fire for her? Or would she be crazy enough to try and do it herself?

Libby sped faster down the road. If only there had been state police, a sheriff's deputy, a policeman watching. She was speeding. It was the only time in her life she'd ever wanted to be caught!

But there were no flashing lights, no sirens. She was going to have to try and stop the perpetrator all by herself. She wasn't a big woman. She had no illusions about being able to tackle a grown man. She didn't even have a weapon. Wait. There was a tire tool in the boot! At least, she could threaten with it.

She turned into the road that led to the house. There was no smoke visible anywhere and no sign of any traffic. For the first time, she realized that she could be chasing make-believe villains. Why would she think that Julie Merrill would try to burn her house down? Maybe the strain of the past weeks was making her hysterical after all.

She pulled up in front of the house and got out, grabbing the tire tool out of the back. It wouldn't hurt to look around, now that she was here.

She moved around the side of the house, her heart beating wildly. Her palms were so sweaty that she had to get a better grip on the tire tool. She walked past the chimney, to the corner, and peered around. Her heart stopped.

There was a man there. A young, dark man. He had a can of gasoline. He was muttering to himself as he sloshed it on the back porch and the steps.

Libby closed her eyes and prayed for strength. There was nobody to help her. She had to do this alone.

She walked around the corner with the tire tool raised. "That's enough, you varmint! You're trespassing on private property and you're going to jail. The police are right behind me!"

Startled, the man dropped the gas can and stared wild-eyed at Libby.

Sensing an advantage, she started to run toward him, yelling at the top of her lungs.

To her amazement, he started running down a path

behind the house, with Libby right on his heels, still yelling.

Then something happened that was utterly in the realm of fantasy. She heard an engine behind her. An accomplice, she wondered, almost panicking.

Jordan Powell pulled up right beside her in his truck and threw open the passenger door. "Get in!" he called.

She didn't need prompting. She jumped right in beside him, tire tool and all, and slammed the door. "He was dousing the back porch with gas!" she panted. "Don't let him get away!"

"I don't intend to." His face was grim as he stood down on the accelerator and the truck shot forward on the pasture road, which was no more than tracks through tall grass.

The attempted arsonist was tiring. He was pretty thick in the middle and had short legs. He was almost to a beat-up old car sitting out of sight of the house near the barn when Jordan came alongside him on the driver's side.

"Hold it in the ruts!" he called to Libby.

Just as she grabbed the wheel, he threw open the door and leaped out on the startled, breathless young man, pinning him to the ground.

By the time Libby had the truck stopped, Jordan had the man by his shirt collar and was holding him there.

"Pick up the phone and call Hayes," he called to Libby.

Her hands were shaking, but she managed to dial 911 and give the dispatcher an abbreviated account of what had just happened. She was told that they contacted a deputy who was barely a mile away and he was starting toward the Collins place at that moment.

Libby thanked her nicely and cut off the phone.

"Who put you up to this?" Jordan demanded of the man. "Tell me, or so help me, I'll make sure you don't get out of prison until you're an old man!"

"It was Miss Julie," the young man sobbed. "I never done nothing like this in my life. My daddy works for her and he took some things out of her house. She said she'd turn him over to the police if I didn't do this for her."

"She'd have turned him over anyway, you fool," Jordan said coldly. "She was using you. Do you have any idea what the penalty is for arson?"

He was still sobbing. "I was scared, Mr. Powell."

Jordan relented, but only a little. He looked up as the sound of a siren was heard coming closer.

Libby opened the door of the truck and got out, just as a sheriff's car came flying down the track and stopped just behind the truck.

The deputy was Sammy Tibbs. They both knew him. He'd been in Libby's class in high school.

"What have you got, Jordan?" Sammy asked.

"A would-be arsonist," Jordan told him. "He'll confess if you ask him."

"I caught him pouring gas on my back porch and I chased him with my tire tool. I almost had him when Jordan came along," Libby said with a shy grin.

"Whew," Sammy whistled. "I hope I don't ever run afoul of you," he told her.

"That makes two of us," Jordan said, with a gentle smile for her.

"I assume you'll be pressing charges?" Sammy asked Libby as he handcuffed the young man, who was still out of breath.

"You can bet real money on it," Libby agreed. "And you'll need to pick up Julie Merrill as well, because this man said she told him to do it."

Sammy's hands froze on the handcuffs. "Julie Merrill? The state senator's daughter?"

"That's exactly who I mean," Libby replied. "She called and invited me over to lunch. Since she doesn't like me, I got suspicious and came home instead, just in time to catch this weasel in the act."

"Is this true?" the deputy asked the man.

"Mirandize him first," Jordan suggested. "Just so there won't be any loopholes."

"Good idea," Sammy agreed, and read the suspect his rights.

"Now, tell him," Libby prodded, glaring at the man who'd been within a hair of burning her house down.

The young man sighed as if the weight of the world was sitting on his shoulders. "Miss Merrill had something on my daddy, who works for her. She said if I'd set a fire on Miss Collins's back steps, she'd forget all about it. She just wanted to scare Miss Collins is all. She didn't tell me to burn the whole place down."

"Arson is arson," Sammy replied. "Don't touch anything," he told Libby. "I'll send our investigator back out there and call the state fire marshal. Arson is hard to prove, but this one's going to be a walk in the park."

"Thanks, Sammy," Libby said.

He grinned. "What for? You caught him!"

He put the scared suspect in the back of his car and sped off with a wave of his hand.

"That was too damned close," Jordan said, looking down at Libby with tormented eyes. "I couldn't believe it when I saw you chasing him through the field with a tire iron! What if he'd been armed?"

"He wasn't," she said. "Besides, he ran the minute I chased him, just like a black snake."

He pulled her into his arms and wrapped her up tight. There was a faint tremor in those strong arms.

"You brave idiot," he murmured into her neck. "Thank God he didn't get the fire started first. I can see you running inside to grab all the sentimental items and save them. You'd have been burned alive."

She grimaced, because he was absolutely right. She'd have tried to save her mementos of her father and mother, at any cost.

"Libby, I think we'd better get engaged," he said suddenly.

She was hallucinating. She said so.

He pulled back from her, his eyes solemn. "You're not hallucinating. If Julie realizes how serious this is between us, she'll back off."

"She's going to be in jail shortly, she'll have to," she pointed out.

"They can afford bail until her hearing, even so," he replied. "She'll be out for blood. But if she hears about the engagement, it might be enough to make her think twice."

"I'm not afraid of her," she said, although she really was.

"Humor me," he coaxed, bending to kiss her gently.

She smiled under the warm, comforting feel of his hard mouth on her lips. "Well…"

He nibbled her upper lip. "I'll get you a ring," he whispered.

"What sort?"

"What do you want?"

"I like emeralds," she whispered, standing on tiptoe to coax his mouth down again.

"An emerald, then."

"Nobody would know?"

He chuckled as he kissed her. "We might have to tell a few hundred people, just to make it believable. And we might actually have to get married, but that's okay, isn't it?"

She blinked. "Get...married?"

"That's what the ring's for, Libby," he said against her warm mouth. "Advance notice."

"But...you've always said you never wanted to get married."

"I always said there's the one woman a man can't walk away from," he added. He lifted his head and looked down at her, all the teasing gone. "I can't walk away from you. The past few weeks have been pure hell."

Her eyes widened with unexpected delight.

He traced her eyebrows with his forefinger. "I missed you," he whispered. "It was like being cut apart."

"You wanted Julie," she accused.

He grimaced. "I wanted you to think about what was happening. You've been sheltered your whole life. Duke Wright's wife was just like you. Then she married and had a child and got career-minded. That poor devil lives in hell because she didn't know what she wanted until it was too late!"

She searched his face quietly. "You think I'd want a career."

"I don't know, Libby," he bit off. He looked anguished. "I'm an all-or-nothing kind of man. I can't just stick my toe in to test the water. I jump in headfirst."

He...loved her. She was stunned. She couldn't believe she hadn't noticed, in all this time. Curt had seen it long before this. He'd tried to tell her. But she hadn't believed that a man like Jordan could be serious about someone like her.

Her lips fell apart with a husky sigh. She was on fire. She'd never dreamed that life could be so sweet. "I don't want a career," she said slowly.

"What if you do, someday?" he persisted.

She reached up and traced his firm, jutting chin with her fingertips. "I'm twenty-four years old, Jordan," she said. "If I don't know my own mind by now, I never will."

He still looked undecided.

She put both hands flat on his shirt. Under it, she could feel the muted thunder of his heartbeat. "Why don't we go to a movie?" she asked.

He seemed to relax. He smiled. "We could grab a hamburger for lunch and talk about it," he prompted.

"Okay."

"Then we'll go by the sheriff's department and you can write out a statement," he added.

She grimaced. "I guess I'll have to."

He nodded. "So will I." His eyes narrowed. "I wish I could see the look on Julie's face when the deputy sheriff pulls up in her driveway."

"I imagine she'll be surprised," Libby replied.

SURPRISED WAS AN UNDERSTATEMENT. Julie Merrill gaped at the young man in the deputy sheriff's uniform.

"You're joking," she said haughtily. "I... I had nothing to do with any attempted arson!"

"We have a man in custody who'll swear to it," he replied. "You can come peacefully or you can go out the door in handcuffs," he added, still pleasant and respectful. "Your choice, Miss Merrill."

She let out a harsh breath. "This is outrageous!"

"What's going on out here?" Her father, the state senator, came into the hall, weaving a little, and blinked when he saw the deputy. "What's he doing here?" he murmured.

"Your daughter is under arrest, senator," he was told as the deputy suddenly turned Julie around and cuffed her with professional dexterity. "For conspiracy to commit arson."

"Arson?" The senator blinked. "Julie?"

"She sent a man to burn down the Collins place," he was told. "We have two eyewitnesses, as well."

The senator gaped at his daughter. "I told you to leave that woman alone," he said, shaking his finger at her. "I told you Jordan would get involved if you didn't! You've cost me the election! Everybody around here will go to the polls Tuesday and vote for Calhoun Ballenger! You've ruined me!"

"Oh, no, sir, she hasn't," the deputy assured him with a grin. "Your nephew, the mayor, did that, by persecuting two police officers who were just doing their jobs." The smile faded. "You're going to see Monday night just how much hot water you've jumped into. That disciplinary hearing is going to be remembered for the next century in Jacobsville."

"Where are you taking my daughter?" the senator snorted.

"To jail, to be booked. You can call your attorney and arrange for a bail hearing whenever you like," the deputy added, with a speaking glance at the older man's condition. "If you're able."

"I'll call my own attorney," Julie said hotly. "Then I'll sue you for false arrest!"

"You're welcome to try," the deputy said. "Come along, Miss Merrill."

"Daddy, do try to sober up!" Julie said scathingly.

"What would be the point?" the senator replied. "Life was so good when I didn't know all about you, Julie. When I thought you were a sweet, kind, innocent woman like your mother…" He closed his eyes. "You killed that girl!"

"I did not! Think what you're saying!" Julie yelled at him.

Tears poured down his cheeks. "She died in my arms…"

"Let's go," the deputy said, tugging Julie Merrill out the door. He closed it on the sobbing politician.

Julie Merrill was lodged in the county jail until her bail hearing the following Monday morning. Meanwhile, Jordan and Libby had given their statements and the would-be arsonist was singing like a canary bird.

The disciplinary hearing for Chief Grier's two police officers was Monday night at the city council meeting.

It didn't take long. Within thirty minutes, the council had finished its usual business, Grier's officers were cleared of any misconduct, and the surprise guests at the hearing had Jacobsville buzzing for weeks afterward.

CHAPTER ELEVEN

JORDAN DROVE LIBBY to his house in a warm silence. He led her into the big, elegant living room and closed the door behind them.

"Want something to drink?" he asked, moving to a pitcher of iced tea that Amie had apparently left for them, along with a plate of homemade cake, covered with foil. "And a piece of pound cake?"

"I'd love that," she agreed.

He poured tea into two glasses and handed them to her, along with doilies to protect the coffee table from spots. He put cake onto two plates, with forks, and brought them along. But as he bent over the coffee table, he obscured Libby's plate. When he sat down beside her, there was a beautiful emerald solitaire, set in gold, lying on her piece of cake.

"Look at that," he exclaimed with twinkling dark eyes. "Why, it's an engagement ring! I wonder who could have put it there?" he drawled.

She picked it up, breathless. "It's beautiful."

"Isn't it?" he mused. "Why don't you try it on? If it fits," he added slyly, "you might turn into a fairy princess and get your own true prince as a prize!"

She smiled through her breathless delight. "Think so?"

"Darlin', I can almost guarantee it," he replied tenderly. "Want to give it a shot?"

He seemed to hold his breath while he waited for her reply. She had to fight tears. It was the most poignant moment of her entire life.

"Why don't you put it on for me?" she asked finally, watching him lift the ring and slide it onto her ring finger with something like relief.

"How about that?" he murmured dryly. "It's a perfect fit. Almost as if it were made just for you," he added.

She looked up at him and all the humor went out of his face. He held her small hand in his big one and searched her eyes.

"You love emeralds. I bought this months ago and stuck it in a drawer while I tried to decide whether or not it would be suicide to propose to you. Duke Wright's situation made me uncertain. I was afraid you hadn't seen enough of the world, or life, to be able to settle down here in Jacobsville. I was afraid to take a chance."

She moved a step closer. "But you finally did."

He cupped her face in his big, warm hands. "Yes. When I realized that I was spending time with Julie just to keep you at bay. If she'd been a better sort of person, it would have been a low thing to do. I was flattered at her interest and the company I got to keep. But I felt like a traitor when she started insulting you in public. I was too wrapped up in my own uncertainties to do what I should have done."

"Which was what?" she asked softly.

He bent to her soft mouth. "I should have realized that if you really love someone, everything works out." He kissed her tenderly. "I should have told you how I felt and given you a chance to spread your wings if you wanted to. I could have waited while you decided what sort of future you wanted."

She still couldn't believe that he didn't know how she felt. "I was crazy about you," she whispered huskily. "Everybody knew it except you." She reached up and linked her arms around his neck. "Duke's wife wasn't like me, Jordan," she added, searching his dark eyes. "She lived with a domineering father and a deeply religious mother. They taught her that a woman's role in life was to marry and obey her husband. She'd always done what they told her to do. But after she married Duke, she ran wild, probably giving vent to all those feelings of suffocated restriction she'd endured all her life. Getting pregnant on her wedding night was a big mistake for both of them, because then she really felt trapped." She took a deep breath. "If Duke hadn't rushed her into it, she'd have gone off and found her career and come back to him when she knew what she really wanted. It was a tragedy in the making from the very beginning."

"She didn't love him enough," he murmured.

"He didn't love her enough," she countered. "He got her pregnant, thinking it would hold her."

He sighed. "I want children," he said softly. "But not right away. We need time to get to know each other before we start a family, don't we?"

She smiled. "See? You ask me about things. You don't order me around. Duke was exactly the opposite." She traced his mouth with her fingertips. "That's why I stopped going out with him. He never asked me what I wanted to do, even what I wanted to eat when we went out together. He actually ordered meals for me before I could say what I liked." She glowered. "He ordered me liver and onions and I never went out with him again."

He lifted an eyebrow and grinned. "Darlin', I swear on my horse that I will never order you liver and onions." He crossed his heart.

He was so handsome when he grinned like that. Her heart expanded like a balloon with pure happiness. "Actually," she whispered, lifting up to him, "I'd even eat liver and onions for you."

"The real test of love," he agreed, gathering her up hungrily. "And I'd eat squash for you," he offered.

She smiled under the slow, sweet pressure of his mouth. Amie said he'd actually dumped a squash casserole in the middle of the living room carpet to make the point that he never wanted it again.

"This is nice," he murmured, lifting her completely off the floor. "But I can do better."

"Can you really?" she whispered, biting softly at his full lower lip. "Show me!"

He laughed, even though his body was making emphatic statements about how little time there was left for teasing. He was burning.

He put her down on the sofa and crushed her into it with the warm, hard length of his body.

"Jordan," she whispered breathlessly when he eased between her long legs.

"Don't panic," he said against her lips. "Amie's a scream away. Lift up."

She did, and he unfastened the bra and pushed it out of the way under her blouse. He deepened the kiss slowly, seductively, while his lean hands discovered the soft warmth of her bare breasts in a heated silence.

Her head began to spin. He was going to be her husband. She could lie in his arms all night long. They could have children together. After the tragedy of the past few months, it was like a trip to paradise.

She moaned and wrapped her long legs around his hips, urging him even closer. She felt the power and heat of him intimately. Her mouth opened, inviting the quick, hard thrust of his tongue.

"Oh, yes," she groaned into his hard mouth. Her hips lifted into his rhythmically, her breath gasping out at his ear as she clung to him. "Yes. That feels…good!"

A tortured sound worked out of his throat as he pressed her down hard into the soft cushions of the sofa, his hands already reaching for the zipper in the front of her slacks, so far gone that he was mindless.

The sound of footsteps outside the door finally penetrated the fog of passion that lay between them. Jordan lifted his head. Libby looked up at him, dazed and only half-aware of the sound.

"Amie," Jordan groaned, taking a steadying breath. "We have to stop."

"Tell her to go away," she whispered, laughing breathlessly.

"You tell her," he teased as he got to his feet. "She gets even in the kitchen. She can make squash look just like a corn casserole."

"Amie's Revenge?"

He nodded. "Amie's Revenge." Jordan paused. "I want to marry you," he said quietly. "I want it with all my heart."

She had to fight down tears to answer him. "I want it, too."

He drew her close, over his lap, and when he kissed her, it was with such breathless tenderness that she felt tears threatening again.

She slid her arms around his neck and kissed him back with fervent ardor. But he put her gently away.

"You don't want to ravish me?" she exclaimed. "You said once that you could do me justice in thirty minutes!"

"I lied," he said, chuckling. "I'd need two hours. And

Amie's skulking out in the hall, waiting for an opportunity to congratulate us," he added in a whisper. "We can't possibly shock her so soon before the wedding."

She hesitated. "So soon…?"

"I want to get married as quickly as possible," he informed her. "All we need is the blood tests, a license, and I've already got us a minister. Unless you want a formal wedding in a big church with hundreds of guests," he added worriedly.

"No need, since you've already got us a minister," she teased.

He relaxed. "Thank God! The idea of a morning coat and hundreds of people…"

She was kissing him, so he stopped talking.

Just as things were getting interesting, there was an impatient knock at the door. "Well?" Amie called through it.

"She said yes!" Jordan called back.

The door opened and Amie rushed in, grinning from ear to ear.

"She hates squash," he said in a mock whisper.

"I won't ever make it again," Amie promised.

He hugged her. After a minute, Libby joined them. She hugged the housekeeper, too.

"Welcome to the family!" Amie laughed.

And that was the end of any heated interludes for the rest of the evening.

THE NEXT FEW days went by in a blur of activity. When the votes were counted on Tuesday at the primary election, Senator Merrill lost the Democratic candidacy by a ten-to-one margin. A recall of the city fathers was announced, along with news of a special election to follow.

Councilman Culver and the mayor were both implicated in drug trafficking, along with Julie Merrill. Julie had managed to get bail the day before the primary, but she hadn't been seen since. She was also still in trouble for the arson conspiracy. Her father had given an impressive concession speech, in front of the news media, and congratulated Calhoun Ballenger with sincerity. It began to be noticed that he improved when his daughter's sins came to light. Apparently he'd been duty-bound to try and protect her, and it had almost killed his conscience. He'd started drinking heavily, and then realized that he was likely to lose his state senate seat for it. He'd panicked, gone to the mayor, and tried to get the charges dropped.

One irresponsible act had cost Senator Merrill everything. But, he told Calhoun, he still had his house and his health. He'd stand by his daughter, of course, and do what he could for her. Perhaps retirement wouldn't be such a bad thing. His daughter could not be reached for comment. She was now being hunted by every law-enforcement officer in Texas and government agents on the drug charges, which were formidable. Other unsavory facts were still coming to light about her doings.

Jordan finally understood why Libby had tried so hard to keep him out of Julie's company and he apologized profusely for refusing to listen to her. Duke Wright's plight had made him somber and afraid, especially when he realized how much he loved Libby. He was afraid to take a chance on her. He had plenty of regrets.

Libby accepted his apology and threw herself into politics as one of Calhoun's speechwriters, a job she loved. But, she told Jordan, she had no desire to do it for a profession. She was quite happy to work for Mr. Kemp and raise a family in Jacobsville.

DIANA PALMER

On the morning of Libby's marriage to Jordan, she was almost floating with delight. "I can't believe the things that have happened in two weeks," Libby told her brother at the church door as they waited for the music to go down the aisle together. "It's just amazing!"

"For a small town, it certainly is," he agreed. He grinned. "Happy?"

"Too happy," she confessed, blushing. "I never dreamed I'd be marrying Jordan."

"I did. He's been crazy about you for years, but Duke Wright's bad luck really got to him. Fortunately, he did see the light in time."

She took a deep breath as the first strains of the wedding march were heard. "I'm glad it's just us and not a crowd," she murmured.

He didn't speak. His eyes twinkled as he opened the door.

Inside, all the prominent citizens of Jacobsville were sitting in their pews, waiting for the bride to be given away by her brother. Cash Grier was there with Tippy. So were Calhoun Ballenger and Abby, Justin Ballenger and Shelby Jacobs Ballenger. And the Hart brothers, all five of them including the attorney general, with their wives. The Tremaynes. Mr. Kemp, with Violet! The Drs. Coltrain and Dr. Morris and Dr. Steele and their wives. Eb Scott and his wife. Cy Parks and his wife. It was a veritable who's who of the city.

"Surprise," Curt whispered in her ear, and tugged her along down the aisle. She was adorned in a simple white satin gown with colorful embroidery on the bodice and puffy sleeves, a delicate veil covering her face and shoulders. She carried a bouquet of lily of the valley and pink roses.

Jordan Powell, in a soft gray morning coat and all the trappings, was waiting for her at the altar with the minister. He looked handsome and welcoming and he was smiling from ear to ear.

Libby thought back over the past few agonizing weeks and realized all the hardships and heartache she'd endured made her truly appreciate all the sweet blessings that had come into her life. She smiled through her tears and stopped at Jordan's side, her small hand searching blindly for his as she waited to speak her vows. She'd never felt more loved or happier than she was at that moment. She only wished her parents had lived to see her married.

JUST AFTER THE WEDDING, there was a reception at the church fellowship hall, catered by Barbara's Café. The wedding cake was beautiful, with a colorful motif that exactly matched the embroidery on Libby's wedding gown.

She and Jordan were photographed together cutting the cake and then interacting with all their unexpected guests. The only sticky moment was when handsome Hayes Carson bent to kiss Libby.

"Careful, Hayes," Jordan said from right beside him. "I'm watching you!"

"Great idea," Hayes replied imperturbably and grinned. "You could use a few lessons."

And he kissed Libby enthusiastically while Jordan fumed.

WHEN THEY WERE finally alone, hours later in Galveston, Jordan was still fuming about that kiss.

"You know Hayes was teasing," she said, coaxing him into her arms. "But I'm not. I've waited twenty-four years for this," she added with a wry smile. "I have great expectations."

He drew her close with a worldly look. "And I expect to satisfy them fully!"

"I'm not going to be very good at this, at first," she said breathlessly, when he began to undress her. "Is it all right?"

He smiled tenderly. "You're going to be great at it," he countered. "The only real requirement is love. We're rich in that."

She relaxed a little, watching his dark eyes glow as he uncovered the soft, petal-pink smoothness of her bare skin. She was a little nervous. Nobody had seen her undressed since she was a little girl.

Jordan realized that and it made him even more gentle. He'd never been with an innocent, but he knew enough about women that it wasn't going to be a problem. She loved him. He wanted nothing more than to please her.

When she was standing in just her briefs, he bent and smoothed his warm mouth over the curve of her breasts. She smelled of roses. There was a faint moisture under his lips, which he rightly attributed to fear.

He lifted his head and looked down into her wide, uncertain eyes. "Women have been doing this since the dawn of time," he whispered. "If it wasn't fun, nobody would want to do it. Right?"

She laughed nervously. "Right."

He smiled tenderly. "So just relax and let me drive. It's going to be a journey you'll never forget."

Her hands went to his tie. "Okay. But I get to make suggestions," she told him impishly, and worked to unfasten the tie and then his white shirt. She opened it over a bronzed chest thick with dark, soft hair. He felt furry. But under the hair was hard, warm muscle. She liked the way he felt.

He kissed her softly while he coaxed her hands to his belt. She hesitated.

"Don't agonize over it," he teased, moving her hands aside to unfasten it himself. "We'll go slow."

"I'm not really a coward," she whispered unsteadily. "It's just uncharted territory. I've never even looked at pictures…"

He could imagine what sort of pictures she was talking about. He only smiled. "Next time, you'll be a veteran and it won't intimidate you."

"Are you sure?" she asked.

He bent to her mouth again. "I'm sure."

His warm lips moved down her throat to her breasts, but this time they weren't gently teasing. They were invasive and insistent as they opened on the hard little nubs his caresses had already produced. When his hands moved her hips lazily against the hard thrust of his powerful body, she began to feel drugged.

She'd thought it would be embarrassing and uncomfortable to make love in the light. But Jordan was slow and thorough, easing her into an intimacy beyond anything she'd ever dreamed. He cradled her against him on the big bed, arousing her to such a fever pitch that when he removed the last bit of her clothing, it was a relief to feel the coolness of the room against her hot skin. And by the time he removed his own clothes, she was too hungry to be embarrassed. In fact, she was as aggressive as he was, starving for him in the tempestuous minutes that followed.

She remembered the first kiss they'd shared, beside her pickup truck at his fence. She'd known then that she'd do anything he wanted her to do. But this was far from the vague dreams of fulfillment she'd had when she was alone. She hadn't known that passion was like a fever that nothing could quench, that desire brought intense desperation. She hadn't known that lovemaking was blind, deaf, mute slavery to a man's touch.

"I would die for you," Jordan whispered huskily at her ear as he moved slowly into total possession with her trembling body.

"Will it…hurt?" she managed in a stranger's voice as she hesitated just momentarily at the enormity of what was happening to her.

He laughed sensuously as he began to move lazily against her. "Are you kidding?" he murmured. And with a sharp, deft movement, he produced a sensation that lifted her clear of the bed and against him with an unearthly little cry of pleasure.

From there, it was a descent into total madness. She shivered with every powerful thrust of his body. She clung to him with her arms, her legs, her soul. She moaned helplessly as sensation built on sensation, until she was almost screaming from the urgent need for satisfaction.

She heard her own voice pleading with him, but she couldn't understand her own words. She drove for fulfillment, her body demanding, feverishly moving with his as they climbed the spiral of passion together.

She felt suddenly as if she'd been dropped from a great height into a hot, throbbing wave of pleasure that began and never seemed to end. She clung to him, terrified that he might stop, that he might draw back, that he might pull away.

"Shh," he whispered tenderly. "I won't stop. It's all right. It's all right, honey. I love you…so much!"

"I love you, too!" she gasped.

Then he began to shudder, even as she felt herself move from one plane of ecstasy to another, and another, and another, each one deeper and more satisfying than the one before. At one point she thought she might actually die from the force of it. Her eyes closed and she let the waves wash over her in succession, glorying in the unbelievably sweet aftermath.

Above her, Jordan was just reaching his own culmination. He groaned harshly at her ear and shuddered one last time before he collapsed in her arms, dead weight on her damp, shivering body.

"And you were afraid," he chided in a tender whisper, kissing her eyes, her cheeks, her throat.

She laughed. "So that's how it feels," she said drowsily. "And now I'm sleepy."

He laughed with her. "So am I."

"Will you be here when I wake up?" she teased.

He kissed her swollen mouth gently. "For the rest of my life, honey. Until the very end."

Her arms curved around him and she curled into his powerful body, feeling closer to him than she'd ever felt to another human being. It was poignant. She was a whole woman. She was loved.

"Until the very end, my darling," she repeated, her voice trailing away in the silence of the room.

She slept in his arms. It was the best night of her life. But it was only the beginning for both of them.

* * * * *

SPECIAL EXCERPT FROM

*Beatrix Leighton has loved Gold Valley cowboy
Dane Parker from afar for years, and she's about to
discover that forbidden love might just be the sweetest…*

Read on for a sneak preview of
Unbroken Cowboy *by* New York Times *and*
USA TODAY bestselling author *Maisey Yates.*

It was her first kiss. But that didn't matter.

It was Dane. That was all that mattered. That was all that really
mattered.

Dane, the man she'd fantasized about a hundred times—
maybe a thousand times—doing this very thing. But this was so
much brighter and more vivid than a fantasy could ever be. Color
and texture and taste. The rough whiskers on his face, the heat of
his breath, the way those big, sure hands cupped her face as his
lips moved slowly over hers.

She took a step and the shattered glass crunched beneath her
feet, but she didn't care. She didn't care at all. She wanted to
breathe in this moment for as long as she could, broken glass be
damned. To exist just like this, with his lips against hers, for as
long as she possibly could.

She leaned forward, wrapped her fingers around the fabric of
his T-shirt and clung to him, holding them both steady, because
she was afraid she might fall if she didn't.

Her knees were weak. Like in a book or a movie.

She hadn't known that kissing could really, literally, make
your knees weak. Or that touching a man you wanted could make
you feel like you were burning up, like you had a fever. Could
make you feel hollow and restless and desperate for what came
next…

Even if what came next scared her a little.

It was Dane.

She trusted Dane.

With her secrets. With her body.

Dane.

She breathed his name on a whispered sigh as she moved to take their kiss deeper, and found herself being set back, glass crunching beneath her feet yet again.

"I should go," he said, his voice rough.

"No!" The denial burst out of her, and she found herself reaching forward to grab his shirt again. "No," she said again, this time a little less crazy and desperate.

She didn't feel any less crazy and desperate.

"I have to go, Bea."

"You don't. You could stay."

The look he gave her burned her down to the soles of her feet. "I can't."

"If you're worried about… I didn't misunderstand. I mean I know that if you stayed we would…"

"Dammit, Bea," he bit out. "We can't. You know that."

"Why? I'm not stupid. I know you don't want… I don't want…" She stumbled over her words because it all seemed stupid. To say something as inane as she knew they wouldn't get married. Even saying it made her feel like a silly virgin.

She was a virgin; there wasn't really any glossing over that. But she didn't have to seem silly.

She did know, though. For all that everyone saw her as soft and naive, she wasn't. She'd carried a torch for Dane for a long time, but she'd also realistically seen how marriage worked. Her brother was a cheater. Her mother was a cheater.

Her father was…she didn't even know.

That was the legacy of love and marriage in her family.

Truly, she didn't want any part of it.

Some companionship, though. Sex. She wanted that. With him. Why couldn't she have that? McKenna made it sound simple… and possible. And Bea wanted it.

Don't miss
Unbroken Cowboy *by Maisey Yates,*
available May 2019 wherever
Harlequin® books and ebooks are sold.

www.Harlequin.com

HQN™

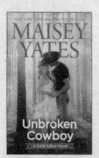

Save **$1.00**
off the purchase of
Unbroken Cowboy
by Maisey Yates.

Available wherever books are sold,
including most bookstores, supermarkets,
drugstores and discount stores.

- ✂

Save **$1.00**

off the purchase of *Unbroken Cowboy* by Maisey Yates.

Coupon valid until August 31, 2019.
Redeemable at participating outlets in U.S. and Canada only.
Limit one coupon per customer.

52616310

5 65373 00076 2   (8100)0 12415

DPCOUP0319